NINE BELLS AT THE BREAKER

NINE BELLS AT THE BREAKER
An Immigrant's Story

a novel

BY

GERALDINE GLODEK

The Barn Peg Press
Iowa City

Published by
THE BARN PEG PRESS
221 E. Market Street
Suite 231
Iowa City, Iowa 52245-2164

Cover design by Brian Treadway
Art and ornaments copyright © 1998 by Brian Treadway

Printed in the United States of America.

This is a work of fiction. All names, characters, places, and incidents are either products of the author's imagination or are used fictitiously.

Library of Congress Catalogue Card Number: 98-73047

ISBN 0-9665943-0-4 Hardcover
ISBN 0-9665943-1-2 Paperback

for

Anna Manley Scicchitano

and

Richard P. Scicchitano

Acknowledgements

I wish to express my appreciation to my family and neighbors in Northumberland County, Pennsylvania, who told of their lives there when so many mines were operating. Thanks to the people preserving our history at the Scranton Public Library, the Mt. Carmel Public Library, and the following Pennsylvania mines and museums: The Eckley Miners Village in Eckley, The Lackawanna Mine Tour at McDade Park in Scranton, The Pioneer Tunnel in Ashland, and Steamtown, U.S.A., in Scranton—places I visited while creating this book. Especially helpful was the publication *When Coal Was King: Mining Pennsylvania's Anthracite,* by Louis Poliniak (Applied Arts Publishers, Lebanon, PA, 1970).

Thanks to my children, Heather and Tom O'Connor, for their readings, suggestions, and helpful explorations. To John Spychalski, Professor of Business Logistics at Penn State, thanks for mapping out Casimir's trip on the Delaware & Hudson in 1910. I would like to thank Ray, a classmate in the Graduate Writing Program at Penn State, for helping me to probe Casimir's reactions to that ride. Thanks to other students in that program and to Professors Tom Rogers and Peter Schneeman.

Special thanks to Brian Treadway at The Barn Peg Press, for his editorial insight on the many revisions and for his own contributions as artist.

Contents

NINE BELLS AT THE BREAKER

1

NOT GOOD MORNING, NOT NOTHING

Casimir was hiding under the bulkhead. His arms scraped against the stone steps leading from the basement of the boarding house as he scrambled out of his flannel robe and into his miner's clothes—a pair of heavy gray pants, a gray shirt, and a gray jacket. A shaft of moonlight, passing through a crack in the bulkhead, shone through the glass panel on the inside door. He kept an eye on that door, watched for the old man's face to appear behind the glass. He hurried to get outside before the mine whistle blew and the whole world was up.

"Dear God," he gasped, "tell me the truth. Was it only a dream? Or was it that crazy old Kraut coming for me? Remember him? His stinking onion breath back in Pottsville? The day Mama's lousy new husband said I could take the train to Philadelphia and back. Alone, like I always wanted. For my eighth birthday, remember?

"I swung my legs from the platform, pretending I was on the docks back home in Gdansk. I know they call it Danzig now, but please don't get mad if I always say Gdansk. I hate that Kraut name! My real papa said I must always call it Gdansk. I pictured his fishing boat just back from the sea, pictured him smiling up at me, showing me the great big catch.

"Then I pictured him in his coffin." Casimir, holding back a scream as he had done that day on the platform, bunched the laces of his boots. "A taxi driver let me feed oats to his horse. That took my mind off Papa. After that, I tossed dice. My first throw was five and four. Remember? The next was six and three. That's when I smelled the onion breath. It was that old man with the bulgy eyes, stooping

3

down behind me. He dragged his finger across my throat. 'Two same numbers,' he said. 'Two nines. Vun more and—'

"I grabbed my dice and tried to run, but he grabbed my wrist. The dice fell. Six and three! He laughed and went for my throat again. I took my dice and backed away. Right off the platform!"

Casimir fell silent, remembering how he had limped home. His mother, Jozefina, wiped her hands on her apron, looked over his foot, and washed the cinder cuts on his elbows as he panted the story. She spoke in English to encourage him to speak American. Her dark eyes and near-black hair added mystery to the words she spoke in a hushed voice as she leaned close to Casimir. "Yes," she said, "there is something in numbers. Three in a row, always bad. Always bad. Remember Mr. O'Grady from next door? He liked to play the cards. One evening he get that ace of spades three times in a row. Ace of spades is death card, you see. That night his appendix busted and he dies!"

"Will that happen to me now? Will I die?"

A train whistle blew and Jozefina said, "Hear that? That is your train. It goes to Philadelphia without you. See, you already got bad luck from those three nines. There will be no more, I think."

"My birthday present train," Casimir whined.

"Shame! You give up. Go look for next train and take it."

"What if the old man's still there?"

"Don't pay your attention to some crazy old Kraut! Stand up. Let me see you walk. Your foot is fine." She pushed him out the door.

Casimir crossed himself and prayed for good luck. At the train station, he found a penny face up on the platform. A penny facing up was a sign of good luck, the widow O'Grady always said. He discovered immediately what the good luck was. The old man was gone. Casimir tossed a kiss beyond the bales of clouds, imagining it landing on the cheek of God.

Remembering that kiss as he put on his miner's hat, helping God to remember it, he began to feel there was some help. "Help me, God. Two nights in a row, that dream! I could even smell the onion breath. Make it so it can't come back a third night in a row."

The mine whistle blew though light had yet to dawn through the cellar windows. Casimir made the sign of the cross and crept back inside for his shovel, auger, and pick. He heard someone raking the johnny stove in the kitchen.

The door at the top of the stairs opened. "Charlie?" the landlady called down to him. "Answer. Yousa there. I know yousa there."

Casimir hid behind the furnace. The door slammed. He heard the landlady go out to the yard and back to the kitchen. He crept out. When he lifted the bulkhead, he saw a lit kerosene lamp next to his lunch pail. On the rag tucked around the food was a note fastened with a straight pin: "Shame for you! No breakfast. You go out with no hello. Not good morning, not nothing. R.M. Gilotti, landlady."

He felt delighted by the small offense he had caused. It was gratifying to discover that he could make something happen, that this day would be more than just the crushing dread of what might befall him if the dream came again that night. He threw a pebble at the kitchen window. The back door swung open. He ran off, smiling.

It was too early to show up for work. He sat on the towering black slagpiles behind the colliery, praying not to have that dream. All morning in the mine he prayed. Finally, as he was estimating the tonnage of a loaded car, his elbow on the edge as he compared the height of the heaped coal with the reach of his fingertips, he felt God give him the saving idea. He must go to the train station and find a penny face up. The idea itself seemed to bring good luck. Around two o'clock the water pumps broke down, and the miners were sent home. There was still plenty of daylight for his search.

He ran home, tossed his blackened boots onto the back porch, flung open the bulkhead, hurried down to the cellar, and washed in the tin tub. He put on his flannel robe and went to his attic room, where he dressed in a black suit. He always wore suits after work. He loved to look nice, respectable, like a person with a clean past.

Casimir left the house and walked to the trolley stop. The Joy Junction station was visible at the edge of Mt. Carmel. Casimir looked to the heavens, trying to get a sense of whether to go to that station or the Mt. Carmel station in town. He felt God prompt him to go to the Joy Junction station, and to go on foot. He followed a path down the mountain through the pines and bare sumac, and he began his quest for the penny in the gravel between the rows and rows of tracks where coal cars sat idle, some heaped with gleaming anthracite, others waiting to be hauled off and filled, probably at his own mine, the Ebony Gem, at the west end of Black Hollow. When he was safely hidden behind a car, he bent forward and squinted at the ground. Whenever he was between the cars and visible to people on the platform, he walked with his head up, his hands in his pockets.

A passenger train pulled into the station. Minutes later, the locomotive belched a cloud of steam and disappeared around the sharp curve at the foot of Manley's Mountain.

The people scattered. Only a girl of about fifteen was left. Casimir was just stepping out from behind a series of Delaware & Hudson cars when he saw her. Their eyes locked like the eyes of two shipwrecked travelers meeting in a clearing. She was tall. Her hair, yellow and straight, trailed from a cheap hat of white rabbit's fur, like the fur on the muff where her hands were tucked and pressed against the belly of her worn brown coat.

Her face showed none of the weathered brazenness of other coal region girls her age, girls with two or three years of factory experience, girls whose roughened hands could break the bones of fingers trying to slip between their buttons, girls who sat at sewing machines, their swift feet rocking on wrought-iron treadles, high-topped shoes ready to shatter the shins of bundle boys with groping hands.

Casimir and the girl regarded one another in silence. A trolley bell clanged on the opposite side of the station. Around the corner a horse scraped at the ground. It snorted and shook its head, the bells around its neck tinkling like falling icicles. From another direction came the sound of someone cranking up a car. The motor coughed. There was silence. Then the cranking began again.

A man in a top hat came from the direction of the horse. "Cab, miss?"

"I'm looking for a patch called Black Hollow. But I'm afraid I got off at the wrong— Is this the Joy Junction station?"

"Yes. Mt. Carmel's the next stop. Every third train stops here first." The man swung his arm in the direction of a village built into the mountainside. "That's Black Hollow over there."

The girl pulled her hands out of her muff and unfolded a small piece of paper. "'Third one up on the west end of the patch,' Uncle Stanush wrote here. But that's too big to be a coal patch. All the patches up Scranton way are a few rows of houses only. You sure?"

The driver shrugged. "Well, time was it was only a tiny patch. Some patches grow. Black Hollow's even got a church and a school. Third one up on the west end, huh?" The driver whisked his top hat off suddenly, revealing a head of greasy, gray hair. He bowed his head in a sort of apology. "Maybe I shouldn't say this, Miss, but the part you want to go to is no place for a handsome young girl like you. All single men in shanties and lean-to's. Rent free almost, you see. Good enough for a man alone. Either saving up to bring their families here, or saving money to take back to the old country. It gets lonely. You oughta tie up that gold hair. Men's just men, you see."

The girl refolded her uncle's note and slipped it back into the pocket inside the muff. She raised her face slowly and turned it toward the mountaintop like a sunflower reaching for light. She tossed her muff and hat onto her brown leather valise. Her fingers gathered the straight strands into a horse tail. "Maybe you're right. I'm here to visit my uncle. That's all." She divided the tail into four sections, which she twisted into ropes and wrapped around the crown of her head like a stack of haloes.

"I'm worried about my uncle," she said, looking all around. "He was supposed to meet me here. He's old." Her eyes searched the platform again, searched the rows and rows of tracks where Casimir, turning away, began to walk among the coal cars, appearing like someone whose job was to inspect them. He nodded approval at some and shook his head at others.

The girl's eyes searched for her uncle. They read the lettering on coal cars: PENNSYLVANIA—PHILADELPHIA & READING—DELAWARE & HUDSON. That last rail line, the Delaware & Hudson, was to become the soul of terror for Casimir Turek.

One day Casimir would recall that he was standing near a Delaware & Hudson car the first time he saw her. One day this girl would have to decide whether Casimir Turek lived or died.

2

NEVER YOU MIND THE WHISTLE

Hey, Charlie," Joe McDonald said to Casimir, "you gonna finish drillin' that hole? You're daydreamin'."

Casimir turned the crank of the four-foot auger, pulled it from the hole, then tamped the powder in with a rod. Joe handed him a blasting squib and Casimir plugged it into the hole. Joe stuck his head out into the gangway to warn of the coming blast. "Fire!"

Casimir lit the fuse. Both men scrambled down the wooden rungs of the manway to the safety of the gangway, where they plugged their thumbs into their ears. The charge blew. The two miners coughed until they gagged. They retreated farther up the gangway.

The cage came down. Caruso Tullio called through the whirling black dust, "Charlie Turek, thatsa you?"

"Yeah?" Casimir answered between coughs.

"Help! That stinkin' mule again!"

"Rebekah?"

"Yeah. Stubborn bitch. Foreman in the stable say, if Rebekah giva you trouble, go getta that Charlie Turek. Shesa listen to you, he say. Only to you."

Joe McDonald laughed. "'Course. She's his girl."

Caruso grabbed Casimir by the elbow. "Come on, Charlie."

Casimir pulled his identification peg, Number 31, from the pegboard, stuck it in his pocket, and stepped into the left cage of the double shaft. Caruso tugged on the signal cord, talking all the way up to the daylight. "You know, the foreman say four pairs of mules to take up for the fresh air. Three pairs, no trouble. Solomon and Sheba, Naomi and Ruth, Jacob and Esau. No trouble. Then Rebekah and Isaac. Oh, that Rebekah! Half in the cage, half in the yard, shesa lay down. Sasha Romanov, he getta that mule to stand up. But then he finds out why. What a kick!"

The cage rose to a clear, cold afternoon. Casimir said to Caruso, "You taking my place in Breast Number Six?"

"Yes." With Caruso aboard, the cage descended.

Casimir plugged his peg into the board in the mine yard to indicate he was working there now. Sasha Romanov's sagging brown eyes glared at Rebekah, who was sitting in the yard. The stubble on his broad cheeks had become fuzzy black stumps. He was sitting on a boulder, rubbing his knee. He got up, limped toward the fence, picked up a branch, and hobbled back with it. He stood squarely in front of Rebekah and whipped the stick from side to side. "Lousy you!"

Rebekah flattened her ears and stood up. Blind like all the mules who lived in the mines, she groped her head about, trying to sense where the man was as he danced around her, waving his stick.

Casimir tore the stick from Romanov's hand and flung it over the fence. "Let her alone, for Christ's sake."

Romanov backed away, whining, "So to you it is okay she keeks me."

Casimir scratched Rebekah between the ears. "Nice going." He wrapped his arm around the animal's face. She nuzzled her mouth against his cheek.

"So he pampers that crazy animal," Romanov grumbled. He shook his fist. "Destroy her! That is what to do!"

Winston Thatcher, a bony-faced man in a suit and vest, charged out of the office shanty, shouting in a British accent. "If there's anything to be destroyed here, it'll be you. These mules cost a fine penny. Next time you shake a stick at a mule, you're out. Hear? Out! Bloody greenies," he muttered as he retreated to the shanty, "they come here to America and think they own the place." He slammed the door after himself. He poked his head out once more and said to Casimir, "Hey, fellow, stop back in here after you bring that mule back down to the stable."

Casimir nodded. He kissed Rebekah between the eyes. Slipping a finger through her halter, he walked her around the yard. Then he returned her to the underground stable and went to the office.

Behind the big oak desk was an oak chair with leather pads. Three maple chairs stood along one wall. Mr. Thatcher looked up and down Casimir's sooty clothes and planted himself between Casimir and the clean chairs. He cleared his throat. "How long have you been with us now?"

"Eight years."

"No foreign accent. Born here, then?"

"Yep. Loup City, Nebraska. My family came from Europe three generations back." Casimir knew he could trust his pronunciation to hide his foreign origin. He whispered a thank-you to God for helping his voice not to shake when he lied. God knew he had a good reason for lying. And God could trust him to tell the whole truth after his plan was completed. A few lies to keep his secret were forgiven.

The office man stared at Casimir as if trying to figure out the face beneath the grit. "Age?"

"Twenty-three."

"Pretty good with those mules, young man."

"We had lots of animals on our farm in Nebraska," Casimir said in a steady voice. He crossed his fingers and muttered a promise to light a candle at St. Hedwig's if God would stick with him through any more lies he had to tell that day. That made two thank-you candles he had to light after work, he calculated—one for giving him the idea to go to the station to find the face-up penny, which had somehow prevented the third onion-breath dream, though he hadn't actually found the penny, and one candle for helping with the lies.

"Well, good, lots of farm animals," the office man said. "I hate to see animals abused. I say, how'd you like to walk that Rebekah more often? Of course, you'll be mining down in, in—"

"Breast Number Six."

"Yes, Breast Number Six all morning and part of—"

There was a knock on the door. An old man with a cane stumbled inside as if he had been given an encouraging shove from behind. He took off his hat, but his hand never left the doorknob. The young girl who had come in on the train the day before slipped in behind him.

Mr. Thatcher greeted the old man with a smirk. "You again. Yes, what is it this time? Sweedok, you said the name is, yes?"

Old Sweedok looked at the girl as if to ask whether his name were really Sweedok. She nodded.

"Yes," the old man said. His voice was filled with courage now. "Stanislaw Sweedok." Stocky, well-built, he was a man accustomed to hard work. But he leaned hard on his cane. His left boot was laced loosely to make room for a swollen foot.

Mr. Thatcher tapped the toe of his own shoe against the visitor's boot. Stanislaw paled with pain but did not withdraw his foot. Mr. Thatcher said, "And you want to work in the mines with the gout or whatever you've got here. No, I told you."

The girl stepped forward. "Sir, it'll go away. Uncle Stanush got this once, years ago. It went away then. It'll go away now."

Casimir could not believe his good luck. He had been praying he would see that girl again. Sweedok. She was Polish, like him, but she had no foreign accent. So maybe she was born here. He could only be with someone who did not come from Gdansk. Someone who wouldn't know about his big sin there. Maybe her family was from Gdansk and had heard about him, though. How could he find out? He backed into the shadows, hoping she didn't recognize his sooty face.

Old Sweedok, as if drawing into himself a spirit set loose by his niece's words, drew in a deep, deep breath. His chest sounded a chord of congestion. He straightened himself up and said. "I want a job."

"You want a job."

"Yes."

Mr. Thatcher's smirk widened. "Tssss."

"I want a job as a miner."

"You want to be a miner. Go home and lie down, old boy."

The girl spoke up angrily. "He doesn't *want* to be. He *is*. He mined up by Scranton over twenty years. Didn't you, Uncle? He mined in Shamokin till that explosion last month shut the place down. He's a good miner. He's been mining most of his life."

Mr. Thatcher chuckled. "Oh, I can believe that. Listen to that wheeze. His lungs have got to be as black as an Irishman's heart. I've seen him around the patch. He can't walk ten feet without stopping to get his wind. Yet he waltzes in here, 'I want a job, I want a job.' Tssss." He opened the door. "Out with you."

"Victoria," the old man said, "let's go."

Victoria put her mouth close to her uncle's ear and whispered.

Stanislaw Sweedok turned to Thatcher. "We'll be back."

The door closed and Casimir stepped forward. "Should I go now?"

The man laughed. "You like her, don't you? You want to see which way they're headed. He lives in one of the lean-to's. The girl, I don't know."

"How about a job for the old man up in the breaker with the kids. Sorting coal. Picking out the slag. He could do that. It'll keep him off his feet. I'll take good care of that mule for you."

"You'll take good care anyway. You like animals, it's plain. Well, I'll think about it. Come back on Monday."

Casimir went out to the mine yard. The iron gate had just swung shut after the girl and her uncle. Casimir watched as they walked along the tracks. Mr. Thatcher stepped out into the mine yard and said, "One more thing before you go back down. Come with me."

A low rumble began. Both men looked up. A coal car, pulled skyward by a cable along narrow rails, reached the top of the breaker and spilled its coal into the tipple.

Casimir followed Mr. Thatcher through the door at the foot of the breaker and up the stairs. Both men blocked their ears from the roar of the great bull shaker, which sized the freshly dumped coal through a descending series of screens, powdering black the faces of little boys as it sent its sooty assortment tumbling down a maze of chutes to the gallery of picking counters, where young fingers prodded and picked out rocks and bits of wood.

When the rumbling stopped, Walter Savitski rose to his feet. He took off his cap and banged it on the counter, sending up puffs of coal dirt. In his deepest man voice he shouted to the pudgy man who patrolled the breaker all day, "Say, Mr. Jones, ain't it time Big Joe blew to send us home? Is he rusty or what?" He folded his arms and worked his mouth into a challenging sneer.

"Never you mind the whistle. I'll tell you when it's time." Mr. Jones spoke with a thick British accent that the breaker boys liked to imitate. They were especially fond of imitating the whistle caused by the man's chipped front tooth.

"But when Big Joe blows—" Walter's voice suddenly cracked and squeaked, betraying him as the twelve-year-old he was.

"I said never you mind." Mr. Jones clamped his hand over the boy's skull and pressed him down to the bench. He grabbed a slab of slate from the coal box and held it under the boy's nose as if he expected him to smell it. "Say now, what's this here in your bin?"

"Coal."

"Anthracite, eh?"

"Yeah, Mr. Jones. Good ol' Pennsylvania anthracite."

"Does it shine?"

"Yeah, when it ain't dusty."

Mr. Jones spat on the slab and wiped it with the corner of Walter's jacket. "Now does it shine?"

"Well, no."

"Then it ain't anthracite. Down the slag chute, dammit!"

The breaker boys, blackened to the bone, picked and poked wearily, their fingertips wrapped in wire so they wouldn't become "cherry reds." Hands that moved too slowly were usually urged on by the poke of a stick, but this was the day before payday, so Mr. Jones shuffled around with a stack of empty brown envelopes and handed them to the slower boys to show how much pay a lad could expect for slacking off at the end of a workday. He had little need for the stick after that.

He craned his neck to scan his workers. Walter swung around and tugged twice on his left ear to warn Emmett O'Reagan, who was slumped two benches behind Walter, his palms sliding up and down his thighs. Emmett straightened his back, slapped both hands onto the picking counter, combed his fingers through the heap, and picked out a few pieces of wood. When Mr. Jones got five rows beyond Emmett, Walter tugged once on his right ear, a signal that it was safe to slack off again. Emmett smiled a thanks, yawned, and stretched his legs, rubbing the soreness out from hips to ankles.

From the top of the gallery, near the landing where Casimir and Thatcher stood, came a yowl. Antonio Corsetti, a very small boy, had dropped a fat rock on his toes. He pulled his fists to his chest and held his breath. "Please, God," he whispered, "don't let me cry."

Emmett whirled around and pointed. "Hey, looka! Looka there! Look at kindergarten baby. His lip's shakin'. What's the matter, Corsetti, gonna cry again?"

The whole gallery started chanting, "Baby, baby, kindergarten baby."

Mr. Jones banged his stick on a bench and fanned a handful of empty envelopes. "This is no playground here. You lads want a pay or don't you?"

Antonio Corsetti stood up and slammed his fists onto his hips. "I ain't a kindergarten baby, I ain't! My sister's five and *she's* a kindergarten baby. I'm seven-and-a-half. I ain't a kindergarten baby. I ain't!"

Mr. Jones shoved the boy back down onto the bench. "You are too."

Antonio began to cry. White streaks appeared on his cheeks.

Mr. Jones raised his stick. "You want something to cry about?"

The stick was pulled from his hands by someone standing behind him. Mr. Jones turned around and found himself facing the office man. "What is it, Mr. Thatcher?"

"No sticks in here, I told you. They're just kids."

"Spare the rod, spoil the child. All the collieries prod them along with the rod."

"Not the Ebony Gem. This is your last warning."

"All right, then."

"I came to tell you that, starting Monday, there'll be an old man working up here. Stanislaw Sweedok. He's got a sore foot. Treat him decently. Understand?"

Mr. Jones frowned. "I understand."

Mr. Thatcher turned to Casimir and said, "If you see the old man hobbling about the patch, tell him six o'clock Monday." Then he took a clean, folded handkerchief from inside his breast pocket and slipped it to Antonio Corsetti.

Big Joe, his steam bursting into the red sky, wailed an end to the ten-hour workday. The breaker boys cheered.

3

IOWA'S FUNNY LIKE THAT

The Iowa River, low for lack of rain, had stranded a chunk of driftwood at the bend beyond the far end of the cornfield.

"It looks like a chair," Victoria told her older brother, Jozef, as she tugged him by the sleeve of his dirty white shirt. "Come, help me drag it out. I can sit on it and read by the river."

"Till Mama catches you. She's still mad at Papa for that half year of schooling he let you have. She says it made you lazy."

"She's just jealous 'cause she can't read. In Polish or in English." Victoria parted the tall prairie grasses with great sweeps of her arms. "It's right around here."

"Maybe it's ice, not wood," Jozef teased, reminding her of their first winter in Iowa when she had begged him to help her carve ice people from the green-edged slabs, thick as mattresses, that the river had heaved in crooked stacks at that same bend.

"You know there's no ice in the summer. Look! There!"

Jozef walked past her and climbed down the bank. The sun-bleached tips of his stringy hair looked like scraps of straw.

Victoria scrambled down after him and pulled a rolled-up magazine from his back pocket. "Where'd you get this?"

"Found it on the train."

"Can I read it?"

"When I'm done. Sunday, maybe." He stuffed the magazine back in his pocket. "Here, help me dig this thing out."

They scraped at the soft soil with sticks, freeing the roots of a tree stump. Four of the larger roots looked as though someone had already begun to fashion them into fancy chair legs. They arched out and upward near the seat, curved down and inward, and came out once more in a way that Jozef said could be carved into animal toes, like the legs of a throne. He promised to do it.

They carried the stump back to the farmhouse they shared with a Czech family and a Swedish family, also hired hands.

On Sunday afternoon, Jozef sat carving on the grass amid a throng of children tossing a ball, shouting in English and in their own languages, while all the parents, relaxing in the shade of the long porch, struggled to chat in English.

Victoria, her rag doll pressed against the magazine inside her blouse, strode out to the back porch and started down the steps.

"Wait!" her mother said, rising from her chair, her thick, square body advancing on the child in the way that drove everyone to silence. "How you walk! Somebody can steal that doll, you think?"

"I just don't want to drop Florence in the mud."

"Mud? Three weeks no rain."

"The dust, then." Victoria ran off and made a zigzag path through the corn, which was up to her waist. She sat on the parched ground at a place where the land dipped low, happily chirping syllables amid the twitter of birds, until she heard rustling in the next row and saw a pair of hands parting the stalks. "Mama!"

Seven years later, she was telling this story in Pennsylvania, in her Uncle Stanislaw's one-room hut of rippled tin, one of nineteen lean-to's strapped and nailed to a line of railroad ties jammed end-up into the black earth and propped against the slagpiles.

The bright afternoon sun poured its light through a single window onto a piece of cracked linoleum that barely covered the mud floor. The four oval holes in it had once lain snug against the squat feet of someone's johnny stove. A pair of wooden crates covered most of the square hole that had been cut around someone's ice box.

In a stove of stones and mud, a pot of vegetables stewed. Old Sweedok, warming his sore foot, which he had propped on a rolled-up overcoat, was sitting on the crate opposite Victoria, who sat brushing her hair as she told her story. Her uncle's eyes danced in the merriment of a long laugh halted by a gasping cough. He rocked and rubbed his chest till he got his wind. He spoke in Polish. "I'll bet she threw you over her knee and gave it to you good."

"Oh," Victoria said, "how she yelled! 'Girls don't need to read, I told you!' She tore her apron off and shook it in my face. 'This is for you,' she shouted, 'not books, not magazines!' I was going backwards on my rear end, pushing myself with my heels. Mama yanked the magazine from under my arm and flung the pages to the wind one by one. I tried to grab my precious treasure, but she raised her arms like a Gypsy dancer and just kept tearing pages. I ran, leaping after them. The corn leaves cut my hands. Mama chased after me, waving that stupid apron like a flag. But she couldn't catch me."

"Good for her, too fat, yes. Did you catch any pages?"

"Only a scrap. It was snagged on a hawthorn tree. I had it in my pocket before Mama was through the last row of corn."

"What did it say?"

"The only words I could read were, 'the—we—sky—little—of.' Simple words. Jozef read it for me later, in the attic, after supper, after he got over being mad about his torn-up magazine. 'Easy come, easy go,' he said in American."

"Well? What did it say?"

"I learned the whole thing by heart. It was part of a story by a man named Stephen Crane. It was in English, of course. Uncle, I'll have to recite it in English to be true." She tried to sound like a man.

> "We are due in Yellow Sky at 3:42," he said, looking tenderly into her eyes.
>
> "Oh, are we?" she said, as if she had not been aware of it. To evince surprise at her husband's statement was part of her wifely amiability. She took from a pocket a little silver watch; and as she held it before her, and stared at it with a frown of attention, the new husband's face shone.
>
> "I bought it in San Anton' from a friend of mine," he told her gleefully.
>
> "It's seventeen minutes past—"

Victoria stared past her uncle's left shoulder as though trying to read the face of a clock in the distance.

Stanush said in English. "Past what? Past what?"

Victoria answered in Polish. "That's all that was left of the paper. But even that little piece was a treasure, though I didn't know the meaning. I was only eight when Jozef taught me to read it. I brought him a quart of mulberries to thank him. I promised him all kinds of berries all season if he would teach me to read better.

"We slept in the attic, me in a room with three Swedish girls. Jozef with two Czech brothers. Everybody worked so hard, they slept like stones. No one heard me creeping out for the berries before sunrise. I ran along the edge of the rows. The farmland was all little hills, up and down and up and down. Iowa's funny like that. It can make you seasick trying to run across a field. But it was good because I could hide from Mama between the waves of land.

"The mulberry tree was next to the hawthorn where the magazine page had snagged. The first time I went for berries, I stole a scrub bucket and hid it in the bushes. I planned to fetch it after my chores were done the next day. I never thought about berry stains until I woke up with purple hands."

"Ah, and your mama saw them and guessed your plot."

"No. She accused me of picking them the day before, hoarding them, and eating them all myself in the night."

"And what was your punishment?"

Victoria laughed. "My punishment? Just for being so greedy, so sneaky, I was to pick a bucketful after my chores. Everyone could have some but me. I couldn't help giggling, knowing that full bucket was waiting for me. Mama called me wise and slapped the smile off my face. But that just made me more determined to barter reading lessons for berries. Oh, Uncle, we had such fun, me and Jozef, reading everything we could get our hands on."

"You were good buddies, you and Jozef."

"Yes, poor Jozef. Mama decided Iowa was jinxed when that corn crib collapsed and he almost got crushed to death. We hadn't been in America two months when little Voychek died in his sleep. He wasn't even a year old. Papa didn't want to leave Iowa. He liked the farm, the big sky. But Mama nagged him. So he wrote to you to find him work here. Here we come to Pennsylvania and Jozef suffocates in a coal slide the first time he blasts in a mine. Aw, there's no use dwelling on the past," she said with a wave of her hand. "So now do you believe me, Uncle? I can read. Please let me see that letter."

"It's in Polish."

"I can read that, too." She shoved his knee and grinned. "I was determined, didn't I tell you?"

Her uncle pointed to a metal box by the stove. "In there. But let me warn you first before you read. It's from your mother."

"Mama! She can't write."

"A neighbor wrote it. It's to find you a—" He broke off, coughing. He rocked back and forth and pounded his fist on his chest. His eyes watered as he gagged, pressing a rag over his mouth. He pushed himself to his feet, stumbled toward the door, went outside, and spat, dragging up phlegm and spitting again and again. Back inside, he slumped against the door, panting, a rattle in his breath.

Victoria helped him back to the crate and put his feet back on the rolled-up overcoat.

He handed her the envelope. His breath rattled on every draw now. "She wants me to help find you a husband. A man from the old country. I am to hand him the description. There's a picture, too."

Victoria looked at the photograph of herself sitting on the front stoop of their house in Dickson City. The features were fuzzy, but clear enough for someone who knew her to identify her, especially that cheap hat with the rabbit's fur. Her black dog was a blur of motion, like her arms, which were flung wide in welcome. The photo was glued to a piece of paper that said, "September 30, 1910. Her name is Victoria Sweedok, age 15, born 1895. Nice, pretty, cooks, sews, obeys. She will make a good wife. Please write to Wanda Sweedok, her mother, at 1050 Main Street, Dickson City, Pennsylvania, United States of America. Please answer soon. Please!"

"Soon! What is this *soon!* Is she in a hurry to get rid of me?"

Stanislaw took both her hands and kissed them. "You poor blind girl. Open your eyes. Your parents were past forty when you were born. Your papa has lungs as black as mine. Your mama is fat and old. Both of them can go any day now. Me, too. Your brothers are dead. And what about you? You have no job, no husband."

"I can find my own husband. Anyway, Uncle, I already found him. An inspector of trains. I'll bet he takes trains everywhere, like the man in the story. We'll go to Yellow Sky! He lives right here in Black Hollow. I saw him yesterday. Give me the letter. I'll rewrite it in English. He must be English with such a good job."

"Your mama said someone from the old country."

"Aw, Mama. Forget Mama. It's my life." Victoria took some paper from her fur muff, stooped down on the floor, anchored her hair behind her ears and made a desk of the crate. "I won't write the *soon* part. Or the *please, please.* It sounds desperate. I'll change my writing, so he won't recognize it after we're married."

"Your mother will kill me if I give this letter to anyone but a Polish man. But my lungs tell me Saint Peter is jangling the keys of the gates for me already. What can she do but help me along? So tell me, where do I find this inspector of trains?"

"On Monday we'll go to the station where I first saw him."

"I'm sorry to warn you, my little niece, that such a man won't want a girl from such a family like ours. Foreigners. *Greenies,* they call us. And poor ones."

"He won't care about that, Uncle Stanush. He saw me, too. He liked me. I saw his eyes."

"All right. We'll find him, then."

As Victoria wrote, Stanislaw leaned back against the pile of garments hanging from a hook and dozed. The breath that rattled in uneven heaves formed English words, "Blasting! Fire!" He startled himself awake. He saw Victoria tying a piece of string around the envelope. "Ah, yes, the letter for the train inspector," he said. "I'll keep it in my pocket. Give it to me. One thing, Victoria, you mustn't tell the train inspector about the magazine in the cornfield."

"Why not?"

"You'll scare him away with such a story. Men don't like brazen women. Let him think you learned to read in school."

A little while after the shack grew dark enough to light the kerosene lamp, there was a knock on the door. Victoria leaned the side of her head against it. "Who is it?"

"Charlie Turek from the Ebony Gem Colliery. We have work for Mr. Sweedok."

Victoria gathered her hair and began to braid it. "Excuse me, I'll open the door in a moment." She took some hairpins from her pocket and pressed them between her lips. One by one, she poked them into her hair. "Stand up, Uncle Stanush!" she whispered. "It's a man from the mine. They have a job for you." She slipped an arm around his back. "Come on, Uncle, up."

She opened the door. The piled hair made her look so tall that Casimir made a show of bending under the lintel as though he really couldn't have gotten inside without doing so. His overcoat had been left unbuttoned to display his nice suit.

Victoria covered her mouth in astonishment. "Oh, sir, you were at the station when I arrived. Inspecting the trains."

He stood so close to her that his warm breath, sweetened with a fennel seed, traced the contours of her heart-shaped face like the fingers of a blind man.

To hide the ugly room, Victoria took a step back and stood next to her uncle. The visitor looked only at her, his mouth forming a smile of restrained delight.

Victoria's eyes darted toward the pocket where her uncle had put the letter. How brazen would it be to hand it to this Charlie Turek herself? Turek, a Polish name. Imagine, a Polish man in such a high position. No foreign accent. Was he born here? Or was he like her, brought to America so young that he spoke like a real American?

She grabbed the wrist of her right hand to stop herself from going for the letter. But, imagining her mother watching her give it to a man she had picked herself, she pressed her fist against her smile.

Casimir looked at her like someone trying to read the hands on a clock that had gone haywire. Then he turned to the uncle and said, "Mr. Thatcher tells me you have a bad foot. Only temporary."

"That's right. I will get over it."

"How'd you like to work up in the breaker till your foot heals? Then, maybe in the mine, depending on how you do in the breaker."

"All children works there. They will sing and make fun."

Victoria said, "Uncle Stanush, it's only temporary. You do good and you'll be back down in the mine. A person can stand anything for a while, even a little teasing."

"No."

"Uncle, it looks like either you take the breaker job or take the train back to Dickson City with me and live with us."

The old miner looked past her and up at Casimir. "My brother, Marek, her papa, he sends her to fetch me because he knows my colliery in Shamokin not can work now because of that fire last week. Marek found out in the Scranton paper. He thinks I am starving here by myself. I am not. Look." He fanned his palm around, indicating a small pyramid of tin cans and a smoked ball of meat in a string sack hanging from the roof. "I can take care of myself."

Casimir said, "Tell you what, Mr. Sweedok, you can think it over. Tomorrow's Sunday. I'll be at nine o'clock Mass. St. Hedwig's. If you're interested, you can catch me coming out of church. The job starts at six on Monday. Think it over."

"We'll come," Victoria said.

"No, we will not. I'll die first! I—" His words were choked off in a spasm of coughing. He staggered back toward the crate and sat down, his back straight and firm, his eyes fierce like an angry king's. His chest heaved and rattled, but he managed to raise his arm and point to the door. "Please. Go."

The next morning Victoria heard the birds before any light came through the window. She lit the lamp, shielding her uncle from the glare with her body. The trousers with the letter still in the pocket were folded on the floor beside him. She wanted to write the name Charlie Turek on the envelope before he changed his mind. But she didn't feel right going into his pocket without asking. She crossed herself and prayed for the patience to wait for him to wake up. In the silence of waiting, she discovered he was not breathing.

"Oh, Uncle Stanush!" She knelt beside him and threw her arms around his chest. She listened for a heartbeat, felt for a pulse in his neck. She closed his eyelids. "Sweet Uncle," she moaned. "Dear sweet Uncle."

Two Lithuanian brothers living in the next lean-to made a coffin from scrap wood. Victoria handed one man the envelope with the words, "Charlie Turek, Ebony Gem Colliery," written on it. She told them that it was in her uncle's pocket, that he must have meant for some Charlie Turek at the Ebony Gem to receive it.

Stanislaw Sweedok's body went to Dickson City by train.

4

WAS HE IN ON IT WITH MAREK?

On Sunday evening after supper, Casimir sat in the dark on his bed. He ran his finger over the holes on the cane chair from right to left, then left to right. He wished Sam's Cafe were open, wished for anything that might make him stop picturing that train heading north with Victoria on it. Until he saw her, he had not allowed himself to think about having a wife. Now that he had let himself imagine such a life—this girl, his wife, waiting for him outside the mine yard at the end of the work day—he didn't know how he could ever again face the lonely walk home to the boarding house.

The white legs of Patches, Mrs. Gilotti's calico cat, slid under his door and cast long shadows in the block of light shining in from the third-story landing.

Casimir went over to the door. He got down on his stomach and began to whisper like a man telling his sins in a dark confessional. "Well, she's gone, Patches. Went back on the train with the coffin, I heard. And a good thing, too. I was on my way to hell for that girl. I was ready to spend all my savings to have her. Every cent saved for my sisters' passage here, every cent for the home I promised them in America."

Patches meowed.

"Yes," Casimir whispered, "you heard right. I do have a family in the old country, two younger sisters, Anna and Krystina. I was born in Gdansk. I can tell *you*. I know you won't tell anybody."

Casimir sat up and opened the door. Patches started in, but paused to yawn and stretch her hind legs out toward the landing. He scooped her up and scrubbed his face on her long, white belly. Then he shut the door and carried her over to the cane chair, where he sat her on his lap and curled over her, rubbing his chin on the orange fur between her black-and-white ears. She rose up on her front legs, pushing her head hard against his chin, soothing him with the sound of her deep, rolling purr.

"Do you ever get lonely?" he asked her. "Ever had a mate? Too bad I didn't know you in Gdansk. We had a tomcat you would've loved. *Muszka,* I named him. Know why? Because right here—" He raised the cat's chin and tapped her neck, "he had a black patch of fur that looked just like a bow tie, a *muszka*. Other than that, he was all white. You would've loved him. We had to leave him there with Anna and Krystina. How terrible that was, leaving him, leaving Anna and Krystina. How could Mama do it?"

Casimir gathered the cat against his chest and began to rock her, as though it were she who needed consoling. His mind replayed the morning the rowboat glided from the docks in Gdansk, carrying him, his mother, two bundles, and the man rowing them out to the big ship in the Baltic. He saw four-year-old Anna shrieking and jumping on the docks, screaming, "Mama, take us! Casimir, come back! Take us!" He saw Mrs. Kopicki, the neighbor, turn the child's face from the sea and into the folds of her skirt. Anna's blonde curls dangled from between the woman's thick fingers. Casimir nearly toppled the boat when he sprang to his knees to pray for forgiveness and wave a guilty good-bye. Little Krystina, just under two, sat in the crook of Mrs. Kopicki's arm, uncurling her fingers in a slow, uncertain wave to mother and brother.

Casimir turned on his mother, hatred in his voice. "Why, Mama! Why can't we take them?"

"You'll understand when you're older, I told you. And don't worry, they'll be along in a year or two. You'll see. Don't worry. I'll send for them as soon as we're settled, and I have a chance to take care of a few things."

Casimir put Patches over his shoulder and began pacing. "Well, I'm older, Patches. Sixteen years older and I still don't understand. She lied, you know. She never sent for them. She broke her promise. She just sits around Pottsville with her new husband and her three new daughters. I have nothing to do with any of them. They don't even know where I live. But Anna and Krystina, they know. We write to each other. Don't worry, Patches, I'll pay their passage here.

To hell with Mama. I'll get them a nice house, nice furniture. The best in America. A farmhouse, just like the one my Uncle Jerzy had a picture of. Just like that. I'll have it built for them. And when it's all prepared, I'll buy their tickets."

Casimir left for work on Monday with a miserable heart. But he hid his misery, so no one would pry. As he was leaving the mine yard at the end of the day, Mr. Jones called to him and tossed him an envelope. "That old man, Sweedok," Jones said. "It was in his pocket. Some greenie in the next shack brought it this morning. I think that's what he was trying to say—it was in the old man's pocket when he died."

Casimir, thinking it was Sweedok's refusal to work in the breaker, stuck the letter in his jacket and figured on glancing at it sometime after supper.

He dragged himself home and went about cleaning his boots on the back porch as though each one weighed a hundred pounds. He removed his jacket and whacked it listlessly against the wire fence, slowly waving away the flying coal dust. He was slow to lift the bulkhead over the three stone steps, slow to go down to the basement, slow to hang his jacket and pants on the hook. He washed slowly.

"Avoiding us?" Mrs. Gilotti yelled down through the closed door.

"Nope. Just getting washed." He dressed, went up to the kitchen, waved hello, and said he wasn't hungry.

"Sneaky Hunkey," Fred said.

"Yeah," Harold said.

Fred and Harold, two retired miners renting a room on the second floor, had a habit of gossiping about Casimir right in front of him. "Boy oh boy," Fred said, "if I ever seen a guy up to something, it's that one."

"You been saying that for three years," Harold said, wiping his mouth. "When's it gonna happen?"

"It will. Mark my words. Them Hunkeys is all alike."

Casimir walked through the parlor and went up the stairs.

"Well, at least he ain't a greenhorn," Harold shouted.

"He might as well be. He's just as sly."

"You're probably greenies yourselves," Casimir muttered as he reached the third-story landing. "Probably murdered your own mothers by the time you were two and managed to get here in time to talk like real Americans. Phonies. I'd like to drag the skeletons out of *your* closets."

He lit the candle by his bed, lay down, and opened the envelope Thatcher had given him. He read it once, read it a second time. His eyes burned with fresh longing as he stared at Victoria's photograph. He stood it against the candle like an icon. Then he ran to the door and threw it open. "Patches? Psss psss psss psss psss!"

The cat galloped up the stairs. Casimir picked her up and swung her in a circle, Wanda Sweedok's letter crumpling in his grasp. "Oh, come in!" He took her inside and tossed her onto the bed. "Look what came for me at work today!" he whispered. "I still have a chance!"

He began to smooth the letter on the table. The candle flame flickered at the touch of his breath. The wavering light made him uneasy, ashamed of his joy, fearful, as though he had been warned of a punishment. He sank down onto the bed and turned his face away from the light. "I mustn't," he said to the cat. "Anna and Krystina."

He turned to Victoria's picture and said, "I'm sorry. I can't answer your mother's letter. Wait. Do you even know what was in the envelope in your uncle's pocket? It was sealed. 'Nice, pretty, cooks, sews, obeys,' it says here. Oh, even without some letter inviting me, I wanted you. You liked me, too. I'm sorry. Anyway, your mother wants somebody from the old country. That's me, but I can't say so. I couldn't. Even to a wife. Not till I make everything right for my sisters. Till then, I'm too ashamed."

Casimir stared at Victoria's picture for a long time. "No use in you going lonely, Victoria, just 'cause I can't marry. There's a new greenie from Warsaw just showed up today at the Ebony Gem. Not a bad-looking guy. Friendly. Fits in easy. Your mother would approve. You'd like him. I could give him the—"

He picked up the cat and pressed it against his mouth, shutting himself up. He blew a warm sigh into the cat's fur. She began to purr.

"Dear God," he said, staring at the candle. "What should I do? I want this girl. I want to do right by Anna and Krystina. Ah, I know!" He flung Patches over his shoulder, stood up, and pulled a penny from his pocket. Uncurling his fingers, he found it face up in his palm. "Oh, Patches, can it be true?" He pulled another penny from his pocket. It was face down. "God, help me! What should I do?"

He knelt down and put Patches on the bed. "There's only one thing to do—leave it in the hands of God."

Turning his eyes to the candle, he said, "Tell you what, God, we'll wait till Friday. That gives you four days to erase that girl from my mind. I'll hide the letter in the basement. The picture, too. I promise not to look at them between now and Friday. If I go all Thursday without thinking about Victoria, I'll pass this letter on to that greenie from Warsaw."

Throughout Tuesday and Wednesday, Casimir managed to push away almost every thought of Victoria. But Thursday racked him with images of her. On Friday after work he sent a letter to Wanda Sweedok, asking when he could meet with them. "Please send a telegram," he wrote. Then he lit the candle in his room and promised God he would stop spending Saturday nights with Cecilia, a prostitute in Shamokin, if he would make Victoria's parents say yes.

After three weeks of waiting for the telegram, he decided they were not interested in him, so he dressed to go to Shamokin. He said a prayer before the candle by his bed and thanked God for trying anyhow. He shrugged and said he felt only relief, but a spiteful spray of spit put out the candle. He left the room.

His landlady was halfway up the stairs. Sniffed me out, he thought. Wants to paw at my mind to know if I'm back to spending my Saturday nights somewhere else.

Mrs. Gilotti was a small, shriveled woman. Her braids, gray and white and black, intertwined on the crown of her head like a nest of snakes. In spite of her age, her movements were quick and wiry, as though she had been set in motion by a big rubber band.

She was carrying a small, rectangular box made of olive wood. Her wide grin seemed to say she had found the box after a long, exasperating search. "Look and see," she said, blocking the stairway.

She put her finger to her lips, beckoned Casimir toward the lamp on the crate, and motioned for him to lower his head toward the box. She looked over each shoulder before sliding the lid from the grooves, "Now," she whispered, "you will learna the secret of the name of my cat, Patches."

She slid the lid out of the grooves, revealing a rag doll with a patchwork skirt. The doll lay with its tattered arms crossed over its chest as though it were dead. In hushed, broken English, Mrs. Gilotti told Casimir that the doll's clothing was made from patches of dresses once worn by her grandmothers. Her eyes narrowed when she tugged on the skirt. "Thissa skirt. The grandmother that wore thissa red, my mother's mother. Whole afternoons she spenda in the barn. A handsome stableboy, they said." She smiled slyly.

Casimir replied with a sly smile of his own as he let her put the doll in his hands. He saw that there were stones in the box, and when he picked one out, Mrs. Gilotti explained that she had taken them from her back yard in Italy and put them there just before they sailed to America. Since her husband died, all she had left that was meaningful to her were these stones, the doll, and Patches. God had not blessed her and Giovanni with children.

She said, "I see how good you are to my Patches. If I die, you keepa the cat, yes?"

"Yes."

And because he was so good to her cat, she knew she could trust him to share the secret of her treasures. After all, what was the good of a secret if it couldn't be shared with at least one friend? She even offered to show him where she kept the wooden box hidden, but he smiled and shook his head, replacing the doll gently among the stones.

"And what about your family?" she asked him. All she could get was what she had already been told—that he was born in Loup City, Nebraska, and that his grandparents were Polish immigrants. He would not even say their names.

"No brothers anda no sisters?"

"Nope."

So frustrated was she at having learned so little after exposing the shame in her own family, she was sorry she hadn't put him out the first time she packed his lunch bucket and saw the horror on his face when he lifted the rag to inspect his sandwich. He peeled the bread apart, undressing two thick slices of roast pork, which seemed to leap out of his hands. He stammered when he asked her never, never to put pork in his lunch bucket again. Harold and Fred sat with spoons of oatmeal suspended between their bowls and mouths, astonishment on their wrinkled faces. Yes, Harold and Fred were right, Mrs. Gilotti had decided that day. This Charlie Turek was strange. She would have bet the stones from her treasure box there wasn't a Hunkey alive who wouldn't kill for a fistful of pork.

Now she slid the lid onto the box and reached into her apron pocket. "Telegram." She handed him an envelope and stood squinting at the backside of it, her treasure box pressed between her breasts.

Casimir gave her no news, but grinned maliciously and placed a nickel in her hand. "For all your trouble," he said.

"Aw, you nasty!" she hissed through her teeth as she threw the nickel at his chest. She ran down the stairs, muttering in Italian.

The telegram said: "Come second Saturday December stop Delaware & Hudson stop Supper stop Marek Sweedok."

Instead of going to Shamokin, Casimir went to the Mt. Carmel station to plot his train route. The man at the window told him the 7:30 a.m. train would get him to Mauch Chunk at 10:07. He said there were three trains to Scranton from there. From Scranton he could take a trolley or another train to Dickson City, which was right on the edge of Scranton. He pointed to a long table with books of timetables from various rail lines. "Take your pick," he said.

Casimir nodded a thanks and started for the table, where the hefty books were chained down. His heart began to pound. Those books, those awful books—they were full of numbers. What if the same numbers came up three times in a row? How could he make himself look at them?

He prayed for the courage to look. Then he took a piece of paper from his pocket and wrote his first option: "Leave Mauch Chunk at 11:43 on Lehigh Valley #1, arrive Wilkes-Barre at 1:17. Leave Wilkes-Barre at 1:50 on Laurel Line Local, arrive Scranton at 2:30.

Leave Scranton at 4:05 on Delaware & Hudson #511, arrive Dickson City at 4:18."

He trembled as he reviewed his choices for the second option, hoping he would find a mistake in what he had written: "Leave Mauch Chunk at 12:43 on New Jersey Central, arrive Scranton at 3:15. Leave Scranton at 4:05 on Delaware & Hudson #511, arrive Dickson City at 4:18."

He slipped his hand inside his coat and twisted his shirt, thinking, something bad is going to happen. Either way, I get to Dickson City on the Delaware & Hudson #511 at 4:18. Wait. Maybe the New Jersey Central continues on to Dickson City. No, Victoria's father said to take the Delaware & Hudson. Better not argue with the man holding the cards. Just do what he says till he says yes to the marriage.

Casimir looked at his first option again, which brought him to Wilkes-Barre. Maybe he could skip Scranton and take an earlier Delaware & Hudson train from there. What if, even then, the same numbers came up a third time? He stuck his hands in his pockets, feeling only nickels and dimes. If only he had a penny, he could prepare himself if it predicted bad luck. Well, he would have to find out, no matter what. He wrote: "Leave Mauch Chunk at 11:43 on Lehigh Valley #1, arrive Wilkes-Barre at 1:17. Leave Wilkes-Barre at 3:10 on Delaware & Hudson #511, arrive Dickson City at 4:18."

Casimir pressed his fists against his cheeks. He was not merely afraid of the repeating numbers. The time and place were the same no matter what he did. Fate, he thought. Fate has made some terrible appointment for me. And somehow, the Delaware & Hudson plays a part. Wait! The man here said there was a trolley from Scranton to Dickson City. He could take a trolley. But her old man said the Delaware & Hudson. How could he explain why he took a trolley instead? Wait! Why did Marek pick that train anyhow? Did he realize how the numbers would come out? Was this a trick? Didn't he want his daughter to find a husband? Maybe he wanted to keep her home to take care of him in his old age. This way, by steering all her suitors to their end, by insisting on the Delaware & Hudson, he could keep her home and never have to admit his scheme.

The air in the station felt thick. He went out and paced the streets. Who needed a wife anyway? There was Cecilia in Shamokin. For him, her handsome Charlie, only fifty cents for a whole night. A wife, a whore, it was all the same. No, it wasn't. I'll have suppers with Victoria, he thought. We'll have a son. She'll wait for me by the mine yard when the whistle blows. We'll walk home together. I won't go to Cecilia anymore.

He stuck his hand in his pocket and felt for the timetable notes. He made up his mind to be brave and take the Delaware & Hudson. Whatever bad luck came from it, he would light lots of candles and pray for a way to protect his wife and the son they would have.

He walked back to the station and sent a telegram back to Marek, saying he would arrive on the Delaware & Hudson #511 at 4:18.

The snow had been falling heavily on Dickson City all day. On the front porch of the train station, an old man in a gray overcoat pushed snow off each end with a coal shovel. He shuffled wearily and continually back and forth, fighting the relentless squall.

Wanda Sweedok approached with her daughter. Short and wide in her thick wool coat and bundled head, Wanda walked clumsily, her heavy body bobbing and swaying like a buoy. Her arm was hooked around Victoria's. When they climbed the three steps to the station porch, the old man, never raising his eyes, tipped his hat and scraped a path before them to the door.

Safely delivered, Wanda let go of Victoria's arm, and with a slight shove, directed her toward a bench near a window. Victoria responded with a frown of annoyance, but said nothing. She crossed the room, removed her coat, and tossed it onto a bench near the fireplace. Her pink dress was made of light, summer material. She sat down and fanned the skirt over the bench. Then she leaned toward the fire, rubbing her arms.

Wanda rushed over and yanked her to her feet. "A summer dress? A summer dress! So that is why you put your coat before I get a chance to see. Sneaky, such girl." Her thick, dark eyebrows were pulled together into one continuous line. She picked up Victoria's coat. "Here, put this back before the man comes off that train and thinks he does see crazy girl."

"Mama, this is my prettiest dress."

"Yes, yes, pretty but crazy, the man will say when he sees. No man wants a wife with no sense." She thrust the coat at Victoria. "Here, put this back before Mr. Lucas comes."

"What Mr. Lucas?"

"The undertaker, Mr. Lucas. That Mr. Lucas. 'Ah, this poor Victoria,' he will say. 'Dead at fifteen. Froze to death in that stupid summer dress in December.'"

"Maybe you're right about Mr. Turek. Maybe he will think it's foolish. I'll cover the dress. Mama, when we get home, will you keep Mr. Turek busy while I sneak upstairs and change to a winter dress?"

"Yes, I will do." Wanda sat down and folded her arms in satisfaction. She pointed to the clock above the mantle. "Four past four. Fourteen minutes till his train comes. Yes?"

"Yes, Mama."

Outside, the old man shoveled a path for Casimir Turek, who had just walked from the trolley stop on Main Street. He had arrived in nearby Scranton on the Laurel Line Local at 2:30. The hour and thirty-five minutes he had to wait for the Delaware & Hudson only maddened him with worry. After wandering in and out of the stores on Lackawanna Avenue until 3:15, he got the idea to buy a gift for Victoria and say he had spent so much time shopping that he missed the Delaware & Hudson, had to take a trolley to Dickson City, and walk to the train station from there.

Casimir said to the old man with the shovel, "Has the Delaware & Hudson arrived from Scranton yet?"

"Five-eleven, you mean. That one. No, that comes at 4:18."

"Thank you," Casimir said kindly. But he felt irritated with the man. He could have said yes or no. He didn't have to remind him of the numbers. Was he in on it with Marek?

Casimir looked in the window and saw Victoria staring into the fireplace, her pale profile played upon by the flickering fire. It was as though the changing hues came from within her, showing a moment of anger, a moment of fear, a moment of warmth, of delight. Until now, Casimir remembered only the friendly glow on her face in Black Hollow. Until now, it never occurred to him that she might feel any other way. What if she didn't like him after all?

When he stepped inside, he was behind the block of benches that faced the fireplace. He watched Victoria rise from the bench. She shuffled toward the window and wiped clear a small circle on one pane. There was something familiar in the way she stood there, the lazy slant of her body, the tilt of her head. The sight filled Casimir with a terrible feeling of longing. He turned away. He looked again and suddenly he knew. It was Tanya in Gdansk that he saw. Tanya, the neighbor girl who sat for him and Anna and Krystina when their mother went off to the market. It was Tanya. Tanya, who went to the window and stood just like that, waiting, her chin raised above the place where the top and bottom windows met. If he were just a little boy again, just for a moment, just to stand to the side of her, looking up at her face, watching her eyes watch for his papa to bring back some of the day's catch. Her hair was just the color of Victoria's. Even Victoria's voice was melodious like hers. Tanya's voice was like a wild, pretty song, especially when she'd cry out, "Here he comes, Casimir! Here comes your papa now!"

Casimir forced himself to smile as he started toward the window. "Victoria," he said, reaching for her. Wanda tried to spring up from the bench and block him. She grabbed the armrest and gave herself a good push. By the time she was on her feet, Casimir's hand was on Victoria's shoulder. Wanda waddled toward him, flapping her hands in a frenzy, as if shooing a flock of chickens from her path. "Hey!" she shouted between loud, heavy breaths. "You!" she wagged her finger in Casimir's face. "You! You! Get out, you!"

The passengers on benches, the people in line for tickets—everyone stared in silence. The ticket seller chewed on his cheeks. He dropped a nickel. It bounced off the counter, rolled across the floor, and went into a semi-flat spin before resting at the feet of a drunk propped in a corner, who picked up the coin, grinned, and stuck it in his pocket.

"Victoria," Casimir repeated softly.

"What Victoria!" Wanda said. She wedged herself between them and pushed them apart. "She don't know you!"

"Mama, quiet! Everyone's staring!"

Wanda narrowed her eyes at her daughter. "Do you?"

Victoria looked from Casimir, to the clock, to her mother.

Casimir's eyes froze on the clock. It was 4:14. Four minutes till the Delaware & Hudson arrived. What if it wasn't enough that he had taken a trolley instead? What if just being in that station when it came was enough to, enough to, Christ! What? What, what, what! He thought he'd go mad right before their eyes.

Wanda kept her palm pressed across her daughter's chest. "Well, Victoria? Do you? Do you know this man?"

"This is Charlie Turek, Mama," Victoria whispered.

"This no can be Charlie Turek. It is not 4:18. The Delaware & Hudson, Number 511, did not come yet."

Casimir felt the color wash from his face at the mention of those numbers. He caught a look of alarm on the mother's face as she took a step back and inched protectively toward her daughter. She glared at him. "Who are you? Something be wrong with you. What?"

"I'm Charlie Turek. It's been a long trip, a long time since I ate." He recited the excuse he had rehearsed in case they asked why he hadn't taken the Delaware & Hudson, as his telegram had said he would, and he held out a tiny package.

Victoria took a small cameo out of the package and smiled victoriously at her mother. "This is Charlie Turek, Mama. I recognize him from my visit to Uncle Stanush. Everything is all right." She unbuttoned the top two buttons of her coat and handed the cameo to Casimir. "Will you put this on me?" She looked around, pleased with the envy she fancied on the faces of young women looking back as they walked out to the platform.

Casimir stood behind Victoria and lowered the black velvet band over her throat. Wanda gasped. Victoria, to her own surprise, jumped at the touch of the icy fingers.

Casimir's smile twitched with fear. He was asking, "How does it feel?" But his voice was lost in the blasting hiss of the Delaware & Hudson, Number 511, coming to a stop.

5

UR COMPANY ASKA

Victoria woke to the creak of the banister as her father eased down the stairs in the dark. Light from the parlor shot up through the iron grate in the second-floor hall, casting a cage-like shadow on the lintel of her open door. Then the light through the kitchen window, thrown skyward by the snowy yard, made a ragged patch of light on her ceiling. She heard her father go outdoors, heard the crunch of snow under his boots. His walk was slow. He coughed.

She knelt at the window, watching him make his way to the outhouse. Moonlight shone on his white hair, which was tossed about when he doubled over in the clutch of miner's asthma. He quieted and went into the outhouse. He stayed in there a long time, too long, Victoria thought, and she went for her robe and shoes. Blackdamp, her dog, began to bark. She saw him pawing at the door of the outhouse. Her father came out and hugged himself in the wind. Victoria shuddered, partly from pity for him, partly from anger at the thought of her mother covered and warm like a lump of rising dough.

Marek went down the outside steps to the cellar. Victoria, fixing breakfast, could hear him raking the furnace and hauling a bucket of ashes out to the pit. She watched him, remembering when he could haul two buckets at a time. Now he carried only one, coughing, switching hands all the way to the pit, stumbling like a clumsy dancer.

By the time he came to the kitchen, Victoria had coffee and oatmeal made. She had packed his lunch bucket with kielbasa, bread, a carrot, and two apples.

Marek watched her tuck a rag over the food. He spoke to her in English. "What good surprise. Good, good surprise."

The five-o'clock mine whistle blew.

"Time to get out of bed," Victoria said, laughing and frisking Blackdamp's curly fur. "We're early. We have time to loaf and talk." She took her father's hands and tugged him toward the table, which was made of mismatched planks, one of pine, the other of maple. Along the sides were two backless benches. At each end was a chair with a plain pine back. Victoria began spooning oatmeal into his bowl. Her face beamed like that of a child presenting a scribble. "From now on, Papa, I'll do this for you every morning. I'll fix your lunch, too. I know Mama should do it, like other wives, but—"

Marek spoke gently. "It is all right with me she don't get up. Such things she did when we were young. Now, she don't. She likes to sleep. It is okay. I am happy alone."

"Alone. But I would like to get up and do this for you."

"To practice on your papa? For this Charlie Turek, you practice."

"I like him, Papa."

"Something be wrong, Victoria. At supper yesterday. You saw."

"Papa, he likes me."

"You will suffer."

"Papa, he has a good job. We'll have a nice house. Our children won't have to wear— Oh, Papa, look!" She jumped to her feet, threw open the bottom of her green woolen robe and stretched out her nightgown. It was made of rough white cotton. Stamped in black and off center were the remains of the words:

GREAT AMERICAN FLOUR COMPANY
OMAHA, NEBRASKA
SHIPMENT NO. 10814

What wasn't lost in the seam along her right leg read:

UR COMPANY
ASKA
10814

"A floursack, Papa. This is a floursack!" The hem was bunched in her fist. Every muscle in her face was stiff with the challenge of daring him to find something redeeming. She saw that he could not.

He should just admit the garment stood for everything that was wrong with their lives. Work, work, and nothing to show for it but a daughter drolling about the house in a floursack.

Suddenly, Victoria broke into a laugh and flopped back down to the bench. Her laugh trailed into a soft moan. She sat with her wrists crossed and limp in her lap, her eyes fixed on a water stain on the ceiling. "Papa, I just remembered the dream I had last night. I don't know whether to laugh or cry. I married Charlie Turek in a cathedral. The Pope himself performed the ceremony. All the cardinals were there in their red robes and red capes and little red beanie hats. Important people came—President Taft, King George, Governor Stuart." She giggled and flushed in embarrassment.

"After the ceremony we went through a big carved door to our own beautiful home. There was a great dining hall all set in candles and crystal. Servants in uniform nodded to us as we passed through the room into another, a bedroom. Oh, Papa, it was so beautiful! It was just like the picture of the princess's bedroom in my little yellow book—the canopy over the bed, the flowing veils."

"Yes. 'The Princess and the Pea.' The first story in that book."

"That one, yes. Wait! You know that picture? You know that book? You know I can read?" She clamped her hand over her mouth.

Marek grinned. His blue eyes, though pewtered with cataracts, glistened with mischief. "I know. I always know. I put that little yellow book by the mulberry tree in Iowa for you to find."

"You! You put it there! All these years you've known."

"I know."

"And Mama?"

"No. I see my little girl hide with books. I see how she enjoys, and I make excuse to make her mama walk some other way, so she don't see. I never tell."

Victoria rubbed her father's knuckles against her cheek. "Thank you, Papa. Thank you."

Victoria stared at him, picturing him sneaking that book to the end of the field and setting it down by the tree.

"And this dream," Marek said. "What happened next?"

"A servant knocked on the door. He set our suitcases down and said it was time for bed. Charlie said he would wait in another room while I changed from my wedding gown. He left the room and I stood before a gilded mirror that went all the way up to the ceiling. I took a long, long look at my wedding dress. Tiny diamonds sewn on the lace threw rainbows in all directions. I looked so beautiful!

"Then I went to the chair where the servant had set my suitcase. And, yes, you can guess what was in it. Nothing but this floursack nightgown! 'Ur company aska 10814,' it said. Papa, I was so ashamed. I burst into tears and—"

Marek pressed a finger over her lips and hung his head. "It is me to be ashamed, Victoria. I am ashamed. What poor, poor life I provide to my little girl. You were happy in Europe. But me and my big dream, come to America. Land of plenty. Streets of gold. Every man can give to his children and grandchildren life like kings. Why not me, I said. And brought you here. And for what? Such poor life that my daughter rather marries a—"

"Oh, no, Papa. I don't mean to blame you. You can't help it that you work so hard and they pay you nothing. I mean—"

Marek swept his hand across the table like someone brushing off crumbs. "Such poor life that she rather marries a crazy man with more money than to live such life."

"Crazy! Papa!"

"Yes. Crazy. Not only this man he tell lies. He tells crazy lies. You will suffer. I cannot say yes to such marriage. Your mama, too. We both can see something be wrong with him. He make lies when he talks. That story about Tim Brennan he tells at dinner yesterday."

"His friend who was killed in the blast."

"That was lie."

"Oh, Papa, why couldn't it be true? I know it would be unusual for a man in a high position like Charlie to be friends with an ordinary miner, but it doesn't mean it can't be true."

"That was lie."

Victoria reached for her father's hands, but he sat back and laid them firmly on his lap.

"Papa," she said, her voice quivering. "I know you're trying to be a good papa and look out for me."

"That was lie. Think about it." He raised his palm to her when she tried to speak, and then he stared into his bowl.

Both Marek and Victoria sat in silence, going over yesterday's supper in their own heads, Marek struggling to guess why a young man would claim to be present at a fifty-year-old event that spawned a ballad, Victoria reliving the glances, the little finger hooked around hers under the table. She recalled signs of hesitation, of struggle even, but she decided they were the mere jitters of a young man naturally nervous about provoking her parents' disapproval.

Neither father nor daughter could know the inner answers Casimir had used to convince himself he wasn't really lying when he replied to Wanda's questions. Wanda had told Victoria to sit in the chair at the end of the table, where her father usually sat. Casimir was told to sit on the end of one bench, close to her, as though they were being sized up as a couple. At his first smile of approval, Victoria's mind sprang into fantasies. She saw herself lying in bed, rubbing her cheek against the cheek of their first-born child. The child's delighted father kissed the infant's tiny hand, then hers. A hired woman was standing by to fetch whatever was needed.

Casimir's mind strayed to the description her mother had written in her bid for a husband from the old country—"nice, pretty, cooks, sews, obeys." He envisioned her waiting for him at the gates of the mine yard with their little tow-haired son. Other miners stood by, staring in admiration and envy. No more jibes about Rebekah the mule. No more doubts about whether he was really a man. Here was the proof. He had a son.

Casimir felt the scrutiny of her parents. But he thought about Wanda's matchmaking letter. Able to read the Polish, and aware that whoever translated it to English had left out the "please, please" and the "hurry," he felt there was room for mistakes. They were old and anxious to find someone to take the girl off their hands. They would overlook things. Still, he must be careful what he said.

"Eat!" Wanda said to him and her daughter, sighing. "You two stare at each other till this food gets cold."

Marek reached across the table and patted his wife's hand. "They just be getting to know one another."

"That is not how people get to know. You want to know somebody? You ask questions. Like this. Charlie, you say in your letter you be working and saving money. What kind of work is it?"

"Mama," Victoria said, "he is an inspector of trains for the Ebony Gem Coal Company in Black Hollow, I told you. I saw him myself walking up and down the tracks when I got off the train there. And he hires people. He offered Uncle—"

"Let him answer for himself," Wanda said.

Casimir scrambled to remember what he had written about himself in answer to the matchmaking letter. He had said he worked for the Ebony Gem. He mustn't have said he was a miner. But he hadn't said he wasn't. He took for granted that they knew. Now he was at their table, and they thought he was some important inspector. What if Victoria realized he was a miner? He'd better not admit it yet.

Wanda leaned into him. "Well? You can't remember what is your work?"

"Not now," Marek said. "We can talk after dinner."

"Now and be done with it." Wanda said.

Casimir made a quick plea to God for help in not letting his voice shake through any lies he had to tell. He promised not to tell any if he could avoid it. Then he forced himself to look calm and said, "I work for the Ebony Gem Colliery."

Wanda folded her arms. "And what do you do there?"

"I keep records of things." Yes, records, he thought. He always carried a slip of paper in his pocket and marked down every carload before it left the gangway. So it was not a lie. He did keep records.

"What kind of records?"

"Tonnage."

"And do you ever go down into the mines?"

"Once or twice a day." Once, if he mined all day; twice, if they sent him up to walk Rebekah in the fresh air and then bring her back to the underground stable.

"And what work you do down into there?"

"Make sure the blasting is done safely." He reassured himself of this truth, recalling how he filled the newly-drilled hole with black powder, tamped it, warned passing miners, slipped a squib into the powder hole, lit the fuse, and got the hell out. Yes, he did it safely.

Marek eyed Casimir. "In our mine, the man that keeps records does not come into the mine to check safety. The inside foreman, the fireboss, he check safety inside."

Casimir felt lucky to have "The Ballad of Tim Brennan" come to mind. It was a local song, probably not known to anyone beyond ten miles of the Mt. Carmel mine where this Brennan guy was killed, he figured. "In our mine, too. But ever since Tim Brennan was killed, I make it my business to check too sometimes. Tim was my friend." Casimir paused, dismayed that he had resorted to an outright lie regarding his job. When he told Victoria later, after they were married, that he was only a miner, he wanted to be able to say he had never lied about his work. But Tim Brennan was buried alive in the last century, around the time those Molly Maguires were hanged for taking revenge on the coal companies. Well, the words were out. He had to continue.

His hand sought Victoria's under the table. He hooked his little finger around hers. "I remember Tim going down in the cage with us that morning. A real friendly guy, that Tim Brennan." Casimir tried to recall the stanzas, recall the story. He asked God to help him switch the rhyming words for something that sounded more natural. "His hat he tipped. The cage went down. His peg he plugged—"

Casimir gulped with embarrassment. Then he turned on God for letting him make a fool out of himself. Are you asleep, God? Nobody talks like that. Even greenies! Help me! Suddenly the words came out just right. "Tim went down the gangway after he lit the fuse. You know when the charge won't blow, how you don't dare go back into the chamber? Well, Tim went back in. Turns out the squib was smoldering. Must've touched off the powder just as Tim bent toward it."

Marek, who had been bending his heart and mind in every direction to give this Charlie Turek a chance, suddenly puffed with rage. Did this young man take him for an absolute moron? He pressed his palms against his stomach as though to keep himself from rising up and scattering the young man's teeth.

Wanda reached over and gripped her husband's leg. "No more questions," she said.

Marek and Wanda eyed the prospective bridegroom, each movement of his hands, each shift in his chair, each turn of the head, each glance at their daughter.

Wanda did not bother to serve tea after the meal. She looked at her husband, who seemed able to read her mind. "Your mama and me will walk Mr. Turek to the door," he said.

The three went into the parlor. Casimir was handed his coat. Victoria heard some whispering. The door closed. Marek and Wanda started up the stairs.

Victoria went in and called up after them. "Well?"

"Tomorrow we will talk," Wanda said. "Clear the table."

Victoria put the dishes in to soak, grabbed her coat, and ran out through the back yard. She ran through the alley and two blocks to Mrs. Zahler's, where her parents had arranged for Casimir to spend the night. She arrived in time to catch him on the front porch steps. "Charlie!" she called softly.

Casimir froze. No one in Dickson City knew him. The moment he had grown up dreading had come. He was going to be just like his Uncle Jerzy in Gdansk, just like his grandfather, his great-grandfather—hearing voices, voices that drove them mad. Did he dare turn around to see who had spoken and find no one?

"Charlie," Victoria said, tugging on the back of his coat.

"Victoria, it was your voice!"

"Of course it was. What did they say, my parents?"

"No."

"It is my life."

"You mean yes?"

"Yes. I will marry you. In the spring. I'll write to you. I have to hurry home before they miss me."

The next morning, as Victoria and Marek sat in silence, reliving the dinner with Casimir, Wanda appeared in the kitchen and said to Marek, "You told her?"

"Yes."

Wanda stood behind her daughter. She leaned over her and wrapped her arms around her, drawing her daughter back against her breasts. "You like this man. You want us to say yes. We be sorry. We find different man for you."

Victoria jumped to her feet. "You're not sorry! You're jealous. I don't want a different man. I want Charlie. I'll get a job, save money, go to Charlie myself. You'll see."

She went up to her room and dressed. She watched from her window till her father went out through the back yard in the opening dawn. Then she marched downstairs and strutted past her mother. She yanked her coat from the peg and swung it in a great, angry flair.

"Where you be going, Victoria?"

"Up the street. They're hiring at the Lady Jane Factory."

Wanda grinned. The gap between her front teeth added a look of impish delight to her taunting. "So, lazy girl go to find job today."

"So?"

"So she can save to marry crazy man. Maybe not bad. Only crazy man will take lazy woman that talk, talk, talk all the time. Talk and argue about everything and no do no work. Don't know how. No cooking, no sewing. Not want to learn nothing to be good wife. How we can find decent man? What he gets to return from you?"

"I'm pretty, Mama. I like children. I'm good with children. I have lots of practice from baby-sitting. And I'll learn to cook and work and sew. Even keep my mouth quiet unless I'm asked."

Wanda smirked.

"You'll see," Victoria said. "You'll see who gets the last laugh."

"This is not joke, Victoria! Something be wrong with that man."

"What?"

"I can feel, I can feel. Victoria, you go and get job. Save money, like I try to tell you for two years. But please no go to that man."

"I'm going, Mama. I'm going to marry him in the spring."

Wanda stood up. Her voice lowered to an angry whisper as she walked past Victoria to the parlor. "You make that bed, you sleep in it. No come crying to Mama and Papa for help."

"I won't."

The Lady Jane Factory, a long building of deep red brick, stood on a corner. When Victoria arrived, a tall, haggard woman was struggling with the padlock clamped on a chain wrapped around the iron handles on the black, sheet-iron doors. The woman glanced at her and said, "Looking for a job, Miss Pretty Face?"

"My name is Victoria."

"I said, 'Looking for a job, Miss Pretty Face?'"

"Yes."

With a jerk of her long, skinny head, the woman beckoned Victoria to come inside. "What can you do?"

"I can learn to sew."

"Rocks can learn to fly. Oh, what the hell. Come up. We're desperate." She led Victoria up a wide iron staircase. The pale green paint was worn down to two dark paths testifying to the daily trudging of women and girls and bundle boys.

In the huge room directly ahead, a broad aisle cut through the center of forty rows of treadle machines. From the right side of each machine rose a thin, T-shaped post with looped ends through which thread was guided from two cones that stood on small plates on either side of the post, as though being weighed on a scale. The yards of looped thread throughout the room gave the appearance of webs constructed in a classroom forgotten by all but a colony of spiders. Snips of thread embellished by dust were caught in the junctures of the wrought-iron legs of the machines.

Victoria and the floorlady stood on the landing, staring into the room. Then the woman jerked her head toward an office to the right. "In there, wait." The woman went into the sewing room.

Victoria hung her coat on a metal clothes tree and sat on a chair alongside a desk. Gusts of cold air blew in as workers held open the door at the bottom of the stairs and filed up to the coat room on the other side of the landing. A freckle-faced girl about twelve stuck her head into the office. "Hey, you gonna work here?"

"I hope so."

"I'm Catherine from Carbondale. There's an empty machine by me. Maybe you'll get to work next to me. My mom packed some candy in my lunch bucket. I'll give you some. We'll be like sisters. We can even be blood sisters! Know what that is? That's what the Indians do with their friends. They stick their fingertips with pins. Then they press them against their friends' fingertips and mix their blood. That makes them blood sisters or blood brothers forever and ever. Nothing can ever change that. Not war or death or anything. They're bound together forever and ever. If you want, we can—"

A loud buzzer sounded.

"Oh, Jesus Christ!" the girl said. "Goddamn floorlady'll be— See you later."

Victoria was given a paper to fill out. Then she followed the floorlady back out to the landing. She hesitated as she watched the relentless darting of needles, the endless rocking of feet on treadles. Her fingers gripped the doorjambs. The floorlady pressed a bony hand on Victoria's back. "You goin' in or not?"

"Yes. Yes, I am."

The floorlady nudged her into the room, up the aisle, past the backs of worker after worker bent over the machines.

Coming toward them was a boy with a huge bundle of cut cloth, his face completely hidden behind it, except for a corner of his forehead and his right eye that peered at her as he stretched his neck to see around the bundle.

A girl at the end of a row jumped out of her seat and backed away from him, her face twisted in alarm, as if the boy were carrying a ball of fire. When he reached the back of the room and dumped the bundle into a canvas cart, the girl sat down again.

The floorlady folded her arms. "What the hell's the matter with you, Susan?"

Susan, a stocky girl about thirteen, pressed her lips together and cocked her head to the side. "Goddamn bundle boy, that's what. Who's this?"

"Miss Pretty Face." The floorlady pointed to the empty place next to Susan and said to Victoria, "There. Sit down there. You'll start as a side-seamer. Piece rate. More you do, more you make. Make mistakes, do it over, lose pay. Sit down and pay attention to the other girls." The woman took some skirt panels from the bin beside Susan's machine and dropped them into the bin beside Victoria's. Then she walked away.

Victoria, looking at the thread dangling from the two cones, felt like crying. She didn't know how to thread the machine, much less sew anything. She tried to copy the threading pattern on Susan's machine. Susan's brown eyes, so fearful in the presence of the bundle boy, had become cold, determined, following fiercely the movement of her own chunky fingers pushing, gathering, guiding the material over the throat plate, rushing to make the best piece rate.

Victoria managed to copy the threading pattern. Then she watched Susan sew panels together and throw them into a bin. Victoria turned to the girl on the other side. She had brown, somewhat bulgy eyes like Susan. Susan's nose turned under a little at the bottom, but otherwise, their noses seemed the same. They each had a bottom lip that stuck out and overlapped the top lip. Susan's hair was a few shades darker than the other's, and the one on Victoria's right looked a little older. They both looked angry as they worked.

Victoria ran her first pair of panels under the needle, but the thread made no stitches. It just made one continuous brown line and slid off the side of the fabric.

Suddenly the lights went out. Workers shrieked about the lost piecework, the lost pay. Those next to the windows continued their work in the dim daylight of a snowy morning.

Susan reached over and grabbed the panels Victoria had tried to sew. Then she slid back the throat plate on Victoria's machine and squinted into the hole. "Ha! No wonder! They didn't put no bobbin in here!" She stood up and shouted, "Hey, what's the idea puttin' a new girl here with no bobbin?"

The bundle boy came her way.

"Oh, shit! Not you! Not today! Get the floorlady."

Susan sat down and whispered to Victoria. "Monthlies."

"What?"

"Monthlies. I have my monthlies. And I bet that bastard of a bundle boy knows I have 'em. He's havin' fun trying to scare me. He thinks he'll get me in trouble and have a good laugh for himself."

"What kind of trouble?"

"Didn't you know? That's how you get in a family way. You know, you get to having a baby."

"How?"

"Jesus, girl, where you from? Didn't you know? If you got your monthlies, and a boy touches you, even if he just brushes against you like this," Susan said, brushing her fingertip over Victoria's arm, "even if his touch is that light, you'll end up in a family way."

"Susan," Victoria said gently, "that's not how you get, you know, pregnant."

Susan traced an X over her chest. "Cross my heart and hope to die." Her eyes drilled into Victoria's. "You can ask my sister. She's sitting right on the other side of you. That's what happened to her."

"What happened?"

"Just what I told you. A bundle boy, too. Chester. Chester works in the mines now. But he worked here as a bundle boy when he bumped into Florence when she had her monthlies and got her in a family way. She told me herself. My father said he'd kill him if he didn't marry Florence. Hayna, Florence?" she asked, looking past Victoria to the girl at the next machine.

"What?" Florence said. "I wasn't paying attention."

"Didn't Chester brush against you when you had your monthlies and you ended up having little Mary Ann?"

"Will you stop telling everybody? Whyn't you just publish it in the *Scranton Tribune?*"

"Maybe I should. If more young girls knew, they wouldn't end up being married to jerks like Chester."

"Aw, shut up."

"No. You."

"No! You shut up!"

The lights went on and the floorlady tossed Susan a small bag of bobbins. Susan took one out and said to Victoria. "For a nickel, I'll show you how to put the bobbin in and make the thread come up through the throat plate. I hate to ask for the nickel, but it's costin' me time to show you."

Victoria took a nickel from a change purse in her pocket. "Thanks," she said. She was glad to give the nickel. She wished she had millions of nickels to hand out. She watched Susan install the bobbin, but looked up when freckle-faced Catherine, sitting two rows ahead, shrieked as the floorlady ripped apart every pair of panels the girl had sewn and told her to do them over. "That's not fair!" Catherine shouted. "What the hell!"

Victoria squeezed the change purse in her pocket. She said a little prayer for Catherine. And she promised God she wouldn't be selfish when she married Charlie. She would not forget where she came from. She would be kind and generous to the Susans and Florences and little Mary Anns and the Catherines from Carbondale.

6

DON'T HE LOOK LIKE MY WALTER?

Deep in the earth, miners, their workday over, strapped their tools to their backs and backed down steep, narrow manways, their feet groping for rotting rungs of wood.

At the central gangway where the tunnels converged, Casimir pulled peg number thirty-one from the board. He chuckled bitterly. "Thirty-one. They should've given me seven or eleven. Might even get outa this coal hole some day." He sat on a boulder next to the cage shaft, set his lunch bucket down, drew a handkerchief from his pocket, and wiped the grit from his teeth.

Donny Wilson, a short, plump mute, grabbed the sleeves of miners gathering to wait for the cage and pointed at Casimir. Smacking a hand over his big belly, he rocked back and forth in a wheezy laugh. He took a handkerchief from his pocket and scrubbed his teeth while dancing a jig in the spotlights from the hats of miners. He bowed low before a chorus of cheers and applause.

"Hey, Charlie," Wilhelm Blankenbiller said to Casimir, "Every day you clean your teeth in here. You cannot vait till you're out of dis mine? Vut you look pretty for? Who?"

"The mules," Joe McDonald said. "He's in love with Rebekah the mule." He hooked elbows with Donny and resumed the jig, tipping his hat and singing:

> *Oh, me sweetheart's the mule in the mine.*
> *I drive her without reins or lines.*
> * On the bumper I sit,*
> *   And I chew and I spit,*
> *All over me sweetheart's behind.*

Caruso Tullio shoved the pair from the spotlight. "Maybe Charlie gotta some nice girl in Pottsville. Shamokin, maybe. If not, my cousin Concetta. She's a nice girl. Hey, Charlie, yes?"

Casimir shrugged.

"Get yourself a girl, Charlie," Karl Spacek said. "Time I was your age, I had four kids. And—"

"Mine were all boys!" all the miners recited along with Karl.

All right, Karl Spacek, Casimir thought. Go ahead, gloat about your weasel-faced tykes. That's what you get from a weasel-faced wife. He smiled to imagine the miners' gaping faces when they saw the woman he got for himself.

A descending cage rattled to a stop on the left side of the double shaft. Casimir swung open the picket gate and got in with four other miners. Two yanks on the signal cord and the cage began to rise, carrying the men outside.

Weary and blackened, the miners pressed their pegs into the large outside board, and like silhouettes in the dusk, they headed for home.

In the mine yard, Casimir slipped behind the office shanty. He waited in the shadows for Antonio Corsetti. The boy appeared and turned his face away when Casimir stooped down next to him. "I wasn't crying," Antonio said. "I got coal dirt in my eyes is all."

Casimir looked at the white smears on the boy's face. "Hope you got it all out."

"I did. It's okay now."

"Good. Say, did you check both boxes at the post office on Saturday?"

"Yeah. I walked by your house and did our secret whistle to let you know about the letters. But you didn't come out. I whistled last night, too. Anyway, there were two letters. Don't worry, I didn't let on to nobody about Casimir, your secret friend. There was one letter in his box, and one in yours. And don't worry, I didn't let nobody see. My mama didn't see neither. I hid them in a tin can under our back porch. I'll bring them right over." Antonio ran out of the mine yard and down the cobblestone street.

Casimir walked home slowly, figuring he'd get there about the same time Antonio showed up with the letters. When he reached the corner of Saylor and Downs, he saw a coin gleaming in the lamplight. If it's a penny, let it be face up, he prayed. He bent over to reach for it. But he closed his eyes and straightened up suddenly, thinking, if it's face down, it's more bad luck than I can face right now. He left the coin there and turned onto Downs Street. A block later he was home. It was dark. He let himself into the yard through the back gate along the alley. He took his boots off on the back porch, grabbed his wire brush from a tin can, sat down on the top step, lit his miner's hat, and began cleaning his boots.

When he heard five short whistles, he stood up, leaned over the fence, and motioned for Antonio to come to the gate.

The boy removed his cap and pulled out two smudged envelopes. First he handed Casimir the one with the American stamps. Casimir stuffed it into his pocket before Antonio could ask about it.

Antonio, handing Casimir the other envelope, said, "This was in your friend Casimir's box. These sure are funny-looking stamps. Where's this letter from?"

The envelope was postmarked, "Danzig, November 18, 1910." Three months it had taken to reach him. It angered him to see the word Danzig. To him it would always be Gdansk.

"Where's it from?" Antonio asked again.

Casimir pointed to the postmark. "Denver. Denver, Colorado. Casimir's brother Patrick."

"Oh, that's right. I see, I see." The boy squinted at the postmark, pretending he could read. "It's hard to tell what it says in this light. Denver, huh? Denver sure has funny-looking stamps."

"It sure does."

"Can I keep them?"

"I'll ask Casimir to save them for you. When's your birthday? I'll give you lots of fancy stamps then."

"February 16th. It just passed. Almost a whole year to wait."

"The more stamps you'll get then," Casimir said to the boy. And, he thought to himself, that's a whole year to recover some of what he was spending to fix up that old company house for himself and Victoria. A whole year to save again for his sisters' house and their passage here. Then, what would it matter who knew his real name, where his letters came from, where he himself came from, that everything got ruined there because of him? Everything would be put right, his shame erased.

"Can't I have just one stamp now?" Antonio said.

"All right. But you must hide it and promise never to tell where you got it if anyone finds it. Even your mama."

"I promise."

Casimir saw that the boy's face had been quickly rinsed. Coal dirt extended the line of his wavy black hair. His dark eyes gleamed as he watched Casimir tear the stamp from the envelope.

Casimir grinned to discover how much joy this gift gave to this little boy. He stooped down and caressed his face. "Gee, you look like your papa. He was a good man, Antonio. A smart man, too."

"That ain't what the company man said when he dumped Papa's body on our porch. He said it was Papa's own fault, the accident. He made Papa sound stupid. He made me feel ashamed."

"No, Antonio. Your papa was the best miner around. Any miner will tell you that. Those timbers were rotten to the core. Don't let the company man tell you different."

"The company man said Papa didn't put those timbers up tight in the first place."

"Antonio, that section of timbers was there since the days of Moses, long before your papa came to the Ebony Gem. The tops were like sponges. The miners put in for replacements, but no, the new timber went to the new tunnels. Why waste them on a section that's nearly mined out anyway, they figured, thinking they'll save a nickel. Well, the pillars gave way before the company got its last nickel's worth of coal from those breasts, just when your papa was walking through that gangway, him and Fred Schmidt." Casimir hugged Antonio. "That's why we have strikes, Antonio. To make them fix things that hurt us and kill us. And to make them pay us something our families can really live on, so little boys like you can study in nice, clean classrooms where you belong. Not pick out rocks in some grimy black breaker."

"So it really wasn't Papa's fault, the accident."

"No."

"I'll tell Mama!" Antonio began to skip away.

"Wait!" Casimir stood up and reached into his pocket. "Say, now, you forgot your quarter for checking the boxes. And an extra nickel for being such a good secret keeper."

"Thanks!" Antonio ran off.

Casimir saw Mrs. Gilotti at the kitchen window. He nodded to her and went directly to the basement through the yard. He washed his hands and sat on the bottom step to read the letters. But before he could open them, an uneasy feeling came over him. What if there was bad news? He was sorry he hadn't stopped to see if that penny was face up or face down. Had he looked and found it face down, he'd feel better prepared to deal with bad news. He stuffed the envelopes inside his shirt, went out through the yard, and ran back to the corner. The coin was still on the ground.

He folded his hands, as if in prayer, then buried his nose and mouth inside the steeple of his fingers. He closed his eyes. "Let it be up. Let it be up." It was.

He went back to the basement, washed and changed quickly, and hurried to the kitchen for supper so he would not arouse Mrs. Gilotti's curiosity. After supper, Patches followed him to his room and rubbed against his shins as he unlocked his door. He stooped down and scratched her under the chin. "Welcome," he said. He opened his door and bowed as the cat strutted past him to the bed. Then he tossed the letters before the cat and said, "Which one shall I open first?"

The cat sniffed Victoria's letter.

Casimir opened it. It said the wedding dress would be ready in time for the first Saturday of June. She would arrive in Black Hollow the night before. Could he find her a room for that night? Her parents still said no. "Charlie, do you have an older friend who can walk me down the aisle in Papa's place? I must accept that Papa won't come, but it would be too sad to walk down alone. Please find someone."

"An older man, an older man," Casimir muttered. "Blankenbiller! He's got white hair like her papa. But he's a Kraut. Imagine, Patches. A Kraut handing over my bride."

Casimir opened his sisters' letter. Anna still working as a seamstress, Krystina still a nanny for a lady across town. They were looking forward to coming over, though they understood it would take time to prepare a home and save for their passage. They could be patient, it said, as usual. A new thing in this letter was asking him if he couldn't find it in his heart to forgive their mother. They had forgiven her. The doctor didn't give her much hope. Six months, maybe. "Couldn't you just go to Pottsville and hold her hand for us once to say good-bye? By the way, Uncle Jerzy died last week. It's sad to think he spent the last seventeen years of his life in that asylum. He was forty-one. Heart failure. Casimir, please go to Mama before she dies, too."

Casimir brooded on the bed, his heart heavy with shame. With his papa alive, Uncle Jerzy could have stayed out of the madhouse. "We could have stayed in Gdansk. It was my fault Papa died, Patches. I didn't tell you that part. My fault we had to come to America in the first place. But Mama, she promised she'd send for—look!" He tapped the letter on the line where his sisters asked him to forgive their mother. "Forgive Mama? Look at me. Look at all I just spent so I could have myself a wife in a nice home. I'm no better than my own rotten mother. Well, I'll start saving again. I will. But the wedding's all planned. I'll marry Victoria. Then I'll send for my sisters."

Casimir carried the cat to the door. "Got to go talk to the priest."

Rehearsing how he would ask Father Kashnoski to reserve that Saturday for his wedding, he headed to the rectory at St. Hedwig's, a Polish Catholic church, the only church in the patch. He went up to the front porch and read the notice telling visiting hours. Fifteen minutes to wait.

He paced on the porch awhile. Then he walked around back to the cemetery, which the full moon lit brightly. He was careful to avoid stepping on anyone's grave. He walked slowly with his head low and his hands in his pockets, following the tracks in the snow made by other visitors. The air, though cold, was still and restful. He found himself glad to be taking this quiet, unplanned walk alone before approaching the priest.

He looked back at the rectory and saw a woman watching him from the window. Her back to the kitchen light, her figure was solid black, like a cavity in the shape of a woman, an entrance to a dark cave, a cursed mine, where a man might go in and never come out. Casimir stood spellbound. He began to feel afraid, as though being drawn in against his will.

He looked away and began walking again. The restfulness of the cemetery deserted him as images of his father's funeral overcame him. Swift clouds cast shadows that made the tombstones appear to move, as if alive, conscious, aware of him and his part in his father's death. They surrounded him like a jeering audience.

Seeing that the woman was still watching him, he fought the urge to run. He strolled to the front porch of the rectory and took a penny from his pocket, squeezing it hard in his fist and uttering a prayer before looking at it. It lay face up in his open palm. He thanked God for this sign and tugged on the bell cord.

In the dark wooden door were three clear, narrow windows forming the shape of a cross. He peered inside, through a tiny, unlit foyer, through a stained-glass scene of Jesus with a lamb slung over his shoulder. He knocked. The woman who had watched him from the back window approached. She looked powerless now, her image fractured by the Good Shepherd.

The female figure collected to wholeness again as she swung open the inner door, and then the outer one. Her welcoming manner was a surprising comfort. Casimir had seen her at Sunday Mass, but had never paid much attention. She appeared to be a little under fifty. She seemed ready to lunge at him with a big embrace, like a woman delighted at the long-awaited return of a child. "Oh, come in! Come in! We are glad! Father is just ready to finish his tea. He does not like to have bother when he haves his tea. His office is there. You can wait in there or out in here."

"Thanks. I'll wait here."

The woman nodded and rubbed her hands in delight as she backed out of the room. It was another half hour till the priest appeared. The room behind him was unlit. Except for an inch of the stiff, white Roman collar exposed at the neck, he was dressed in black. He was a short man with a short, broad face and a thick cap of solid gray hair with such a low hairline that he appeared to be peering out from under a rock.

He spoke in a flat tone, as though trying to conceal irritation. "My housekeeper says you want to see me."

"Yes. I want to arrange for a wedding."

The priest turned around and hollered, "Mrs. Wozniak, come into the office and take notes."

Casimir and the priest sat facing one another across a broad desk. Mrs. Wozniak took her place on a stool in the corner behind the priest. The priest, heavy-hearted in the discharge of his sacred duties, looked back at her. She seemed to will herself into the proper attitude, drawing in her smile and letting her back and shoulders fall into a frumpy sort of slump, like a punished pupil who had been caught making faces at the rest of the class.

"Well? Where is *she?*" Father Kashnoski said. He bobbed his head in all directions as though he expected someone to emerge from behind the drapes or a piece of furniture.

"Who?" Casimir said, flustered before the demanding stare.

"The woman you plan to marry. I like both parties to be present to make sure both understand the sacred duties of marriage and family."

Casimir explained that the girl was from away. She was alone in the world, except for him. He told himself that, since her parents had abandoned her, she really was alone. It was no lie.

"Well, then," Father Kashnoski said, "I must have some way to know she understands her duties as a wife and mother. Now—you're a coal miner."

"Yes. What are you getting at?" Casimir's heart began to pound. Did this man know Victoria didn't know he was a miner?

The priest puffed up his cheeks and blew out a mouthful of exasperation. "Does she understand the lot of a coal miner's wife?"

A coal miner's wife, Casimir thought, any coal miner, he means, not me especially. That's what he means. Casimir tried to sound confident. "She comes from a coal mining family. She knows what kind of life it is. Hard work and no reward but the love of her husband and children."

"And God."

"Yes, Father. That goes without saying."

"No, it doesn't. If the people in this patch said that out loud a little more often, instead of praying for more and more—more money, more advantages, more, more, more—you'd all feel a little less downtrodden and a lot more glad for the cross you've been given to help you earn your way into heaven."

Casimir wanted to slug the man as he remembered him standing with the company during the last strike. The man didn't even have the shame to make a secret of the free groceries and supplies he got at the company store. Priests depend on the charity of the community, this one always told the parishioners. More, more, more. What the parishioners prayed for most was that the bishop would transfer Kashnoski to hell and replace him with a priest like the one in Tamaqua, or the one in Locust Gap, or that Father Matsko in Coal

Township, priests who saw the suffering of the miners and their families and helped them. But no, Black Hollow was stuck with Kashnoski, a company man through and through. A man who never went without like the miners' families.

"And you," the priest continued, "as a husband, are to provide for her and the children. Both of you, under pain of hell, are obliged to train them up in the teachings of the one true Church."

"Yes, Father."

The priest turned to his housekeeper. "Mrs. Wozniak, start a clean sheet of paper and— Mrs. Wozniak, what's the matter with you? Why are you smiling? You've been smiling since this man arrived!"

The woman smoothed back her thin brown hair and adjusted the combs on the sides, as though she had been caught looking sloppy. She closed her eyes and bit her lower lip, but still she could not conceal her delight.

"Mrs. Wozniak?"

"Don't he look like my Walter, Father? His eyes—"

"Yes, yes. A little. Now take a clean sheet of paper and write—"

"Those eyes, almost turquoise like my son's. Until I saw so close this man, I think only my Walter has such color eyes." She said to Casimir, "He's dead, you see. Did you know him?"

Casimir nodded. "He worked in Breast Number Four when the accident happened. I work in Six. I'd see him waiting for the cage in the gangway. He only worked there a month or—"

Mrs. Wozniak, shrinking before the glare of the priest, cut him off. "I am sorry, Father. I will write."

She pulled a clean sheet of paper from the bottom of the stack and placed it on top. The priest asked Casimir for the young woman's name, and then began to dictate:

> Dear Miss Sweedok,
>   It has come to my attention that you wish to marry one of my parishioners, Charles Turek. Before I can agree, I must ask you to reply to some questions. First,—

"'Questions,' Father. How you must spell?"

The priest spelled the word and others she asked about, looking more exasperated at each interruption. Casimir, wondering why he didn't just write the letter himself, decided that the priest liked having the woman at his command, no matter how much trouble her poor English was.

They struggled through the rest of the dictation:

> First, are you a practicing Catholic, faithfully receiving the sacraments and attending Mass every week? Second, describe the lot of a coal miner's wife. Third, are you prepared to love, honor, and obey your husband? Fourth, do you know the parents' obligation to school their children in the teachings of the Holy Mother Church? Until you answer these questions properly, the Banns will not be announced.
>
> Faithfully yours in Christ,
Rev. Joseph Kashnoski

Well, Casimir thought, relieved, he didn't ask what she understood *her* lot to be as a miner's wife. Maybe she wouldn't get it. He would go home and write his own letter to her, make sure she thought he meant the people she would live among.

Father Kashnoski stood up and said to Casimir, "If I receive a proper reply, it will be my duty to announce the Banns of Marriage three times. If I don't, well—"

Casimir rose to his feet. "Three times?"

"You know that the parish where the wedding is to take place announces the Banns of Marriage on the three Sundays before the wedding."

"Three in row?"

"I thought you said you're a Catholic!"

"I am."

"Then you should know—"

"Three in a row? Couldn't you skip a Sunday?"

"Why should I skip a— What's the matter with you?"

"It, it's just that if there's some mix-up, some delay, the wrong train, or the wrong— Who knows? It might take an extra Sunday."

Mrs. Wozniak put a finger over her lips and patted the air to shush him. She jerked her head toward the door to let him know she would talk to him privately outside.

The priest said, "Make sure you plan properly, and there will be no need to bend the rules of the Holy Catholic Church."

"Yes, Father."

"Mrs. Wozniak, see this man out."

"Yes, Father."

Mrs. Wozniak grabbed a woolen shawl from the clothes tree by the door and walked Casimir out to the porch. "I know what you mean about three in a row. Father does not believe such things. He tells that I have a sin to believe them. But I do believe. I will help you. I will sit in the last row in our church and bring salt each Sunday of the Banns. When the priest he tells the Banns, I will throw the salt over my shoulder. No one will see."

"Thank you."

"I am glad to help so you don't end up to get dead like my boy. I threw the salt for him, but he don't listen to me about the other thing. He does not believe. Like Father Kashnoski."

"What other thing?"

"Not to look upon his bride the night before the wedding."

"Oh, God!"

"What!"

"Victoria is coming on a train the night before the wedding. I was going to meet her at the train station and walk her to some place she'll spend the night."

"No, you must not. I will meet her at the train. She can stay with me. I will protect both of you."

"Thank you. God bless you."

7

LET THIS CUP PASS FROM ME

On the morning of the wedding, Mrs. Gilotti came to Casimir's room. She looked down at her shoes as she spoke. "I am ashama to ask on such a day, but—but, remember, you tell me—you say when I die, you keepa the cat? Now you will be married and don't live in this house no more. You and your bride in the new house, if I die—"

"Of course, we'll come and get Patches!"

Mrs. Gilotti's thin face eased into a smile. "And I have a gift for you anda the new missus. I know how they do with the dolls for the Polish wedding feast. For you the dolls I mada myself. You will see. The neighbors will bring things, too. I talked to many. Food. Music today in your new back yard, that corner house everybody sees you breaka your back to fix for the new bride. The talk of the patch, you and that house. Every night after work, every weekend, fixa, fixa, fix. Today, a celebration in that yard after the wedding."

"You arranged a big party?"

"You hava no family here. The girl is not from here. Who can have a wedding and no celebration? You were a good tenant. Clean. Always paya the rent. I do the celebration. I am glad."

Casimir stared at her, too stunned to say thank you.

She turned to leave. "And before you go, let me say how sorry I was so crabby sometimes." She offered her hand, and Casimir shook it. She backed out of the room.

Casimir listened for her to close the door of her second-floor bedroom. Then he went out, dropped his belongings off at his new residence, and headed for St. Hedwig's, though the wedding would not begin until ten. He had arranged to meet Donny Wilson there early, and he had to get there before Victoria to avoid any chance of looking upon his bride before the ceremony.

He walked up the center aisle and gazed at the large wooden crucifix behind the marble altar. He genuflected, turned right and knelt before the altar of St. Joseph, which was much closer to the altar rail than the central altar in its receding sanctuary. On a pedestal attached to the wall, above a small marble altar, St. Joseph stood in brown sandals, a white tunic, and a green robe draped over one shoulder. A solemn, barefoot toddler in a white tunic sat on his left arm. His hair was sandy brown and curly, his eyes light blue. Like the carpenter holding him, the child gazed, expressionless, beyond the empty pews.

Before St. Joseph's altar, close to the rail, was a wrought-iron tray of red votive candles with a coin slot and a card that said it cost one cent to light a candle. Casimir took two pennies from his pocket. He could not bear to look whether they were face up or down. Besides, there was no telling how they would land in that dark chamber once he slipped them through the slot. He put one penny in and lit one candle. He pressed his clasped hands against his mouth and whispered, "Dear Saint Joseph, you were the head of the Holy Family, just like I'm about to become head of a family. Help me to be a good husband and father. Please ask God to forgive me for letting Victoria think I'm not a miner. And please, please help her not to hate me when she finds out. I didn't mean to trick her. I didn't even know she thought I was somebody important till that dinner with her parents. And—well, you saw the whole thing. You know it wasn't really my idea. All right, I should've spoke up, I confess. Anyway, please ask God to help."

He put the other penny in the slot. "One more thing. The worst thing of all. Saint Joseph, please ask God not to let me go crazy like my grandfather and uncles, like Uncle Jerzy with his mouth stuck in that crazy O-shape. How the children of Gdansk laughed at him! Don't let it happen to me! Remember Aunt Marta said madness was the curse of the males in our family? Remember I asked if that would happen to me when I grew up? If I'd hear voices and my mouth would get stuck in that O? She said, 'Not if you're good.' I'll be good. I'm saving money again to make up for the bad thing I did in Gdansk. I'll get Anna and Krystina here. I want to be a good husband

and father. But I can't if I go mad like the others. Please get God to help."

Casimir looked at the crucified Jesus behind the center altar. Jesus was good, but it didn't save him from his fate. "Is madness to be my fate no matter what I do?" he asked Saint Joseph. "Am I a passenger on the Delaware & Hudson, ending up in the same place at the same time, no matter how I start out?"

Staring at the crucifix, he thought about the agony in the Garden of Gethsemane. He remembered how Jesus had prayed to be delivered from his fate, how the apostles, his best buddies, had fallen asleep while he agonized and prayed alone. *Let this cup pass from me.*

The image of Jesus sweating and wringing his hands in dread wrenched him deeply. For the first time in his life, Casimir really felt for that suffering Jesus of Nazareth, felt sorry for him, really sorry. He was no longer some stranger from long ago when men wore dresses, some stranger who sacrificed his life so that sinful little boys like Casimir Turek could go to heaven when they died. He was somebody doomed to suffer no matter how good he tried to be.

The image of his sisters on the dock flashed in his mind. What if he made a life for them in America and the voices came anyway because the voices really were a curse passed from grandfather, to sons—yes, all the sons, to Ignacy, Casimir's own father, not just to Casimir's uncles. No use pretending it hadn't happened to Papa. Mama and Aunt Marta whispered about it. It was starting with him, too. No use pretending. Was it mercy, after all, for him to die before the neighbors saw? Before the other fishermen saw? Before the O-mouth happened and the children of Gdansk laughed at him, too?

Casimir joined his hands into a single fist and pressed them against his forehead. He rocked on his knees and squeezed back tears. "Let this cup pass from me! Let this cup—"

Suddenly, he shuddered, tried to shake the thoughts from his mind. He rose and ran down the side aisle, through the recessed area at the back of the church, past the baptismal font, and up the spiral staircase to the choir loft, where he was to meet Donny Wilson at nine-thirty.

In the center of the loft was an organ. There were five pews on each side. Casimir circled the organ a few times, paced in and out of the pews, flipped the kneelers up, set them down, flipped them up, and set them down again. He paced the length of the loft and counted all the organ pipes lining the back wall.

"Come on, Donny. Come on, Donny," he muttered. He sat down in a pew. His eyes traveled along the last seven stations of the cross protruding from the walls between the stained-glass windows. Station number nine snagged his gaze. It was there that Jesus fell for the third time. Jesus fell three times, Casimir thought. Three in a row. "Oh, what's the use trying to stop anything!" He got up and started pacing again. "Come on, Donny. Come on!"

Donny, who had crept up the stairs, sneaked up behind Casimir and began to shadow him, step for step, breaking into a wheezy giggle when Casimir turned around to face him.

Donny's round face was full of merriment. He stepped back and spread his arms, encouraging Casimir to behold his neat black suit and bow tie. He raised his arms over his head and turned a full circle.

Casimir grinned. "You look great! The best best man a guy could ask for. And your sister. She still says she'll be the maid of honor?"

Donny nodded.

"What about old Blankenbiller? Did he find a suit? Does he know to walk Victoria from Mrs. Wozniak's house at 9:45?"

Donny gripped the lapels of his own suit and stuck his chest out proudly. He patted his hair as though pushing down the bushy, white hair of Wilhelm Blankenbiller. He raised his chin, strutted over to the organ, and knocked his fist on it as though knocking on a door. Then he bowed from the waist and offered his arm to an invisible woman, walked her over to Casimir, bowed again, and stepped back.

Casimir nodded and said, "So it's all arranged. Good. Good. Jeez, I never thought I'd see the day I'd ask a Kraut to hand over my bride. But she wanted somebody to give her away. Her own father's too sick to come, like I told you. And Blankenbiller looked the part. What the hell. And, and what about Mrs. Wozniak? She was supposed to let you know Victoria arrived all right last night."

Donny nodded.

"And what about—did you know that, oh, Jesus, Donny, I hate to ask you this, but I'm depending on you. Did you know, did Mrs. Wozniak tell you why I couldn't meet Victoria at the train myself?"

Donny shook his head.

"Promise you won't laugh?"

Donny pressed his hand flat over his heart.

"Mrs. Wozniak said it's bad luck for a man to look upon his bride the night before the wedding."

There was laughter in Donny's eyes, but he managed to hold back a smile.

"Say, Donny, do you suppose it means I can't look at her until the moment Blankenbiller hands her over?"

Donny shrugged.

"Well, just in case, help me out, will you? If it seems I might accidentally catch a glimpse of her, be a curtain or something, will you?"

Donny laughed into his hand and patted Casimir's chest as though begging for forgiveness.

"Go ahead. Laugh, if you think it's stupid. But will you do it anyway?"

Donny nodded. Then he raised his finger to indicate he had another solution. He walked away and came back swinging his hips, his standard way of imitating a woman. Then he put his fingers on top of his head and pretended to pull a veil down over his face.

"Ah!" Casimir said. "She'll have her face covered."

Donny nodded and shoved Casimir. He waved his hand as though to say, don't worry, and he walked off.

Alone again, Casimir paced the loft. Then he went downstairs, walked up the center aisle and positioned himself in front of the altar rail to practice not turning around, just in case she forgot to pull the veil down.

He heard someone walking up the aisle behind him. Victoria? Too early. *Don't turn around!*

"Mister?" a man's voice called.

Blankenbiller? No. No greenie accent. *Don't turn around!*

"Mister?" a child's voice said, followed by a giggle. "Mister?" the child said again. "Mister?"

Don't turn around!

"Excuse me, sir," the man said, stepping in front of Casimir. "You the bridegroom?"

A tall, dark-haired man stepped in front of him. A canvas bag hung from a shoulder strap. He set a wooden tripod on its feet and spread the legs.

Casimir's face gave way to an easy smile of relief.

A little girl about three stood behind the man. She leaned her head from around his hip and peeked at Casimir through the fingers of one hand. Jumping sideways suddenly, she said, "My name is Gina Diomira Valente." A rag doll with a thumb-shaped head fell to the floor. Clusters of loose black curls tumbled over the child's face as she bent down to pick up the doll. "And her name is Sarina." The child's dark, dark eyes were full of joy and trust as she held Sarina up to Casimir.

Casimir grinned and patted the doll on the cheek.

Mr. Valente stooped down next to Gina Diomira and put his arm around her. "Tell Mr. Turek why we're here."

"We came to take a picture of you and your new bride at the altar."

Casimir said to the father, "But I didn't hire a—"

"Your mother hired me."

"My mother! Is she here?"

The photographer spoke in a whisper. "She came with us on the same train from Pottsville. She's in the last pew back there. I told her the groom's family is supposed to sit up front on the St. Joseph side, but she says she wants to stay back there." Mr. Valente glanced back at her. "She's awfully sick, I'd say. If you want to say hello, I'll wait up here and explain how I'll do the photographs when you come back."

The doors at the back of the nave opened. Victoria? *Don't turn around! Don't look!*

The little girl began tugging on Casimir's hand. "Come, I'll show you where your mama is."

Casimir flung her hand away. "Stop!" he whispered. "You'll ruin everything!"

Gina Diomira stumbled and retreated behind her father. She clung to his coat. Her father pressed his hand against her cheek. Her dark eyes fixed themselves on Casimir from around her father's hip.

"Mister," the photographer said, "You're lucky we happen to be standing in a church right now. It's not my business why you won't go to your mother, but you didn't have to treat my little girl like that." He stroked his daughter's hair. "Come on, sweetie, we'll go outside. We'll go for a nice walk, watch the birds. Mr. Turek's mama really wants a picture. She's a nice lady and she don't feel good. She'd be real sad if I didn't take a picture for her. We'll come back in when we see the people coming out. We'll take one quick picture and go home."

The child, her suspicious eyes still on Casimir, nodded. Her father tucked the tripod under his arm and led her outside.

Casimir stood before the altar rail with his eyes closed. The door opened again and again. The pews were filling up. Two altar boys came out of the sacristy and swung open the brass gates at the center of the altar rail. One of the boys, pointing to the two kneelers placed just inside the sanctuary, told Casimir he was to escort the bride to the kneelers after the father handed her over to him and the maid of honor lifted the short veil from her face.

The boys went back into the sacristy until organ music began to play and they were led out by Father Kashnoski. When the priest saw Casimir facing the altar, he twirled his index finger for Casimir to face the center aisle with his profile to the altar. Casimir pretended not to notice. The priest whispered to an altar boy who went out to Casimir and told him to turn and face Mary's side of the church.

Casimir turned his body, but stared at his shoes. The people in the pews had become still and attentive, as the wedding party approached. Donny took his place beside Casimir. Donny's sister Margaret stood opposite him.

Casimir closed his eyes tightly, not daring to open them until Wilhelm Blankenbiller placed Victoria's hand into his. Even then he was careful not to look directly at her. Oh, why didn't that stupid Mrs. Wozniak tell him the exact moment it was all right to look?

Margaret took a step forward, lifted the short veil from Victoria's face, and stepped back. The priest, with a nod and small movement of his fingers beneath the open book he held, beckoned the couple to come forward to the pair of kneelers in the sanctuary. Still looking straight ahead, Casimir looped his arm through Victoria's and walked with her to the kneelers.

The Nuptial Mass was laced with special prayers for the bride and groom. Casimir promised to love, honor, and cherish his wife; she promised to love, honor, and obey. At the nod of an altar boy, Victoria rose and walked over to the altar of Mary, placing a flower from her bouquet at the feet of the statue. She knelt there while the organist sang, "Mother, at Your Feet Is Kneeling."

When the service ended, Casimir looked at his bride for the first time as he turned to kiss her in the sanctuary. They started down the aisle to the vestibule, Casimir forcing a smile while dreading that his mother would step out from a pew and call him by his greenie name.

In the vestibule, people hugged and kissed them. "Rebekah will be jealous," one man said.

Casimir assured Victoria that Rebekah was only a mule.

Victoria blushed before the stares of the men, who ribbed Casimir about how long it would take him to produce a son. She waited for the last one to go out before turning to Casimir with a look of sly delight. She took a small drawstring sack from inside her beaded purse and placed it in Casimir's hands, saying. "This is all the money I saved from the factory, all but what I spent on this gown and the train to come here. It's yours to decide how it is to be spent."

"Casimir," a woman called from behind him. He felt a hand on his shoulder. It traveled down his arm, gripping him tightly near the elbow. He turned around and found himself looking into the weary eyes of a hollow-cheeked woman, her skin lifeless, almost gray. Dressed in a shabby, black coat, she was so thin that her shoulders seemed to come to points beneath the cloth. A few gray hairs sprang from under her brown babushka.

Casimir turned his palms up and shrugged. "Wait here," he whispered to Victoria. "This woman doesn't look too steady. I'll sit her down in there and see what she needs."

He motioned for the woman to follow him back inside the main part of the church. He walked her halfway down the nave and sat in a pew with her. "Mama?" he whispered.

"Casimir, I had to see you," she began in Polish.

Casimir put his finger up. "Speak English, Mama. And whisper. No one must know I speak Polish. People think I was born here. How did you know where to find me?"

"For years I know. Since you left us in Pottsville. But I leave you alone like your note told. Sometimes my neighbor visits her relation here. She looks at you in church to say me you are all right. She told about Banns of Marriage. I must come to get this to you today. And to see you once before I die. I don't have so much time."

She handed Casimir a small object wrapped in a red cloth. "Your papa's watch, this was."

"Stanislaw's? He's not my papa! Your new husband, maybe, but not my papa. He was never my papa. I don't want his watch."

"Not Stanislaw. Ignacy, your papa. His watch. You will know it. The one he showed you to teach to tell time. I brought it from Gdansk. I mean to give it to you when you become a man. But I stay away like you wanted." She brushed her son's cheek with her fingertips. "What a handsome man you grow up to. You be good husband to such lovely girl out there."

Casimir glanced back at Victoria, who was peering curiously from the vestibule. Without unwrapping the watch, he stuffed it in his pocket, turning in such a way that Victoria would not see.

"You are really sick, Mama. Dying! I wish—" He lifted his hand to touch her face, but let it fall to his side. He looked at the statue of Mary. Please, please help me to forgive Mama. Help me to take her hand and say good-bye for my sisters as they asked. Oh, I can't. I just can't.

Jozefina lowered her eyes. "I go now." On the way out, she took Victoria's hands and kissed them.

"Who was that woman?" Victoria asked.

"I don't know. The photographer's mother, maybe. She got out of a cab with him and the little girl," Casimir said.

"She called you Casimir."

"See? She doesn't know me either. She's just crazy, I guess. You know how old people forget and mix people up."

"She doesn't look so old, but she looks awfully sick."

"Yes. That's why I took her inside the church and sat her in a pew. Looked to me like she was going to pass out."

"She handed you something."

"She wanted to give me her husband's watch. Imagine. But I didn't want to take advantage of her. I handed it back." A lie, another lie, he thought. First, the lie about some folk song hero being his friend. Then the lie about not being a miner, even if it wasn't an outright lie. Now the lie about his mother, and about the watch. Already I'm building a life of lies, he thought.

"I'm asking too many questions," Victoria said. "My mother told me you would be sick of me in a month because I talk too much, argue too much. I'm sorry."

They went back inside for the photograph before the altar. Gina Diomira Valente glared at Casimir the whole time. He would never forget those dark, dark eyes and that cold little face. She glared back at him one final time as she climbed into the horse-drawn cab with her father and Casimir's mother while Casimir and Victoria sheltered their eyes from a storm of rice.

They got into a motorcar, which Casimir had hired, and headed for 255 West Saylor Street. The car, jostling them as it rumbled over the cobblestones, moved slowly. Casimir's fingers groped over his papa's watch in his pocket.

The driver, as instructed by Casimir beforehand, turned down the last alley and drove along the makeshift shacks, a move that was supposed to make the home he had prepared for Victoria look like a palace by comparison.

A one-armed man, who was sitting on an upside-down bucket, peeling a potato held by his bare feet, shouted in Polish, "Ah, the bride and groom! Congratulations! God bless you! Sorry I can't come to your party. I drank myself sick last night."

Casimir pretended to be puzzled by the words, and Victoria translated for him.

The car stopped in front of the house on Saylor and Girard, and the driver opened the door for them. Casimir chuckled to cover up the dread he felt at her seeing the house. "Come around to the back," he said. "Mrs. Gilotti's putting on a big party for us in the yard."

Victoria, thinking the house belonged to some Mrs. Gilotti, who was kind enough to prepare a feast for them, tried not to show any displeasure at what she saw. The once-white exterior was caked with coal dirt. Even as they stood before it, a coal wagon rumbled past and drove over a rock, which made the wagon tip from side to side, jolting the slide-up door at the little chute in the back, causing a thin, glimmering stream of coal dust to fall to the ground. Victoria looked from the little sooty mound, up the hill to the breaker of the Ebony Gem, and then to the house again.

Casimir watched her eyes discover each little horror. To the sides of each window were vertical rectangles of not-so-black wood, revealing the places where shutters had once adorned the home. A lone third-story window still boasted one red shutter, but it hung from a twisted lower hinge. Casimir cursed himself for not removing it.

Victoria said nothing as he led her alongside the house toward the side gate of the yard. Cinders crunched under their feet. A little blonde girl with red ribbons threaded through her braids leaned over the banister of the back porch, pointed to Casimir and Victoria, and yelled, "Here they come! Finally!" A cluster of little heads appeared over the banister. The gate swung open, and four men stepped out of the back yard, one with a mandolin, another with a bass fiddle, one with a horn, and the fourth with an accordion. A blast of polka music greeted the bride and groom. Donny Wilson and his sister stepped out, stood to each side of them, and nudged them toward the make-shift trellis that had been hurriedly constructed and arched over the gateway and decorated with colorful paper flowers. A boy and a girl rag doll dangled from bright ribbons tied to the top of the flowery arch. Someone handed Casimir a paring knife. The musicians held one long note. The crowd waited. Casimir, having no idea what was expected of him, blushed and shook his head.

"Cut the dolls down," Victoria whispered. Casimir cut them down and held them up, puzzled.

"That's what you get when you keep to yourself and turn down wedding invitations," someone shouted. "You act like a big dummy at your own."

Victoria put her hands out. Casimir placed the dolls gently into them. She returned the boy doll to him.

Somebody punched Casimir on the arm. "That's so you getta least one son anda one daughter."

Donny and his sister crossed the arch first and were handed shots of whiskey. Casimir felt so lost for what to do next, that he wanted to grab the whole bottle from the miner who handed him the glass. A long table stood in the center of the yard with foods representing almost every part of Europe. The musicians made a stage of the back porch and people threw coins into the bass fiddle with each request for a song. Casimir saw his bride whisked away from him again and again as pennies were dropped into her white silk beaded bag and she was whirled through the grass.

On her next waltz with Casimir, she said, "All the men I dance with tell me they're miners. It was nice of you to invite miners. We never got to go to bosses' weddings in Dickson City. I wish the girls from the factory in Dickson City could have come. They helped me make this dress and we were good friends."

Casimir began to feel overwhelmed by the drinks, the whirl of polka dances, the whirl of lies and worries in his own head. Chatter whirled around him. There was a phrase in German, in Polish, in Lithuanian, in Russian, in English, Italian, Croatian. He was flung back to Ellis Island, flung before the panel of American doctors at long tables. They made chalkmarks on people's coats, strange marks—circles, squares, X's. His mother had shaken her head in confusion when she saw the marks. And little Casimir would not ask this Stanislaw Gombrowicz, her new husband, what the marks meant. Stanislaw, a strange man with smiling blue eyes, who, an hour after meeting them, took Casimir's mother for his wife in front of some businessman. Not even a priest! So what if some priest in some Pottsville, Pennsylvania, would perform the ceremony later!

It angered Casimir to remember that smiling, already American Stanislaw saying in Polish, "I sure am happy to have a son like you." Casimir chuckled, recalling how he had put that man in his place right then and there, breaking free and shouting, "*Nie!* You are not my papa!" Even now Casimir would not admit how good it felt later to hold that tall, strong man's hand in the crowd that babbled in so many strange and frightening tongues on Ellis Island. Stanislaw Gombrowicz, a man who could speak Casimir's way and the American way. "No," Stanislaw had said in Polish, "I am not your papa, and you don't have to call me that. You had a papa in Europe and he was a good man. I'm sorry. I just meant to say welcome, and I'll help you and your mama all I can."

The backyard musicians played on into the night. Casimir led Victoria into the kitchen. The couple threw pennies to children who stood outside the window, beating on turned-over washtubs that had held blocks of ice for the refreshments. Casimir closed the window, lit the coal oil lamp, pulled down the shades, and said, "I guess they'll be banging on those tubs every two minutes. But I've had enough."

"Me, too. Let's go home."

"What do you mean?"

"To our own house."

"Victoria, this is our house."

"Not Mrs. Gilotti's?"

"No. She only arranged the celebration. You mean you thought all along that this was her house?"

Victoria didn't answer, but looked about the room in stunned silence. Both the window to the back yard and the one facing the school field across Girard Street had crisp, new, orange cafe curtains, a gift from Donny's sister. The wall above the beige wainscoting was newly papered in a pattern of trailing nasturtiums, orange and yellow. She could still smell the fresh glue.

"See, Victoria? I just finished the walls. And the kitchen table here. I sanded it and got one coat of finish put on. The chairs still need sanding, I know, but I'll get to them. What do you think?"

Victoria nodded and offered him a weak smile that didn't fool him. He could see she hated the place.

He led her into the parlor, where a shabby green sofa, the only piece of furniture, stood near the front door. "Men are coming on Monday with a beige carpet. It's beautiful. Wait till you see! And see, I painted these walls myself. I replaced the rotted wood in the windows. Wait till you see our bedroom!"

He was afraid to look at her face. He was tired. He pictured himself as a clown dancing frantically before a bored princess.

8

IN!

No, no pork," Casimir said.

"But it's really good. And there's at least two pounds left from the celebration. We mustn't let it spoil."

Casimir bent over to tie his shoes, while Victoria, standing tall in the royal blue velvet robe he had given her, held out the plate of pork like a benevolent queen bestowing a gift on a humble subject.

"No pork," he said. "No pork. Ever."

Victoria frowned and shook her head. Obey, she reminded herself. She had promised at the altar to obey. "Beef, then?"

"Good." Casimir buttoned his vest and put on a black tie. He was wearing the same black suit he wore when he first saw Victoria at the Joy Junction Station.

"Where's your lunch bucket?" she asked.

"In the cabinet. There. Under the washtub."

Victoria opened the door. "This?" She pulled out a bucket and lowered her head to look farther back into the cabinet.

"Yes, that. You won't find any others in there."

The bucket was shiny except for the coal dirt caked where the handle was joined and the seam ran from rim to base. Victoria pinched the handle and stood up, holding the pail away from herself, as though she had never in her life encountered such a dirty thing. She set it in the basin and pushed up her sleeves. "Did you bring any water in? This bucket can use another scrubbing. I never thought men who work in the office would end up with coal dirt in their lunch pails. I guess you just can't avoid it. My father brought his home as black as the ace of spades after a whole day in the mine."

Casimir thought of Mr. O'Grady dying of a ruptured appendix back in Pottsville after being dealt the ace of spades three times. Did Victoria know about that? What else did she know?

"Did you bring any water in?" she repeated.

"Four jugs. There. On the floor by the ice box."

Victoria dug the coal dirt out with the point of a knife and began to scour the bucket.

"You don't need to go through all that trouble," Casimir said. "It's only a lunch pail."

"The boss's lunch pail. You can't show up looking like, like—"

An ordinary miner, Casimir wanted to say. He was losing patience, picturing Donny Wilson waiting for him in the bushes with his real work clothes. He had to get out the door before the other miners saw him leaving in a suit and made a clown out of him. They'd tell their wives, make a big joke. And the joke would get carried back to Victoria. He knew she had to know the truth, but not like that. He wanted to grab the bucket, throw the food in and leave. He decided he would buy a new lunch pail to hide in the bushes and fetch on the way home every day after washing and changing at the Hungarian boarding house. For now, he hurried things up by gathering the food while she wiped the bucket dry.

"That was *my* job," she said when she saw the carrot, the celery and apple stacked on a sandwich.

"Tomorrow you can do it. I like to get to work early on Mondays. There's extra planning at the beginning of the week."

"Where are the rags?"

"Same cabinet, on the little shelf in back."

Victoria stooped down and reached in. She pulled out four crumpled, frayed patches of cloth. "These?" she said, frowning. "They're all wrinkled."

Casimir shook his head and chuckled. "They're clean. What the hell, a rag's a rag. Yeah, those."

"Where's the iron?"

"In the cellar stairway. You want to iron the rags?"

"Well, Charlie—"

"There's no time for that. Just cover the food any old way. I have to go." He watched her tuck a blue cloth tightly around the food, stretching the wrinkles out, her lips tight with determination.

When he took the bucket from her, she stood back and looked him over again, nodding in approval. "Can you wait a minute till I get dressed?" she said. "I'll be quick. I'll walk you to the mine."

"The colliery's no place for a woman. I'd rather you didn't go there. I forbid you to go there." Before she could protest, he went out into the dark morning, restraining his steps to a fast walk, feeling her eyes on him. Once he turned the corner, he ran.

Outside the mine yard, Donny Wilson waited in the bushes with Casimir's tools and a burlap sack with his work clothes. Casimir changed, then hurried through the alley behind Dombi's boarding house. He crept through the gate and draped his suit on the banister of the small porch of the wash house at the end of the yard.

He walked back toward his own house, tempted to parade by the window and let Victoria catch him in his miner's clothes. It was his first day of pretending, and already he was tired of it. He had a mind to march into the house, yank off that fancy blue robe, toss it in the trash, and say, "Listen, Victoria, your princess days are over. I'm a miner and that's that."

He did walk home, determined to tell her. He crept alongside the shanty at the end of his own yard and watched Victoria through the window, as he tried to decide what to say. She was sitting at the table, snipping strings from the lunch pail rags. The iron was heating on one of the cast-iron plates of the johnny stove.

He heard the voices of miners coming up the alley behind the shanty. One of them called to him, "Hey, bridegroom, can't take your eyes off that little beauty?"

"Yeah, Charlie. Never I seen such bride so red in the face in church on Sunday morning. Some Saturday night you spend, huh?"

"Notta you business, you guys. Charlie, dona listen to them. Pigs, they are. Yes, pigs!"

Casimir grinned and walked with them to the Ebony Gem.

Victoria sat with a piece of brown grocer's paper across her lap to catch the threads she trimmed from the rags. Soon tears spilled onto the paper as she imagined her mother grinning, beholding the dump this brazen girl found herself in after thinking she was so much smarter than her greenie mama and papa.

She crumpled the paper, stood up, flicked the tears away, and tossed the rags onto the ironing board. Then she sat down with a cup of coffee. The table was up against the window that looked out on the school field across Girard Street. No one was there. She wished she had something to read. She wished she knew someone.

She looked around the kitchen. It needed a thorough scrubbing, she decided. Every room in the house needed something except for the bedroom where they slept. The other two rooms on the second floor were a museum of cobwebs and water stains.

The image of her gloating mother came back to her. She began to imagine answers to Wanda's taunting. Yes, there was work to be done. But, as Charlie had explained, he'd been a boss only for the past year, had spent a few years in the mines, as a miner first. No wonder he couldn't bring her to one of those big homes with the lovely porches that went around to the side, homes with dormers and turrets, homes with huge rhododendrons, lovely shade gardens. It would take time to catch up to the other bosses' homes. Besides, she had promised, in the presence of God and witnesses, at the altar of a Catholic church, to take him for richer or poorer, until death. It was just going to take time not to feel poorer than she had felt under her father's roof.

She rubbed her palms up and down her thighs, remembering the blood on them on Sunday morning. There was no turning back, even if her parents didn't gloat and simply welcomed her home. She was not the same, would never be again. The blood had sealed her union to this Charlie Turek, as when children prick their fingers and press their wounds together—like the Indians Catherine had told her about in the factory—and declared a blood bond forever and ever.

Victoria picked up the iron and spat on it. The spittle danced to her satisfaction. She ironed the rags. Then she brought down all her husband's clothes to iron. Feeling lonely, she moved the ironing board closer to the window that looked out into the back yard. Through that window she could see the side door of the James Buchanan School. The school had already closed for the summer, and the handles of the door had been chained shut.

Victoria took a long look at the shanty in the back yard. She pictured how it might look with the weeds gone and some flowers along the foundation and some by the three wooden steps just inside the wire fence that went along Girard Street. Some sort of shrub alongside the outhouse, which stood where the other end of the shanty met the neighbor's fence, might be a good way to hide it.

She heard cinders crunching alongside the house. Women's voices grew louder. Several women with wheelbarrows reached the gate near the back porch and stopped. In two of the barrows sat small children in sun bonnets. Older children walked beside the barrows, burlap sacks draped over their arms. The women waved at Victoria. She waved back. One woman wearing a brown kerchief let herself in the gate, ran up onto the porch, and knocked on the door.

Victoria, blocking the view through the glass pane of the door with her body, opened the door halfway, then pulled it against herself, hoping the woman wouldn't look past the kitchen into the dreary parlor. Why couldn't they have come later in the afternoon, after the delivery men had a chance to bring the new carpet? She wished she had thrown a blanket over the shabby sofa until she had a chance to make a presentable cover for it.

These women probably want to sell me some coal on their way back from the slagpiles, she thought, glancing at the wheelbarrows.

"You comin'?" the woman said. She was a very tall woman, very thin, her face a long, narrow oval framed in a colorful scarf of red, black and gold. The red fringes lifted lightly in the breeze.

"Me? Where?"

"The culmbank."

"Culmbank?"

"Yeah, the slagpiles. You know. To pick coal. Where's your barrow? The shanty?"

"No, no. I'm not going. My husband's having coal delivered. Wednesday, he said."

"Delivered! Really? Huh. I'll be damned. Lucky you."

Victoria was stunned. It was surprising enough to find these miners' wives at her wedding reception. And that was all right. But to think that they expected her to go gleaning bits of coal with them from the slagpiles! What kind of coal patch was this anyway? It was still the Pennsylvania anthracite region. Eighty miles south of what she was used to, but still, it shouldn't make that much difference. Yet here were these miners' wives expecting the boss's wife to come home like a sooty doll so she could heat her own home.

The woman put out her hand. "Oh, I'm Vera Urkov. Urkova, really, if you want to say it the Russian way for the wife. But I like to do like Americans, the same for the husband and wife, the same for the sons and the daughters."

Victoria pressed her foot against the door to keep it from swinging wide open as she shook hands with her neighbor. "Hello, Vera. Russian, you say. You sound like you were born here."

"Almost. I was only two when I came. My husband, Vladimir, he came just last month. We were married on Ellis Island. Arranged it through a marriage broker like a lot of folks. Vladimir speaks only two words of English, 'Good' and 'morning,' to be friendly to the other miners. He says he doesn't want to learn English. His hands are speech enough if he has something to say, something to ask."

"I'm sure he'll pick it up."

"Yes, you can't help picking up some. Say, we're goin' for water this after. Around two. Manley's Mountain. Good springs up there. The water's a lot better than the patch pump. Wanna come?"

"No, thanks. My husband said he'd take care of filling the water jugs."

"Oh." Vera frowned and looked sideways, as though trying to work out a puzzle before speaking again. "You mean he's gonna lug your water after working all day in—"

Victoria felt impatient with all this questioning. She cut her off. "He says he wouldn't have me doing it."

A look of shame crossed Vera's face. "Well, then, I guess you don't need anybody to—" She looked down at her own hands and made a gesture of brushing off her skirt. She seemed to shrink. She shifted her weight in a moment of clumsy silence, like a ragged pickpocket caught weaving among a ballroom of wealthy guests and flung at the feet of the lady of the house. Her eyes darted as though she were searching for a space to dash through.

Victoria, struck by a flash of shame herself, said, "But the store. I need to go there before Charlie gets home."

Vera's face brightened. "Sure. Soon as we get back with the coal, I'll come by."

"I meant I'd like to go now. If you'll just tell me where, I can find my own way."

"There's a few. I think you can find them." Vera turned abruptly and left the yard.

Victoria went back to the ironing board and saw the group of women make their way along her fence as Vera spoke to them. They glanced coolly back at her.

After work Casimir slipped away from the group and ducked into the yard of the Hungarian boarding house. He was pleased with the place. Columbine in every color lined the fence. Clumps of daisies sprang up alongside the outhouse, which was freshly painted light green like the washing shanty. The shanty windows were so clean that Casimir pressed his finger to a pane to see if there was really glass in it. Good, he thought. It was going to be worth the nickel a day to wash here. He stepped behind the line of seven other miners who took their boots off in the yard, set their hats on them, and ran into the shanty, where four big pots of water were boiling on a johnny stove.

The men tore their clothes off. They raced for the stove, shoving each other. Four men claimed pots of hot water to dump into the cold water already in the tubs, which sat on a gray linoleum floor newly tracked with silty black footprints.

Casimir and three other men, all boarders in that house, were left standing naked in the center of the floor. The three Hungarian boarders who had lost the race to the tubs shook their fists and grumbled in that Magyar tongue he could never figure out. He couldn't understand why they were so upset. They'd get their turn. He followed them to a narrow space behind a four-foot-high panel. When they rested their arms on the panel, he did the same.

He heard someone coming up the steps and figured it must be Mr. or Mrs. Dombi with more water to heat. But it was a little boy about four years old. His dark eyes were huge and close set, his eyebrows thick enough to be on a young man. He had a tambourine full of soaps, which he handed to the men in the tubs. Then, quiet and somber, the child stood like a little sentry against the back wall. His feet and legs were bare. Only his toes moved at first, curling in, curling out. Then he began to bounce his plump little rump off the wall until he discovered Casimir. Casimir smiled at him from behind the panel. But the child became motionless and stared with those huge, dark eyes. Gina Diomira eyes, Casimir thought, remembering the photographer's little girl at his wedding. Stop staring!

The child stared and stared at the newcomer, his fingers spinning the discs on the tambourine. Little Gypsy brat, Casimir thought. Stop. But the child continued to stare until his mother appeared at the door. A tall, husky, tidy woman with her hair concealed in a kerchief, she had a marching way about her. Casimir saw that she had brought no water to heat. Maybe Mr. Dombi was going to bring it.

Mrs. Dombi grunted a greeting as she passed Casimir. She knelt down by the nearest tub and gave a Magyar command. The man in the tub, who had already lathered his hair and washed all but his back, fished around with both hands. Mrs. Dombi stuck her arm in behind him, pulled out the soap, grumbled something, then smeared circles of lather over his back. She pointed to one of two small jugs next to the tub. The man picked it up and poured some clear water into a tin cup Mrs. Dombi had taken out of her apron pocket. He tipped his head back and let her rinse the soap out of his hair. They repeated this until his hair was clean.

When she finished, she curled her fingers into a fist, raised her thumb and jerked it toward the door. The miner frowned and whined something to her. "Out!" she said, the first word Casimir heard in English since he got there. She covered her eyes while the miner went for a towel dangling from a nail on the wall.

Then she raised her index finger to Casimir, beckoning him to the tub that had just been vacated. "In."

"In there?"

"In!"

"But the water. It's black!"

The woman dried her hands on her apron. "Out then," she said, pointing to the door.

"Okay, okay, I'll get in."

The woman covered her eyes. Casimir slipped out from behind the panel and dashed toward the tub. The little boy jumped in front of him, skipping backwards and shaking the tambourine, drawing attention to Casimir's nakedness. "Shhhame! Shhhame! Shhhame!" the child said, shaking the little tin disks that seemed to echo his words.

The miners laughed. Mrs. Dombi kept her eyes turned until Casimir landed in the tub. Then she spun around and slapped the child five times on the bare legs. He ran out the door, wailing.

Good for you, you little Gypsy brat, Casimir thought, closing his eyes as he dipped himself into the water, which was now only luke-warm. He soaped his chest as fast as he could. He ran the bar of soap over his head.

The huge man in the next tub bellowed with laughter. His black eyebrows rose to a high arch. His wet hair was slicked back with soap. His four front teeth were missing.

"Vampire," Casimir muttered.

"Say?"

"Nothing."

"Say!" The man held up a fist.

"I'm tired," Casimir said, trying to make his pronunciation sound something like "vampire."

The man shrugged and offered a soapy hand, leaning so far out of the tub that Casimir thought it was going to tip over. "Franz."

Casimir shook the man's hand. "Charlie."

Mrs. Dombi did Franz next, then the other two miners who had made it to the tubs for the first round, then Casimir. Pressing the heel of her hand on his neck, she shoved his head forward and slapped the bar of soap onto his back. Casimir could have sworn there were bits of glass in it. He wished he could go home to his own tub in the cellar. Imagine. A nickel a day for this, money he could be putting toward his sisters' passage. But no, he thought resentfully, Victoria wanted to believe he was somebody. Why did he ever marry her? It was clear she wanted somebody else, somebody important, well-off.

9

SO IT'S REALLY, REALLY TRUE

Come on, girl," Casimir said, leading Rebekah from the cage to the mine yard. "Have a little fresh air."

The July sun was a welcome change from the dripping, dark mine. Casimir turned the mule toward the south side of the yard and made three loops around. On the fourth loop, he caught sight of Victoria looking in over the wooden fence as she was walking by.

Casimir turned away. Oh, God, he prayed, hoping to be saved by the coal dirt on his face. Don't let her recognize me. What the hell's she doing here anyway? I told her never to come here.

He hurried the mule across the yard. Pretending to be scratching his face, he looked through his fingers and saw that Victoria had stopped in front of the iron gate as if she were thinking of coming in. Casimir walked the mule to the other side of the shanty. He made the animal stand still for a moment. When he came around the other side, he saw that Victoria had started up the road. She glanced behind her once before turning onto Girard Street.

The office man poked his head out of the shanty. "You don't have to be afraid to say hello to her. It won't reflect badly on your work. You can walk a mule and say hello to your wife at the same time. And by the way, Charlie, if I were you, I'd keep a beauty like that barefoot and pregnant, as they say."

"Swine!" Casimir muttered as he walked away. "Like I haven't thought about that!" He walked Rebekah a few more turns around the yard, then took her to the underground stable and returned to Breast Number Six.

The workday dragged, but his mind raced. He'd told his wife, told her not to come here. What did she think she was doing? Didn't she promise to love, honor and obey? Obey. What if she recognized him walking Rebekah? He pictured her standing on the back porch with her suitcase packed when he got home.

After work, he ran from the mine yard. He was first on the steps of the Hungarian bath house. He washed quickly, grateful that Mrs. Dombi noticed he was in a hurry and that she rinsed his hair first.

He hurried home and went into the yard from the side gate near the back porch. He cupped his hands around his eyes and peered over the cafe curtains. Pots were steaming on the johnny stove. Victoria, her back to the window, was wiping a spill from the kitchen floor. He was glad she was down there. It would be easier for him to say his piece.

"What were you doing watching that man walk the mule in the mine yard today?" he said as he came through the door. "I saw you from the shanty office."

Victoria's hand, gripping the rag, was suddenly motionless on the floor. "Watching the— I was, I was just passing by." She twisted her head around and looked up at him.

"No, you came and stood by the gate and watched him. You acted like you knew him. How do you know him?"

"I, I didn't." She reached up to the counter to pull herself up. "For a minute I thought—"

Casimir walked around and stood in front of her, speaking as she began to rise. He tried to speak gently. "Didn't I tell you the mine yard was no place for you?"

"You did. But I get so lonely here. The other bosses' families live up by the highway. I have no one to talk to all day. I just got lonely and thought I could stop in the office and say hello. Maybe meet the other bosses. Maybe they'd offer to introduce me to their wives."

"There'll be time for that. But I'll say when." His look softened. "Victoria, I'm sorry. I saw you looking at him. I didn't know what to think. Men notice you. They ask me how I found such a beautiful— I couldn't help feeling jealous. Don't you see how it looked?"

"I never thought about how it looked."

"I know. I got a little jealous, that's all. I'm sorry. Forget about it, okay? And no more coming to the mine yard, all right?"

"All right."

"Come here." He sat by the table and pulled Victoria onto his lap. He rubbed his palm over her belly. "Did it start yet?"

"No." Victoria's face colored. She turned away like a shy child.

"You said it was always like clockwork. How late is it?"

"Two weeks. I guess I should go see a doctor."

"The only doctor around here is the company doctor, Dr. Kirk. They dock the miners' pay to cover Kirk's salary. Plus he charges the poor miners extra for delivering babies. I don't like the idea of dealing with him. Besides, it makes me a little jealous, the thought of a man doctor touching you there."

Victoria's face colored again.

"Tell you what, Victoria, there's a midwife in the patch, Mrs. Anderson, an old woman."

"Very old?"

"Old, but healthy and strong as an ox, don't worry. I'm pretty friendly with her son-in-law, Joe McDonald, a miner who works down in Breast Number Six. He's always bragging about the million babies she's delivered in half the time of our big-shot company doctor. He says she never charges money. But, of course, I'll insist. And, say, what about this? If you're lonely while I'm at work, she'll be good company."

Victoria got up and stirred the stew, thinking maybe a midwife wasn't such a bad idea. Some company, at least. The other women in the patch, after the third invitation, had stopped inviting Victoria to glean coal from the slagpiles. No one invited her to the store. No one invited her to the Tuesday and Thursday morning sewing groups in their homes. No one invited her to the water pump anymore.

When she needed water, she either asked Casimir to go for it, or she went herself between eight and noon when most of the other women were on the slagpiles. She felt ashamed of the way she had snubbed the miners' wives. After all, she herself had come from a miner's home. Yet, she couldn't understand why they expected her to pay attention to them. She gave every penny she could spare to the needy families fund at St. Hedwig's. It wasn't as though she had altogether forgotten where she had come from.

Why didn't the other bosses' wives make some effort to welcome her? It was a whole month since the wedding, and not one had stopped by. This wasn't how things were supposed to be. She turned to Charlie. "Yes, I'd like to meet this Mrs. Anderson. But the other bosses' wives, I'd like to meet them, too. Will you do something about that?"

"First, let's see about Mrs. Anderson. Then we'll talk about the others. I'll stop over her place tonight."

After supper, Casimir went to ask Mrs. Anderson if she could stop by the next morning. Victoria, clearing the table, would stop walking, as if she had forgotten where she was going. She'd stand thinking on her way to the sink—holding a pair of plates, a handful of flatware, the cups, the glasses—feeling a little crazy as she tried to match up what she had seen at the mine yard with what her husband had said about the same event. She scolded herself for not being able to forget about it as he had told her to. She had promised to obey. But that man she saw looked so much like her Charlie.

She heard the gate swing shut and she looked out the window. Casimir was coming up onto the porch with a chubby, rosy-faced woman, whose fluffy hair was carelessly rolled into a cottony bun. As though abruptly called from the kitchen, she was wearing a flower-print apron that looped around the neck, covering much of her plain gray dress. The apron was wet and wrinkled in two spots where she had dried her hands. She was laughing a carefree laugh and patting Casimir's shoulder as though reassuring him.

Victoria opened the door. She almost cried at the sight of the old woman's warm smile with its promise of friendship.

Casimir, seeing his wife's delight, smiled with a kind of pride, as though he had just fished the woman out of a pond.

Victoria said, "Oh, Mrs. Anderson. I didn't think you'd come till tomorrow. I'm so glad."

"I'm glad to come," Mrs. Anderson said. She lifted Victoria's hand and placed it in her own, patting it. Her thick fingers were becoming misshapen with knotted joints that became more prominent when she set one hand down on the back of a chair.

She winked at Victoria and said, "Let's talk alone, just us women. Tell me everything, and I'll tell you—if I can so soon—if it means you'll be having a baby." She said to Casimir, "Can you give us a half hour to ourselves?"

Casimir grinned. "I was just on my way to shoot pool with Donny Wilson at Sam's Cafe."

When he left, Victoria and Mrs. Anderson sat at the table. "Now, dear," Mrs. Anderson said. "Your husband says you're two weeks late. What else can you tell me?"

"My breasts," Victoria said with great embarrassment. "Suddenly, they're huge, and there's this brown line going from between my breasts all the way down to the bottom of my stomach."

"Ah, yes," Mrs. Anderson said. "The dark, fuzzy line. Saint Sebastian's Arrow. Don't see too many of those. But they happen. Means the baby will have tons of hair, dark hair, probably. Anything else? Do you get sick in the mornings?"

"It only happened once. Usually, I'm okay. My back hurts a little, way at the bottom of my spine."

A serious look came over Mrs. Anderson's face. "It sounds to me like there's a baby on the way. I hate to have to ask you this—and believe me, I'll keep the answer to myself—but is there some chance this baby got started before the wedding night? I'll need to know if you want me to give you an idea when it's due."

Victoria stood up, offended. "Mrs. Anderson!"

"Sit down, dear. I'm sorry, but I had to ask."

Victoria sat down. "That was my first time with anyone. Ever!"

"I'm glad," Mrs. Anderson said. "Then I'd say the baby's due around the middle of March, just in time for spring. Imagine that."

Victoria recovered from the question and said, "Spring. A wonderful time to have a baby. You know, Mrs. Anderson, I love children. When I lived in Dickson City, I often looked after children. I can't wait to have my own. I picture myself making little dresses and pants and hats for them. I learned to sew last year. Sure, they'll be wearing store-bought clothes, but I want to make some with my own hands." She was so glad for another woman to talk to, that her words poured out like water from a broken dam. She noticed Mrs. Anderson looking around the kitchen and said, "See how nice Charlie had the place fixed up for me? He even did some of the work himself, he said. Come upstairs and have a look. First, take a look at the parlor."

They stood in the archway to the front room. "Don't mind the sofa," Victoria said. "I'm making a cover for it. I guess our children will mess up this beige carpet. But kids will be kids. Men. They should let their wives pick out something more practical. But I guess I shouldn't complain about having something beautiful."

Mrs. Anderson wagged her finger. "No, you shouldn't. Compared to the other wives, you live like a queen. Why, they couldn't begin to dream of having what you have already."

The two women paused at the bottom of the staircase. They stared at one another in confusion, as though each had been talking to someone else and found herself suddenly beholding the face of a completely different person. As they started up the stairs, Victoria said, "Mrs. Anderson, I've seen the bosses' homes around Scranton. I baby-sat for some. This is good for a man just new at being a boss, I suppose, but I'm sure the others here must have oriental rugs and china cabinets and all sorts of things we don't have yet."

They walked past the closed doors of the back bedroom and the middle room and went into the front bedroom.

Victoria dragged the rocking chair to the bedside for Mrs. Anderson and lay down. She sighed through a wistful smile.

Mrs. Anderson, her face a picture of confusion, sat in the rocking chair. Her lips parted as though she wanted to say something.

Victoria said, "Look at you. I must be talking too much. Too fast. I'll shut up. Mama told me yacking would be my downfall. I'll drive a man crazy, she said, talking, talking, talking. For weeks before the wedding, I practiced holding my tongue. I talk to Charlie only when he asks me something. Trouble is, he's the only one I have to talk to. I guess I dammed up my mouth so much that I'm pouring it all out on you. I'm sorry. I should let you get a word in."

Mrs. Anderson said, "Victoria, I don't understand why you compare your house to the ones bosses' families live in."

"Why shouldn't I?"

"You'll only end up resenting your lot."

"My lot. My lot, did you say?"

"Yes. Maybe you don't have oriental rugs and china closets. You probably never will. You must accept that and learn to be thankful to have it so much better than the other miners' wives."

"Other! But, Mrs. Anderson, Charlie's not a miner."

"What do you mean?"

"How could you think— Would a miner go to work in a suit and come home looking like he spent the day in an office?"

"Charlie comes home that way because he stops at that Hungarian boarding house to wash up first. It's the talk of the patch. Why, just this morning Catherine, my youngest, says to her man, 'Friday's my birthday, Joe. How 'bout washing up before you come home, like that handsome Charlie Turek from Saylor Street. Only don't come home with a knife in your belly.' Oh, those Hungarians! Nobody talks like them. That Magyar talk. You can't tell what they're up to. But they must be up to something. Your man's takin' an awful chance going there. You. You could heat a kettle for him at home."

"So that's what the neighbors think goes on! I think they're jealous." Victoria propped herself on her elbows. "Mrs. Anderson, does this look like a coal miner's bedroom? Look at this carpet. You're a midwife. You've been in lots of miners' bedrooms. How many have carpets? Or big mirrors?" She moved her head about, jutting her chin to point. "Look! One—two—three. Three mirrors in one room." She lay back down and closed her eyes, giving Mrs. Anderson an opportunity to take it all in.

Mrs. Anderson said, "That only goes to show you how hard your man works. Everybody knows what a mess this house was before. People saw your man working till all hours. Fixing, painting. He didn't tell a soul what he was up to. He's a very private man, your Charlie. Friendly now and then. Answers when he's spoken to. The only friend he really has is that Wilson fellow that lost his voice when his throat was cut in that mine accident. It was your Charlie that saved him. Charlie'll help anybody. But he keeps his mouth closed and goes his own way when the work is done. He's a real worker. I heard he done gardening in Mt. Carmel to help pay for all the work he done in this house. Maybe I'm wrong about that. But, Victoria, I can tell you for sure your man's a coal miner."

"Well, yes, he was. And that Donny Wilson friend of his must have had that accident back then. Charlie's a boss for a year now."

"He's still a miner. He works down in Breast Number Six with my son-in-law, Joe McDonald, Catherine's husband. Charlie blasts and digs and shovels just like Joe."

Casimir returned from Sam's and came in through the kitchen. Donny Wilson, following, gave Casimir a shove, pushing him toward the parlor. Casimir stumbled forward. He turned around. "Don't. I told you I'd tell her today. I will. I'll do it now. Come on, wait at the bottom of the stairs. If I know you're listening, I won't back out. If I do, you can tell her I'm a miner."

Donny turned his palms out in a gesture of helplessness. Casimir said, "I know—you can't talk, you can't read, you can't write. Find some way. You can get my miner's clothes from the basement. Show her the clothes and point to me. She'll get the idea."

Donny nodded. Casimir went up the stairs. He crept through the hall and ducked into the bottom of the stairwell that led to the attic. Peeking around the molding of the bedroom door, he saw Victoria propped up on her elbows, shaking her head.

Mrs. Anderson said to Victoria, "I'm sorry you found out like this. It wasn't my place to tell you. But it was out before I realized I was tattling, and so—"

Victoria, all but wagging her finger at Mrs. Anderson, looked at her like someone trying to get a child to confess to a fib. "I think you're jealous, too. But that's all right. I'm not making fun or accusing you. So please don't be angry. I don't blame you. You probably had to deliver your own babies. And here my man is, paying you to take care of me." She lay back against the pillows and sprawled on the bed, massaging the back of her left hand, as though she had nothing better to do than admire the smoothness of her own skin.

Mrs. Anderson straightened up and tipped the rocking chair forward, a look of indignation hardening her face.

Victoria rolled over and began to sit up. Mrs. Anderson laid her hand on Victoria's arm. She sighed and shook her head, half smiling. "Why don't you just lay back, dear, till we talk this out."

Victoria sat straight up. Her voice became thin, childlike, whiny. "I want to open the curtains." She twisted around and pushed open the curtains alongside the bed. She folded her arms and said, "See, Charlie put that big mirror on that dresser, that big wide one opposite this window. He put it there special for me, so I could open the curtains beside the bed here and see the birds land on the top of the maple tree. Just lying here, I see everything going on behind me through that big mirror. In the evening, I get to see the sun go down behind the mountains. Sometimes Charlie brings me tea."

Watching through the vanity mirror facing the side of the bed, Casimir could see Victoria stack and plump the pillows before lying back down. He could see her profile, her turned-up nose, her bottom lip jutting out just a little. Propped up on the pillows, she was literally looking down her nose at the old woman on the rocker.

Victoria pointed at the dresser mirror. "See? There's a robin, see? And there's some little sparrows!"

"Victoria, I think Charlie hired me because you don't mix with the neighbors. You must be awfully lonely, keeping to yourself the way you do. He feels sorry for you, I bet."

"None of the bosses' wives mixed with us in Dickson City."

"Nobody hires midwives here. We help each other. I didn't want money. Charlie insists on paying me. That man has an awful lot of pride, it seems. But I didn't realize he had so much pride that he told you he's a boss."

"Not told me, exactly. I saw him in a suit the first time. I took it for granted."

"But he never straightened you out on it."

"No. That's because it's true. Why should he straighten me out? Well, I did look a little disappointed when I first saw the house. I asked him why we live here and not in one of those big single homes along the highway like the other bosses' families. That's when he told me he'd only been a boss for a year and needed time to do more with this house. He's done so much, just in the month since I moved in." Victoria studied the troubled look on the midwife's face. "Mrs. Anderson, you don't seem comfortable here. Maybe you should leave. Maybe I should have a doctor, not a midwife."

"Sending me away won't change the truth. But if you're asking me to leave your home, I'll go. I don't force my services on anyone. I'm sorry I was the one to tell you. It wasn't my place. But I can't take it back." She stood up. "If you change your mind, I'll be glad to deliver your child. I'll be glad to keep you company sometimes, too. Let me know."

"Wait. Sit down." Victoria took in a deep breath and held it, as though preparing to speak a stream of words. After a while she said, "There were signs. I—"

Mrs. Anderson raised her palm. "Maybe it's your husband you'd rather say it to, not me. It's not my business, everything that goes on in a couple's house where I've come to deliver a child."

"I guess he was afraid I wouldn't marry him if I found out." Victoria rolled toward Mrs. Anderson. "I helped my mother pick coal from the slagpiles from the day I moved here from Iowa. I promised myself I'd never marry into a life like that."

"Oh, but you see, you did. You did exactly that. You married a coal miner. Come on, now. You'll see it won't be so bad, picking coal. You'll get to know your neighbors on the slagpiles. And when you know everyone has it the same as you, why—why, you don't feel so beat down by it all. Really, Victoria, you don't. You say, 'This is how it is,' and you get down to the business of living. Believe me, dear, no matter how hard the truth is to hear, it's never so hard as fighting it all the time. Once you know what's what, you're in a good spot. You're free to figure what to do from there. Without the truth, it's like playing poker with the cards in your hand facing out, away from yourself. Now, you wouldn't want that, would you?"

"I guess not," Victoria mumbled into her pillow, her back to Mrs. Anderson.

"Of course not."

Victoria cried long and hard. "I never imagined it would turn out like this!"

"I know, dear." Taking a brush from her apron pocket, Mrs. Anderson brushed Victoria's hair slowly.

"You'll make a good life of it after all," Mrs. Anderson crooned. "Dreary as a coal patch can be, there are little ways to be happy. But, Victoria, you've got to get off your high horse and mix. You can join in on the quilts, for example. You mentioned you can sew."

"Some. Nothing fancy. I worked in a factory."

"And food. Jarring food doesn't have to be a lonesome, boring chore. Why, you can invite a neighbor and put the jars up together while your men are in the mines. And imagine the fun we have every fall when the pigs are butchered. The men making the sausage. The women making the sauerkraut. You'll never know, though, if you don't come out. And say, I'll bet you're a little scared about taking care of a new baby—"

"I didn't say I was scared."

"Oh, everybody is. It's no shame. If you mix with the neighbors, you'll see how they manage before you have to tend to your own. Will you try?"

"I'd feel like a fool. I haven't looked at the miners' wives since we settled in. I can imagine what they think of me now. Besides, I took care of lots of neighbor children in Dickson City. I enjoy children and I know how to care for them."

"All right, then. Maybe you don't need neighbors for that reason. But everyone needs company."

"Please, Mrs. Anderson, don't tell anyone I didn't know Charlie was a miner. Like you said, it's the talk of the patch, how he comes home all cleaned up like a businessman. How they'd howl if they found out!"

"I promise I won't tell anyone."

"And don't coax me to mix. I'm too ashamed."

"All right. I won't. But if you change your mind, I'll be glad to introduce you."

Casimir appeared in the doorway. "I heard most everything. The truth is out and I'm glad. I'm only ashamed I didn't get the nerve to tell you myself, Victoria. Every day I meant to do it, but I didn't. Mrs. Anderson, if Donny Wilson's still down there, tell him I'll see him tomorrow."

Mrs. Anderson nodded and went out. Casimir's eyes followed her down the hall. He listened for her footsteps to reach the parlor. Then he shut the door. He was so terrified that Victoria was going to say she was leaving him, that he almost dropped to his knees. But the thought of himself begging after all the work he had done angered him. He would ask her forgiveness for lying. But he would not beg. He clasped his hands over his stomach and stood before her. "Do you forgive me?"

"Charlie."

He tried to sound calm, but he heard his own voice, fast, shaky, loud. "I let you think I was somebody important. Now you know. I'm just a coal miner. Do you forgive me? I didn't think you'd want me if you knew." He thought he was going to fall to his knees after all. "I was going to tell you, after I fixed everything, after I painted and fixed and put nice things here for you. And I did that, didn't I?"

"Yes."

"Do you hate me now that you know what I am?"

"Charlie—"

"Well, do you? Do you hate me now?"

"So it's really, really true."

"And you never suspected until you saw me with that mule today."

"So that *was* you."

"Yes."

"The first morning you went to work, I was surprised to see the coal dirt in the seam of your lunch bucket. But I decided you couldn't help picking up some coal dirt when your office is right next to a breaker. I couldn't understand why you never let me walk you to work, even part way. But I never guessed the reason. Even today, when I saw you with the mule, I tried to make some excuse. I was glad when you said it was someone else. Yet, I couldn't put it out of my head."

Casimir sat on the rocker next to the bed and stared at the floor. After a while he said, "Your mother and father. They guessed."

"They didn't guess you were a miner. They said you lied about Tim Brennan. Papa said you got that story from an old ballad. I told myself that even if Papa was right, it was only a white lie. You wanted to impress us by showing us what a sympathetic office man you were, going down into the dangerous mines when you didn't really have to, just to make sure the miners were okay. Once in a blue moon there is such a decent company man. Why not you? Why couldn't the death of your friend move you to look out for other miners, though it was a little hard to picture an office man being friends with a miner in the first place." Victoria sat up. "Oh, Charlie, I wanted to believe in you!"

"You hate me then."

"I hate the way you pretended."

Casimir stood up, grabbed Victoria's hands, and pounded them on his chest. "You hate *me!*"

"How can I hate you for being a miner? My daddy's a miner. Uncle Stanush was a miner. But Charlie, you should've told me. Oh, Charlie!" She freed her hands.

Casimir sat in the rocker again. "You wouldn't've married me if you knew. If you knew all you'd ever be was a poor man's wife in a plain, bare house with nothing but a husband and children to show for all your work."

"Charlie, this is America. It's not supposed to be like that. People leave their home of generations back in Europe for a better life, not a life that's just as bad or even worse. Yes, worse. In Europe, we had stables, not our own, of course, but Papa tended them. We had open space and fields to run in. I was only three, but I remember. Papa wanted something of his own. America promised something for everyone. We ended up in Iowa, working on another man's farm. I was happy there, whether it was our own or not. But little Voychek died in his crib and Jozef was nearly crushed when a corn crib collapsed four years later. Mama decided Iowa was jinxed, farm life was jinxed. She wasn't going to lose her only other son. She was longing to live where there was a big Polish community, where people would understand each other and help each other improve their lot. But we ended up in a mining town, where Jozef got crushed in a coal slide in the mine. We're worse off than we were in the old country.

"Charlie, I don't want my sons dying in breakers and coal mines. I don't want my daughters in factories at twelve. I pictured them having a real childhood, time to play and run and sing, not pick coal from slagpiles every morning, just to keep a johnny stove going so their mother can cook and they can eat. So their father can feed a furnace and they won't freeze to death."

Casimir and Victoria sat in a thick silence for some time. Then, leaning forward in the rocking chair, he said with a smirk, "And so you can have fancy things in the house and nice clothes."

"What's wrong with wanting something nice? This is America, Charlie, America! It's supposed to be nice! It's supposed to—" Her voice trailed into sobs.

"This is Black Hollow, Pennsylvania. This is where you can barely afford to keep alive, though your husband works ten hours a day under the ground. This is where you say good-bye to him in the morning, not knowing if he'll be crushed or blackdamped to death or come home with only half his fingers. I don't say this to feel sorry for myself. It's the truth, and Mrs. Anderson was right. It feels good to say the truth out loud." He pressed his face against his hands and sat with his elbows on his knees, rocking slowly. "You don't know what hell it is to hide things, Victoria. Leave me, if the truth of this life is too much for you. I'm sorry I lied. I know it wasn't fair. It was wrong. I can't turn back the clock and give you a chance to choose beforehand. I can only promise to do my best. If you can't forgive me and promise to do your best, it's better that you go. I will send you money to take care of the child. I won't come around. You know, though, as Catholics, we will always be married."

"I know."

"But I will stay away till the day I die if you want. Decide."

"Where could I go? When I told my parents we were getting married, they said, 'If you make this bed, you sleep in it.' I can't go home. I have no money to go anywhere else."

"You can stay in this house, and I'll go back to Mrs. Gilotti's boarding house, if you want. But it would be hard to live in the same patch and not come around. Maybe I love you already, I don't know. But if you don't want me, it's better for you to go away and I'll stay here where I have work. I'll sell the things I put in this house. The money's yours. I'm sorry, I already spent the money you gave me in the back of the church after the wedding. I spent it fixing more of this house. But you can have every penny of what we sell."

Victoria remained silent for a while. Then she said, "If you hadn't gotten that photograph and my mother's letter about finding me a husband, would you have tried to marry me?"

"No."

Victoria looked offended. "No?"

"No." Casimir thought about his joy in seeing her for a second time at the mine office when her uncle came looking for a job. And yes, he had to admit he went to her uncle's lean-to, hoping to encounter her again, even thinking how wonderful it would be to have her as a wife. But he had his sisters to provide for. Forgetting now that it was Victoria's departing on the train with that coffin that had prompted him to resign himself to not having her, he remembered himself as having firmly rejected her so he could save toward a farmhouse and furniture for his sisters, having saved almost enough for their actual passage.

He wished he could tell Victoria this, but his shame over his stranded sisters was too deep. He would hurry and save to make up for everything. Then there would be no shame in telling how his papa had died on account of him, and how his little sisters got left behind in Gdansk.

Victoria said, "But when you saw me at the train station and at Uncle Stanush's shanty, you looked at me like—"

"I didn't say I wasn't interested. I just wouldn't have had the courage to ask. What did I, a coal miner, have to offer?"

"Oh, Charlie. As long as we're coming out with the truth, I have some truth to tell. I sent my picture and my mother's letter to you."

"You?"

"Yes. Mama sent it to Uncle Stanush, and he showed it to me. I begged him to give it to you on Monday. He agreed to do it. When he died, I took it from his pocket, as if I'd discovered it there. I printed your name on it. I gave it to a neighbor to give to some Charlie Turek. I let you think it was my uncle's idea and I didn't know anything about it."

"And I let you think I wasn't a miner."

"Charlie, I will stay. We must make something good of this life. For ourselves, for our baby." She rose from the bed. Then she stood at the window, looking out.

Casimir took his shoes off and lay down on the bed. He looked up at his wife, watched her eyes search the horizon. He propped himself up and let his eyes trail hers along the rounded ridges of the Appalachians that entrapped people like arms with bulging muscles. He watched her eyes. Despite her saying she would stay, her eyes seemed to be searching the horizon for a way out. He looked away. Through the mirror opposite the window, he saw a sparrow fly into the upper pane. It flew away, but then returned, flying into the pane again and again. Flecks of blood dotted the glass. The sparrow dropped out of sight, but in a moment it was back again, beating itself to tatters.

Victoria gnawed at her knuckles. "Charlie, look at that poor little bird. Stop him!"

"Victoria."

"Charlie, stop him!"

"I can't!" Casimir shouted. He leapt from the bed. He cupped one hand against the side of his wife's face, turning her from the bird, pressing her against his chest. He spoke softly. "I can't. Birds do that sometimes."

10

THE LAST GOOD DAY IN GDANSK

Break, break, break,
At the foot of thy crags, O Sea!
But the tender grace of a day that is dead
Will never come back to me.

—TENNYSON

It was a funny sort of porch for Gdansk, the best copy Casimir's father was able to make of one in a photograph Uncle Jerzy had found on the street. It stuck out at the end of a row of two-story brick structures that had one square slab of stone and two stone steps at each front door. In the photograph was a Nebraska farmhouse with a porchful of smiling young women posing stiffly, some standing, some sitting on chairs, some sitting on the steps. Familiar Polish embroidery patterns could be seen on the skirts of the women on the bottom step. Everyone's eyes squinted into half-moons in the late afternoon sun, which threw their shadows into zigzag patterns on the clapboards. Their hair was tamed in kerchiefs, the sleeves of their white blouses rolled up to the elbows. It was plain to see that these young women were "accustomed to hard work and prepared to continue doing it cheerfully," as the accompanying letter from a marriage broker pointed out.

The space beneath the dark porch was filled in with white latticework. The head of a dozing white dog was visible in the space where a tiny door stood open next to the three steps.

"A wife for me," Uncle Jerzy said one evening at supper, pulling the muddy envelope from his pocket. He sat back, his mouth reverting to its chronic O-shape while Ignacy, Casimir's father, read the announcement published by W.J. Murdek, Marriage Broker, of Loup City, Nebraska, serving Europe and America.

For weeks, Uncle Jerzy pestered to go to Nebraska. Holding out the envelope, he pestered in single words, "Wife. Nebrushka. Ameddika." Ignacy, satisfied with his life as a fisherman, had no great wish to go to America, only a slight curiosity about that magic land, not enough to send him sailing over there. Besides, he wanted to witness the scraps of Poland ripped from the grip of Germany, Russia, and Austria, and stitched back together as Poland. No country, however full of promise, was worth more than that dream.

Ignacy told his brother he would bring Nebraska to Gdansk. Then maybe the wife would come. But he couldn't promise. He built the look-alike porch, which was much smaller, and duplicated the latticework and steps the best he could, even down to the little latticework door with the dark frame and push-down latch.

Casimir loved to play under there. One summer afternoon he was under the porch on a rag mat, trying hard to stay clean. If he did, his mother would take him down to the docks to watch his father unload the catch while Anna and Krystina took afternoon naps.

Tanya, the baby-sitter, was coming up the walkway, humming. He heard the wooden porch steps creak as she walked up them. Pretty Tanya. She opened the front door and called in, "I'm here to stay with Anna and Krystina now." He liked the sound of her voice, every sentence like a line from a song, a soft kind of song that could put you to sleep. His mother wasn't ready. Tanya waited outside and fussed over the cat in her song voice.

His mother came out to the porch and called him. He got to his feet, stooping under the porch beams. He slid the mat over to the little door. Then he knelt on the mat to keep his knees clean. He pressed the latch. Jozefina stood on the steps just beside his head. Her black hair hung in a very heavy braid, each of the three plaited strands as thick as a dock rope. She wrapped the braid into a ball at the base of her neck while she walked around Casimir and inspected him. "Nice and clean," she said. "Good boy!"

Casimir ran up the steps to kiss and pet Muszka, who had been gazing smugly on the banister, having been crooned to contentment by Tanya. The cat raised its back end as Casimir's hand traveled to the tip of its tail. "See you later, Muszka." A kiss on the animal's head, and Casimir turned to the steps to join his mother. But as he turned, he caught sight of his Uncle Jerzy's haggard face, brown stubble along the jaw and around the mouth, pressed on the glass window of the door. The turquoise eyes, exactly the shade of Casimir's, were aglaze with longing. Long, bony fingers had come to rest at the base of the glass. The man's mouth formed a perfect "O".

"Let's take Uncle Jerzy," Casimir said.

Jozefina went to the top step and reached for Casimir's hand. "You know he won't behave."

"Yes, he will. Won't you, Uncle?"

Jerzy slid down and pressed his lips to the glass, leaving a greasy, circular lip print on the lower right corner. He pulled his face back and traced the print with a trembling finger. His mouth still forming an O, only his eyes smiled in approval. He clapped for himself, then proceeded to frame the whole glass with lip prints.

"See?" Jozefina said. "Look at the mess he's making."

"Because he's mad we're going without him. Look, now he's sad." Jerzy pressed his forehead against the pane, his eyes downcast and glazed.

Casimir pulled on his mother's arm. "Mama, can we take him?"

"You remember what he did last time. Remember how he said his voices told him to sit on the bronze horse in the park and wait till the angels brought him a sword?"

"To kill the Germans. He won't do it again." Casimir ran to the door. "You won't climb up on the horse again, will you, Uncle?"

Uncle Jerzy stepped out. His pants were buttoned wrong, leaving a gap in the middle. The child turned his uncle away from Jozefina and pulled him down, whispering in his ear. Both of them giggled. Casimir petted the cat while his uncle rebuttoned his fly.

When Jerzy finished, he reached into his pocket and took out a crumpled envelope. "Nebrushka," he said. "Ameddika. Wife."

"Yes, Uncle."

"Wife," he said, pointing to one of the women on the bottom step in the photograph.

"Yes, Uncle. Maybe she'll hear about our porch and come."

Jerzy nodded, looking at the photograph with longing. Suddenly he laughed with delight. He held the photograph up and positioned his arms for a waltz. He began dancing across the porch.

"Let's go," Casimir said, tugging his uncle down the steps. It wasn't until they were halfway down that Jozefina noticed Jerzy was wearing one brown shoe and one gray bedroom slipper. Casimir was about to go inside for the other shoe when Tanya appeared on the porch with a pastry. "Jerzy," she called in her song voice. "See what I brought for you? Cinnamon. Your favorite kind. Come stay home with Tanya. We'll have fun." She held out a slender hand with the pastry, her face bright with the promise of a fun afternoon.

Jerzy, one foot on the top step, one on the porch, reached for the pastry. Tanya took a step back, luring him toward the door. He looked from the pastry, to Casimir, to the pastry, to Casimir.

Jozefina bent toward her son. "Tell him it's okay to stay here and eat it," she whispered.

"But he wants to come with us."

"No, he wants the pastry. He just doesn't want you to be mad if he stays. Tell him it's okay."

"You stay and have a treat, Uncle. We'll take you next time."

Jerzy nodded. He took the pastry, turned to the brick wall of the house, sat down, folding his legs in front of him, and tore off small pieces of the pastry, slowly slipping them through the O.

Casimir was not convinced he had done the right thing, but his mother had whisked him off so fast that it was too late. He felt guilty thinking about all the sights Uncle Jerzy would miss on the way to the docks. He didn't think it was right for him to enjoy them if poor Uncle Jerzy couldn't, so he said to his mother, "I want to play blind man. Will you tie your handkerchief on me and lead me?"

Jozefina did as he asked. Casimir listened to the clopping of hooves and the rumble of carriage wheels over the cobblestones. Now and then, when they waited to cross at a corner, he could hear a horse scrape the ground and flap its lips. He knew when they were nearing the docks, for the smell of the salty Baltic air and wild roses grew so strong that it hugged him. Now he could smell the fish.

"Off with the blindfold," his mother said. "The docks."

Casimir had wanted to see if he could make it all the way to the boat without stumbling. But he slipped the handkerchief over his head and made up his mind to be good all day so he wouldn't spoil his mother's friendly mood.

In America, he would come to look back on this day as his last good day in Gdansk.

The tide was out, and the boats lay low along the pilings. They were barely visible from the wharf. Ignacy, standing halfway up a ladder, his forearms resting on the dock, grinned at his wife and son. The gray along his front hairline gleamed silver in the sun. "We're back early. Stosh got seasick. Imagine, forty years on the waves and he heaves his lunch all over the deck. I was just cleaning it up here."

"Shall I climb down and help you?" Jozefina said.

"And drag your skirt through this stink? No. I'm almost done. We'll walk in the park then." Ignacy lowered a pail with a rope and pulled up water several times, pouring it onto the deck, going over it with a broom. "She's just about clean. Just a minute."

Casimir let his feet dangle over the dock and held his nose.

"There. Finished," Ignacy said.

Afterwards, Casimir walked between his parents in the park, holding their hands, hoping his friends from school wouldn't see him doing that. After all, he was seven. They'd say he was acting like a baby. But it felt so good to be like they were before Uncle Jerzy started hearing voices. Friendly, not fighting. Just as he thought about his uncle, he noticed the bronze horse where Jerzy had sat waiting for the angels to bring him the sword. Casimir frowned. If they thought about Uncle Jerzy, they might start arguing. He let his knee give out and pretended to twist his ankle so they'd have to hurry past that horse to the benches beyond the next section of trees. Though his trick got them away from the bronze horse, it also meant that the walk was over, and they would have to take him home.

On the way back, they stopped in a church, Casimir having hopped on one foot, his arms linked through his parents'. They left him sitting in the back pew. They held hands as they walked up the nave. His mother lit a candle on the tray behind the railing at the altar of Mary; his father did the same before the altar of Saint Joseph. They both knelt with their faces buried in their hands. Then they met at the top of the center aisle and walked down together like a new bride and groom.

Casimir could not remember a day when everything went so right. At supper, Jerzy ate with a fork and closed his mouth as he chewed. He sang with everyone on the front porch after the children's tub baths in the kitchen. He went to bed at eight-thirty, like Anna and Krystina. Usually, all three of them had trouble falling asleep in the white nights of the Baltic, but on this night they drifted into sleep without a fuss, leaving Casimir sitting on the porch between his parents, relaxed and drowsy.

Ignacy said he had to run around to the back of the house and set his gear up for the morning. It would only take a few minutes.

Casimir rubbed his bare feet on the wood between the posts of the porch banister, waiting. His head rolled sideways against his mother's arm. The wind picked up, and the salty breeze wafted the smell of wild roses. His mother began to hum an old Slavic tune. His lids fluttered with the weight of sleep, and through them he saw the bright light of the sun. The clock tower in the square rang nine bells.

Casimir heard his papa's boots land firmly on the wooden steps. They crossed the porch. Two strong arms slid under him, and he felt his papa's breath on his cheek. "Up you go, *muy synku*."

"Papa?" Casimir sat up in the darkness of Black Hollow. In so many dreams he relived some part of that day. This time it was the moment when Ignacy's boot came down on the first step of the front porch. Sometimes it was Uncle Jerzy eating with a fork. Sometimes it was Tanya and Muszka. His papa's boots never got past the third step. Casimir always woke up, his heart sinking, longing to feel his papa's strong arms pick him up, longing to hear his voice.

Victoria stirred. She rolled onto her side, away from him. Casimir thanked God she slept so soundly. He could give himself away, dreaming, calling out in his sleep. He pressed himself curve for curve against her, like a shadow, and put his arm around the rising mound of her belly. He wondered if the child was sleeping, too.

11

THAT'S HOW I COULD SAY YES

The snow came down hard. But it stopped as suddenly as it had started, adding little to what was on the ground and not slowing the train down at all. Casimir cursed the sky. If only the snow would stop the train, he would have an excuse for not visiting his mother in the hospital. He could write back to Anna and Krystina and assure them he had really, really tried to hold Mama's hand and say good-bye for them, as he had promised in his letter. Then, if she died before next Saturday, his next chance to go to Pottsville, well—

"Pottsville! Pottsville!" the conductor called out. Casimir hurried off the train, ran into the station, and asked about the next train back to Mt. Carmel.

"Not for an hour," the ticket seller mumbled without lifting his jaw from his palm.

An hour. A whole hour, he thought, pacing. If he didn't make himself walk up that hill to the hospital, he would have to spend a whole hour in this station where that crazy old Kraut with the onion breath saw him throw those three nines in a row. He couldn't stand to wait there.

He went back to the teller's window. "The next town ahead, then, Schuylkill Haven. When's the next train to Schuylkill Haven?"

"Two minutes. Back on the same train."

Casimir purchased a ticket and got back on the train.

The day was growing dark. As the train approached Schuylkill Haven, Casimir looked out at the outline of the silo and the moonlit snow on the immigrants' cottages at the poor farm. His heart raced as it had done the day he left his mother's and Stanislaw's home. He had thought of going to the poor farm to work, but the farm being a mere few miles from Pottsville, it was probably the first place his mother and Stanislaw would look for him. How odd that he should be looking at it now, for it was the poor farm that grew the food for nearby hospitals. Had he settled there, it would be his toil providing his mother with her last meals. He pictured his mother picking at soggy morsels of food on her hospital plate.

He had to go see her. He had to. He could never face his sisters if he didn't.

He went into the Schuylkill Haven station and bought a ticket back to Pottsville. Another ride on the Reading Railroad. Since he'd been able to avoid the Delaware & Hudson, maybe the visit to his mother wouldn't go so badly. He seized that thought, consoling himself with it over and over. But what could they talk about? Something safe, it had to be. You never knew who might be listening at the door. Remembering that last good day in Gdansk, the night before his papa died, he decided they could talk about that. The good day. Yes, they'd talk about the good day, nothing else.

It occurred to him that she would call him Casimir. Casimir—he had not worn the name for so long. He took a walk behind the station, mumbling his own given name, "Casimir, Casimir," trying it on, staring at his own vague, moonlit reflection in the back window of the station. He had an urge to scream, "Here I am!" as if he had been lost in the bottom of a well and some search party was groping in a nearby field, calling, "Casimir, are you there?"

. He paced to one end of the building, then to the other, peeking around each end. No one could see him. He broke a twig off a bush and walked to the center of the back of the building, where he stooped down and leaned forward, extending the twig toward a smooth mound of snow. "C-A-S-I-M-I-R," he etched in the snow. He sat on his heels, staring at his own name. There. He was used to the name. He would not run out of the hospital when she said it.

The Reading pulled in. Quickly, he scooped up two fistfuls of snow and pressed it over the lines of his name. Then he got on the train. Feeling less afraid, he sank into the seat, and the moment the train stopped, he stood up, and stepped onto the platform. He walked through the station, then headed toward the hospital.

Halfway up the hill he noticed a light on in a little corner store. He should bring his mother some food that was not from the poor farm, something with a little dignity to it. *You must take care of your own,* he remembered his papa saying whenever Jozefina tried to insist he put Uncle Jerzy in an asylum. His mother was "his own," no matter how he felt about her. Yes, he should buy her something. He knew it was the right thing to do, for he felt his father smiling down on him when he crossed the street and tried the knob of the store.

The storekeeper looked up from his paperwork, smiled, and unlocked the door. "Just in time," he said. "I was just about to close up." He was a husky middle-aged man who looked as if he should be wielding a sledgehammer. "What can I get you?"

Casimir spotted a shelf of jarred cherries. He took one jar down and traced the raised glass design with his fingers. It was a little bird nibbling at a cluster of berries. The design put a smile on his face. "Where did you get these?"

"My own backyard. My wife cans them every fall. Want some?"

"Yes. They still make these jars, huh?"

"They sure do. My mother used them when I was just a little kid."

"Mine too. My mother put elderberry jam in them. I used to spoon it into my mouth right from the jar." Casimir gave the man a silver dollar. He stared at the jar while the man got his change and a bag. Then, armed with the jar of cherries, he left feeling a little braver. It was something safe to talk about.

Casimir paused on the hospital steps and asked God to help him keep his voice from shaking through any lies he had to tell, assuring God he wouldn't tell any lies he didn't really, really have to. Then he went in.

The ether smell made him swoon. At a desk in the lobby sat a sleepy young woman who twirled a lock of her red hair.

"I'm here to see my aunt, Jozefina Gombrowicz," Casimir said.

"Oh. Her nephew. You wouldn't happen to know where we could reach her son. 'Casimir Turek,' it says here." She showed him a scrap of paper. "I'm supposed to send him right to her room no matter what hour he comes. She calls for him round the clock."

"My cousin, yes. He moved to Denver. But can I see her?"

"Sure. Room 214. But her doctor's in with her now. No, wait. That's him there. Doctor Stauffenberg!"

The doctor hurried over. He was a tall man who pulled his lips in pensively under a dark mustache.

"Mrs. Gombrowicz's nephew," the receptionist said. "Her son moved to Denver, he said."

Casimir reached for the doctor's hand. "Charlie."

"She's near the end," Dr. Stauffenberg said. "Death could come tonight. But it could have been last night. Or the night before. It should have been. I think she's hanging on for her son. She says she knows he'll come. Do you know anything about her son?"

Casimir's voice quivered. "What do you mean, know anything about him? What do you want to know about him?"

"Maybe you could tell her something, some news that would satisfy her and get her to let go. She's in great pain. She'll be better off to let go. Every night her husband comes to take her home to die. But she says her son would never go to that house. So she waits for him here in the hospital."

"Casimir sent me a wire asking about her," Casimir said.

"Good, good. Tell her that, will you? She'll be glad to know."

"I will."

"Would you like me to go up with you?"

"Thanks, no. Let me just sit a minute and think about what to say."

"I wouldn't delay too long." The doctor walked down the hall.

Near the end, Casimir thought. Death could come tonight. Why did he have to say it that way? As if a figure with a black cloak and sickle were to— The thought of death in the image of the Grim Reaper he had seen in sketches made him shudder. He shuddered to think of his mother opening her eyes in the moonlight through the window and seeing the cloaked figure standing over her bed.

The receptionist stood in front of him. "A penny for your thoughts."

"A penny?" Yes, a penny, he thought. I might as well have some idea how it will go, for better or worse. He stood up and pulled a penny from his pocket as he walked toward the stairs. The penny was face down.

Somewhat prepared for the worst, Casimir went up to the nurses' station on the second floor and asked about Room 214. A nurse with sad brown eyes half smiled at him and pointed the direction to the room. It seemed to Casimir that everyone walking through the hall had stopped to watch what he was going to do. He walked down the corridor, keeping close to the wall. When he reached Room 214, he stopped to the side of the doorway.

From where he stood, he could see the contours of bony knees and feet under a white sheet. On top of the sheet was an arm with sagging flesh, and thin, restless fingers pinching the sheet into a tiny mound and then smoothing it out again. The fingers pinched and smoothed the sheet over and over.

Casimir felt a hand on his shoulder. The nurse with the sad brown eyes said to him, "It's all right. You may go in. Would you like me to go in with you?"

"I'd like to be alone with her."

"I'll be at the desk if you need me."

Casimir nodded. He watched the fingers pinch and smooth, pinch and smooth. Suddenly, the knees rose. Fists pounded on thin thighs. I must tell her I forgive her, Casimir told himself, having decided that her agony was due as much to her need for his forgiveness as to the cancer. I will go in and say, "Mama, I forgive you." He got as far as the doorway and looked to the right. Those dark eyes, though sunken into her ashen face, widened with joy. Her black and silver hair hung down over one side of the bed. "I pray and pray you come. Every night, Casimir."

Seeing the slow, peaceful way she closed her eyes before she looked at him again, he smiled back. She gazed at him as gently as at the end of their last good day in Gdansk. He remembered her laughter on the docks, her humming on the porch, his father's strong arms. But when Jozefina struggled to sit up and reach for him, all he could see was her hand reaching to comfort him night after night back home, after his papa was dead. He remembered how he'd grab her wrist and push it away.

If you would just hold Mama's hand for us!

Ashamed of his own impulse to draw back, he took the jar of cherries out of the bag and set it on the stand near her head. "Just like the jars you used when I picked the elderberries here in Pottsville."

Jozefina glanced at the jar and smiled. "Still too angry to touch me, Casimir?" She was speaking to him in Polish now. Casimir shut the door so no one would hear. She smiled understandingly, but continued in her native tongue. "Like that night on the German steamship. Seven days and seven nights already. People vomiting.

Filthy straw berths in the steerage. I tried not to cry out. But I did. I was full of fever. You woke up and reached up to my berth. My hair, a big, long lock of hair, was glued to my cheek with sweat. It weighed so heavy on my face. You reached to brush it back for me."

Casimir looked to make sure the door was still closed before speaking in Polish. "'Anna, Krystina!' you screamed. I didn't know till then that you didn't want to leave them in Gdansk."

"Want to leave them there! No, no! Anna just turning four. Krystina not yet two. How could I want to leave them there? Come sit by me." Casimir sat on the bed but slid his hand away when she tried to take hold of it. She continued. "That night on the steamship. I felt your fingers close to my face. You were going to lift that lock of hair from my cheek. But you couldn't get yourself to touch me. Just like tonight. Still too angry. Casimir, I had to leave them in Gdansk."

"Why, Mama? Why couldn't we all come to America?"

"The marriage broker, the man who arranged the marriage, he said, 'What man in America wants a woman with three children to provide for? A man wants some of his own. Especially a son. Pretend you have only one child. Only one. Then when you give him his own child, a son, then you tell him you have two more children to bring over and beg him to send for the others. Only then.' Casimir, I explained that to you when we got here."

"Yes. But you never sent for them. Never. You never even told Stanislaw you had two girls in Gdansk. And you made me promise never to tell him."

"And never did I give him that son. Three baby girls I had in America. By then his lungs were getting bad. He's a lot older than me. I couldn't ask him to raise two more when I saw how he was. He is a kind-hearted man. He would only have felt terrible to learn I had left them in Gdansk so I could give him a son first."

"Oh, Mama, how could you agree to marry a man you never even saw?"

"I could tell from the letter Stanislaw wrote the marriage broker he'd be good to you. That's how I could say yes to a man I never even met."

Casimir watched her hands grip the sheets. "You have a lot of pain, Mama."

"Yes, but let's talk. I'm so happy that you came, that the pain is nothing, as long as we talk."

"Can't they give you something?"

"I said no. I said I wanted to hear and talk and not be half crazy with medicines when somebody special came to see me."

"Meaning me."

"Yes. Now we can talk. Face it, Casimir. I'm dying. What you say dies with me. Go on, tell me all you kept inside. All the things you wouldn't say in Gdansk after your papa died. How you kept to yourself after that!"

"Why me, Mama? Why didn't you leave me there and bring Anna? For months after we left I dreamed about her sobbing on the docks after us."

"But you were the one I had to save."

Casimir's face colored with embarrassment. He felt exposed in a way he couldn't name. Anger came to his rescue, restoring his power, shielding him. He glared at her and rose to his feet, turning toward the door, threatening to leave. "You're talking nonsense."

"Don't look at me like that. You were the one who lived under the front porch after your papa died."

Casimir sat down again. "Because Papa built that porch. Sitting under there made me feel close to Papa."

Jozefina lifted her hair from the side of the bed and began braiding it. She had never thought it decent to be seen with her hair hanging. It was like being caught in a nightgown.

"Oh, Mama, let your hair hang. Be comfortable." But Jozefina went on braiding it anyway. "I know," she said, "you loved that porch. But you wouldn't come out from under there after he died. And you wouldn't even let Anna in. She'd set your dinner on the street. You'd wait till you couldn't see her feet before you'd open the door. She'd lean over the banister, watching for your hand to slide the plate through that little door. I was scared for you, Casimir. If a child could go mad, I thought you were going to be the one."

"I know, I know. Madness runs in Papa's side of the family. Uncle Jerzy. Grandpa Turek. How you and Aunt Marta went on and on about that! Like it was okay for madness to be in the family, as long as your side wasn't to blame. All you wanted to do was put Uncle away. You didn't waste any time doing it after Papa died, did you?

One day after the funeral, gone! Off to the asylum! Poor Uncle Jerzy. Papa would have cared for him all his life."

"No, Casimir."

"Mama, you could have managed. Uncle was so good the last day we were all together. The day we went down to the docks and you and Papa stopped in the church and lit those candles."

Jozefina sat up again, took the jar of cherries from the night stand and ran her fingers over the design. Her voice was weaker. "You wished every day could be like that."

"That was the last good day for everybody."

"A good day, but not such a good night. Not for your papa."

"What do you mean?"

"The voices. They were starting with your papa, too."

"That's a lie!"

"That night. I heard him myself, talking back to them."

"Talking in his sleep. That's all."

"No. I tried to hide it from you, but you overheard me telling your Aunt Marta about it the next morning. It's only a dream to think your papa could have cared for Jerzy all his life. The day was coming when he would be just the same. He heard the voices, too."

"Sleeptalk, that's all. But you and Aunt Marta had to go whispering about it. And Papa was dead before the day was through. Mama, I can still see you pacing alongside the supper table, glaring at him. You *had* to get out of the house, you told him."

Casimir sighed and shook his head. "Mama, I'm sorry. Here you are in your last days, maybe even your last hours. I promised Anna and Krystina I would come to give you comfort, and here I am accusing you. I better go." His hands squirmed in his pockets. *If you would just hold Mama's hand for us.* He reached for his mother's hands, pressing them inside his own. "Good-bye from Anna and Krystina," he said. Then he released her hands and put his own safely in his pockets.

Jozefina cried. Then, after a long silence, she said, "You cannot make my last hours worse by saying what I tried to get you to say instead of holding it all inside, hiding under that porch. You blamed me. Say it. Get it out. It's better for both of us."

"Mama, after all these years of silence—"

"Yes, go ahead, say it. You can't hurt me by saying it. I know what I did. Yet I have made peace with myself. With God. Say it, and then get on to *your* part."

"*My* part! Mama, you're mad. I had no part in Papa's death!"

Jozefina set the jar of cherries on the night stand and slipped her fingers through her long braid as if putting on a glove. "If you can't forgive me, Casimir, I don't blame you. And it's all right. I told you I've made my peace with God. But you don't forgive yourself, and that can make you crazy."

"Forgive myself for what?" He made himself smile. He shrugged. "What have I got to forgive myself for?"

"For laughing."

Casimir's face reddened. Jozefina sat up and tried to reach for his arm. He stepped away, and she lay back down. "Casimir, you were laughing when your papa was dying."

"No! You weren't even in the house. So there, how would you know?"

"After you ran away, Anna wrote and told me. But she couldn't remember why. She was only three. All she remembers was everybody laughing. So I know. And now I know why you wouldn't mix with the Polish children when we came to America. You thought one of them might be from Gdansk and recognize you. Casimir, that terrible boy who laughed when his father was dying. You left Pottsville, pretended to be somebody else. A new name. Some American Charlie. No foreign accent. Who would know?"

"Mama, it was Anna that was laughing. And Krystina. Slapping her fat little hands on her highchair tray. It was them, not me!"

"Casimir, tell me why you were laughing."

"I wasn't! Mama, it was your fault Papa died. If you'd stayed home, if you were there, you could have stopped Papa from choking, but no! You had to run next door to see Aunt Marta. You couldn't wait till after supper. I guess you had more whispering to do about Papa hearing voices. You let Papa die! Then you came to America and found a new man and got new daughters. You left Anna and Krystina behind. I hated you for that!"

Jozefina looked up to the ceiling and said, "Dear God, I can't help him. I failed. I hope you will take me as I am."

Her jaw hung loosely and her slow breathing rattled. Her eyes were only half open. She seemed to be staring at her feet.

"Mama?"

Her eyes rolled upward and then down again. Her breathing became a loud gurgle.

"Mama?"

Casimir took hold of her fingertips and shook them, but she seemed not to notice.

"Mama? I lied. I did laugh."

A smile crossed Jozefina's lips.

"Mama?"

Jozefina's jaw dropped and her hand fell over her son's.

He felt for a pulse. He left the room quickly, picturing the Grim Reaper gathering her up and carrying her down the fire escape.

Casimir could barely remember the train ride home from Pottsville. He seemed to have just appeared in front of his own house, where he stood looking up at his bedroom windows. The shadow of a hunched figure covered much of the wall and part of the ceiling. The head dipped below the window sill. The shadow straightened up, then, its arm extending downward, toward the night stand. Then the light went out.

Death could come tonight, Casimir thought. Has he come for Victoria, too? Dazed, he walked around to the back yard and let himself into the kitchen. He did not light a lamp. Instead, he groped along the counter and rummaged in the dark for the candles in the middle drawer. He found one and lit it, dripping wax in the center of the table till he made a soft pool large enough to stand the candle in.

He took a bottle of whiskey from the cabinet, opened it, and poured a shot. He envisioned himself standing in his bedroom doorway, beholding the dead body of his pregnant wife. One more shot of hooch and he'd have the courage to face it.

Someone coughed lightly on the way down the stairs and through the parlor, as if trying to avoid startling him. "Charlie?" It was Mrs. Anderson's voice. She had come after supper to visit Victoria.

Casimir was surprised that she was still there. She stood in the archway between the kitchen and the parlor, her hand resting on the knob of the cellar door. Her voice was almost a hiss. "You look ghastly."

"Just tired. Why you here so late?"

"Victoria asked me to sit awhile, tell her things about Black Hollow, who'd lived here the longest, and so on. So I told her about the old grocer." She laughed lightly. "I didn't want her thinkin' I was the oldest person in the patch, see. She's asleep now. I gave her a peck on the forehead, and out she went like a light."

"That was you? A moment ago, I was outside and saw a shadow leaning over her. That was you?"

"Why, of course. Who else?"

"Never mind. You say she's all right?"

"If she takes care, that baby won't come till March, like it's supposed to." Mrs. Anderson sat down. "Now, tell me about you. You look ghastly pale. What's on your mind?"

"Nothing." Casimir was aching to tell someone his mother had just died. He looked at the old woman opposite him. She leaned a little toward him. Her head was tilted to the side, resting, as if she had nowhere to go and all night to listen. Her eyes, drooping wearily at the corners, caught the candlelight, which danced tirelessly in them. "Talk to me," she said. "I can keep a confidence. Something happened tonight. Something bad. Tell me."

He tried to dodge her glance, but her face followed his, as if she were his image in a mirror. He shook his head. "Tomorrow, maybe."

"Things have a way of eating at your heart if you don't get them out."

Casimir felt Mrs. Anderson's eyes follow his hand as he poured another shot. He held the glass lightly against his lower lip, waiting for her to lecture him. She said nothing. He drank the shot in one swallow. Then he poured another one and sipped it like brandy. He could feel the cloaked figure with the sickle lurking about the room. He watched the old woman's eyes for some sign that she sensed it, too. But from her he sensed a righteousness. There she sat, so smug and smart, so all-knowing and right. He mocked her in his mind, wagging his head. *Something happened tonight. Something bad.* What was she anyway, a mind reader? So smug, so steady, while he trembled, barely able to pour another shot. He felt her waft her righteousness over him like a priest with one of those gold incense cans on a chain. Puffing a holy, smoky cloud like they do at dead people in coffins and anything else in need of God's mercy and forgiveness. He lifted the bottle. "Want some?"

"I'll have a shot," she said. She remained seated and allowed Casimir to wait on her. Each sat sipping and trying to read the other's eyes. He liked watching her sip the whiskey. It brought her down a notch. Finally, Mrs. Anderson said, "You're not going to tell me anything tonight, are you?"

Casimir threw another drink down his throat. He could still feel the cloaked figure staring at him from somewhere in the kitchen. The centers of the nasturtiums on the wallpaper above the wainscoting looked like so many eyes, all watching to see what he was going to do.

"Tell her about me," he heard his mother's voice say in Polish. He jumped to his feet, his head turning, his eyes searching every corner of the dark room.

"What is it, Charlie?"

"I thought I heard a noise."

"I didn't hear anything. Won't you tell me what's on your mind?"

Casimir sat back down. He rubbed his palms along his jaw, carefully slipping a finger in each ear as his elbows came to rest on the table. He slid his chair away from the light. He tried to steady his voice. "I'm tired, Mrs. Anderson. Tomorrow, maybe. I'm tired."

"All right. I'll be going then." She stood up and put her coat on and went out.

"Casimir, why didn't you tell her about me?"

"Mama?" How could this be? He took the candle over to the mirror on the cellar door and held it near his lips, expecting to find them in that Uncle Jerzy O. They were straight and closed, yet he heard his dead mother talking. Was she trying to punish him for not forgiving her? Was she going to haunt him now?

Her voice was clear and strong. "Tell Victoria about me."

"Speak English, Mama! We don't speak Polish here."

"Not to tell everything to her. She thinks I live in Nebraska. Tell her you get this wire to announce my death. Tell her. Tell her something. Somebody's mother dies, someone should hear it."

He felt the cloaked figure follow him up the stairs. If he went into the bedroom, would it follow him there and take his wife? Don't think about it. Anger rescued him again from the fear. He thought about Mrs. Anderson, the nerve of her, asking what was on his mind. What was it to her!

He gripped the jambs of his bedroom door. In the moonlight, he could see Victoria sleeping, and his rage leapt from Mrs. Anderson to his wife. Why did she need that old woman around so often, so late into the night? Three months till the baby was due. He shook Victoria awake, immediately regretting that he had, unnerved by the sight of his own shadow. He should have let her sleep. What if the Reaper punished him? He'd show that he was sorry. He helped Victoria sit up. He hugged her tenderly, as if that was what he had meant to do in the first place.

"Casimir! Casimir, tell her about me," his mother's voice said.

Victoria rested her forehead against her husband's neck. She squeezed his fingers. "You're shaking." She reached toward the foot of the bed, where a woolen blanket was folded along the edge. She slid it toward him and spread it over his shoulders.

"Casimir, tell her."

He leaned forward and let his face come to rest on Victoria's lap. She began to stroke his hair. "You're shaking real bad."

"Tell her! If you tell her, I promise I won't bother you no more."

Across the room was the vanity dresser. Casimir expected to look in the mirror and see the reflection of Jozefina standing somewhere in the room. But all he saw was himself looking like a helpless child, his one arm wrapped around his wife's calves, one hand clutching her wrist, his cheek on her thighs. He could feel her belly pressing against the back of his head. The child shifted against him.

"Victoria," he murmured. "My mother was buried today. In Nebraska."

12

GUESS WHICH ONE

Victoria panted as the powerful push of her muscles tried once more to force the baby out. "How much longer, Mrs. Anderson?" Her toes clenched the covers at the bottom of the bed.

"Soon, I think. Soon." The midwife folded a washcloth into a rectangle, dipped it into a pot of warm water, wrung it out, and patted Victoria's forehead.

At the next contraction, Victoria drew her feet up and sucked in a breath through her teeth. The next was so powerful that she bunched her hair and screamed. Big Joe, as though mocking her, screamed into the sky—three long blasts forecasting snow.

"Not more snow," Victoria whined. "It's almost the end of March. This was supposed to be a spring baby."

Five contractions later, Big Joe blew an end to the workday.

"Thank God," Victoria said. "Charlie'll be home soon!"

"I'll listen for him," Mrs. Anderson said. When she heard men's voices outside, she went to the window. A parade of miners, their backs and arms burdened with tools, some walking with a hand on the shoulder of a coal-blackened son, marched up Saylor Street. Several men broke away at the school field and turned onto Girard Street. Mrs. Anderson was able to pick out Donny Wilson, his pudgy frame all but dancing. He had begun to walk backwards, facing the others. His arms and hands were waving about in some story he was trying to tell.

Mrs. Anderson opened the window just high enough to stick her head out. "Donny, is Charlie with you?"

"I'm here," Casimir yelled. He came and stood directly below the window and looked up, his turquoise eyes like little lakes on a charred landscape.

"The baby, Charlie! Any minute now! Hurry and get washed. I'll call you as soon as it's born."

"I'll wash and be right up!"

"It's no place for a man, I told you. Just get washed. I'll call you." She shut the window.

"Hear that?" Casimir said to the other miners. "Our baby's coming!" He ran through the back yard and into the cellar, tore off his clothes and dumped the jugs of warm water into the tin tub. He scrubbed himself wildly.

Hearing miners' boots crunching the cinders along the high cellar windows, he wished Victoria would let out such a scream that the whole patch would hear. Then they would know he was a man. He could make babies as good as any other man around here.

"Shame!" a woman's voice said in English.

Casimir froze and listened.

"Shame, to wish such bad pain she screams, so you can brag." He knew that scolding tone, that choppy, foreign way of sounding out the words. "Mama!?"

"Shame."

"You promised not to torment me if I told Victoria you died! I told her. I thought you were satisfied. Go away."

"What was that thing your Aunt Marta told?"

"I forget."

"Liar. She said you if you are bad, then the voices come."

"Go away." He waited to hear something more, but heard nothing. He wiped the black grit from his teeth with a salty rag, and rinsed his mouth quickly. He dressed, ran halfway up the stairs, and spun around. "You stay down here, Mama, hear? Leave us alone." He pressed his palms together in prayer. "Please let her rest in peace. Make her leave us alone."

He ran up to the kitchen and slammed the door behind him, pressing his back hard against it. He stood frozen by the archway to the parlor, praying, wishing, begging God to help him.

Mrs. Anderson came running down the stairs. "Charlie! A girl! It's a girl!" She came through the parlor and yelped with surprise to encounter Casimir just on the other side of the archway. Her white chignon, having been knocked loose by the bundle of soiled linens slung over her shoulder, had slid to the tip of her chin like a beard. "Charlie, you have a beautiful little girl. Bald as a pumpkin!"

"Name her Anna Krystina," Casimir heard his mother say from behind the cellar door. His heart was a lump of ice.

Mrs. Anderson laughed. "Don't look so shocked. Lots of baby girls are born bald. She'll get hair. I promise. Come see her. Victoria's already calling her Felicia. She says it means joy."

"Casimir, name her Anna Krystina, something to show you don't forget about your sisters in Gdansk, just so you have baby boy to brag about first."

He had not considered any girl's names before the baby was born. It was going to be a boy, and his name was going to be Frank. But now he was stuck with a girl, and his dead mother was declaring the child's name from behind the cellar door. Her voice was loud, loud enough for Mrs. Anderson to hear. Casimir studied the old woman's face for some sign that she, too, heard the voice. But she just stood there grinning and promising the little girl would get hair. It was clearly a voice only he could hear. He was being punished. If he wanted the voice to stop, he'd better do as his mother said.

"Anna Christine Turek," he said, suddenly realizing Krystina would sound like a greenie name in America. People would wonder how he came up with such a name. There would be questions. "I want the baby to be called Anna Christine."

Mrs. Anderson went out to the kitchen. "I'm sure you'll want to talk that over with Victoria. I'll busy myself down here if you'd like to go up now. I'll get supper for you and take care of this laundry." She went out to the porch to get the wash tub.

Casimir remained pressed against the cellar door. "A girl, not a boy, smart man," the voice said. "The miners still will laugh." Casimir tipped his head forward, away from the cellar door, and found that the voice grew fainter. When he pressed his ear against the door again, the voice was louder. "Maybe them American doctors come from Ellis Island and put big, big chalk mark on your clothes. Maybe X, maybe square, maybe circle."

Casimir opened the cellar door. The voice grew louder. "One of them marks mean you be only half real man. Can't make a boy baby. One mark means crazy man, Casimir. Guess which one."

"I don't know. Please, Mama, leave me alone."

"Come back down later. Maybe, if you are good boy, I will say you which one."

Casimir slammed the door, reliving the day he asked his Aunt Marta if the voices and the O-mouth would happen to him one day, like Uncle Jerzy. "Not if you're good," she had said.

He turned to the mirror nailed to the cellar door. His mouth was straight. Maybe there was still time to fix his life. But, did the voices come because of what he had done to his papa? Because he had spent the money for his sisters' passage and the farmhouse he had promised to have built for them? Because he had made a girl instead of a boy? He had satisfied his mother's demand to tell Victoria about her death. So that couldn't be it. Maybe it was the lie he had told. Nebraska. He had said she died in Nebraska. How would he ever figure out which thing brought on the voices? If he couldn't make them stop, how could he keep his promise to Saint Joseph to be a good husband, a good father? I should ship myself someplace on the Delaware & Hudson, he thought. Get myself killed and be done with it. Marek and Wanda had the right idea, trying to trick me into getting on that train.

"It is sin to take your life, Casimir. That's what you be doing if you take that Delaware & Hudson."

"I know."

"You must stay on this earth and care for your family. You must promise to love this baby, girl or not. Do you hear? You must promise, or I don't go away."

"All right, all right!" He took in a deep breath and held it. "All right. I promise."

Casimir opened the cellar door. "Mama?"

He heard nothing. He closed the door again and crept through the archway into the parlor, as though trying not to wake a nasty dog. He listened hard with each step and found that the voice did not follow him. Was she going to stay in the cellar? Maybe no one would know about her then.

He went upstairs to the front bedroom. Victoria, her cheeks red and wet with tears, smiled as she glanced sideways at the bundle by her side. Casimir hesitated in the doorway.

Victoria nodded to encourage him. When he got close to the bed, she laughed and said, "Sorry, but our little girl's got a head like a peeled pear. She's sleeping. Come look."

Victoria lifted the corner of the little cotton blanket from her face.

Casimir's eyes widened. "Sucking her thumb already?"

"Mrs. Anderson says some babies learn to do that before they're born. Did she tell you I was thinking about calling her Felicia?"

Casimir tugged the baby's thumb from her mouth. The little hand curled around his finger in a tight grip. He felt her sucking on the knuckle of his index finger. He avoided Victoria's eyes as he spoke. "You know, I was thinking of another name. Anna Christine. Is it all right?"

Victoria was so relieved that he was willing to think of a girl's name after all, that she agreed immediately, pleased with the name herself. "That's a beautiful name. Yes."

"And you," he said, lifting strands of her hair and laying them gently across his palm. "It must have been very hard, very painful. I'm sorry."

"It's over. I've already forgotten that part. But you, you look so worried. I'm all right. Anna Christine's all right. What about you? You're pale. Your hands, they're shaking."

Casimir dropped the strands and shoved his hands into his pockets. How could he answer? He had one ear cocked for his mother's voice, afraid he would jump at the sound and his wife would guess what was wrong. Maybe his mouth would snap into that crazy O-shape. He imagined himself glancing at the vanity mirror and seeing a white-coat doctor sneaking up on him with a piece of chalk.

Victoria sat up and pulled his head against her shoulder. Casimir could feel her waiting for an answer.

"I feel stunned," he said. "I feel like a miner clunked on the head with a rock. I can hardly believe it's true, Victoria. We have a child." He pulled away from her and lifted the veil of the bassinet he had made and painted white, its dome, which covered about a third of the bottom, a basket weave of willow branches. "Do you think she'll like the bed I made for her?"

"Let's find out."

Casimir lifted the child from the bed and put her in the bassinet. She barely stirred. When he put her on the little mattress, she pulled her knees up to her belly and folded her arms over her chest as though she had never left her mother's womb. Casimir tugged the white nightgown down over the tiny, red feet and replaced the cotton blanket. At the bottom of the bassinet was a small, bright yellow afghan crocheted by Mrs. Anderson. Casimir pulled it up to Anna Christine's shoulders. A warm wave of love washed over the lump of ice that was his heart. "Anna Chrissy," he said. His child was a girl, and he found that he would love her, after all. He wouldn't have to promise to try, so that his mother wouldn't haunt him and taunt him. The love just came on its own.

He pulled the veil over the bassinet and lay down beside his wife, praying silently that his mother would leave him alone.

Victoria and Casimir, exhausted, each aching from their day's labor, gathered one another in a soothing embrace and fell asleep.

The next day Casimir thought he heard his mother speak while he was raking the furnace. But when he called out to her, there was no answer. Weeks went by and he heard nothing. But he could not feel sure she would not be back. Just in case she caught him by surprise by speaking to him in front of Victoria, he made a point of muttering aloud on purpose, saying things like, "I know I had a hammer in my hand a minute ago. Did I leave it in the cellar? Up here?"

When Victoria uttered a thought aloud, he laughed and said she was just like him, talking to herself. He tried to be as good as he could, thoughtful and kind, willing to do anything to keep the voices away, keep his mouth straight.

He still ached for a son. Another mouth to feed, though. It would be harder to save money for his sisters' passage. Would he be punished if he tried again for a son before sending for them? Would the voice come back to torment him? An idea came to him. He wrote to his sisters and asked their permission to try for a son before making arrangements for their passage.

His sisters' reply took months. "What man wouldn't want a son?" they wrote. Considering Victoria was three months pregnant when he received their letter, he was thrilled with their understanding. He went down to the cellar and waved the letter in the air. "See, Mama? It's all right with them. See? Mama, are you still here?" Though he had not heard his mother's voice since the day Anna Chrissy was born, he sensed that his mother's spirit was lurking somewhere in the cellar, threatening to speak again if did something bad. He knew she could hear if he spoke. "Here, Mama," he said into the musty air. "Look at this letter. If it's okay with them that I try for a son first, why should you torment me about it? There's nothing wrong with a man wanting a son. Even Anna and Krystina agree. So don't think I'm bad and start making me hear your voice."

Receiving no answer, he fell to his knees and said a prayer of thanksgiving. Then he prayed that this second child would be a boy so he wouldn't have to keep putting his sisters off until he had a son.

Though he ached for a boy, he could not imagine loving a child more than he loved Anna Chrissy. After supper, he'd lie on the parlor floor and play with her. She'd fall asleep on his chest like a kitten while he petted the curly little sprouts of white-blonde hair on the back of her head.

Victoria often sat and mended as her husband and daughter dozed at her feet. One October evening, while they napped, she sat re-reading a letter she had just received from her parents. They had decided to forgive her for disobeying them and marrying that strange man. They asked if they might please see their grandchild. They hoped they could visit at Christmas.

Victoria thought of asking Charlie if he'd mind pretending to be a colliery boss during their visit. But she decided to try writing a letter saying he was a miner, the most caring one in the patch, in all of Pennsylvania. She began with a description of the nice furnishings in their home. And by the way, Charlie's job as a miner was pretty steady. Six-day weeks for the past two months. And he was so thoughtful. "Really, mother," she wrote, "did Papa ever pick wild-flowers for you on the way home from the mine?" As she wrote, she became more convinced herself that, miner or not, he was perfect, and she was still the envy of the patch.

When Casimir awoke, she showed him her parents' letter.

"You know I don't know Polish," he said. "Or am I so groggy that I can't read English either right now."

She translated the letter, which was in her father's hand. Casimir didn't want them coming to his home, but he saw the wishful look on Victoria's face when she asked if he'd mind if they came for Christmas. What if he said no? Would that be a bad thing? Would he hear a voice?

But how could he stand them when he knew they hated him? He pictured Wanda scoffing at him as he came through the gate in his miner's clothes. She would laugh and mock him, singing "The Ballad of Tim Brennan" in that grubby greenie accent of hers. But he was afraid to say no.

"All right. Let them come, but there's just one thing. Don't let on I'm a miner. I'll wash at Dombi's boarding house like I did before. It's only for a few days I'm asking you to pretend."

"It's all right with me. I was thinking the same thing. It's not worth the trouble. Knowing Mama, though, she'll want to come early to prepare for the holiday and stay a few days after."

"That's all right, I guess." He looked around the parlor. "We have to do something with this room. A rug, a couch, that's all we have." He brushed his hand over the back of the couch. Victoria had made a cover of expensive material, two shades of green brocade.

"Don't you like it?" Victoria said.

"I do. It's beautiful. But we need chairs," Casimir said. "Two, at least. I have a little money. You know that second-hand store up along the highway? Where rich people toss things just to have a change. I'll look there. It'll be cheap. It'll only look expensive."

The black velvet love seat and the deep green wing-backed chair Casimir bought drained him of every penny and left him with twenty-seven dollars to pay off at a rate of two dollars a month, plus interest. His salary averaged $3.10 a day. From that the Ebony Gem deducted the cost of blasting powder, squibs, drills, anything a miner needed to do his job. Once a month a dollar was taken out to pay the company doctor.

On November 20, when the first payment was due, Casimir took the payment book from a drawer in the kitchen and counted out the cash. He was alone and sitting in the chair at the head of the table, close to the cellar door. He thought he heard the doorknob rattle. He listened for a moment, then got up and opened the door. He poked his head through, listening as he peered down into the darkness. "Casimir," a woman's voice said in a whisper.

He ran down the steps, pulling the door shut after himself. "Oh, Mama, please! Please don't torment me."

"Look how you did with your money. Forty-seven dollars each it costs now for a boat from Gdansk. How you can save it? How you can buy them a farmhouse like Uncle Jerzy's picture? How!"

"Mama, I had to do this. If I say Victoria's parents can't come, maybe you will punish me with your voice for that, or maybe she will get mad and leave me. But if they come and don't see a good life, that rotten Wanda will torment me worse than you. Maybe she will convince Victoria to leave me. She mustn't leave now. We have another baby coming. A boy, I hope, a good boy, much better than me. A good boy to make Papa smile down on me finally. Mama, please leave me alone."

"Not till you pay, like purgatory, where you don't get punishment forever, but just till the venial sin burns off. Then I go."

"When, Mama?"

"Christmas, maybe."

"Maybe! Tell me for sure!"

"December twenty-sixth. Victoria's mother be here for Christmas. I be, too."

"All right. But will you stay in the basement?"

"On Christmas Day?"

"Yes."

"Till Christmas Eve. Then I don't know. We will see."

Wanda arrived a week before her husband, so she could make sure Victoria had all that was needed for the courses of a traditional Polish Christmas Eve dinner. She trollied about to every neighboring town, buying from this store and that.

On Christmas Eve, Casimir bought a bundle of straw from the wagon parked in the school field by the Lithuanian family who made the straw available for the Slavic families who needed it to celebrate in the traditional way. He carried the bale through the yard, grinning.

Victoria watched him from the kitchen window. "Mama, look. Charlie has the straw for the table."

"So, big news. That is his job." Wanda grabbed a long wooden spoon and stirred the contents of a huge pot with steely determination, as if she were stirring a cauldron, the awful effects of its contents to become manifest in good time.

Victoria tried to make light of everything. She tried to make her mother notice anything good her husband did. She ignored her mother's cold comment and tried again. "He looks like one of those bundle boys in the factory, peering around that bale of straw like that. I hope he doesn't trip."

Wanda continued to stir the pot. "He already do trip."

"What do you mean?"

"He trip in his own lies. All week he trips. He thinks I don't see."

"Oh, Mama," Victoria laughed uncomfortably.

"'Oh, Mama!'" Wanda mocked. "I see you don't say, 'What lies, Mama?' You don't want to know what lies I mean. You don't want to face there is something wrong with that man."

Casimir set the bundle of straw down on the back porch, came directly into the kitchen and lifted his wife almost to the ceiling. "Gotcha!" He put her down and sniffed about the room. Victoria covered his eyes with a pair of quilted red potholders. "You're not supposed to look."

"I don't have to." He sniffed again. "Pickled herring in sour cream. How do you say that in Polish?"

"Sledzie marynowane w smietanie."

"And almond soup."

"You looked."

"I did not. I can smell it. Say it in Polish."

"Zupa migdalowa."

"That's a good little greenie," he said, patting her on the head.

Victoria removed the potholders from over his eyes and smacked him on the chest with them. "So what if I'm a greenie. I don't have an accent."

Wanda lifted the spoon from the pot and banged it dry. Then she wagged it in Casimir's face. "Yes, Victoria is greenie. But just the same, we have three greenies in this kitchen." She thumped the end of the spoon between her breasts. "Me, one greenie. Victoria, second greenie." She stared at Casimir, her eyes screwed tight to knowing little points.

Casimir thought he would melt before her. He shoved his shaking hands into his pockets. His knees all but buckled. How did she know? Had his mother's voice spoken to her, too?

Wanda banged the wooden ladle on his shoulder as if she were dubbing a knight. "You Greenie Number Three." Then she asked him in Polish if he was from Danzig.

Casimir laughed and said to Victoria, "What did she say?"

"She asked if you're from Danzig."

"If I was, I'd have better sense than to call it by its Kraut name. Ask her if she's from the moon."

"Mama," Victoria said in Polish, "are you from the moon?"

Wanda scowled. Victoria laughed and hugged her husband.

He pulled Victoria closer and kissed her. "I hear Anna Chrissy babbling in her crib upstairs," he said. "Want me to get her?"

"She's been awake from her nap for a long time. I'll go."

"I'll go." Casimir went upstairs. Anna Chrissy clapped when she saw him. He whisked her out of the crib and pressed her to his chest, twisting his body from side to side. "Oh, baby, baby, little baby. I love you so, little baby. We have such a good life now. No more voices, Mama promised me yesterday. But your Baba downstairs, she'll ruin everything." Tears escaped from his eyes.

He held Anna Chrissy until he felt calm again. Then he changed her. He took her into the front bedroom and played with her on the rug. After a while, Victoria came upstairs, wearing a heavy coat and scarf. She had coats for Casimir and the baby. She took Anna Chrissy from him and laid her on the bed, bundling her in the warm clothing, speaking softly to her. There was laughter in her voice. "Guess where we're going. Not far. Just out to the porch. But the porch is a very special place tonight. It's time for the *wigilia*, our Christmas vigil. Grandpa just got here from Dickson City. Me and you and Daddy and Grandpa and Grandma—we'll all go out and wait for the first star. And when we see it, we'll know the Christ child was just born. C'mon, now. Up we go!"

They went down to the back porch. Marek and Wanda were already out there. Wanda's face softened in the moonlight when a hush fell over the family as they stood in expectant silence. Anna Chrissy looked from one face to the other. She put her arms out for Casimir.

He took her from Victoria and the child nuzzled the crown of her head against his neck.

"There!" Casimir called out. "I see the first star! There!"

Victoria turned Anna Chrissy's face toward the spot. "See? A star. *Gwiazda.* Star."

Anna Chrissy smiled.

Casimir opened the door and they all went inside to the table, where a cloth covered the layer of straw as a symbol of the way Mary might have covered the infant Jesus in the manger. As tradition would have it, the table was set for an additional person, the extra plate there for a stranger who might happen by, maybe Jesus himself, disguised as a humble beggar.

On all but Anna Chrissy's plate, Victoria placed an *oplatek,* a sacred unleavened wafer formed over a baking mold that created an impression of the stable with the Star of Bethlehem spreading its beams from above. Marek held his out to his wife and said, "Blessed and happy Christmas." She broke off a corner of the wafer and ate it. He offered a piece to Casimir, then to Victoria, then to Anna Chrissy, wishing each a blessed and happy Christmas. He ate the remainder of it himself. Then Wanda offered hers around the table, and Victoria and Casimir each offered theirs. Victoria put an *oplatek* on Anna Chrissy's plate. The child took a bite.

Marek served the foods, announcing whether each was bitter, sweet, tart—each dish intending to mirror one of life's many moods and conditions.

Wanda smiled slyly at Casimir and said, "Let's pull straws."

"No!" Casimir said, remembering his last Christmas in Gdansk, when Uncle Jerzy sat there slipping scraps of everyone's *oplatek* through that crazy O, his eyes smiling mischievously, as if he knew something nobody else knew. Ignacy had never permitted the pulling of straws from under the tablecloth to see who would die first. He said the whole custom was a slap in the face of the Christ child, but Uncle Jerzy pulled one anyway that last Christmas. Ignacy let it pass, but then Casimir wanted to pull one, too. "Oh, why not?" Ignacy had said, shrugging. "It's only a silly superstition. Even the Christ child would laugh at it." It was Ignacy who got the shortest straw, and by the next summer he was dead.

Wanda reached for a straw. Casimir grabbed her wrist, his eyes wild. "I said no!"

Marek separated their hands and took his wife's hand. "This is not our home. We do like this man in this man's home. Even in our home we don't pull straws. Never. Suddenly, you get idea to do it here. You just like to stir up trouble like a witch stirs a pot in the woods."

"Yes, I stir up trouble. But I don't make this trouble. I just stir the pot so Victoria can see and smell it before times get so late, she cannot get out. Victoria, come home with us on the train."

"Mama, I have a husband and baby here, and another baby due in March. We have no trouble here."

"I tell you outright, Victoria. Yesterday I come home from store and see light in your cellar. I look through the window and see this man, his arms waving about like he want to hit somebody. Inside the house I go, into the kitchen. I put my ear to the cellar door. I hear something. I open the door a crack. 'You promised, Mama,' he says, only he say it in Polish, perfect Polish, like somebody born there. 'Go back to Gdansk,' he say. So I go back outside and look in window and look to see maybe there really is somebody there. But his arms go, his mouth go, but nobody to hear him but me. Huh! And this crazy man call my little girl, 'That is good little greenie.' Huh!"

Casimir smiled. "Victoria, go home with them on the train, she says. Won't it be nice for them to have a daughter in that old bare house to care for them in their old age?"

Victoria stood up. "Charlie's right. You're jealous of my nice life here, Mama. You make up stories so I come home and keep you in your old age. I won't go, Mama. For three years you tried to get me to work in a factory. I remember. I won't go. And if you cannot respect my husband, maybe you shouldn't come here."

"I will not."

13

THE RUG

Casimir paced the kitchen with Felicia, two weeks old. Her black hair reminded him of his mother's, but only in color. Felicia's ringlets were like puffs of smoke; his mother's braids, cables of heavy rope. The infant, her knees pulled up, her arms crossed over her chest, smiled in her sleep. Casimir kissed her on the cheek, but he shook his head, thinking, why couldn't you be a boy?

Anna Chrissy pulled herself up on the bars of her playpen and grinned at her father. She was soothing her tender gums on a brown biscuit, which oozed from the corners of her mouth and pasted the tips of her short, blonde curls to her cheeks. Casimir stooped before her and said, "So what do you think of your baby sister here?"

Anna Chrissy let out a loud squeal and tried to cram her soggy biscuit into the baby's mouth. Felicia threw her arms apart, shuddering, her blue eyes wide. A yelp escaped from her lips. Her father jostled her gently and stood up, rescuing her from Anna Chrissy's reach. The infant crossed her arms again and sank into frowning sleep. Casimir studied her face. He looked confused, as if the child had suddenly appeared in his arms from nowhere.

He grabbed Victoria's sleeve as she carried a stack of plates to the table and said, "When did you have Felicia?"

"Two weeks ago. March 20th."

"That's Anna Chrissy's birthday!"

"Yes, you know that."

Casimir turned pale, thinking, the twentieth, the twentieth, both on the twentieth. Same day, same month. "Victoria, and this is 1913. Thirteen!"

Victoria laughed. "Thirteen, yes. Superstitious?"

"Aren't you?"

"A little. I guess if we had a baby on Friday the thirteenth that would make me a little nervous. You know how you hear scary stories when you're a kid. And when something awful happens to you when it happens to be Friday the thirteenth, it makes you wonder.

"Once, when I was living in Iowa, we were in the loft in the barn. It was winter. A Friday, the thirteenth. Papa was forking hay down for the cows lined up along a trough below. I was four, a little skinny kid. I was leaning over the hole, watching the hay slide down the chute, and oh! Down I went! Papa grabbed my foot, but my shoe came off. I ended up stretched out stiff in that trough, terrified, staring up at the big, fat face of a chewing cow. The stalks of hay sticking out of her mouth were getting shorter and shorter. It made me think of the straws sticking out from under the tablecloth at Christmas, how each person grabs one to see who gets the shortest one, to see who's doomed. God, how I screamed!"

"How did you get away from the cows?"

"Edward, the owner's son, heard me screaming. He rushed in and yanked me out of the trough by the arm. 'Dumb greenies!' he kept shouting, 'Damned, dumb greenies!' He picked me up and flung me onto a pile of straw. Then he kicked a milking pail clear across the barn and cursed. I was shaking and sobbing, lying in the straw, saying, 'I'm not a dumb greenie, I'm not a dumb greenie!'

"By then, Papa was down from the loft. He hugged me and said not to pay attention to such a stupid, bossy, big-mouth boy. 'Empty barrels make the most noise,' he said."

"And that was on Friday the thirteenth," Casimir said. He paced the floor in silence.

Victoria stroked Felicia's cheek. "But this little girl being born in 1913. Well, here we are in 1913. A whole 365 days long. Something has to happen in all these days. People get born. People die. Life happens just the same. There's no getting out of it."

Like the Delaware & Hudson, Casimir thought. You end up arriving on train number 511 at 4:18. There's no getting out of it.

"Might as well have a baby," Victoria said.

And she might as well be born on the Delaware & Hudson, Casimir thought.

Anna Chrissy dropped her biscuit over the side of the playpen by the stove. She began to stamp and cry, and when Casimir tried to put Felicia in her mother's arms so he could tend to Anna Chrissy, Felicia started to cry, too.

"Can't you hold her till I'm done here?" Victoria said. She picked up Anna Chrissy's biscuit and gave it back to her.

"All right. But you're the mother." Casimir bounced Felicia to silence. Anna Chrissy was happily teething on her biscuit again. Casimir stepped into Victoria's path. "It takes nine months to have a baby, right?"

"You're not thinking of—"

"What's today?"

"April 3rd. Charlie—"

"So if we started another baby now, it would be born—Let's see, May, June, July." He counted on his fingers and mumbled the months in the middle. "November, December, January. Are babies ever two months late?"

"No, but we can't—"

"Okay, then. This is a good time. A son this time. I want a son."

"You hear that, God?" Victoria wiped her hands on her apron, as if it were sacrilegious to raise them up with baked bean sauce on them. "Charlie wants a son this time."

Casimir reddened. "Don't make fun of me. I'm the only married man at the Ebony Gem without a son."

"I doubt that."

"I am, and everybody knows it. Victoria, I want a son."

"Mrs. Anderson said not to get pregnant for six weeks."

"Mrs. Anderson don't wear the pants in this house."

Within the month, Victoria was pregnant again, and this third pregnancy was so troubled that Mrs. Anderson had to spend more time at the house. Casimir still insisted on paying her. It showed who was in charge. And it made him feel she'd be less inclined to gossip about anything she saw in his house. You never knew. If his mother's spirit came back to the basement, or worse, upstairs, and she overheard, like Wanda, there was no telling who she'd blab it to. He remembered the children of Gdansk laughing at his Uncle Jerzy.

Though Mrs. Anderson still told him she did not expect to be paid, she kept a small leather change purse in her apron pocket, and it seemed to Casimir that she always kept a few loose coins jingling as a hint that she really did intend to be paid. Never mind what she said about doing it for free. Whenever she put the money in that little purse, she smiled, he noticed, and shut it with a satisfied snap. And he resented her for it. Every penny he paid her was one less toward bringing his sisters to America.

Victoria went into labor on a bitter winter day. Casimir fed the furnace and the johnny stove. He set two extra buckets of coal in the kitchen, four altogether, so he wouldn't have to run back down to the coalbin. He asked the next-door neighbor, old Mrs. Stutzman, who kept a boarder from Tyrol and one from Wales, to take care of Felicia for a few hours. But he wanted Anna Chrissy to keep him company and wait with him for her new brother to be born.

Anna Chrissy, almost two, sat on the rug stacking wooden blocks on her father's chest. He heaved his chest, then he let the air out with a rush, sending the blocks tumbling to the floor. Anna Chrissy looked at him with puzzled blue eyes. When Casimir laughed and shook her hand playfully, she smiled. Then they laughed together. He picked up a block and put it on his chest. Anna Chrissy added one. Then he added one. When the little girl tired of the game, she snuggled against him on the floor. He stroked her pale hair until she fell asleep in the crook of his arm. "We'll name him Frank," he whispered. "A plain, simple, American-sounding name. Frank."

It was almost dark when Mrs. Anderson shook him awake. She looked like a shadow leaning over him. He could see the shape of her sloppy chignon against the dim window light. Though he couldn't see her mouth, he knew she had to be smiling when she said, "Another girl! Victoria wants to name her Julie."

Coins jingled in her change purse. They reminded Casimir of the little victory bell Miss Mason used to tinkle for the first pupil to finish the spelling words on the blackboard. Feeling Mrs. Anderson's breath come down on him now, he could feel Miss Mason's impatient sighs on the crown of his head as she tapped her foot and waited for him to catch up with the others. "Casimir Caboose," she would call him. The newest boy in the class, and knowing little English, he was always the last to finish, and the children laughed at his bad spelling. Now the miners would laugh when they saw he still did not have a son. The last man in the patch to have one. Casimir Caboose, he thought bitterly, dragged along by the Delaware & Hudson.

"Name her anything you want," he said to Mrs. Anderson. He sat up and put Anna Chrissy on his lap. Her dress was turned up at one part of the hem. Casimir smoothed it down and told her to be a good girl while he went out to do something. He could see that Mrs. Anderson was about to scold him, but he waved his hand at her and went out the door.

He walked down to the end of the patch. He passed the makeshift shanties and climbed up to the slagpiles. "Don't say a word," he warned his mother, expecting her to return and reprimand him, though he had heard nothing from her since December 26, 1912.

He sat on the highest peak of the culmbank and dug the heel of his boot into the dirt, sending an avalanche of black pebbles down the bank. He picked up a slab of slate and, smashing it into its separate layers, flung the ragged disks at passing crows, whose caws seemed to mock him as they flew by untouched.

He waited and waited for his mother to scold him, but he heard nothing. He had just done something bad, but heard no voices. It worried him. If voices came because somebody was bad, at least a person had a chance to figure out what the bad thing was and not do it anymore and make the voices go away.

He had done two bad things—walked out on his new baby and thrown rocks at birds. Where was the voice?

After he thought about it awhile, he began to feel a sense of power. For two years he'd been kowtowing, afraid to be himself, afraid to provoke the voices. He was sick of it. Sick of it. He was sick of having girl babies, and he wasn't going to pretend to love this one just so his mother wouldn't haunt him. "I don't want this baby girl!" he shouted, tempting God to punish him with voices. But no voice happened. He went home, feeling cocky and proud.

Casimir paid little attention to Felicia and Julie. What feelings of love he could still muster went to Anna Chrissy. Victoria began to seem a stranger to him. He felt like a boat detached from its moorings, drifting apart from them all.

All day in the mines he brooded over his situation. He wasn't one son closer to having the kind of son he should have been, a son who would make Ignacy smile down on him. He wasn't one son closer to gaining the miners' respect, and with the expenses of the babies, not one penny closer to building that farmhouse he had promised his sisters, or even paying their fare to America. He had a constant feeling of wanting to smash everything in his path. The feeling nagged him so much that he left for Sam's right after supper every night, for fear he'd start doing just that.

He could not enjoy his house because he felt he had no right to it. It was all fixed at the expense of bringing Anna and Krystina over. He hated himself for what he had done, and when he could not bear the torment, he blamed Victoria. She was the one whose face drooped the first time she saw the house he'd slaved to fix. He could still see the crown of her head against the padded headboard, while she looked so snootily down her nose at Mrs. Anderson when the old woman was trying to tell her he was a miner. Yes, the whole mess was Victoria's fault. Trying to be a princess in a coal patch.

"I'll make her pay," he muttered one afternoon as he was leaving the mine yard. Instead of letting himself into the basement through the yard door, he marched to the front of the house. He banged his boots hard on the steps of the front porch. Forgetting that Victoria kept the front door locked to keep Anna Chrissy from wandering outside, he rattled and rattled the knob.

Victoria opened the door.

"Give your coal-miner husband a kiss," he said. He spread his arms out as if displaying his miner's clothes to her for the first time.

"Is the cellar door jammed?" she asked him. She fingered the buttons on the front of her dress to close them. She was cradling three-month-old Julie in a sling. A thin stream of milk trickled across the baby's cheek. Her face reddened angrily as she nuzzled unrewarded against her mother's covered breast.

"No, the cellar door is not jammed. I want to come in this way."

"But your boots. You'll track coal dirt right across my rug!"

"Your nice beige rug?" He took a step forward. Victoria blocked his way, laughing nervously.

"You think I'm playing." He wrapped a gritty, black hand around her arm. He kissed her hard on the mouth. Then he pushed her aside.

He stepped inside the parlor and planned his path. He headed for the archway leading to the kitchen where the cellar door was. "I'm walking right across this rug to that cellar door. Then I'm going down to get washed and changed. How do you like that? I'm the man of this house. A man's home is his castle. And today I don't feel like coming in through the dungeon door."

He stopped here and there to twist his heels, grinding in the dirt. He turned around once to admire the trail. Then he looked at the sofa and two stuffed chairs Victoria had made covers for. "Maybe I'll take a nap on the couch first," he said. "Sooty it up a bit."

"My God, what's wrong with you!"

"Daddy," he heard Anna Chrissy call from the kitchen. Looking in on her, he raised his index finger and said, "I'll be right back as soon as I change." He winked at her and went down into the cellar to wash. When he came back up, he whisked Anna Chrissy into the air and waltzed her around the kitchen. "Daddy's girl, Daddy's girl," he sang. And the wispy strands of her white-blonde hair would rise as her father dipped her down on every third beat.

Felicia smiled from behind the bars of a playpen. She raised her hands to be picked up. "Me, Fisha, Fisha!" she said. Casimir frisked her black hair, but he did not pick her up.

"I'll dance with Felicia," Victoria said. She put the baby in the playpen, picked up Felicia, forced a smile, and began to hum while she danced the child around. When Casimir stopped waltzing with Anna Chrissy, Victoria set Felicia in the playpen again.

"Time to eat," Casimir announced.

"It isn't ready yet," Victoria said. Her face was flushed, her eyes glassy. She turned toward the stove.

"Gee, you look just the way you did the day I brought you here," Casimir said. "My blushing bride." He stood behind her and began to remove the hairpins that kept her hair off her back in the June heat. He kissed the side of her neck as locks of her hair fell over his cheek. "My blushing bride," he whispered.

"Stop it!" she hissed. "Not in front of the girls!"

Casimir turned to Anna Chrissy. "How old is Daddy's girl?"

The child held up two fingers of her right hand in the manner he had taught her. "Two!" she said.

"See? She's only two. She doesn't know what's going on." He pressed his chest against Victoria's back and began to kiss her neck again. His hands kneaded her breasts. He made a trail of soft kisses up over her chin and along the corner of her mouth. He felt a tear come to rest on his lips. "What's this?" He scraped the tear from his lip, studied it, then sucked it off his finger. He turned his wife around and regarded her smudged face. Black tears rolled over her chin. He heard her swallow hard.

"Mama cry," Anna Chrissy said, pointing.

Casimir pressed his lips to Victoria's throat.

"That is enough, Casimir!" he heard his mother call from behind the cellar door.

Casimir pushed Victoria away and ran down to the cellar. "Okay, Mama, I'll stop. Just please, please, don't go up there. Stay down the cellar. I'll take my punishment down here."

For fifteen minutes he sat on the bottom step, listening to a tirade about how he laughed when his father was dying, how he spent all his sisters' passage money, how he acted like a filthy pig in front of poor little Anna Chrissy, how he tormented his wife about the fancy things in the house after he had gone out and bought those chairs on his own, long after she knew he was a miner and couldn't afford them. Words came at him like blows from all sides, but he sat there muttering, "Yes, yes, I did it, I did it."

When the cellar was quiet again, he said, "I'll go up and help get supper on the table."

He sat Felicia in the high chair. Anna Chrissy sat in his chair, waiting to sit on his lap, while he heaped food on each plate. The infant Julie was falling asleep in the playpen.

Casimir picked up Anna Chrissy, sat down, and sat her on his lap. They ate off the same fork, taking turns.

Victoria got up and took a saucer from the cabinet. She selected a few beans and cooked carrots from the mound of food Casimir had placed on Felicia's plate and put them on the saucer. She diced the carrot and set the saucer on the tray of the high chair. Then she sat with her hands on her lap. She stared at the school field across Girard Street. Her manner was brooding and silent, like a captive on a slave ship, looking back, watching her homeland shrink on the horizon. Now and then her eyes would shift toward the back door.

Casimir noticed this and it made him angry. It made him want to hurt her. Let his mother complain. He was ready for her now, and he wasn't about to kowtow to her, now that he had gotten over that first surprise. He said to Victoria, "Getting ideas there, lady?" Depending on how she answered, he might leave her alone, and he might not.

Victoria looked down at her plate and said nothing.

Casimir removed Anna Chrissy from his lap, stood up, and then sat the child in his chair. He shuffled along the table and stood behind Victoria. He began to massage the back of her neck. "You'd like to walk away from this life, wouldn't you?"

She stood up and faced him. She said nothing. She pulled her lips together tightly.

Casimir wagged his finger at her. "Well, you can't. You got three babies and a man to look after. And another baby by next spring."

"Charlie, no. No more babies. We can hardly feed the ones we have."

"Don't tell me who I can feed! I'm a man! I can feed ten! And I will. Victoria, I want a son."

"Charlie! Charlie, listen." Victoria wrote on the table with her finger as she spoke. "This is June, 1914. We were married in May, 1911. Do you realize that's just three years ago? Only three years, and already we have three babies."

Casimir felt weak. Three babies, three years in a row. Three girls in a row. What good could come of it?

"What's wrong with you, Charlie? You come storming across the rug in your sooty black boots. A half hour later you talk of making more babies!"

"June, you said. June what? What's today? June what?"

"Charlie!"

"June what!"

"Fifteenth."

"Fifteenth. June fifteenth. July, August, September. Wait a minute." He walked into the parlor to think things out. He sat on the sofa and closed his eyes when he saw what a mess he had made of the rug. My God, he thought, a few days off the mark and we could have a third one born on March 20. Well, wait, March 20, yes, that's three. But not three in a row. Julie was born last February, so maybe it would be okay. No, better not take a chance. Let the bastards taunt me at work. I won't take a chance. The same number three times. The kid might as well be born on the Delaware & Hudson. "All right," he said, walking back to the kitchen, pretending to compromise, "You have your hands full already. We'll wait awhile to start on a son." He shuffled across the kitchen, back into the parlor, and then to the kitchen again. "I'm sorry I ruined the rug."

He left the house and went straight to Saint Hedwig's, where he raced up the aisle on St. Joseph's side. He knelt at the rail. He reached into his pocket and pulled out a penny. When he saw it was face down, he pulled out another one. It too was face down.

Did he dare try another one? Three pennies face down in a row. What could be worse? He felt in his pocket for a nickel, put it into the coin slot with a plan of lighting only one candle, thinking the overpayment would find him more favor with Saint Joseph. He picked up the lighter stick and drew from the flame of another candle. On the way to his own candle, the flame on the stick went out. What did that mean? Was Saint Joseph so disgusted with the ruined rug that he wasn't going to accept his offering? He thought of Cain in the Bible. God didn't want his offering. Casimir felt too humiliated to try again. He said his prayer without his own flickering light. "I'm sorry I was so mean. Sorry I was such a rotten husband and father. I promise to be more like you. I promise I'll be good. Now will you make it so I don't hear Mama's voice?"

For days Casimir shuddered whenever he thought how close he had come to having a third child born on the same date. A son yet! All day at work his mind played horrible images of what might befall the boy. He imagined him at eight years old having to work as a door-boy in the mines to take care of Anna Chrissy, Felicia, and Julie because their parents had been killed in an accident, maybe run down by the Delaware & Hudson. Like the best door-boys, Casimir's son opened the tunnel doors at exactly the right moment to let the rail cars through. He'd close the doors promptly to keep the ventilation going through the right passages. But as door-boys were known to do, Casimir's boy fell asleep against the doors. When the next carload came, he was trampled by a blind mule and crushed by spilling coal and broken boards. Casimir dreamed this scene one night and cried out. He grabbed Victoria by the shoulders.

"Who's Frank?" Victoria asked.

"Why?"

"You just yelled, 'Not Frank. He can't be dead!'"

"I was dreaming some door-boy was crushed to death. A handsome boy, a strong boy with guts. The poor kid fell asleep, and that was it for him. His name was Frank."

It frightened Casimir to think he had acted this scene out with Victoria but had no memory of it. What else did he do in his sleep? He could have started that kid and not even known it! "Victoria, do I always sleep restless like that?"

"Sometimes."

"We didn't— I didn't touch you, did I? You're not going to have another baby, are you? I didn't mean to touch you. I told you we could wait for a son."

She did not understand his decision not to have a son just yet, but she was glad for it. Mrs. Anderson had said there were ways women could prevent babies and still satisfy their men, though it was nothing you'd want your parish priest to know. But if leaving her alone was going to be Casimir's way of not making babies, she wasn't going to argue with that.

"Maybe we should sleep apart for awhile," Casimir said.

Victoria said, "I'll sleep down on the couch if you're willing to come down and wake me when you hear the baby cry up here."

"I'll sleep up the attic," Casimir said. "There's heat up there in winter if I uncover the grate. It's just a matter of making up a cot on the floor."

14

Once Casimir made himself at home in the attic, he decided it wasn't such a bad place. It was one large room that ran the whole length of the house. There was good window light. He could plaster the holes in the walls and put some nice paper on it. Why, two people could share that room, he thought one night as he lay on a straw mat, watching the full moon weave through swift clouds. Two people, Anna and Krystina. They could live here. Here, with us! Why didn't I think of this long ago?

"Because," he uttered, "because I promised them a big farmhouse, their own, like the one in Uncle Jerzy's photograph of Nebraska."

No, that wasn't the reason, he decided. He had let his sisters down because he was trying to please Victoria. Princess Victoria. She had taken up all his attention. All his attention, not just his money. It was her fault he never thought of offering them the attic before.

"And you did just what I did," he heard his mother say. Her voice came from the dark rafters. "Just one more baby in America. Then I send for Anna and Krystina. You hated me for that. Now you do same thing. Your sisters be old maids by now. Wait and wait for you to send for them. Then they get too old and no one wants them."

"Stop!" he hissed.

"It is true. Already they be in their twenties. Old maids. No one wants them now."

"Stop! Stop! Stop! What are you doing up here? You promised to stay in the basement!"

"All right. For sure, I promise. If you promise to visit me there."

139

"All right, all right, I promise. But first I must go down to the kitchen and write them a letter, tell them to pack their stuff. I need to do that right now. I'll visit you after work tomorrow."

"All right."

He lit a candle and went down to the kitchen. He would have the money for their passage in six months. But where would he get it? "Dear Anna and Krystina," he wrote. He stared at the paper. Where would he get the money? Work extra jobs? He must plan it all out first. He'd think about it all day in the mine, then write the letter.

His eyes strayed to the issue of *Republika Gornik Pennsylwanski,* a Polish weekly. Victoria must have been reading it before she went to bed. He was glad to find it. It made him feel closer to Poland. Most of the articles were about things of interest to Polish anthracite miners in Pennsylvania, but there was news of the home country. He read it again and again. Austria had already declared war on Serbia, which he had heard, but thought of as something going on far, far south of Gdansk and of no concern to him. Germany had declared war on Russia. It sickened him to imagine the Germans and Russians tramping over Gdansk to get at one another. Now it appeared that France, Great Britain, and Italy might join in.

"And you left your sisters there to be stuck in this, Casimir," he heard his mother yell in Polish from behind the cellar door. "They could be forced into the streets by now!"

Casimir rushed over and opened the door. "Mama," he whispered, "help me get them out of there. Tell me what to do. But not up here. Please don't yell through the door anymore. When you want to talk, wait till I come down. How will it look if you startle me in the kitchen?"

"Like crazy man you will look. Even though me and you, we know it is my spirit, my true spirit, speaking. Not some crazy voice."

"Yes. And speak English, Mama, in case Victoria hears you."

He went down to the cellar. "Mama, does Papa know about the war?"

"Of course he knows about it. He is glad. When it is over, Poland will be Poland again, not divided up like pie by greedy countries."

Casimir reached behind the furnace for Ignacy's pocket watch, which he had hidden there the day Jozefina gave it to him. Carefully, he unwrapped the red cloth. He knelt down and pressed the watch to his lips as if it were the relic of a saint offered to the parishioners to kiss at the altar rail. "Papa?" He heard nothing. If his mother's spirit could speak to him, why not Papa's? "Please, Papa, tell me what to do." After a few minutes of waiting, he wound the watch, as if doing so would make his father speak. "Papa, please."

Frustration fueled into rage. He pointed into the air and said, "It's *your* fault, Mama! He won't come into this room as long as you're here. Not after what you did. Get out of here!"

He looked down at the watch. Five minutes. That should be enough. With his hands over his face, he rocked back and forth on his knees and waited for a sign. He looked at the watch. Seven minutes had passed. "You blame me too, don't you, Papa?"

Casimir waited a long time for an answer. Then he got the idea a confession might help. He said, "Okay, Papa, I admit it, I laughed when you were dying. But see, I didn't realize you were dying. Neither did Anna. We thought you were playing that pantomime game with us, a gorilla that time, the way you were beating on your chest. We thought we were supposed to guess what animal you were. You know, how you always did to make us laugh."

"Laugh, and not fight," he heard Jozefina say. "Yes, fight. Admit it, Casimir. You kicked Anna under the table and made her scream and made your papa have to holler. Then he—"

"You weren't even there, Mama! You were out visiting in the middle of supper. Out whispering to Aunt Marta behind Papa's back. How would you know?"

"Then your poor papa choked on that piece of pork, trying to holler at you to stop kicking Anna."

"Shut up, Mama. You weren't there."

"Yes, on a piece of pork he choked. All on account of you! No wonder you don't eat pork. Ha!"

"Shut up!"

"If I shut up, you think your papa don't know what you did? You deny your big sin. Then you leave your poor sisters to perish in that war. No wonder your papa don't answer."

"If you can't tell me how to get them over here, then just shut up!"

Casimir ran back up to the kitchen and closed the door. He jammed the back of a chair under the doorknob to keep his mother in the cellar. Then he stood in the middle of the kitchen, pressing his fists against his temples, trying to think, wishing his mother would stop accusing him of things and just help him figure out a way to get his sisters here.

After awhile it occurred to him that it was stupid to ask his mother the best way to get the girls over. After all, if she gave a damn, they'd have been in America years ago, in Pottsville. He'd have to think it out himself. The thing to do, he decided, was to take a trolley to the railroad station in Mt. Carmel, send them a telegram, and find out what kind of passage could be arranged from Gdansk in six months or so. But he had to go to work. Victoria would have to go to the station. If he had to tell her a million lies to get around the real story of who Anna and Krystina were, he was going to do it.

He couldn't imagine himself falling asleep and calmly waiting till morning to tell Victoria what to do. He unjammed the chair from the cellar doorknob, then rushed upstairs to wake her, forgetting for a moment that he had passed himself off as American-born. He had told Victoria his grandparents had refused to teach him Polish because, they said, America was for Americans. So how could he explain his alarm over an article written in Polish?

"Victoria," he said when he got her downstairs, "what does this article say? Something about Gdansk, I know. I can figure out Gdansk."

She was about to protest being awakened for such a thing, but she saw a wild look in her husband's eyes. His fingers pinched the corners of the newspaper tightly as he held it up to her. His whole body seemed to tremble. Victoria translated the headline for him: "Poland in the Crossfire."

"Read me the whole thing."

When she finished translating the article, he said, "My father has relatives in Gdansk. Two young women. We must save them from the war."

"What! And bring them here? Charlie, how can we can we do that? We can barely afford to feed—"

"Don't tell me who I can feed, I told you!" Casimir found that he had raised a fist. He stood there holding it up and looking at it with surprise, as if someone else had raised it on him. Victoria cringed. Casimir turned and walked to the window, his hands in his pockets.

"Just help me get them here. We can send them on to Papa in Nebraska later. Just help me get them to America. Write them a letter. It has to be in Polish, of course." He turned and faced her. "Will you write it?"

"Right now?"

"Yes. Sit down."

Casimir sat at the end of the table by the cellar door, half listening for his mother's voice. He gestured for Victoria to sit at the opposite end, afraid his mother might call out to her from behind the door and tell her about the pork.

Victoria sat down and wrote what he dictated. The letter said their passage could be arranged for about six months from now. They should choose the date and let him know as soon as possible. Victoria, besides mailing the letter, was to go to the Mt. Carmel train station in the morning and send a telegram with the same message.

The next day, when he came home from the mine, Victoria told him that the man at the station said it was impossible to make passenger arrangements through the port of Danzig at this time.

"Danzig?" Casimir said with a belittling smirk. "What are you? A goddamn Kraut? It's Gdansk. Don't call it by its Kraut name!"

"I'm just telling you what the man said, Charlie."

Casimir rammed his hands into his pockets and paced the floor in silence while Victoria prepared supper. Now and then, as he passed Anna Chrissy, who was kneeling on a chair and watching a sparrow strut across the window ledge, he'd kiss her on the top of the head.

He stooped down by the playpen. Julie, at six months, had a full head of straight hair, chestnut, like his. It sat like a helmet on her head and made him think of the war. She had been sitting and playing with a hand-me-down toy Casimir had made for Anna Chrissy two years before, a U-shaped piece of wood with an arch of wooden beads. The baby became still. Her dark eyes, glittering like anthracite, stared at him. There was no joy in them, no anticipation of being talked to or picked up. Her father had not picked her up since the day she was born. He had never put one spoonful of oatmeal into her mouth. He had never touched her, never spoken to her. He merely looked at her from time to time the way one might regard a neighbor's potted plant growing taller in a window.

Felicia, almost a year-and-a-half old, was standing in the playpen with her back to Casimir. She was watching an orange cat on the back porch licking its fur. Felicia's puffy black hair had become coarser, the curls dragged low by the weight. She turned around when the cat, leaping over the porch railing, left abruptly. Casimir was struck by Felicia's turquoise eyes, exactly the color of his own, looking out from the heart-shaped face so much like Victoria's. He looked from Felicia to Julie to Anna Chrissy, noticing how each one had some feature of his or Victoria's or his mother's. It seemed as though each child was assembled from bits of broken people whose parts had been tossed into the same junk drawer.

Casimir stood up, and began to pace again, stopping in the archway to the parlor and staring at the black track he had ground into the rug. What would his sisters think when they saw it? He turned to Victoria and said, "After supper, scrub that coal dirt off the carpet. I'll keep an eye on the girls while you do it."

"That dirt'll never come out."

"Try."

"I did. Twice."

"Let me try. Where's the bucket?"

The next morning Casimir told Victoria that he would be ordering only one ton of coal at a time this winter, not two. The coalbin was full now, and since it was only August, they wouldn't have to worry about it yet. A ton at a time might be enough to keep the furnace going, but not both the furnace and the johnny stove. She'd have to start picking coal from the slagpiles to keep that going. She should consider herself lucky their house had a furnace at all. If she didn't want to pick coal, that was all right, but then she'd better be ready to get by with only a johnny stove for cooking and heating, like most of the other families in the patch. He was willing to buy coal for that.

"I know it won't be easy picking coal with three small children," he said. "You'll have to start by October, though." He grabbed his lunch bucket, went down to the cellar, put on his miner's clothes, and went out the door.

The children were still asleep. Victoria sat with a cup of coffee, remembering the cold mornings in Dickson City when she and her mother would join the parade of women and wheelbarrows and children too young for school or work.

Though she could picture those days as clearly as if they were happening now, she couldn't imagine herself facing those women at the slagpiles of Black Hollow, not after the way she had snubbed them the three times they invited her to join them. "My husband's having coal delivered on Wednesday," she remembered saying. They must have felt like slapping her face. "My husband brings the water," she had said, when they invited her to the patch pump. How could she face them now?

She went to the bottom of the stairs and listened to see if the girls were stirring. All was quiet, so she went to the shanty to see what shape the wheelbarrow was in, to try to make herself plan this coal-gleaning task no matter how humiliating it was. The shanty looked exactly as it had the first time she went in there four years ago. The floor was covered with badly cracked linoleum, which was full of coal dirt. A few lumps of coal were strewn about. A wheelbarrow and a blackened wooden wagon were parked in one corner. A sledge hammer and two shovels lay in the center of the floor. Two metal screens, one with small holes, the other with large holes, stood against the wall. Some coal bootlegger must have been using this shack to crack coal, she thought. A few wooden boxes and boards were heaped near the door to the alley. Two eight-paned windows faced the school across Girard Street. Coal dirt lined the panes like black snow. She remembered thinking that one day she would hire someone to clean up that awful mess and make a playhouse for her children.

She walked toward the wheelbarrow, intending to bring it out to the yard. But she turned away from it and went back to the house. No, she wouldn't do it. She couldn't face the women she had snubbed. She hopped over the banister to Mrs. Stutzman's porch and knocked on the door. The old woman's back had become so hunched that she had to tip her head back to see straight ahead. "Ah, you, hello!" she said.

"I can only stay a minute. My girls will be awake any moment now. Mrs. Stutzman, we're having trouble keeping up. Please don't tell anyone. I'll need to take in laundry this winter. It has to be someone who wouldn't go talking about it to people, somebody who would just bring it. Remember last week that man who came and asked if you'd do his laundry in exchange for coal?"

"Yes, I know. Jinx Evert. A single man living in a lean-to."

"Yes, him. He bootlegs a little coal on the side, he said."

"'I cannot,' I told him. Bad hands. Bad back."

"Did he find somebody?"

"I don't know. Maybe not. He lives in the one with the three big rain barrels in front, he said, in case I change my mind."

Without telling her husband, Victoria bartered with Jinx Evert for the coal, telling him to bring the coal through the shanty door that opened to the alley. Jinx, a pillar of a man whose blonde hair was always in gritty clumps, built a small bin in the shanty, walling off one side of it. He came by several times a week, bringing enough coal to keep the johnny stove going.

Once the deliveries were underway, Victoria told Casimir about the arrangement. He said he didn't care how she got the coal, just so she didn't expect him to provide it. Meanwhile, he was saving up money by doing errands for bosses' and merchants' families in Mt. Carmel—hauling ashes, carting water, running errands. He did things that he could do alone, always fearful that his mother's spirit would speak to him in front of someone. But he heard nothing from his mother since he had put his plan in place and began his dogged efforts toward his sisters' passage. He was being good, and God was taking notice.

During the months he waited to hear from his sisters, Casimir worked on the attic. He plastered the holes in the walls. He looked through the Sears & Roebuck catalogue for wallpaper most like the paper he remembered to have been on the walls of the girls' bedroom in Gdansk—delicate ladies in pale blue gowns, being escorted through a garden by handsome young men. The trees on the Gdansk walls were willows, he recalled, while the trees in the catalogue were sycamores. The dancing ladies in the catalogue paper wore blue gowns, pink gowns, yellow gowns. He was sure Anna and Krystina wouldn't mind those little differences. They'd be pleased to see the arched bridge crossing a stream, like on the old paper. He laughed to recall how Anna, her feet dangling from the side of the bed, would call him into her room and ask him to pretend he was a handsome prince and dance with her through the royal gardens. "Boys don't dance with their sisters," he'd say. But he'd pity her, the way she lowered her face and stared up at him, her turquoise eyes little lakes of tears. "Oh, come on," he'd say. He'd yank her off the bed with an exasperated sigh so she wouldn't think he was soft. "Bow first," she'd say. And he'd bow from the waist.

Winter came and went. In May of 1915, Jinx Evert was found dead in his bootleg hole at the foot of Manley's Mountain. Done in by blackdamp, everyone supposed. Victoria put a vase of yellow columbine on his grave.

Around that same time, Casimir received a letter that had been mailed from Copenhagen. He ran all the way home from the post office and let himself into the basement through the yard. Sitting on the dirt floor in front of the furnace, he opened the envelope, took the letter out, and kissed it. He rose to his knees and took a penny out of his pocket, squeezing it hard and begging God to let it be face up when he slapped it onto the back of his hand. It was face down. He shook his head and sat down on his heels. Then he read the letter.

> Dear Casimir:
>
> I have just received one of your letters, the seventh you said you had written. I don't know what became of the others. I did write to you several times to say only that Anna and I are all right, because it was not safe to say what we do. I can see you do not get these letters. I hope this letter finds its way to America.
>
> I don't know how much truth you get to hear, but the Polish people in Europe hear promises from Germany, Russia, and Austria, each urging us to side with them and someday we will be an independent Poland again, not divided up among those three. Germany has been trying to get control of Warsaw from Russia and destroys our towns and cities as she advances. To stop her from advancing, Russia burns our crops and shells our buildings. Everywhere Poles, little children and all, roam for a place to live,

like a lost plague of locusts, as some journalist called us.

Starvation and destruction are everywhere. We have heard how Papa always hoped to live for the day when Poland would again be Poland, free and united. So Anna and I do what we can here, in his memory and his honor, helping to bring supplies and information from one place to another. We hope our work will help him rest in peace. It is the thought of Papa's spirit smiling down on us that keeps us going, for we cannot count on each other for encouragement now. We have separated. There is no sense in us being caught and killed together. One of us must be left to carry on what Papa would want.

I'm happy to hear you have three fine little girls in America. All the money you've saved to bring us there, spend it on them to make them comfortable and happy. When I see the children starving here, it is a consolation to know your children are in America.

We want to remain here now, to marry here someday, if we survive the war. Raise a new generation of children in a free and independent Poland. Maybe, after the war, we can manage to come to visit on our own. In the meantime, we will visit you in spirit.

Soon you will receive a separate envelope containing only an address. Write to us there. It will take long to hear back and forth. God bless you, Casimir.

Krystina

Visit? Not be brought to America to live? Casimir could hardly believe what he had just read. Visit! His whole life he had planned for the day he would wave them ashore on Ellis Island. Now they were just going to visit. How could they do this to him? Did they get tired of waiting? It wasn't his fault it took so long. Okay, he admitted, he got a little sidetracked trying for a son. But what man wouldn't? They should understand that. They said they understood it. He still had their letter to prove it. Goddamned women. The other delays, why, they were Victoria's fault. Wanting everything, poor deprived princess.

He had worked to save his sisters. What thanks did he get for all his efforts? What did he have to show for it all? A fancy beige carpet with a streak of coal dirt from the front door to the kitchen. A wife content to sleep in an empty bed. He had a mind to run up and throw her down on the kitchen floor and give it to her good right then and there. So what if it made a third baby born on March 20th? How could his luck be any worse?

Look what was left of his lifetime of efforts to set things right. Two smug sisters someplace in Europe, telling him to enjoy his comfortable little life in America while they ran about setting the world right so Papa could rest in peace. Oh, and when the war was over, maybe they'd visit. Maybe. "In the meantime," Casimir translated aloud, "we will visit you in spirit."

He opened the door of the furnace and threw the letter into the fire. "Damn your spirits, both of you!"

He sank to the floor and wept.

15

PATCHES IN THE NIGHT

Why sleep in the attic? What did it matter if he made ten babies to feed? His sisters didn't need him or his money. Let them all be born March 20th! He had no good luck no matter what he did.

Casimir dismantled the cot he had made for himself in the attic, kicked the parts around the floor, and flung the blankets into a corner. Then he went down to the second floor, vowing never to go up there again.

He found no special pleasure in sharing a bed with Victoria again. There was no difference between her and Cecilia, the prostitute in Shamokin he spent Saturday nights with before he got married. She meant no more to him than a way to relieve himself of rage and tension. He no longer cared what she thought about him or felt for him, which seemed to be nothing. They were even, then. They lived in the same house and provided care for the same children.

When Victoria became pregnant again, he thought of the child as some vague responsibility coming his way, and thinking Fate, or worse yet, his mother's spirit, would spite him if he hoped too hard for a boy, he would not let himself care what it was going to be.

It was months after Krystina's letter that the envelope arrived with the promised address for her and Anna. His first impulse was to burn it. But he folded it into a square and then took Ignacy's watch from behind the furnace. Peeling back the red cloth, he pressed the little square paper against the watch and wrapped them together. Then he hid them behind the furnace.

He sat down on the bottom step, his elbows on his knees, his chin in his hands, and waited. For what, he didn't know—to hear a voice, perhaps. He had not heard a voice for more than a year, since the night he read about Germany declaring war on Russia. He had come to expect that, if he ever heard one again, or ever heard from his father at all, it would be in the basement. In a way he was glad he wasn't hearing any voices, voices that could mean he'd end up just as crazy as Uncle Jerzy. Yet he longed to hear something. He was isolated in his own home. There was Victoria tending to her three children and waiting for a fourth, and there he was, watching her feed and dress and cuddle them, and then submit coldly and quietly to him at night.

His family, his real family, was down in the basement behind the furnace. Angry as he was at Anna and Krystina, he thought of them as part of that real family, so he allowed their memory to exist there, their address wrapped in that red cloth with Papa's watch. Mama wasn't quite so deserving of the red cloth. He thought of her as a loose spirit flitting about the cellar and perching upside down from a beam like a bat.

He would stay in the basement after work until Victoria called him for supper, when he'd go up and eat in silence. Silence was safety. His words, his thoughts, so clear and organized, so meaningful in his own head, had become harder and harder to speak in ways that didn't leave other people scratching their heads, especially since he had to keep so many parts secret, like his mother's spirit. She was right. They would not understand it was really her spirit, her actual presence. Someone would want to put him away out of their own foolish ignorance. Or even burn him at the stake like Joan of Arc. He bet if Joan of Arc could do it all over again, she wouldn't tell anybody about the voices that led her to lead France to victory.

But if she didn't tell that part, he realized, she'd be in the same fix as him, making speeches that looked like torn slices of Swiss cheese with bites missing.

Silence was safety. Being alone was safety. But if he never came out, people would wonder, ask questions. He continued to dress in a fine suit in the evening, go to Sam's for a shot and a game of pool with Donny. Then he'd come home to the cellar, where he'd sit on the bottom step, feeling purposeless and lost. At night he would wake up, restless and angry, dreading how miserable he would feel when the whistle blew to wake the miners at five, just about the time he was finally drowsy enough to sink into a deep sleep.

One night he was awakened by a sound he heard on the front porch roof outside his bedroom window. The sound was unmistakable. It was the distressed meow of Patches, Mrs. Gilotti's cat, who used to search the house for him whenever she was harassed by Harold and Fred. Hearing her now, Casimir remembered how he'd rescue her, take her into his room and settle her across his chest, petting her till she purred herself to sleep.

Poor animal, Casimir thought, throwing off the blankets. She must be really miserable to search me out halfway across Black Hollow. He was flattered to think she had chosen him to be the one to save her. Maybe Anna and Krystina didn't want to be saved, but Patches appreciated him anyhow. He opened the window. Victoria sat up and pulled the blankets up to her chin. "Charlie, what are you doing? It's ten degrees out there!"

"Letting the cat in."

"We don't have a cat. You're dreaming again. Please shut the window. It's bad enough to be pregnant without getting pneumonia, too."

"The neighbor's cat. It was crying on our porch roof."

"I've been lying awake and didn't hear any cat. Charlie, you were dreaming. Please shut the window."

Casimir closed the window. He could not fall back asleep. He went down to the basement to get warm by the furnace. At the little rectangular window above his head he heard something scratching, picking at the caulking around the pane. He heard Patches meow. Setting a crate below the window, he stepped up and lifted the hinged board he had installed after Wanda had spied on him through that window. He looked outside. He heard a dog bark and didn't hear the cat after that. He pounded his fists against the cellar wall. "Gone!" He cursed whatever mongrel it was that had scared Patches away. She'll probably never come here again, he thought. Well, he'd go there then. Yes, that's what he'd do. If Harold and Fred had to treat her so goddamned bad that she ran across the patch to find him, then he'd go there and save her from those rotten bastards.

The next day after work, Casimir bought a wash basket, a small pillow, and a piece of red flannel cloth. In the cellar, he cut a U-shaped opening in the side of the basket, placed the pillow in the bottom, and spread the red cloth over it, tucking the ends and carefully smoothing every wrinkle. He put the basket beside the furnace to warm. Then he set out to rescue Patches.

Mrs. Gilotti's windows were steamed from cooking, but even so, Casimir, standing in the back yard, had no trouble seeing that they were eating. He wondered what they talked about at the table now without him to pick on. Harold and Fred probably picked on Patches all the more.

High on the panes the glass was clear. Casimir crept up onto the back porch to get a better look. He chuckled at the sight of them eating in the same pattern—slice, shovel, chew, listen. Slice, shovel, chew, listen, as though listening for the food to drop into their stomachs. Finally, they were all wiping their mouths. Muffled as their voices sounded, Casimir was glad that he could at least hear something and maybe pick up a clue as to where to find Patches. Mrs. Gilotti pointed to the floor and looked sternly at Fred, whom she accused of having dropped a piece of meat. "Waste! I should adda the cost to your room and board."

What surprised Casimir was that the meat was still on the floor to be noticed, since Patches always ate whatever was dropped. Maybe she's in the basement, he thought. Soundlessly, he went to the bulkhead, lifted it, went down the stone steps, and lowered the bulkhead. Taking his miner's hat from the sack he had brought, he lit the light and put the hat on his head.

He moved his head around, shining the dim light into the basement through the glass panel. He thought he saw Patches sleeping on the floor near the furnace. Trying the door, he found it locked. He took an iron skeleton key from his pocket and pushed it into the hole till he forced out the key inserted from the other side. The clang it made when it fell to the concrete floor sounded to him like a hammer hitting a tin washtub. For sure, they heard it in the kitchen, he thought. He took his hat off and put the lamp out. After sitting quietly for what felt like an hour, he lit his miner's hat again and let himself into the basement. "Uncle Charlie's here," he whispered. He searched and softly called the cat's name. Thinking he might have scared her when the key clanged, he figured she must have hidden behind something. He managed to pull things away from the walls without making noise. After a long search, he realized Patches was not in the basement.

In the yard again, he looked up at the high porch and thought of climbing up the post to check the upstairs. Only what if he got caught? The police would come. There would be questions. Lots of questions. He decided to make an excuse to go in. He left his sack in the yard, went around the front of the house, and limped up the porch steps as if he had fallen and twisted his ankle.

Standing on one foot, he knocked on the door. Harold opened it. "Well, it's the Hunkey! Come in!" He called out to the kitchen. "It's Charlie. Put some water on for tea!"

Casimir hopped inside and limped through the parlor, leaning on the furniture. "My foot, I twisted it. I think it'll be all right if I stay off it for a few minutes."

"Sit, sit!" Mrs. Gilotti said.

"Thanks. By the way," Casimir said, trying to sound only half interested, "where's Patches?"

The three others were all sitting on the same side of the table, opposite Casimir. His heart began to race. He felt as if he were sitting before a panel of judges, all of them knowing he had some hidden reason for asking. It was just a matter of tripping him up, making him admit to his scheme. It seemed to take forever for one of them to speak up. "Buried out back," Fred finally said.

"What?"

"Buried outa the back," Mrs. Gilotti said.

"Where out back?" Casimir asked as calmly as he could.

Harold leaned forward and asked, smiling, "Why? You wanna put flowers on her grave? Okay. She's right underneath where we set the ashcans."

"Yes," Mrs. Gilotti said. She lowered her eyes and shook her head as if the mere talk of Patches was going to bring her to tears.

"When did she die? How?"

"Seems she had a little accident 'bout two weeks ago," Fred said. He bumped elbows with Harold, and they both snickered.

"Accident my eye!" Mrs. Gilotti said.

"Now, Mrs. G.," Harold said, "we didn't mean to hurt your kitty. She got a bit underfoot and we didn't see her there."

Casimir wanted to tear the smiles off their faces and smash their heads together.

He placed his hand between Mrs. Gilotti's shoulder blades. "I'm sorry," he said. "She was a wonderful cat."

Mrs. Gilotti nodded, her eyes full of tears and gratitude.

Casimir left, but he came back in the middle of the night with a pickax, a digging fork, and a shovel. He loosened the very top of the partly frozen ground with the pickax, tapping it lightly, carefully. Then he poked farther down with the fork and shoveled the loose soil aside, finally probing with his bare fingers till he found the wooden box, which he slipped carefully into his sack. Then he shoveled back the dirt, dragged the ashcans over the spot, and left.

When he got home, he dug up the dirt floor next to the furnace. He scooped out a grave for Patches, carefully squaring the corners. He removed the wooden box from the sack and saw that it was the same padlocked box that had once held Mrs. Gilotti's mementos from Italy. He wondered if her patchwork doll was still in the box, but out of respect for the dead and for Mrs. Gilotti, he did not open the lid.

"Poor Patches," he said. "It was her spirit calling out to me, her spirit. Crying for a decent burial." He lay on the floor and set the box on his chest awhile, remembering how Patches liked to nap on his chest when he lived at Mrs. Gilotti's boarding house. Then he placed the box into the hole and covered it with dirt. For now, he dragged a crate over it. Some day he would make a little monument for her, a little stone.

The next day he took the bed he had made for Patches up to the attic. Then he brought some boards and nails from the basement and hammered them across the attic door from jamb to jamb. At supper he announced that no one was ever to go into the attic again.

16

MUMBLY PEGS

The next evening, after Casimir dished the food onto the girls' plates, he held a serving spoon full of mashed potatoes over his own plate for a long time. Then he stabbed it back into the bowl and said, "I'm going to Sam's."

Anna Chrissy, three now, said, "Can I come?"

Casimir stooped before her. "No, sweetie. Taprooms ain't for little girls."

"What's a taproom?"

"A beergarten, where men drink beer and whiskey and get good and drunk and stagger across the floor and—"

Victoria sighed. "Charlie, she doesn't need to know all that."

"Why not? That's where her daddy's headed." He kissed Anna Chrissy on the top of the head and went out the door.

At Sam's he had little to say to Donny. He headed home after one beer and let himself into the basement. On the following nights, he did the same, sometimes not even going to Sam's at all, but climbing the slagpiles, sitting far into the night, letting Victoria think he was drinking with the men.

On Saturday, he just sneaked down to the cellar after breakfast. He sat and sat in the dark. As the morning wore on and the children of the patch finished their chores, the school field across the street began to fill up with children playing games. Casimir could hear shouts and squeals and laughter. What could anyone have to laugh about?

When he got restless, he stood up and walked toward a basement window and stepped up on a crate. He lifted the hinged board and hooked it to a ceiling beam. Then he put the candle out so no one would notice him. He watched some children playing kick-the-can. Then he pulled the board back down and sat on the bottom step in the dark for an hour or two. Maybe three. He didn't know. An hour felt as long as a day.

Late in the afternoon, he put the board up again and saw Anna Chrissy sitting on a braided rag mat which she had set on the cinders alongside the house. Shielding her eyes from the sun, she watched a group of older children playing mumbly pegs, a game of whacking whittled sticks into the air with wooden paddles, trying to see who could keep their peg in the air the longest.

Anna Chrissy, her blonde braids tied with green ribbons, rose to her knees. She picked up a red cinder and tried to keep it airborne by hitting it with her palm. She couldn't seem to hit the same cinder more than twice. After losing several cinders in all directions, she sat down again and shook her head, disgusted. Casimir felt sorry for her. He wanted to make her feel better, wanted to go out to her, but he felt as though his blood had turned to molten lead and it was just too much effort to move. He pressed his palms against his forehead, ashamed that he could not make himself go out to her.

As if she had read his thoughts, she turned around and saw him at the window. She tapped on the glass and motioned for her father to come out. Crawling closer, she hollered, "Will you make me one of those?" She pointed to the mumbly pegs and paddles the children across the street had.

"Oh, God," Casimir muttered. "She needs me. Give me a push."

Anna Chrissy tapped on the window again. Casimir nodded and stepped down off the crate. He tore off one slat from it and took it outside. Sitting on the mat with Anna Chrissy, he began to whittle with a pocket knife. Anna Chrissy squirmed her way under his arm and leaned against him.

He kissed the top of her head. "Shall I tell you a story?"

"Yes!"

"Okay. Once in a faraway kingdom, called Russia, there lived two beautiful princesses. Their names were Antonia and Karina."

"Antonia and Karina." Anna Chrissy closed her eyes and smiled a wide closed-lipped smile, as though she had just tasted something delicious. "I like those names!"

"And they had a brother named, named—named, uh—"

"You forgot."

"No, named Caruso. He was a handsome prince with blue eyes. His sisters had blue eyes, too. But Antonia's hair was chestnut. Like his. Karina's was black like her mother's. They lived in a beautiful farmhouse in Moscow with a big front porch and their own special playhouse under the porch, behind all criss-cross boards. It had a little criss-cross door with a push-down latch. Inside, there was a little rag mat Casimir's mother had made for him."

"Casimir!"

Casimir dropped the board he was whittling and grabbed Anna Chrissy's shoulders. "Why did you say 'Casimir'?"

"You said it first," Anna Chrissy whined. "You said Casimir's mother made him a little rag mat. I thought his name was Caruso."

"I said 'Caruso'! You heard wrong."

Anna Chrissy stretched backwards, trying to pull away. "Daddy, you scared me."

"I'm sorry." He let go of her shoulders. "Caruso was his name. I said 'Caruso.'" He started whittling again, but Anna Chrissy did not lean against him this time. She folded her legs and clasped her hands in her lap.

Casimir continued the story. "The house belonged to their Uncle Patrick, a fisherman. 'A man's home is his castle,' he said. Just like a farmhouse he saw in Nebraska, which was just west of Russia. He had a picture of a wife, and he always kept it in his pocket. But Uncle Patrick took a ride on the Delaware & Hudson. It made his mouth go round and he couldn't work in the coal mine anymore."

"Daddy, what's the Delaware and— A coal mine! You said he was a fisherman!"

"He fished in the mines."

"Oh."

Casimir was flustered. He was picturing the docks in Gdansk where his papa had fished, but his mouth talked about the mines. He knew what he meant to say. He hated when his mouth played tricks on him. It was probably his mother. Oh, yes, she was keeping her mouth shut, letting him think he wasn't crazy after all. But he was starting that Uncle Jerzy talk, mixing things. Mixing things, though he knew what he meant. Fish in the mines. Wait! Were there fish in the mines? He tried to remember. Were there fish?

Anna Chrissy cupped her hands around Casimir's knee and shook it. "And then what happened?"

"There's lots of water in the mines. It drips down red from the tunnel roof with iron ore and makes rusty streams alongside the tracks where the mules pull the coal cars. That's where his Uncle Patrick fished. And the daddy of Antonia and Karina and, and—"

"Caruso. Remember?"

"And Caruso. Their daddy couldn't pay for the house by himself, and he was worried sick, because a man's home is his castle, so he heard a voice. And his wife knew, and her sister Marta. If that wasn't bad enough, Caruso, stupid, goddamned Caruso, went and left his toys on the front steps one night. He was too damn lazy to put them away. And in the morning, his father stepped on the toys and fell down the steps."

"Did he hurt hisself?"

"Yes, sweetie. He broke his neck and died."

"What's 'died'?"

"That means his body couldn't move anymore and it melted away in the ground like ice in the summer. But his soul—the part you think and see and hear with—that part went to live with God in Heaven. The daddy's soul was happy. Do you know what I mean?"

"No! What color was it?" There was irritation and frustration in Anna Chrissy's voice. "How comes it didn't melt?" She looked at her father's hands with impatience as he paused in his whittling project.

"It looks like a puffy white cloud in the shape of a person. It's like a rock on the slagpiles. It never melts. If you're good, it floats up to Heaven with God after you die. It goes very, very slowly."

"How far is Heaven?"

"High in the sky. Higher than the breaker. It's good because there's no Delaware & Hudson. All the pennies are face up, and nothing happens more than twice in a row. But people who love you don't get to see you anymore, or have supper, or tuck you in, or play mumbly pegs. They don't see you till they die and their body gets put in the ground and melts, and their souls go to heaven."

"Oh." The little girl's face was sad and bewildered.

"So let me tell you what happened after the daddy died. There was nobody to buy food for the family. Caruso felt terrible. It was all his fault, but he couldn't help to make it better. He was only seven. He was too little to get a job."

"So what did he do?"

"His mother was sad and lonely with no husband, so she went to a faraway land to find one. She took Caruso with her. She kissed the girls and promised to send for them soon. But when she got to the faraway land, she had lots and lots more babies and forgot all about the little girls she left behind."

"Did they die and melt in the ground?"

"No. Caruso wrote them a letter and said he would save them when he was big and got a job and enough money to build a boat to bring them to the faraway land to live in a big farmhouse he wanted to make for them."

"Did they like the boat he made them?"

"Sweetie, he never made the boat. He got so busy in the new land that he never made the boat. So he never brought his sisters to the new land. They waited and waited so long that they got sick of waiting for Caruso, and they didn't care about him anymore. They would not come to the new land to see him."

"Then did they die?"

"No. I think they just got busy and forgot about their brother. And he was sad and sorry. He felt ashamed that he had never built the boat. Plus, he got punished with a voice. He would never, never be happy again."

"Is that the end?"

"Yes."

"Good. I didn't like that story. Let's just play mumbly pegs."

"In a minute. There. The paddle's all carved. Here, hold it. Let me see how the handle fits your hand." He wrapped the child's fingers around the wood. "Perfect. Now I just need to whittle some twigs on the ends to make mumbly pegs. Let's go find some twigs."

17

VALENTINE'S DAY

Every morning when Big Joe blew at five to wake the miners, Victoria got up before Casimir, fixed the fire in the kitchen, and made breakfast. It used to be that Casimir got up at the same time, dressed, went to the outhouse, came back and fixed fires in both the kitchen and the basement. But now he brought a bucket of coal to the kitchen at night and set it on a pair of stacked crates near the johnny stove so Victoria wouldn't have to lift it so high to dump it into the fire in the morning.

She seemed to expect less and less of him, letting him sleep till breakfast was ready, and reminding him gently that the furnace still needed tending. "Won't you tell me what's eating at you?" she'd say across the table. His only response was to stir his coffee in silence. Lately, he'd have two or three days of stubble on his face before he'd bother to shave. His hair lay in oily clumps, coal dirt caked at the roots.

One morning, Victoria reached across the table. His fingers made no effort to hold onto the spoon as she tugged it out of his hand and set it down. She pulled both his hands toward her and said, "I cannot stand this. A stranger sits across from me every morning. I know I expected too much when we were first married. I was still a child, fifteen, wanting everything to drop into my life, like in fairy tales. I thought I loved you as soon as I met you. But then I didn't know what love meant. I thought it meant that this handsome man came along and gave me everything and made me happy. Mrs. Anderson helped me see how hard you worked for me. She helped me to accept my lot as a miner's wife. Now you slip away from me, from our

161

children. You live in the basement. You never talk. You have troubles that you won't tell me."

"Mrs. Anderson," Casimir muttered. "Mrs. Know-It-All. She tried that what's-on-your-mind stuff with me. Old busybody. Wasn't it Mrs. Know-It-All who told you I was a miner?"

"You know Mrs. Anderson told me."

"Did she put you up to this, 'Charlie, what's on your mind? Charlie, what's on your mind?' You'll drive me crazy with such a stupid question. Everybody has a mind. Everybody has somethin' on it."

"Mrs. Anderson didn't put me up to anything."

"Your mother, then."

"I forbade Mama to say anything about you after that Christmas dinner. Papa, too. They write and tell me how they are. They don't ask about you. They don't ask to visit. They invite me and the girls."

"Not me."

"No."

"Why don't you visit them?"

"If you're not welcome, then neither am I."

"What a loyal little wife!"

"Stop it, Charlie. Tell me what's on your mind."

"Why does Mrs. Anderson want to know?"

"I'm not asking for her. I'm asking because I care."

"You care. It makes you feel like a better wife to ask me that. Now you don't have to run to confession every week to tell Father Kashnoski what a selfish princess you are. You cook and sew and scrub like a good little miner's wife. 'Look at me, what a good wife I am!' you can say."

"Look at yourself, Charlie. Go! Stand up. Take a look in the mirror there on the cellar door."

Casimir stood up and ran his finger along his lips. Did she see that crazy O? Is that what she meant? He tried to look calm as he shuffled over to the mirror. He smiled to see his lips in a straight line. "There's nothing wrong with the way I look. Say, where's my lunch? Did you pack my lunch bucket?"

"It's on the counter, Casimir."

Casimir froze.

"Yes, I called you Casimir," Victoria said softly. "Casimir. I know that's your real name."

"You're crazy." Casimir walked back to the cellar door and smiled into the mirror. "What a handsome coal miner you are, Charlie Turek." He ran his palms across his cheeks. "You could use a shave. Other than that, you look just dandy."

Victoria stood behind him. "How many nights you've shaken me awake now, yelling, 'Mama, it's me, Casimir. Answer, Mama!' For weeks now, you have the same nightmare."

"Dreams mean nothing."

"That woman who stopped you in the vestibule after our wedding, she called you Casimir."

"What woman? That crazy woman? That sick, skinny woman? You're just as crazy as she is." He opened the cellar door, closed it after himself, went down, and began raking the furnace. He heard the door at the top of the steps open. Then he saw his wife start down. "Don't come down here!" he shouted. "You don't belong down here. You have your own family upstairs. You don't belong down here." When he saw that she made no move to return to the kitchen, he started up after her. "I said go back upstairs!"

"But not as far up as the attic! You've boarded up the attic. The cellar windows. Will you board up the cellar door, too?"

"I will if I have to. Don't make me force you up those stairs."

Victoria faced him in silence, the child inside of her overdue. Casimir glared up at her. She turned away and started back upstairs. But she was not fast enough to suit him. He put his hand flat on her back and shoved her through the door.

He slammed the door and stood with his ear pressed against it, his hand on the knob.

"She knows your name," he heard his mother's voice say in Polish. "You might as well tell her everything, Casimir."

He ran down the stairs. "Oh, *now! Now* you talk to me, Mama! Well, you waited too long. I have nothing to say to you."

"She wants to listen to you. Think what it would mean not to have to lie and sneak and hide all the time."

"Speak English, Mama." He sat down, folded his arms on the step above him, and buried his face in them.

He heard footsteps approach from behind the furnace. "Think how it can mean. You don't wake up asking, 'What do I give away in my sleep *last* night? Or the night before?' Give it all away. Go tell her your papa died on account of you make him choke on that pork. Tell her you left your sisters to be rotting in Gdansk. Then, if you be talking in your sleep, she will understand what it's all about. She will not nag, "What's on your mind, what's on your mind, what's on your mind, what's on your mind, what's on your—"

"Shut up, Mama! Go away. You're never here when I need you. Only when you feel like butting in."

"I promise I be here any time you need me."

"Here, in the cellar. Only in the cellar."

"Only in the cellar. Casimir, think about telling her. Think about it at work today."

"I will."

All day at work, Casimir brooded over the way Victoria must have laughed at his nightmares all night. Laughed at *him.* By the time the whistle blew, he had worked himself into a rage.

He rushed home ahead of everyone, fuming all the way to his back yard. The points of the picket gate were covered with huge, airy snowflakes that sprang upward like a fountain with a slam of Casimir's boot. He stormed toward the bulkhead.

Anna Chrissy rapped on the kitchen window. She was smiling and holding something up to him. He could barely make out her face behind the red smudges on the glass. It angered him to see the smudges. It was bad enough to have to crawl and drill and blast and breathe in coal dirt all day without having to come home and see filth on the windows!

Instead of going to the basement to change and wash, he went right in through the kitchen. He scowled at Anna Chrissy. "Look what you did to the glass!"

"Daddy, I made—"

"Look what you did!" He opened the toy box. Grabbing the mumbly peg paddle he had made for her, he raced to the chair she was kneeling on by the window. He clamped one hand over her shoulder and whacked her on the bare thigh.

He had never struck her before. They stared at each other, fear and disbelief on their faces. Anna Chrissy's chin quivered, but the look in her eyes changed from fear to hope as she held up a wet, red paper heart to him. Streaks of red were smeared on her cheeks, and along her temples. The red, pasty concoction had flattened her yellow curls like dried blood. A broad red patch appeared on her thigh.

Casimir looked away from her leg. He saw that the table was covered with newspapers. On the newspapers were scraps of paper and cups of red finger-paint Victoria must have made up for her.

He stepped away from Anna Chrissy so he wouldn't hit her again. "Where's your mother?"

"In bed," Anna Chrissy said with a tremble in her voice. Tears were slowly oozing over the smears of red paint on her cheeks, but like her mother, she cried in silence.

"In bed! In bed and leaving you to make this mess down here!"

"The new baby's coming. A Balentine's baby, Mama said." She did not move from the chair. Still kneeling, she put her arms down, the red heart dangling from her fingertips.

"Where's Felicia and Julie?" Casimir said.

"Mrs. Anderson took them next door to Mrs. Stutzman."

"Why didn't you go?"

"I wanted to give you my Balentine first." She hugged the soggy heart to her chest. The muscles in her throat moved with gulps that stifled her voice.

Casimir stared at the paddle mark on her leg. He felt a confusing mix of pity and contempt for her, and guilt. He wanted to slap her for making him hate himself. But he forced himself to go over and take the paper heart from her and say something nice. "Thank you," was all he could get himself to say.

"Are you still mad at me?"

"No." He wanted to say he was sorry he hit her. He read the expectant look in her eyes as one of waiting to hear him say it. But he didn't. He couldn't make himself do it. His heart bunched with such hatred for himself that he felt like running all the way to Wilkes-Barre and throwing himself in front of the Delaware & Hudson. "Go next door," he said, afraid he'd hit her again.

Anna Chrissy got down from the chair, went over to the table and began to clean up the mess.

"I'll clean that up," Casimir said. "Hurry. Wash your hands and face."

Anna Chrissy opened the cabinet as quietly as she could. She took out her two-step stool and got washed. Then she crept across the room and set the stool below the peg rack, took down her coat, put it on, and went out. Casimir watched her climb over the banister to the neighbor's back porch.

While he was clearing the table, Mrs. Anderson came rushing into the kitchen. She looked shocked to see him there in his miner's clothes, but said nothing about it. "Hurry and get Doctor Kirk," she said. She was wiping her bloody hands on a towel.

"What for?"

"The baby won't come. It's breech, I think. Hurry! And find someone with a car on the way back. We might have to take her to the hospital if he can't deliver the child here."

"She doesn't need a man doctor touching her. Even you said a room with a woman giving birth is no place for a man. You deliver that baby. That's what I pay you for. Now go and do your job."

"She needs Doctor Kirk. Now!"

"She doesn't need a man doctor touching her, I said."

Mrs. Anderson went out and climbed over to Mrs. Stutzman's porch. Moments later, Anna Chrissy was running through the yard and out the back gate. Mrs. Anderson climbed over the banister again. She glared at Casimir as she passed him on her way back upstairs. "Women can die in childbirth, you know."

"Then get up there and do your job!"

Casimir left the mess on the table and went down to the cellar. He took his work clothes off and flung them across the room. He looked around as if he expected his mother to holler at him for doing that. He filled the tin tub with the jars of water he had left to warm by the furnace and got in. He decided he would wash exactly one half of his body. If Victoria didn't like it, it was too bad.

He drew a wet line across his stomach, just under his ribs and lathered himself from there to his toes, being careful not to cross that line with any suds.

He spent a lot of time on each toe, massaging each one. While he was doing this, he heard a door slam. Fast, heavy footfalls went through the kitchen, through the parlor, and up the stairs.

"That skinny, greedy company doctor," Casimir said. "Pig. Touching other men's wives with his skinny, man-doctor hands. Well, let him. To hell with him. To hell with her."

He did not like the feel of the grit in his mouth, and he wanted to clean his teeth. He didn't know if he could do it without dripping water on his chin or chest or arms, places above the line. He picked up the rag he used for cleaning his teeth and sprinkled some salt into the palm of his hand. He leaned his head over the side of the tub, rinsed his mouth with water from a jar, dipped the rag into the jar, and then into the salt, and began scrubbing his teeth.

He heard the doorknob rattle at the top of the cellar steps. His first thought was that Anna Chrissy had told somebody how mean he had been to her, and they were coming to get him and put him away. He kept glancing up the stairs as he cleaned his teeth.

The door opened. "Charlie?" Mrs. Anderson's voice.

"Don't come down here!"

"Charlie? You have a son. Do you hear? I said you have a son. And Victoria's okay, thanks to Dr. Kirk. I have to get back upstairs and help. Come up!" She closed the door.

Casimir twisted around and looked toward the spot behind the furnace where he had hidden his father's watch. "Oh, Papa! Did you hear that?" He wished his papa would answer. "Papa?" Nothing.

He slid down into the tub, holding his breath, bending his knees till the water covered his chest and face and head. He frisked the coal dirt from his scalp and face and dug it out of his ears. Then he sat up and rubbed a bar of soap over his head, scrubbed it quickly, and rinsed it with water from a tin pitcher.

He dressed and raced up to the second floor, past doctor Kirk, who was coming out of the bedroom. A thin, balding man with glasses and long fingers, he handed a bundle of bloody towels to Mrs. Anderson and said to Casimir, "She'll need lots of rest."

"A son? I have a son?"

Dr. Kirk smiled and nodded. Then he followed Mrs. Anderson downstairs.

Casimir went into the bedroom. Victoria smiled at him from across the room. It seemed to take great effort for her to speak. "Finally, I gave you a son! That's why you pulled away from us, isn't it? Because you thought I'd never give you a son. Look at him, how dear." She turned her head to the side and looked at the veiled bassinet alongside the bed.

Casimir tiptoed toward it.

Victoria laughed lightly. "Go on, look. It's okay."

Papa, look. Casimir lifted the veil and felt his face drain white. Swaddled in a white bunting, the child turned his little face inside the hood. His lips puckered and flattened and puckered again, sucking at the air. Then they stayed pursed, completely rounded, as he half opened his eyes. Casimir could have sworn the baby smiled with those eyes. Mocked him. *That crazy O! That crazy, crazy— The kid is mad! It happens to the males, happens to the males!* No, wait! It must be that skinny doctor's kid. It can't be mine! *Papa, don't look! Don't look! It isn't ours!*

He leaned over the bed and ran his hand up Victoria's thigh. "How did you like that skinny man-doctor touching you here?"

"What!?"

"You heard me." He closed the door. He took his shirt off and threw it on the floor. Then he took his shoes and socks off, and then his pants. He stood naked before his wife and said, "Kinda skinny, that doctor, ain't he? Not like a coal miner. Coal miners are husky and strong, see?" He slid under the blankets and lay next to her, running his hand all over her body. "Was it fun with the doctor?" He shoved her nightgown up to her waist.

"Charlie, stop! What's the matter with you?"

"Was it fun laughing at me last night? And all the other nights I talked in my sleep?" He slid on top of her.

She tried to push him away and scream, but he clamped his mouth over hers.

How easy she was to pin down.

18

The next morning, Casimir crept from the bedroom before the whistle blew. He went straight to the outhouse, then to the cellar through the yard door, and put on his miner's clothes. He sat on the bottom step and hurried with his boots, hoping to be gone before the whistle got Victoria out of bed.

But he heard her walking through the parlor and out to the kitchen. Her feet dragged. Her steps were uneven. She yanked open the utensil drawer with such force that everything spilled out. She seemed to be looking for something among the spoons and knives and forks scattered about the floor. She went back through the parlor and upstairs again.

Casimir threw open the lower furnace door and shoveled the ashes out, hurrying madly. He slammed the door, opened the upper one, threw in two shovelfuls of coal, poked the fire with swift, frenzied jabs, and shut the door.

He saw that the lace in his left boot had come undone. He sat on the step again and hurried to tie it. Suddenly the door opened at the top of the steps. Casimir looked straight ahead and said in a cold, single tone, "I told you not to come down here."

Victoria's voice was little more than a whisper. "Casimir, I hid a knife in the bedroom. If you ever force me again, I'll cut that thing off."

She closed the door. Casimir heard her remove the iron plates from the johnny stove and drag the poker from its cast-iron stand. He listened to her stabbing the hot coals in slow, labored thrusts. She attached the raking handle. The usual rough, fast, back-and-forth raking was a slow, strained pull, once this way, once that, before the

169

handle fell off the nub. She replaced it and began again. Casimir counted the pulls on the handle—seven—eight—nine. When she added coal, it sounded as though she were scooping it from the bucket with a cup, not dumping it in. She replaced each burner lid. Her slippers scratched along the linoleum. The legs of a chair scraped the floor as it was pulled away from the table. There was silence. Then sobs.

Casimir remained on the bottom step. The damp, musty, basement smell on the far end, away from the furnace, wafted itself toward him. He thought he saw a rat leap up into a space between two stones in the wall. "A filthy rat," he muttered. "That's what I am."

"You are disgusting," he heard his mother say. "Cruel! How you can do such thing? Think such stupid thing? A little baby. All babies make funny faces with their mouths."

"Leave me alone, Mama."

"Why I should not to bother you? Your Aunt Marta, she warned you. Good boy, no voices will come. Bad? Then—voices for you!"

"I'll tell Victoria I'm sorry. After work. After I've had a chance to figure out how to say it, how to face her."

"Maybe you be lucky. Maybe you wander into blackdamp. The light on your hat, it will go out. Then you suffocate, just slip into death. In that black, black mine where nobody can see nobody. You don't face nobody. Not one miner. Not one living—"

"Oh, shut up, Mama."

"You don't face your wife. The ugly thing you do. Listen to her."

Casimir listened to Victoria sobbing at the table. He knew she was not one to cry aloud. There were always soft, silent tears. The sound frightened him. Was it really *her* voice bursting from her own throat in such terrible gulps? Or was it some other voice come to punish him? "Which is it, Mama?"

"Guess."

"I can't. Mama, if you must punish me with your voice, please stay in the basement. Don't follow me to work."

"Only if you promise not to do that ugly thing again."

"I promise."

It was still dark when he left for work.

At the mine yard he was greeted with punches of congratulations. "So tell us," they said. "Is he bald? Does he have hair? Does he smoke a pipe, or what?" The men clutched at their chests in the cold. Some stamped their feet, frosty breath spewing from their nostrils.

All Casimir could remember was the O-mouth. "I don't know."

"Vut? You don't know? All dis time you vait for a son and you cannot tell us is he bald?"

"I mean I don't know if he smokes a pipe." He laughed along with them so they'd forget about him and go on to something else.

The cage came and took them down. Rats squeaked and raced through the gangway. When the cage gate opened to release the miners, the foreman crept over to a rat that had stopped to sniff something. It looked up just as he picked up a rock. It seemed to Casimir that the rat looked deliberately at him, as if it expected him to save it, like a relative in a new country expecting the first arrival to take care of his own. He felt exposed. He took a whack at the animal with his pick, but it got away. The foreman put a hand on Casimir's shoulder. "Now here's a smart miner. The only one with sense enough to kill those diseased things. The rest of you are fools!"

"Charlie's the fool," one man said. "As long as we got rats alive at our feet, we know we're all right down here."

"That's right," another man said. "When the rats clear out, we clear out. Charlie knows that, too. He's not himself today, that's all."

"Up all night and waita for that baby boy."

"You don't need rats here," the foreman said. "Why do you think we bring these canaries down every morning?" He held up the little brass cage, swinging it from his fingertips at each miner like a thurible of incense. "If this little guy drops dead first thing in the morning, we all wait in the yard till the fans clear the place out."

Every rat Casimir saw made him think of the darkness of what he had done, brought fear of more punishment, more voices. "I'm sorry," he would whisper to God. But at lunch, when he took his pocket knife out to cut off the soggy tip of a carrot, he remembered Victoria's threat. Cut that thing off. Huh! Who gave her the right? She was his wife. It was her job to lay there when he wanted her. She should cut Dr. Kirk's thing off, giving her a kid with a crazy O-mouth.

Casimir would get back at both of them somehow. In the course of blasting and digging and loading, an idea came to him. He'd plan a big christening party, with Dr. Skin-and-Bones and the whole patch invited. None of this small, sneaky stuff with Victoria inviting those factory-girl godmothers and their godfather brothers and husbands from Dickson City so she could avoid the patch women she had snubbed. Her snubbing was the talk of the patch. What if the patch women saw the coal dirt on the princess's nice beige rug, saw the proof of how her husband had put her in her place?

Satisfied with that plan, Casimir spent the rest of the day trying to guess where Victoria had hidden the knife, wondering if she'd really do it. In his mind, he lifted each pillow and felt under the edges of the carpet. He peeked behind the curtains and ran his hand along the back of the headboard. It shouldn't be that hard to find.

When he got home, he washed quickly in the cellar, then raced up to the bedroom and searched in all the places he had rehearsed. He found nothing. He would make her tell. He brought the rocking chair down to the kitchen, determined to sit on it and stare Victoria into confessing where she had hidden it. Yes, he would rock and stare her down while she fixed supper. But it was Mrs. Anderson who was fixing supper while Victoria lay on the couch in the parlor. He had passed them on the way upstairs and not even noticed. He stepped between the old woman and the stove. "I didn't hire you to stay on and make supper."

"I know," she said coldly. She brushed past him to the sink.

"I hope you don't expect to be paid."

"I don't. I never did." She marched back to the stove, rammed a spatula under a piece of meat and flipped it, splattering grease.

"What are you doing here then?"

"Your wife was hemorrhaging today. Anna Chrissy came and got me. I would have stopped in anyway. Doctor Kirk had to come, too. He wanted to put her in the hospital. She wouldn't go. She hasn't said a word all day. She just whimpers on the couch."

"You look at me like I did something to her."

Mrs. Anderson wagged her finger. "You should've gone for Dr. Kirk right away yesterday, like I told you."

"Yeah, maybe so. But if you'd done your job right in the first place, we wouldn't've needed him yesterday or today. So there!"

He went upstairs, ignoring Victoria on the couch. He put on a suit. He admired the fit before the vanity mirror. My body is strong and fit. Not like that skinny doctor. He smiled, then headed down to Sam's Cafe.

Every time the door opened, he announced to the newcomer that he had a son, and everybody was invited to the christening on the last Sunday of March. He clung to men's jackets as they tried to leave, until they promised to bring their families to the christening.

"I hate to tell you, Charlie," one man said. "My wife won't believe me. Even if she did, she wouldn't come. Your wife don't invite nobody to your house ever since she got here. No insult meant, but all our wives say she thinks she's better than the rest."

"Well, she's sorry. She wants people to come now. Will you come? My wife's a dyed-in-the-wool Hunkey. We'll do the whole Hunkey tradition for her. You know, putting the kid under the table and all. Okay?"

On the last Sunday of March, 1916, the little boy was welcomed into the Roman Catholic Church. Donny Wilson and Margaret, his sister, were the godparents. After Mass, the rite was performed at the marble baptismal font at the foot of the stairs to the choir loft.

The somber voice of the priest washed over the infant. "I baptize thee, Frank Valentine Turek, in the name of the Father, the Son, and the Holy Ghost."

Casimir pressed his lips to Victoria's ear. "Frank Valentine! Where in the hell did you get a name like that?" He liked the Frank part, the name he was going to give one of the girls before he knew she'd turn out to be a girl. But he had never told Victoria the name. He resented her using it. Once it could not be used on that particular baby, it was not to be used at all. It was something to be stored forever in the attic, like the wallpaper with the ladies in blue gowns, like Patches' bed. Victoria had no business dragging it down. The Valentine part? It sounded like a girl's name. What the hell!

After the baptism, the godparents left the church and walked ahead, carrying Frank, preparing to put him under the parents' kitchen table according to the Polish tradition. The real mother and father were to retrieve the child to show they were the rightful parents.

Casimir, having written the doctor a note of appreciation and invitation, could hardly wait to get home and find that skinny adulterer among the guests. Let him claim his O-mouth kid.

Victoria, taking Felicia's and Anna Chrissy's hands, led them from the church. Casimir wedged himself between Victoria and Anna Chrissy, separating their hands. He leaned against Victoria's arm and put his mouth on her ear. "Frank Valentine! What the hell, Victoria."

"How many times I asked you what you wanted to name him," she said. "You had no interest, so I picked something I liked."

"Valentine! It sounds like a girl's name. And that lacy dress you put on it! Are you sure it's a boy?"

"A christening gown. Boys and girls wear the same."

Victoria quickened her pace. Anna Chrissy and Felicia whined for her to slow down. Traces of snow still lined the streets. Felicia stepped in a puddle made by the morning sun. Casimir yanked the child from the water. She glared up at him, showing a defiant face.

"Felicia," Victoria said, "will you run ahead to Mrs. Stutzman's? Ask her to bring Julie home. Tell her we'll be there in a minute. Anna Chrissy, you too."

The little girls ran ahead and turned the corner.

"Frank Valentine," Casimir said. He smirked and shook his head. "Figures you'd pick a name like that. Sounds like the sort of name a tart would pick."

Victoria stopped and folded her arms. "If you wanted me to name him Casimir, after you, you should have said so."

Casimir laughed. "Only a crazy woman would call a child after a name she heard in her husband's nightmare. Huh! I go and have a dream about some greenie getting off the boat, and you go and name your baby after him. Wouldn't *you* look like the fool!"

"Did the greenie teach you Polish in your sleep?"

"Now you're really talking crazy."

"No, you're talking Polish in your sleep. I told you, I'm learning all about you. Mama was right about you. I'm glad she won't come here. She won't get to rub my face in my mistake. She was right about Gdansk. I know you're from Gdansk and your real name is Casimir. You never set one toe in Nebraska, but you tell me you lived on a farm there and your mother died there just before Anna Chrissy was born. That woman in the back of the church after our wedding, she was your mother, and she died right here in Pennsylvania. You were with her when she died."

"The lies you tell yourself. All because you didn't get to live in the palace you wanted."

"The lies you tell me. And now you're angry because I found you out, so you call me filthy names like whore, and you force yourself on me like a pig five minutes after Frank is born."

"Have I touched you since that time? No! But still you go on about it."

"Like you go on calling me whore because a man doctor had to deliver Frank."

"You liked it."

"Casimir, look. On the day I found out you were a miner, you said something that never left me. You said, 'You don't know what hell it is to hide things, Victoria.' You sounded like a man trying to push a boulder up a hill, and I got the feeling you were talking about more than the secret of being a miner. I didn't know what you meant, and I didn't want to know. If I didn't know, I could pretend it wasn't so bad, whatever it was."

"Suddenly, you want to know all about me."

"Tell me the rest. Tell me where you came from, who you are. Get it out and be done with it. Whatever you're hiding, I don't care. We have four children to raise. We have to get along. Get it out of your system and stop tormenting me and the children."

Casimir curled his index finger and ran the knuckle softly along her jawbone. "What about the knife?"

"What about it?"

"First, tell me where you hid it."

"Then you'll tell me everything?"

"Yes."

She looked hard and steadily into her husband's eyes. "You know my royal blue robe that I hang on the bedpost? The velvet one with all the gathers at the cuffs?"

"The one I bought you for a wedding present."

"Yes. The knife is in the left sleeve between the lining and the velvet. The point of the knife is in the cuff."

"Damn! I checked the pockets of that thing a thousand times! Anyway, you're lying. I would've felt a knife in the sleeve."

"It's only a little knife. The one I use to slit the chickens' throats before I cut their heads off."

"What chickens?"

"The ones I buy at the market."

"You buy live chickens and kill them?"

"It's cheaper that way."

Casimir stopped walking. "You kill them yourself? You really cut their heads off?" For the first time, he was sure she would have used that knife on him. Slit his throat in the night. Or cut that thing off. Who the hell was she to threaten him with it?

"Now," Victoria said, "after the neighbors leave, you'll tell me your part?"

He grinned. "Say, do you threaten Doctor Skin-and-Bones with that knife when he's up in our bedroom, going at it with you while I'm at work? Ask *him* what's on *his* mind, why don't you?"

"You! You tricked me into telling you. I thought you might. But I took a chance so you'd spill the truth and we could get a new start."

"I don't want a new start with you. Enjoy that skinny, spectacle-faced— Why would I want to roll in the hay with you again? Princess of the Patch! Princess with the royal blue robe. La-di-da!" He pulled a square brown bottle from his coat pocket, took a swig, and blew a blast of boozy breath into her face. "How do I smell?"

"Stop it! You stink! The neighbors'll think you're drunk!"

Exactly, he thought, taking another swig. If he could not make his words come out right, they would blame it on the booze.

They reached their back yard. A stringy-haired boy standing stiffly like a guard on the porch said, "My dad said to wait outside till the godparents get the baby settled under the table."

Casimir saluted him. The boy saluted back and went inside. Casimir guzzled some more whiskey and pressed the bottle flat against the center of his chest as though displaying his very heart.

"Put that away!" Victoria said.

Casimir wagged his body. "No."

"Please, put it away."

"Why? Afraid the neighbors will see? What will they think of a royal princess with a staggering old soak for a mate?"

"Please don't ruin it. People were decent enough to come, after the way I shut them out. It's a miracle they came at all. A godsend!"

"A godsend! It was *my* doing. I begged them to come."

"Yes, I am thankful to you for it. I've been so lonely. I've been wanting to break the ice and ask people myself, but I was too proud. I'm glad you did it." She reached for the bottle. "Please don't ruin it. It'll be hard enough showing my face."

The door opened and the little guard said. "Ready! Here comes the real parents to fetch their baby!"

Casimir whispered to his wife, "Ha! The big moment! Victoria and Dr. Skin-and-Bones claim the little tyke they made."

"What are you talk—?"

"I know the kid is his. Shall I smile nice for the people?" He turned his back to the guests so they wouldn't see how he tormented her. He tucked the bottle under his arm, stuck an index finger into each end of his mouth and stretched his lips. Victoria walked in ahead of him, trying to look calm and happy.

Casimir walked in, swigging the whiskey. He made a point of stumbling over the threshold. His flamboyant grin faded when he looked over the guests. "No Doctor Kirk?"

"Don't be silly," one of the women said. "Company doctors don't come to miners' celebrations. You invited him?"

Casimir sent Anna Chrissy to run and get Dr. Kirk. "Hurry!" Casimir said. "Tell him to hurry!"

The table had been pulled out to the center of the kitchen and a lacy white cloth covered it. Pastries were piled on plates. A small pile of wrapped gifts was in the center of the table. There were ten adults and some children. Mrs. Anderson stepped to the head of the table, smiling proudly, announcing the names of the visitors: "Vera Urkov, Concetta D'Angelo, Mary O'Neill, Greta Blankenbiller, and Catherine McDonald, my youngest. They brought these lovely cakes."

Victoria felt her eyes filling up. "They're beautiful."

"And these are their husbands, Vladimir, Antonio, Michael, and you know Wilhelm from your wedding, and Joe, my son-in-law."

The men all nodded.

The infant under the table began to cry. Casimir bent toward him and said, "Just wait for one more guest, that's all."

The door opened and Doctor Kirk, winded, appeared with his bag, looking puzzled to find a kitchen full of smiling people. He looked under the table. The infant's face had become purple with demanding cries. Joe McDonald jabbed Casimir. "Well, ain't you gonna claim your boy?"

Casimir turned to Dr. Kirk. "Maybe you better have a look at him, Doc. Look at his color."

Dr. Kirk stooped down and picked up the child. Casimir grinned at Victoria and twitched his eyebrows.

"He looks fine to me," the doctor said. "Mighty hungry after a long time in church, I'd guess. But otherwise he's fine."

Casimir smiled. "Yes, a fine healthy son."

Victoria took the baby. "Dr. Kirk, can you stay and celebrate with us? If it wasn't for you, little Frank might not be here."

"He sure wouldn't," Casimir said, chuckling. "Here, Doc, would you like a tart?" His hand made a gesture toward Victoria before picking up a small plate with a blueberry tart and offering it to the doctor.

Dr. Kirk put the plate on the table. "No, thank you, I can't stay. I was just about to take a drive with my family. I thought you had an emergency here. The baby's fine." He nodded to Victoria and left.

After a few moments of clumsy silence, Victoria said over Frank's loud wailing, "I need to go upstairs and feed Frank. Go ahead and start without me. I—" She stopped speaking. She felt her face flush as she tried to say what she wanted to. "I want to ask all of you to forgive me. You were so friendly when I came to live here, but I kept to myself. I don't know how to make up for it. I'm just glad you're giving me another chance." She looked at Vera. "Especially you. You came up on the back porch how many times and invited me to glean coal from the culmbanks. But I said no, and—well, I'm sorry."

Vera, still as thin as the first day Victoria saw her, said, "Let's forget about that."

"Thanks." Victoria turned and left the room with Frank.

Casimir wanted to make a joke about Doctor Kirk claiming the baby from under the table, but everyone seemed to have forgotten that event. Everyone was silent. Casimir could tell that people were taking in what Victoria had said, really thinking about it. She had ruined his whole day with her stinking apology.

What if those patch women really, really forgave her? What if they started coming around sewing, chatting, taking up Victoria's time, bringing their own brats over to sticky up the walls? Supper would be late. She'd get behind on the laundry. Worst of all, what if his mother came upstairs and spoke to him in front of one of them? How could he ever control it all? One friend in here. Two friends in here. Three. She didn't deserve friends anyway. If she did without them this long, she could go on doing without them.

He planted himself in the same spot where Victoria had spoken, as though taking his turn at the podium during a town meeting. "Well, she finally got the words out," he said. "I warned her she better apologize."

Mrs. Anderson glared at him. "I'd say she meant those words."

"I'd say she meant to save her fancy belongings," Casimir said. "She knows I won't put up with her snubbing the christening guests." He beckoned the women to the archway leading to the parlor. When they were all clustered by the cellar door, looking into the front room, Casimir said, "See that rug? I lost my temper one night and sootied it all up to teach that princess a lesson. Too good for everybody else around here. Thought I'd give her a little less to show off about. Bring her down a notch." His whiskey breath spewed all over them. They stared back with sour expressions as he went on. "Even then she wouldn't apologize. Guess what. She thought I was a boss at the Ebony Gem when she married me. A boss. Not an ordinary miner like your husbands, but their boss, some big shot boss much better than them. That's why she wouldn't be seen chumming around with you ladies."

The women looked at each other, frowning.

Vladimir Urkov said to his wife in his deeply rolling voice, "*Shto znachit,* 'chummink'?"

"Being friendly," Vera said in English. Then she summarized in Russian what Casimir had said.

Vladimir, a solid, broad man, a little shorter than Vera, drew his heavy eyebrows together.

Mrs. Anderson wagged her finger at Casimir, "You let her think you were a boss. Went out in a suit. Came home in a suit." She looked over at Donny Wilson, who nodded in agreement.

Casimir shot him a look of resentment.

Mrs. Anderson looked at each of the women and said, "You all remember how he washed at that Hungarian boarding house."

Casimir smirked. "Oh, I played along a bit. Let her down easy, I figured. But even after she knew, she stayed up on her high horse. Finally, I invited everybody and made her apologize."

"So she isn't really glad to have us," Catherine McDonald said. She had square blue eyes, puffy cheeks and a rosebud mouth that gave her the appearance of a Victorian doll with a perpetual expression of surprise.

"She is so," Mrs. Anderson said.

"I see," Casimir heard his mother's voice holler from behind the cellar door. "Try to spoil everything on her. You don't fool nobody."

Six women stood between Casimir and that door. He feared it would burst open any second. He elbowed his way through the women and pressed his back to the door. "Don't look!" He pointed at Vera. "You! 'Some broomstick stopped by!' Victoria said. 'Go for coal? Go for coal? Huh! Go for coal with some sooty broomstick! Don't make me laugh!' That's how she liked your invitation."

"*Shto znachit,* 'broomsteek'?"

Vera translated for her husband, who puffed himself up and marched his wife out the door.

Casimir, his back still pressed against the cellar door, heard the knob rattle behind him. "Don't look! Fools at her feet. You can, if you want. Take your cakes. Take your presents." He opened the door and pulled it shut after himself. He stood on the top step, pulling on the knob so no one could open it. He listened to people go out.

Casimir ran down the steps, flailing his arms as though pushing aside curtains to expose an intruder. His voice was a hiss. "Mama! Why did you do that? You agreed to stay down here!"

"I did not open the door."

"Don't even come up the steps from now on." He etched a line in the dirt floor in front of the steps. "This is where you stop. Hear?"

"Why you don't say so before?"

"Shut up, Mama!" Casimir went up to the kitchen, surprised to see Mrs. Anderson. She was holding two plates heaped with little cakes. She turned and stared at him.

He took long, slow strides toward her, thumping his thumb on his chest. "This is *my* house. I say you stay out!" He grabbed the plates from her hands. The cakes bounced and rolled along the floor.

Mrs. Anderson stood motionless and pale. Her arms remained stretched out, her thumbs and fingers still positioned as though holding plates.

Casimir, rage stiffening every muscle in his face, advanced. He held up the liquor bottle as though he were going to smash it on her head. "Now, out!"

Mrs. Anderson backed toward the door to the porch. She lifted her coat from a wall peg and held it up like a shield. "Charlie, why did you drink so much?"

"Oh! What's on your mind, what's on your— I said *now*, out of my home! A man's home is his *shto znachit!* His *shto—* Oh, is it round?" He tapped his fingertips over his mouth, feeling its shape. "No. Good." He caught Mrs. Anderson looking at him. "Out!" he hissed. "Don't come back! Don't ever come back!"

Mrs. Anderson's heel caught the door as she tried to back out to the porch. She staggered outside.

Casimir laughed. "Drunk? What's on your mind, what's on your mind, what's on your mind?"

Mrs. Anderson hurried out the gate.

Casimir stood in the open doorway, feeling his lips as he watched his daughters playing in the yard.

"What a draft!" Victoria said, coming down the stairs. Now her voice was behind him in the archway from the parlor. "Where's that draft coming— My God, where are they? Where did they go?"

Casimir kicked the pastries around the floor. "Your fake apology. It made them mad." He laughed and went down to the cellar.

19

FOLLOW THIS WITH YOUR EYES

The next morning Victoria lay still as she listened to her husband get up and go out in the dark morning before the mine whistle blew. Her heart, her stomach, everything ached. She remained in bed until she was satisfied that he had not come back into the house.

She sat up and slid her legs off the bed. She moved like a carved figure brought to life and trying out its limbs for the first time. She made her way down the hall and looked in on Anna Chrissy and Felicia in the middle bedroom. She wept at the sight of the quilts rising and falling with the breath of the two little girls.

She went into the back bedroom and slid Julie's blanket farther up, over her shoulders. Then she took the baby from the crib and carried him downstairs. The mine whistle blew. The girls whimpered in their usual moment's complaint and fell silent again. Frank burst into a wail.

Victoria took him out to the kitchen. She pressed him against herself, swinging her body from side to side, shushing him to silence as she lifted the cast-iron plates on the johnny stove. The fire was almost out. The kitchen was cold. She laid Frank on the table and covered him with a coat she took from a peg by the back door. Then she tended the stove.

She saw that Casimir had left the coffee pot on the warming area at the back of the stove. She got a cup from the cabinet. The coffee came out in a mere trickle. She opened the lid and saw that Casimir had packed newspaper inside. It had absorbed most of what he couldn't finish himself, leaving her almost nothing.

She sat at the table and took Frank to her breast. "Franush, Franush," she said softly. "What are we going to do?"

Cinders alongside the house crunched under miners' boots. Victoria, remembering her first morning in Black Hollow, remembering the first time she heard that sound after Casimir left for work in a suit, wept.

When Frank fell asleep, she took him back upstairs and put him in his crib. Then she went out to the outhouse, came back in, and sat down again at the kitchen table. She sat staring at the floor for a long time. She heard the cinders crunching under the boots of children going to the school across the street, and later, under barrow wheels and boots of women on their way to glean coal from the slagpiles. It sounded as though the whole world were marching off without her.

She heard someone tapping on the window pane. She stood up and looked over the cafe curtains. Mrs. Anderson was motioning for her to come out.

Victoria went out to the porch and said, "Come in. I'll make some coffee."

"I daresn't come in," Mrs. Anderson said, standing alongside the porch banister. "Your husband forbade me."

"Forbade you!"

"The rage in his eyes! I thought he'd kill me if I didn't go."

"What happened? One minute the house was full. The next minute— What in the name of God happened?"

"He insulted everyone, made it sound like he forced you to apologize, like you didn't really want to, like you didn't really want neighbors coming around. He told them you thought he was their husbands' boss, not one of them, when you first came here, and that's why you couldn't be bothered with your neighbors."

"My God, he told them that?"

"Victoria, you meant it when you apologized, didn't you?"

"Of course I meant it."

"Well, I don't think they'll ever believe you now. I tried to reason with my Catherine when I got home, but she wouldn't hear it. I'm afraid your Charlie spoiled everything for good. What's got into him? Ever since little Frank was born. I just don't understand it."

"He got some notion that Frank isn't his. He suspects Dr. Kirk."

"So that's it!" Mrs. Anderson said. "So that's it," she repeated in a mutter, slowly nodding her head. Then she said, "You know, Dr. Kirk was having himself a time with Stosh Moleski's woman two years back. I delivered the child myself. To this day I'm not sure if the little boy was his or Stosh's. I know I came in one afternoon to check on her. I crept into the bedroom, thinking she was asleep."

Mrs. Anderson covered her eyes and gasped as though discovering the shameless pair at that very moment. "She was asleep all right, and the doctor right next to her. Oh, I tiptoed out, kept my mouth shut, but Stosh caught them himself. He put an end to that. Moved the family to Philadelphia. I hate to have to ask you, Victoria, but I know how disappointed you were to find out your Charlie was only a miner. A doctor, why, now that's a man with a little more stature."

"How dare you, Mrs. Anderson!"

"I'm sorry if I guessed the wrong thing. But Victoria, you must have done something to make him so—so spiteful, so—so— I don't know what. All I know is that he gave you the world at first, and now he takes it away, threatens to spoil your nice things, spoils your nice christening party, fixes it so nobody wants to come around. Think back, Victoria, maybe something you said, something you did. You must have done something! If it was Dr. Kirk, you can tell me. I won't repeat it. It's no good holding it in. Come over to my place and we'll talk. I daresn't come in your house."

"No, you daresn't," Victoria mocked bitterly. "And I won't be coming to yours." She turned to go inside.

"Wait! Be reasonable, Victoria. Facing the truth will help you."

Without looking back, Victoria said softly, "I don't deserve this." She went inside and closed the door.

Casimir began to spend even more time on the slagpiles, hiding. Words were driving him crazy, playing tricks on him, threatening to humiliate him in the streets. Sometimes they behaved properly for weeks, like obedient children in church pews. But just when he thought he could trust his tongue, it was suddenly a basketball up for grabs by thoughts leaping and stamping past each other from all sides. Then there was a phrase from this notion, a word from that as his tongue was passed from thought to thought.

The next thing he knew, those words might come flying through a hoop-mouth like his Uncle Jerzy's. Oh, how the children of Gdansk laughed at Uncle Jerzy, mocked him! He knew that's what Victoria did in the middle of the night. He bet she even caught a glimpse of the O-mouth, something he could never control in his sleep.

Every morning Casimir checked his lips to see if they had become stuck in that crazy O. Throughout the day, in the darkness of the mine, he checked his mouth with his fingers. He hid from the people of Black Hollow at every opportunity, and he kept his breath all whiskied up to explain how the tongue betrayed him.

As for his family, he cared nothing for any of them now, and he didn't care whether they cared about him. He scarcely looked at his son, who was slow to put on weight. At six months old, he wasn't much bigger than the girls were at three months. At a year, though the child had taken steps on his own, he looked more like a baby of nine months. This, to Casimir, was all the more reason to taunt Victoria about scrawny Doctor Skin-and-Bones. "Why, all he needs is a pair of those silly-looking spectacles on his skinny little face, and there you have it, a chip off the old block. No wonder the doc was so quick to get over here and deliver the kid. It's his. Doc, be nimble. Doc, be quick. No! Doc, be quack. Ha!"

Sometimes Victoria would defend the child, pointing out the turquoise eyes, exactly the color of Casimir's. The child had his high cheekbones, his chestnut hair. In answer to her, he'd repeat the list of likenesses to Dr. Kirk. Then he'd revert to his usual method of harassment. He would sit in the rocker and stare at her and grin. Sometimes he'd jump up and stare long and hard, inches from her face, grinning, trying to provoke a reaction. She kept her eyes on her work, cooking, washing, ironing, diapering—all in hard silence. He always set the rocker right at her heels, sometimes getting up to imitate her movements.

When she went into the parlor, he went into the parlor, dragging the rocker behind him, dragging it back to the kitchen when she went back out there. Sometimes she'd get Anna Chrissy to help her lug the rocking chair up to the bedroom before he got home from work, but Casimir would always bring it back downstairs.

One afternoon the mine closed early because the air circulator pumps had broken down. Casimir came home and crept up onto the back porch. He saw that Victoria's face was buried in her arms at the kitchen table. The ironing board was set up by the stove, the iron reheating on one of the burner plates. Over the chairs were draped some clothes she had already pressed. There was one white shirt left in the basket to iron, one of those he wore with a suit when he dressed up to go to Sam's at night. Casimir watched her stand up and look at the rocker. She seemed to glare at it. Then she marched over to it, picked it up by the arms, carried it into the parlor, and came back to the kitchen. Taking the shirt from the basket, she spread it over the board and yanked the iron from the stove, slamming it onto the shirt. She bit her lower lip and blinked back tears.

Casimir waited for the tears, but they did not come. He wondered if she had seen him there on the porch and was determined not to give him the satisfaction. If she hadn't had enough, then he was going to give her something to cry about.

He stamped hard on the porch and knocked on the window, grinning through the panes. He was pleased to see her startled eyes. She walked over and pointed to the yard, indicating that he should come in through the cellar. He opened the kitchen door, stepped inside, and smiled at his wife, as if expecting her to offer to take his sooty coat and miner's hat and hang them graciously on the rack. He put on a British accent. "Not going to ask me to sit for tea?"

Victoria turned from him and started removing the clothes that were draped over the chairs. She folded them on the table, then stacked them in the basket while Casimir shadowed her. He saw that her face was stern again. She lifted the basket and raised her chin. Casimir stepped in front of her and put his blackened hands over hers. "Let me carry this upstairs for you," he said. When she tried to pull it away from him, he slipped his hands through the wire handles and yanked the basket from her. Then he held it away from himself, showing her how careful he was being not to get coal dirt on her clean, newly pressed laundry. Victoria was biting her lip again, but stopped when her husband's eyes fixed themselves on it. Her eyes met his with anger. He smiled and carried the basket into the parlor. "By the way, where did you stash the kids?"

"Anna Chrissy's playing next door, visiting Mrs. Stutzman. The others are napping. Don't wake them, Casimir, please." She called him Casimir all the time now.

He pounded up the stairs. "Oop!" he said, laughing. And the basket came bouncing down, clothes littering each step. Victoria ran to the stairs. "Don't bother," Casimir said. "I'll pick them up." By the time he tramped his black boots over each garment on his way down, Victoria had managed to rescue two little dresses. When he got to the bottom, he started back up the stairs again, picking up the blackened clothes as he went. He pulled the basket along his side. At the top of the stairs, he folded the clothes neatly with his sooty hands and stacked them in the basket.

Felicia and Julie appeared in the hall, pressing their backs against the wall. Felicia put her arm around Julie and glared at her father. Frank was wailing in his crib.

Victoria walked halfway up the stairs and extended her arms, as if preparing to catch the girls. "Come to Mama. I want you to go next door. Anna Chrissy's there. Tell her to stay till I come for you. Don't tell the neighbors anything's wrong. It'll be all right. Mama and Daddy are just busy and need help watching you today."

Julie stared at her father with frightened eyes, dark eyes that Casimir had always thought came down the line from Jozefina. "Maybe you're doctor Skin-and-Bones' kid," he said to her now, and laughed. The child lowered her head all the more and raised her eyes. Suddenly Casimir remembered Gina Diomira, the photographer's little girl at the wedding. Little Italian brat, acting scared of him for nothing. Maybe Julie was the photographer's daughter.

Neither child pulled away from the wall when their mother urged them again to come down. They could not do it without passing their father, who was sitting on the top step.

"What," he said, "do you think I'm the ugly troll under the bridge? Nabbing little children by the ankles?" Felicia sucked in her lips, knitted her eyebrows and took in a breath. She hooked arms with Julie and said, "Mama wants us downstairs. Let's go." Casimir ground his knuckles into their ribs as they ran by. He kept looking at Victoria, watching the pain in her eyes. Good, Casimir thought, it gets to her when I upset the girls.

Julie screamed and ran to Victoria's arms. Casimir threw the basket at his wife and daughters. On his way down, he stepped carefully around the clothes, and went into the cellar.

"Go ahead," he challenged his mother. "Tell me what a slob I am, picking on her children. Notice I said *her* children, not ours. Who knows who the fathers are? Except Anna Chrissy. I know that one's mine. She's the only one you suggested a name for. Never said one word about the others' names. Never said one word since, since, I don't know when. Oh, I know, since that damned christening. Almost ruined the whole event, yelling like that. Nothing to say now? To hell with you, then. I don't need you. I never needed you."

He went and stood by the furnace, looking at the spot where he kept his father's watch hidden. "Papa? What about you? Why don't you talk to me? I come down every day, and nothing. Nothing. Is it the place? Maybe you don't like America. Or maybe you hate me. You hate me, don't you? I turned into a monster."

Casimir kept more and more to himself at work. "Traitor" was the only word he had for Donny Wilson. On the day after the christening, Casimir had chewed him out for nodding in agreement when Mrs. Anderson brought up the Hungarian boarding house. Casimir had given him to the count of ten to apologize. He waited for Donny's familiar gesture of apology—clasped hands pressed against the chest, three quick bows, and a sheepish smile. But, instead, Donny folded his arms and shook his head. He kept his stand even when Casimir reminded him who had saved his life once in the mine.

No one paid much attention to Casimir either. Now that he had a son, there was little to tease him about, except having more sons. Even that didn't interest the miners much, for they had other things to discuss. Congress had declared war on Germany in April; in early December, Austria-Hungary.

Suddenly, the war "over there" was of concern to everyone here. "Making the world safe for democracy," as the President had put it, was on everyone's lips, and to many of the miners, reason enough to risk abandoning their families, possibly forever, should their lives be lost in the cause.

Casimir, waiting for the cage in the gangway one day, and hearing all this talk, listened especially to two Polish miners talking in their native tongue about the Bolshevik Revolution.

"Yes, yes, Russia fights on the same side as the United States, but she is so busy with her own mess, she won't be able to keep her claws sunk into Poland much longer."

"And with America in the war, there's a real chance of wresting the pieces back from Germany and Austria. I'm signing up!"

"You? You're not a citizen yet. I don't think they'll take you. Besides, you're a miner. Low on the draft list, even if you were a citizen. They need our coal for the war effort."

"I'll beg them to take me! If they won't, I'll go back to Warsaw and fight."

Casimir thought, why not me? Why not join the Army? Make the world safe for democracy! The world? To hell with the world. It was Poland he'd save. Finally, his papa would be proud of him. He would be to Poland what Joan of Arc was to France. His voices would coach him.

He paced the gangway in a frenzy till the cage came. He ran all the way home, flinging the bulkhead against the fence, bounding down the stone stairs and through the door into the basement. "Finally, you get the idea," he heard his mother say. He had to catch his breath before he could answer. There was laughter in his voice. He stepped out of his work clothes as he talked. "Yes, yes, now I know what my part is. So that's why it didn't work out to bring Anna and Krystina to America! And here I've been taking it out on everybody. Do you forgive me, Mama?"

"Yes."

"Papa? Do you hear, Papa? I'm joining the Army! Putting Poland back together!" He heard no reply, but he did not allow himself to become frustrated. There must be a purpose in making him wait to hear that voice. Yes, hear a voice. Hear a voice that no one would believe could be heard, a voice that everyone, if they knew, would say he was crazy for hearing. But now he was sure the voices were real. Real and good. Aunt Marta was wrong about them being a punishment. If others didn't hear them, it was because they were not meant to hear. The voices were only for those with a special, God-given mission, like Joan of Arc. "Isn't that right, Mama?"

"Yes. You be Casimir of Arc when you get to Gdansk."

"And Uncle Jerzy. What about him?"

"He was like John the Baptist who come before Jesus, come first to prepare the way. Uncle Jerzy came first to prepare the way for our Casimir. Nothing was wrong with Uncle Jerzy. Yes, the town think he was crazy how he sat on that bronze horse, wait and wait for the sword to rid Gdansk of them stinking Germans. But he had a vision, a private vision, like Saint Joseph, how he take Mary and the infant Jesus to Egypt to save them from Herod."

"Yes. Just like Saint Joseph. What if Saint Joseph told the people an angel came to him and told him to flee from Bethlehem?"

"They would say he was crazy."

"You're damn right, Mama! They'd lock him up. Put him away."

His mission clear, Casimir took the red cloth from behind the furnace and unwrapped Ignacy's pocket watch. He kissed it and squeezed it in his hand, raising his eyes, and saying, "Thank you, Papa. Thank you for giving me this chance." He unfolded his sisters' address, which he had wrapped along with the watch, memorized it, and wrapped it up again. Then he ran up the stairs with the intention of sneaking up to the bedroom to write to Anna and Krystina for the first time since he received the address.

Victoria was filling the washtub in the kitchen to bathe the children. She was stooped beside it, swishing her hand through the water to make suds. Little Frank, naked, was peering into the tub. He scooped up a handful of suds and put them into his mouth, frowning miserably and looking accusingly at his mother as if she had tricked him into tasting them. The child backed toward the sink when he saw his father come up from the basement. Casimir rushed over toward him, clamped his little head between his hands, and kissed him hard on the forehead. He did the same to Victoria and said, "Something wonderful is going to happen!" Then he ran upstairs and wrote to his sisters, revealing his plan.

He did not go to work the next morning. Instead he went to the post office to ask where he could sign up for the Army. He was told he'd receive a notice to take a physical in a few weeks. A few weeks. He mustn't let that upset him. His day was coming.

He was determined to find some good in having to wait, and to make some good of the time himself. He lit candles every day at St.

Hedwig's and prayed for the strength to be kind to his family. Now his family seemed much different to him. Suddenly he liked them again. At supper he looked from child to child, memorizing their features, fixing pictures of them to take along in his mind to Europe: Anna Chrissy, her hair almost white on the ends from last summer's sun, would be six, come March. He brought her little heart-shaped cinnamon candies every day after work.

Black-haired Felicia would not relinquish that mistrustful stare from her pale blue eyes. "Put out your hands. Like this," Casimir would say, kneeling before her and cupping his hands in front of himself. At first she'd let her hands hang at her sides while her father held peppermint sticks out to her. Then she'd hold her hands out, but then spread her palms apart, letting the candy fall to the floor. Sometimes she'd clasp her hands behind her back, wrinkle her nose and shake her head.

"Okay," Casimir would say, "I'll give them to my buddy here." Little Frank would toddle over, snatch the peppermint sticks, and race across the room, hiding behind the couch, as if he expected his father to snatch them back.

Julie, meek, three-year-old Julie with Jozefina's dark eyes and his own chestnut hair, barely whispered thank you when she took the bonbons he offered her. She'd back away and nuzzle her face into Victoria's skirt and would not eat until Victoria petted her head and told her it was all right to eat the candy.

He did not tell anyone about his mission. Realizing he could get killed in battle, he was glad for whatever time he had to make up for the mean ways he had treated everybody. He had an idea that his father had struck a bargain with God to give him this chance, so he had better live up to it. He insisted on washing the dishes after supper and then filling the washtub to bathe the children.

He spoke very little. It was easier for everybody if he just kept quiet. When he didn't have a chore to occupy him upstairs and save him from idle conversation, he retreated to the basement. He was sure his father would speak to him directly soon, and it would happen down there. Evening after evening he waited, and when the voice did not come, he would tell himself that Ignacy must have some purpose in his silence. Yet he was steeped in a deep pool of longing.

Victoria did not know what to make of Casimir's change of heart. Where once she had refused to suspect anything wrong about him, now she was afraid to trust anything good. She wished she had someone to confide in. There was no one. Mrs. Stutzman next door was someone to speak with over the fence while hanging clothes, or over the porch banister on summer evenings while the children played in the yard. She was fond of faulting anyone who "aired their dirty laundry in public." So she discussed weather and favorite memories, never private troubles.

It was late January when Casimir received a notice to appear in Sunbury, the county seat, for a physical examination the first week of March. How would he ever stand the wait? Ah, he thought, there is one good thing about this. I'll get to celebrate Frank's second birthday on Valentine's Day. And Julie's is February something. She'll be four. Anna Chrissy and Felicia, both March 20th. There would be time for them, too, before he got shipped off. God really did have a purpose in making him wait.

On the morning of the physical, he dressed in his best suit. It was a mild, but misty day. It seemed to him that each tiny speck of moisture carried a balm that seeped through his skin, settling inside, in his heart, bringing him a great sense of peace.

When he sat down on the trolley, he noticed how comfortable the seat was. He wondered if the trolley company had guessed his mission and wanted to surprise him with the newly padded seats. Most comforting of all was knowing that the train he would take to Sunbury was not the Delaware & Hudson. The world was right. All except for Europe. And he would make the difference there.

His recruiting place turned out to be what served as a farmers' market on weekends. The smell of sweaty animals reminded him of the unwashed passengers who had sailed in the steerage section of that ship, sleeping night after night on the same dirty straw.

Casimir was not prepared for such a huge assembly of men waiting to be examined. Some of those wanting to fight could barely speak English and were not yet citizens. They pleaded with the clerks to give them a chance to sign up and help. Everyone seemed so tall, so massive. The babble of broken English and foreign tongues made him sweat. It was too much like landing at Ellis Island. The place was not only stuffy, but dark. The only light inside came from two skylights thwarted by dark gray clouds, and from six small, horizontal, rectangular windows high up on the walls. If those windows had been just a little lower, he might have charged toward one and dived right through it. At least a dozen men stood in line ahead of him. How could he last that long?

He felt a hand on his shoulder. "Don't worry," he heard his mother whisper in his native tongue, "I'm right here with you. Right behind you."

"And so am I," a man's voice said, also in Polish. It was the voice of Stanislaw Gombrowicz, the man his mother had married on Ellis Island. "And I sure am glad to have a son like you now."

"*Nie!*" Casimir screamed. He swung around and pounded his fists at the air as though beating a giant on the chest. "You are not my papa!" He had shouted in Polish.

All the babbling in the room stopped. Two doctors in white coats hurried down the line toward Casimir. They squinted at him and then looked at each other. "Come with us," one of them said, and led him to a small room containing only a dusty wooden desk and two wooden chairs. He sat down as he was told to, furious at himself for crying out like that, furious at his mother for showing up, and worse yet, for bringing that new husband of hers along. The older doctor dragged the other chair over and sat in front of Casimir. He took a tongue depressor and held it straight up. "Now watch this stick when I move it. No, no. Don't move your head. Just your eyes. Yes, yes, like that."

Then the doctor took out his pocket watch and unhooked the chain from his belt. He raised the watch and made it swing from side to side, saying, "Follow this with your eyes."

Casimir tried to follow. He wished the doctor would swing it more slowly. He felt his eyes snag along the path of the swinging watch, as if they had to leap over invisible hurdles. The doctor exchanged a serious look with his colleague. Casimir expected one of them to take a piece of chalk from his pocket and make a strange mark on his sleeve, the meaning known only to them. Then they would laugh between themselves when he left the room. Anyway, what was the idea of making him stare at the watch? Had they guessed he kept his father's watch hidden in the basement? Were they going to tell him he wasn't fit to join the United States Army, and taunt him with the watch, hinting cruelly at the decision they were about to pelt him with?

"What's your name?"

"Charles Turek. Charles Patrick Turek."

"Who were you yelling at out there?" They spoke as if talking to a little child who had just spent a half hour in the corner to ponder what he had done wrong.

"Nobody. I mean somebody, but nobody. Oh, you know what I mean. Thinking out loud. Daydreaming a man. Only nothing."

"What language was it? Russian? Polish? Lithuanian?"

"English. I know it. Put I before E, except after C, or when sounded like A, as in reindeer or weigh. I know it, see? I was born in Nebraska. Loup City with my parents. But my birth certificate was lost in a fire. My baptismal certificate, too. I was born here. All I know is English."

"I see. Well, you just go back into the assembly room and get back in line for the general physical."

"Really? Back in line?"

"Yes."

During the weeks of waiting for the Army's decision, Casimir could hardly keep up the kindness he had begun toward his family. He knelt by the furnace every evening, asking Ignacy to give him the strength to be nice to everyone. He made a small wooden altar, which he covered with doilies he had taken from the parlor chairs. Then he took the wrapped watch and the paper with his sisters' address and stored them on the shelf beneath the top of the altar. He slipped into Saint Hedwig's church one evening, removed a half dozen votive candles from the tray in front of the statue of Saint Joseph, and put six fifty-cent pieces through the coin slot. For sure, when the priest found them among the penny offerings he'd know it wasn't an outright theft and wouldn't have him arrested.

Each night he lit one candle for seventeen minutes (Ignacy had died on the seventeenth of the month), timing the flame with Ignacy's watch. While the candle burned, he asked his father to help him be a good husband and father and to give him the strength to carry out his mission in Europe. If it wouldn't be too much to ask, would he mind speaking aloud just this once? If not, that was okay. Casimir would accept that it just wasn't the proper time. When the seventeen minutes were up, he blew out the candle, closed the watch, kissed it like a relic, and put it away, fortified for the next day's efforts at kindness.

He still spoke very little. But the words he did say were always respectful. It seemed to him that the children had begun to trust him again. If he died in Europe, he would be remembered as a good husband and father, like Saint Joseph.

It took a whole tormenting six weeks for the United States Army to send him a notice. He picked up the letter and ran right from the post office to the slagpiles, running with one hand in his pocket as he dug for a penny, barely able to resist tearing open the envelope on the way. He squeezed the penny hard as he scrambled up the embankment and ran across the summit till he reached a place where the slagpiles met the trees on the adjoining hill. He sat down on a rock and slapped the penny onto the back of his left hand. It was face down. He cursed the penny. Then he cursed himself for being so foolish as to put his faith in a stupid coin.

He opened the letter. Not fit to serve, it said. The news left him numb. He could barely feel the rock beneath him. He stood up and looked behind him to see if it had disappeared, somehow leaving him to sit suspended on air.

Rain came down, at first in a fine mist, then in big, slow, heavy drops. The letter drooped in his hands, but he could not feel the wetness of the rain, only light, airy taps. The wind picked up. The leaves of a quaking aspen rattled like the little tin discs in the Hungarian boy's tambourine—"Shhhame, shhhame, shhhame."

20

I WON'T LET ANYTHING HAPPEN TO YOU

Casimir checked every inch of the basement. He crawled along the floor, poking his fingers between the rocks in the walls. He climbed on crates and barrels, inspecting the ceiling beams. Someone must have interfered with his mission. Had someone defiled the altar? The doilies were still in place, the candles still there. The red cloth with his papa's watch and his sisters' address were still on the shelf below. He had done everything right. Someone else had ruined his mission.

It must have been Victoria. Somehow she had tampered with things. And what a fool she was to do it! She might have been rid of him. Yes, she'd like to be rid of him. She wasn't at all moved by the help he had been giving her with the children since Christmas.

With bitterness, he sat on the bottom cellar step, reviewing the parting scene he had rehearsed. He uttered his announcement that he must leave to serve his country, meaning Poland, but knowing she would take his words to mean the United States. He would kiss her and each of the children. They would all walk to the trolley together and take it with him to Mt. Carmel, waiting solemnly with him for the train to Harrisburg or Philadelphia or whatever city he would be ordered to for his induction. The train would be the Reading or the Pennsylvania Railroad, the New Jersey Central or the Lehigh Valley. Anything but the Delaware & Hudson.

She must have done something. He searched the cellar again. What was different? How clever she was to hide her tracks so well. All the same, he knew she was the one. She had defiled the sanctuary and made it displeasing to his papa, made him think her husband wasn't good enough to partake in the mission to piece Poland back together. Had she convinced his papa her husband was really an American? Born in Loup City, Nebraska? Whatever she had done, he was going to be stuck here in America, while Anna and Krystina, those smug know-it-alls, created a new Poland for Papa. "I should just go jump in front of the Delaware & Hudson," he muttered.

"No," his mother's voice said. "Don't destroy yourself."

"I'm already destroyed, thanks to you. You and your big mouth in Sunbury. You and Stanislaw."

"It wasn't Mama's fault," a different female voice said. It spoke in Polish.

"Who's there?"

"Krystina. Me and Anna. I told you we would visit you in spirit."

"You waited too long. Go to hell."

"Casimir, listen. Victoria was down here rooting around the minute you went out the door. It made Papa angry. She went to Sunbury to warn you. Stanislaw went along to help."

"So Victoria *was* down here! I'll make her pay! I won't give her a minute's peace."

"Casimir, wait!" his mother's voice said. "Listen! Don't—"

"Shut up, Mama."

He paced the dirt floor, devising means of torment. He decided that this would be his last night of kindness. The morning mine whistle would be the signal to start his campaign of revenge.

When the whistle blew, he whisked the blankets off of Victoria, dragged them out to the hall, and threw them over the banister on his way to the back room, where Frank and Julie slept. He burst into their room, shouting, "Hello! Good morning!" He marched in a military goose step. "Up, up, time to get up! Up, up, time to get up!" He slid back the bolt lock high up on the door to the porch overlooking the back yard. Then he yanked the children's covers off and threw them down into the yard, chanting, "Up, up, time to get up."

Victoria scooped Julie from her bed and went for Frank, who was reaching for her with one hand and gripping the side of his crib with the other. He couldn't seem to let go when she lifted him over the side. She had to set Julie down and peel his fingers from the bars.

Casimir ran past them into the middle room, where Anna Chrissy and Felicia slept, repeating the same march and shouts, throwing their blankets down the stairs.

He did this every day until the children got up on their own when the whistle blew at five. They ran down and huddled by the johnny stove in the chilly late-spring morning. Casimir shouted up the stairs, "Your children are up and ready for breakfast. Get down here and fix them something!"

Victoria, coming down the stairs, said, "I know they're up."

"And just think, Victoria, nice and early every morning now. No more quiet cups. A coal-miner husband and his lunch bucket."

Victoria ushered the children to the table and kissed each one on the top of the head. As she cooked oatmeal, Casimir dragged a chair over, climbed up on it, and kissed her on the top of the head.

When she turned to reach for a pair of potholders on the wall, Casimir tipped over the pot. He stooped down and marveled at the patterns of oozing oatmeal that worked its way across the plates of the stove and down the front. He beckoned the children. "Look, children, come! Nifty designs!"

Victoria stooped down. "Charlie, what's the matter with you? Why are you doing this to us?"

"Oh, so we're back to Charlie now. No greenie name?"

"Is that why you're doing this? Because I call you Casimir?"

"Greenie, greenie green. He maketh me to lie down in green waters." Casimir took his lunch bucket from the cabinet. He stuffed it with things from the ice box and shelves. He stuffed his pants pockets, stuffed his coat pockets, took a burlap sack from the bin and stuffed that. He grinned, "Mighty hungry, those rats in the mine."

Casimir began giving Victoria less and less of his pay. By July, he gave her no money at all. If she wanted groceries, she could buy at the corner store on tick, he told her, and maybe he would pay the bill at the end of the month. Maybe, maybe not. She bought on tick till mid-September, when Mr. Jackson told her he was sad to say she'd have to make some payment before he could give her more on tick because her husband had not paid anything.

One evening, in his usual habit, Casimir went into the kitchen to pick up the lids from the pots and smell what was cooking. There was one cast-iron pan on the stove. Casimir found it empty.

"So, what's this?" he said, swinging the pan.

She stood with her arms folded. "Our supper."

"Our supper."

"We're down to flour and water, a cup of sugar, apples, and carrots. No more tick at Jackson's store. You didn't pay."

Casimir swept the pan across the pots and pans hanging on the wall, sending them crashing and bouncing in all directions. The children ran in from the parlor and huddled by the cellar door. Casimir threw his arm around Victoria's head and grabbed a fistful of her hair. He yanked her face toward his and hissed, "No more tick at Jackson's store. Tick-tock, tick-tock! You just find somewhere else to get tick."

Victoria, aware of the children watching, put her arms around Casimir and kissed him.

"We heard the crash," Anna Chrissy said. Her voice was thin, warbling. "We thought you were fighting."

"No," Victoria said. "We weren't fighting. I tripped and knocked some pots off the wall." Her whole body trembled beneath the calm shell she presented to the children. She slipped from Casimir's arms and stooped down to pick up a pot. She had to press her knee against it to stop it from wobbling in her hand. She made her voice sound cheerful, almost musical. "Say, children, I was just going out to the store. Here," she said, taking their jackets from the wall pegs. "Play in the yard till I come out. We'll all go."

Casimir wagged his head and mocked her in a high voice, "Play in the yard till I come out. Play in the yard till I come out." He clasped his hands in mock delight as the children walked cautiously by him and out the door, their jackets only half on. "Ah, Papa plays with children," Casimir said, reaching for his coat.

Victoria blocked his way. "Let them alone."

"So let them alone, and they'll come home, wagging their tails behind them."

Victoria closed the door after the children and remained standing in front of it. "You need a doctor," she said, fearing he would strike her for saying it.

"'Oh, Doctor Skin-and-Bones, my wife makes me sick.' Should I tell him that? I don't need a doctor! Especially not that skinny company doctor."

"A priest, then. I don't know if you're sick or just plain cruel and evil. Some of both, I think. Some of both."

"Father Company-Man? Shall I go see him? Everybody knows who butters his bread."

"I don't care what doctor, what priest. Find somebody to stop you if you can't stop yourself."

Casimir lunged toward Victoria. She pulled up her shoulders, turned her face toward the wall. He reached past her and grabbed the doorknob. "I'll see a goddamned doctor. Then he'll tell you what's what. Maybe he'll put *you* away." He went out to the porch, picked up a bucket, ran back in with it and threw it at the johnny stove. It came flying back at his feet. He thrust it into Victoria's arms. "Scrub that coal dirt out of the rug." He went out. He walked toward the Ebony Gem and climbed up the slagpiles. He paced up there until it was dark. A doctor. It was happening then. His mouth was making that crazy O. In his sleep it had to be, when he couldn't check in the mirror to make sure his lips were straight. Victoria must have seen it in the moonlight coming through the window. What if she brought that skinny doctor to the house in the middle of the night to see it for himself?

He got an idea. He went to Sam's and asked for a whole bottle of scotch. "A big, fat bottle," he said. He swished a swig around his mouth before swallowing it. Then he took the bottle and left for Dr. Kirk's office, gargling scotch and spitting it out as he walked. If he couldn't make the words come out right, the doctor would get a whiff of his breath and blame the hooch. So there, Victoria.

Doctor Kirk was just going up the steps of his front porch when Casimir reached the house. "Doctor, wait, please!"

The doctor, his medical bag in his hand, turned around. "Is this an emergency? I just got back from delivering a baby. I haven't had supper. Can it wait?" He tried to make out Casimir's face.

"It's me, Charlie Turek. I just need a minute." He made a show of staggering and downed a swig of scotch.

"Come back tomorrow, when you're sober."

"Please, only a minute give me. My wife. Something's wrong with her. She lost her balance tonight. She knocked all the pots off the wall. Scared the children. Scared me."

"She's probably expecting again. Some women get dizzy. Pass out, even." The doctor opened the door.

"No, wait. Her temper. It's way out of hand. Tonight, the bucket flying through the air, crashing off the stove. She's mad I can't keep buying things for her. Like before the children came along."

"You spoiled her."

"Spoiled her. Doc, I can't please her. Can't please her no matter what I do. More and more she wants. She ran up a big, big bill at Jackson's store. How can I ever pay it?"

Dr. Kirk took the bottle from Casimir's hand. "You won't pay it by spending your money on this stuff. Get hold of yourself. And put your foot down on that woman. I don't know why you came here. I'm a doctor, not a priest."

"Yes, Doc. I'll talk to a priest." He headed for the rectory.

Victoria bought on tick at Genovese's store until she was told she could have no more credit unless something was paid on her bill. Then she moved on to another store, and then another, working her way to Mt. Carmel. Having no money for trolley fare, she walked, pulling Frank in a wagon. The girls walked alongside it.

Every night she asked her husband for money. Casimir liked when she begged him for it. Sometimes he'd throw a nickel on the floor. She'd pick it up and put it in her apron pocket. She had made a secret bank by snipping a few threads from the hem of her winter coat. She slipped every third nickel into that hem.

When she pleaded that they had four children to feed, he asked her how she'd like five. And would she rather have one from him or from Doctor Skin-and-Bones? He promised that some night he would come up and give her another child. One night he tore the sleeves off her blue velvet robe. He ripped the lining away and probed for a knife. He sat on the bed and kneaded Victoria's breasts, grinning. "Now see how you like me," he said, rubbing his stubbly face against hers. She did not resist him. Night after night he took her the same way. She did not get pregnant, something he thought a suitable punishment for spoiling his mission in Europe. "Did Doctor Skin-and-Bones do something to keep you from giving me my own son?"

"You did it, Casimir. You ruined me minutes after I had Frank."

"Doctor Skin-and-Bones' kid."

"Believe that if you want."

Casimir could see that, despite her brave, brazen look that Felicia copied so well, she was breaking down. A little quiver of the lip, a clenching of the fists when she thought he didn't see. Oh, but he did see. He was making her pay. She was feeling it.

He followed her around, chuckling, dragging the rocking chair, sitting on it and rocking wildly, banging his boots on the floor. He'd lean forward on the rocker, pat her stomach and grin. "Got any buns in that there oven? Skin-and-Bones buns, maybe? What's for lunch? Flour and water? No more stores to buy on tick?"

He had converted all his earnings into silver dollars. He jangled them in his pockets as he followed her around the house. One day he put the coins into a little cloth sack and attached a string to it. He dusted his shirt with the last bit of flour left in the house. "I'm a doctor," he said. "See? See my nifty white doctor coat? I run the whole world with my chalk." He scraped some flour from his shirt with his finger and drew circles and X's and squares on Victoria's sleeve. "Guess which mark means you're crazy."

Victoria went on cooking as though she took no notice of him. But Casimir watched the muscles in her throat, watched her swallow each scream. She didn't fool him. She was feeling it. He inserted himself between her and the stove and swung the sack of coins from side to side. "Follow this with your eyes."

Casimir stopped going to work. After the second absence, a breaker boy brought a letter saying he would be fired the next time he missed a day. Dressed in a suit, Casimir showed up at the mine yard the next morning, threw the crumpled note at the foreman, and said, "Keep your goddamned job!"

He strolled through the patch and strutted into his house, grinning as though he had just won some sort of prize. "Well, princess, I am now unemployed. What do you think of that?"

Victoria, who was scrubbing the kitchen floor, did not look up or answer. That evening, she served even smaller portions for supper. Casimir gobbled his share. Then he scooped Victoria's potatoes from her plate, shoved them into his mouth with his hands, and threw her plate across the room. Fragments bounced off the stove. He ran over to the cabinet and yanked out the drawer of utensils. Spoons and knives and forks flew out as he spun back toward his family. He raised the drawer above his head and slammed it on the table. The children shrieked and covered their faces. Their mother pulled their chairs away from the table. "Out to the back yard," she said. Casimir clanged a ladle against a frying pan behind her head as she ran out after them with their coats.

Victoria shooed the children into the shanty and locked the door. She bundled them in their coats, kissing and patting them as she guided them past the coalbin Jinx Evert had built for her. She led them out the back door into the alley. Lamps lit the main streets, but she made the children walk in silence through the dark alleys to the trolley stop. She dug the fare from the hem of her coat. When they got off the trolley in Mt. Carmel, she bought them cheese and apples, which they ate on the trolley ride back.

Instead of going home, she went to Dr. Kirk's office. Her knock went unanswered. She pounded on the door. The housekeeper opened it. Her weathered face was angry. She hoped it was a true emergency, for the office was closed and Dr. Kirk was at supper. What was the nature of the call?

"Please, just get the doctor." Victoria walked the children inside. Holding Frank, she told the girls to sit quietly on the bench in the hall while she talked with Dr. Kirk.

"I'm sorry, but you'll have to take them into the office with you," the housekeeper said. "I don't watch children out here."

"Nobody asked you to. My children know how to behave. I'll take the smallest one in with me."

The housekeeper went to the back of the house.

Victoria stooped down in front of Anna Chrissy. "You'll mind Felicia and Julie, won't you?"

Anna Chrissy nodded.

Dr. Kirk came down the hall, dabbing a napkin at his thin mustache. His look of annoyance turned to outright disgust when he saw Victoria. "Turek's woman," he said. "What is it?"

"Can we talk in your office?"

The doctor headed toward the examining room. Victoria sat Frank on her hip and followed him. Tears fell when she tried to speak. "It's my husband. He was a good man, but he's become so mean, cruel."

Dr. Kirk's look softened. "I'll ask my wife to watch your child so you can undress and show me where he hurt you."

"I can't show you. He doesn't hit me. He doesn't— He keeps all his money. He follows me around the house and—"

"Follows you around the house? A man's got a right to walk around his own house, Mrs. Turek."

She raised her hands to her face. Her fingers groped about her cheeks as though the words she was trying to find were there in Braille. "It's the way he follows—"

"Let me make sure I understand. He follows you around. Does—he—hit—you?"

"No. But he—"

"Well, then, you haven't been hurt, now, have you?"

"Yes, I have! My children have! If you saw the rage on his face, heard the filthy names he calls me—"

"Sticks and stones will break my bones, but names will never— Mrs. Turek, there are men who really hurt their wives. Let me tell you, I have women come in here to be patched up every other week. I've never seen *you* in here. But I've seen your husband. You've driven him to drink! The poor man can't please you no matter how hard he tries. I've been to your house. There's not a miner's wife from here to Scranton that wouldn't give her all for half of what you have in your house. And now you say your husband's cruel because he doesn't shower you with every penny since the children came along. And he gets angry sometimes. Who can blame him?"

Victoria stood up, holding Frank. She pressed her cheek against his head and swung him gently from side to side. "Oh, Franush, let's go. There's no help here."

She took the children out. Where, she asked herself, could she take them? What good was it to go home? He'd be sitting on that rocking chair, waiting to pounce on the first one in the door. If it was Anna Chrissy, he'd wave her homework in her face and make fun of her printing until she ran up the stairs in tears. He'd scream the highest note he could hit in Julie's face while she pressed her fingers in her ears and begged him to stop. He'd run after Frank, clapping behind his head until the child would stumble over something and hurt himself while looking back at his father, who'd scold him then for not watching where he was going. Felicia would keep a brazen face for as long as she could while her father banged a metal ladle against a pan right above her head. In time, she would cry. Victoria would be breathless from trying to step between each of the children and their madman of a father. How could she take them home to another evening of torment?

But where else could she go?

"I'm cold," Julie whined.

"Me too."

"Me too."

"All right. I'll take you home. But I want you to go into the shanty first, while I go in the house and see how your daddy is. Anna Chrissy, try to keep Frank quiet. Lock the shanty door with the bolt inside. Don't open it unless I say it's me, okay?"

"I'm scared," Julie said.

"I won't let anything happen to you."

21

IF TO BE HUNGRY

Victoria crept up onto the back porch. Peering over the cafe curtains, she saw Casimir asleep in the rocker. She led the children out through the back of the shanty, through the alley and to the street, so that the cinders alongside the house would not be crunched as she ushered the children to the front porch. They all tiptoed through the dark parlor and up the stairs.

The girls were halfway up, Victoria carrying Frank behind them, when Casimir rushed into the room, clanging two pot lids. "Yaa! Yaa! Yaa! Yaaaaa! I fooled you! Ha, ha! You thought I was asleep. But I saw you. The shanty, the shanty, to hide, ha, ha. Sneaking to the front. You can't. No. Come on, girls. Come down and sing with your daddy. We'll join hands. A circle. Then pee on the rug. Mama dabs it up."

Victoria set Frank down on a step and patted his rear end. "Upstairs with Anna Chrissy. She'll put you to bed." She sat down sideways, blocking Casimir's way.

"Move," he said. "Kisses good-night."

He tried to step over her. She grabbed his belt and pulled him down.

"Bitch! Whore! Tart! Miner's wife! Let go!"

Victoria, clenching the belt, said, "Children, run! Into the front bedroom! Lock the door. Hide the key!"

"Bitch! Teaching them to hate their father!" Casimir struggled to his feet and climbed over his wife. He ran up the stairs, Victoria behind him. The bedroom door slammed. The key turned. Casimir rattled the knob. Suddenly he turned and tore the pins from the braids wrapped on the crown of Victoria's head. He held the braids out like reins. "Whore! Whore! Whore! Whore! G'dyup, g'dyup, g'dyup! Make me something to eat. Ya, ya! G'dyup! Down to the kitchen. Make the coal-miner husband a meal."

Victoria let him drive her away from the children and down to the kitchen. He shoved her toward the stove, dragged the rocker up to her heels, sat down, and grinned.

Without a word, she made hotcakes and plain sugar syrup, all she could come up with, given the little left on the shelves.

Casimir clasped his hands behind his head and rocked in great swings as if trying to see how far forward he could tip without landing on his head. He hummed and grinned and whistled. "Ah," he said, "that's what I like, a little woman that goes about the kitchen with no talk."

When the meal was ready, he grabbed the plate from her as she was heading for the table with it. He remained on the rocker and put the plate on his lap. He pushed the rocker in circles with his heels as he chewed with his mouth open and smacked his lips.

Victoria sat at the table and stared at her feet.

Casimir licked the empty plate. "I noticed there's not much food, miner's wife. Guess you could use some money." He dropped the plate on the floor, stood up, and reached into his pockets, pulling out two fistfuls of silver dollars. "What's this! Money to give!" He shuffled toward the back door.

Victoria stood up. "Where are you going with that?"

"Follow me and see."

She followed him across the street to the school field, where he flung the coins in all directions. He dug into his pockets again and again. Victoria leapt at his flailing arms as he squealed and danced in the lamplight, scattering coins here, there, a shower of tiny stars.

Casimir laughed. "Some lucky little boys and girls will get real rich at recess tomorrow!"

Victoria picked up one, two, three, four silver dollars. Casimir dug the coins from her fists. He threw them over his shoulder. He dragged Victoria back to the yard and flung her onto the grass. "Children and kisses good-night," he said. "I'll break that door down."

"No! Let them alone!" Victoria ran past him into the kitchen and blocked the archway to the parlor. Casimir came in and stood grinning at her. Then he sat in the rocker.

Victoria remained in the archway. Every few minutes, Casimir would grab the arms of the rocker and pretend he was going to stand up and race past her. Victoria would jerk her body and press her hands tighter against the sides of the archway. He'd point at her, sit back with a smirk, and say, "Ha, ha. Fooled you, didn't I?"

After nearly an hour of this, Victoria began to feel a soft rumbling around her heart, something like the faint vibration of railroad tracks carrying the feel of an oncoming train. Her feet ached from pressing them into the corners of the archway. The muscles in her legs burned. Her wrists hurt. The rumbling spread through her whole body, which was wedged in the archway like a part of the house itself. Like a stressed support, it seemed about to bow and snap. She pulled the chair out from the end of the table, centered it in the archway, and sat down.

She felt Casimir staring at her from the rocker. She felt him watch her chin drop into her hands. Her eyelids fluttered. Her head tipped to one side, then the other. She felt as if her mind were whirling away like a top. I'm going crazy, she thought. I can't hold up anymore. I'm going mad. She covered her eyes.

Casimir stopped rocking and slid to the edge of his seat. Victoria watched him through her fingers. His chin was raised, his neck stretched, his eyes wide, his lips parted, his eyebrows rising in anticipation. He looked like a spiteful child watching his mother's favorite teacup totter on the edge of a table.

Seeing his delight, Victoria was suddenly filled with rage. It flared in her chest and rose to her face, burning away the weak, sick, floating-away feeling she was sure she was going to succumb to only moments before. She stood up.

"Sit down," he told her.

"I have work to do." She opened the utensil drawer and let Casimir watch her slip a knife into the pocket of her skirt.

Casimir smiled and began to rock in wide swings, stiffening his legs straight out, banging his heels on the floor. "Planning on slitting some chickens' throats?"

Victoria picked up the empty plate from the floor. "Do you want any more hotcakes?"

"No, whore, I don't. Why don't you run over to Dr. Skin-and-Bones' kitchen? See if he wants anything."

Victoria washed the dish and pan and pot in silence.

"My, oh, my," Casimir said. "The little tart washes dishes."

Victoria wiped the table and swept the floor. Then she slid the chair she had placed in the archway back to its place at the table. She stood in the archway, staring at her husband, her hand pressed over the knife in her pocket.

Casimir grinned and rocked slowly, flapping his elbows and making clucking noises like a chicken.

Victoria backed out of the room. She got the key she had hidden under the couch. She backed up the stairs and down the hall to the front bedroom, let herself in, locked the door, and lay on the floor by the bed, listening to her children breathe.

The next morning, when the colliery whistle blew at five, Victoria kept the children locked in her bedroom while she searched the up-stairs for Casimir. He was not there. She took a rubber ball from the middle bedroom and bounced it down the steps. She listened at the top of the stairs for several minutes.

She felt her way down in the dark. She stood still, listening. She lit the candle on the table at the foot of the stairs, raised it above her head, and looked all about the room. She looked behind the couch, behind the chairs. She listened at the cellar door and heard nothing. She looked around the kitchen.

She jammed the back of a kitchen chair under the cellar door-knob. After filling everyone's coat pockets with apples, she brought the children down and took them out to the back yard, where they took turns using the outhouse. Then they went into the shanty. Victoria opened the door to the alley and rolled the wheelbarrow and wagon outside. Sitting Frank in the wheelbarrow, she told the girls to take turns pulling the wagon. They went up Girard Street to the bush path alongside the railroad tracks.

In the moonlight they followed the tracks to the mine. A long trail of loaded coal cars waited to be pulled out by the locomotive. With rumors of a wildcat strike, the company, anticipating theft by families stocking up, had the train well-guarded. A two-coach train of Coal & Iron Police stood behind the coal train. Rifles held by uniformed guards stuck out at every window. Even the cook, his chef's hat tall and bright white, went about his work with a rifle strapped across his chest. Several guards paced alongside the coal train.

Victoria and the children hid quietly until the whistle of the coal train blew. The air brakes let out a loud hiss. Frank began to cry. Victoria covered his mouth and bounced him to silence as the guards who had been patrolling hurried into the passenger train.

Falling coal could be heard while the train swayed over a large section of switching tracks. "Coal," Victoria whispered to the children. "Spilling from the cars. Be quiet and listen for more."

After both trains pulled out, two Coal & Iron Police remained standing along the tracks. They looked in all directions. "All clear," one of them said. "Let's get some coffee before the place fills up with miners." They lowered their rifles, went through the mine yard and into the shanty office.

Victoria led the children from the bushes and told them to keep to the ground and fill their sacks with the coal along the tracks. She looked into the mine yard and saw some boulders at the bottom of the tracks that went up to the tipple. She went around to the side of the fence and looked in through the back window of the shanty. The men were sitting around a table drinking coffee and laughing.

She opened the gate just wide enough to slip through and scrambled, half crawling, half running, to the chunks that lay at the mouth of the mine. In the darkness, it was only by weight that she could tell which were rock and which were coal, the coal being far lighter than a rock of the same size. If she could wrap her arms around it and still budge it, it was coal. She managed to roll two big ones outside the gate before someone came out of the office. She pushed them into the weeds and beckoned the children to lie down next to her.

The man who came out of the shanty had a small cage with a canary that chirped as he carried it toward the double mine shaft. He opened the wooden gate to the left shaft cage and got in. Another man came out of the shanty and set the sheave wheels in motion, sending the cage rattling down the pit. The man at the controls, responding to the buzzing signals sent by the foreman below the ground, transported him from level to level.

The children helped Victoria push the coal boulders across the tracks and into the nearby mountain laurel, its firm, broad spokes of leaves full among the bare trees and briars. She heaved the sacks the children had filled into the wheelbarrow and sat Frank on top. Propping two white birch branches against the wagon, she created a pair of rails and rolled one big chunk of coal up the branches and into the wagon. She nudged the other chunk behind some thicker brush. "If we can't get back here before it gets light, we'll come back for that one tomorrow," she said. "Anna Chrissy, when we get home, let me check the house before you go in to get dressed for school."

She pushed the wheelbarrow, and the girls took turns with the wagon, one pulling while two pushed. They didn't last more than thirty or so yards. Pulling the wagon through the coal dirt was like dragging it through black sand. Victoria let them hide the wagon among the laurel. They smoothed over the wagon tracks. Then they walked alongside the barrow with their mother.

By the time they got back to Girard Street it was getting light. Victoria told the girls she dreamed some angels had come in the night and scattered silver dollars about the school field for them to buy food. She said maybe the dream had come true, that they should look and bring the money to the shanty. "We'll buy lots of food. Surprise your daddy. Don't tell him you found money, no matter what he asks. You mustn't spoil the surprise."

She left the wheelbarrow by the shanty and hurried back for the wagon, leaving Anna Chrissy in charge of the younger girls. She took Frank along. She pulled the wagon out from the bushes and started back. A group of miners on their way to the Ebony Gem saw her. "There's Charlie Turek's wife!" one of them said. She nodded and tried to hurry by.

Joe McDonald began to walk with her. The others stopped and waited for him. "I don't mean to mind your business," he said, "but I know Charlie ain't working and I wonder how I can help."

"You would help us?"

"We heard how he lost his temper, lost his job. Maybe he can get it back. You know, a lot of men signed up for the war. We're short-handed at the colliery. Maybe they'd overlook Charlie shootin' off the way he did—you know, give him his job back. We really need the help."

"He'd never ask for it back."

"I'll go to Mass at your church on Sunday. Talk to him a little afterwards. See if he'll let me ask for him."

"I have to warn you, he's not himself."

"A man out of work, of course he's not himself."

"No, no. Worse. I don't think he can manage anymore. You couldn't trust him with explosives, with anything."

"Oh, sure you can. Whatever's eating at him, he'll get over it. I've worked with Charlie down the hole. I'd put my life in Charlie Turek's hands any time. Don't give up on him. I'll meet you next Sunday after church."

Vladimir Urkov came over and stooped down by the wagon. He pinched the visor on Frank's cap and jiggled it playfully. "Nice boy," he said in a gentle, deep voice. He lifted the rag from his lunch bucket, pulled a carrot out, and placed it in Frank's hands. "For you, nice boy. So sorry if to be hungry."

When Victoria got back to the shanty, her daughters, their hands and pockets full of coins, danced up to her. She gave Anna Chrissy a silver dollar to take her sisters to the store with after school, to spend on anything they wanted, and she put the rest in her own pockets. "Wait in the yard till I put these sacks in the shanty." She went in and pried up a corner of the linoleum. She hid the silver dollars there and dumped coal over the spot. She took the apples from her pocket, wrapped them in her scarf, and hid them in the coalbin.

She asked the children to wait just a little longer in the yard. Then she went into the house and checked every room for any sign of Casimir before letting Anna Chrissy inside to get washed and dressed for school.

She fed the children hotcakes with sugar syrup for the fifth day in a row. Then she took them back out to the yard. As soon as Anna Chrissy crossed the street to the school, Victoria went into the shanty. She sighed, picturing the task she had set for herself. Already she felt tired. Already she felt envious of the women who would glean their small pieces of coal from the culmbanks that morning and every morning, maybe taking a crack with a carpenter's hammer at an occasional piece too big for their stoves, while she would have to take a sledge hammer to the coal boulders she brought back from abandoned bootleg mines, small caverns dug out of hillsides.

Tears and bitter laughter burst forth together as she remembered girlhood dreams of being carried away from the coal region by some handsome, pitying stranger. Now, not even twenty-five, she felt like an old, bent widow as she stared at the mound of anthracite that was to save her and her children.

She pushed a boulder of coal to the center of the floor, picked up the sledge hammer, and brought it down hard.

"What's this?" Casimir said, having appeared in the doorway behind her. "Bootlegging coal, are you?" He bent down and picked up the black nugget that had come to rest against his shoe. He bounced it in his hand like a toy. There were striking dark circles under his eyes, which were fixed wide with fear, despite his smile.

"Yes, I am," she said softly. She brought the sledge hammer down on another lump of coal. Casimir laughed and said, "Huh, at that rate, you'll be here till Christmas making your first wagonload."

She didn't answer, but struck another blow at the coal.

"And who will buy your little wagonloads?"

"All the grocers from here to Mt. Carmel, all the ones we owe money to."

"Ah, Saint Victoria, Honest Abe, paying her debts. Saint Abe! You think they'll buy your two-bit wagonloads? Can I watch you beg: 'Please oh please oh please, buy these!'"

"If you want."

"If you want, if you want. La-di-da-di-da, if you want. I'm hungry. Make the coal-miner husband some breakfast."

Victoria put down the sledge hammer and left the shanty, Casimir following right behind, his mouth on her ear, saying, "La-di-da-di-da. Honest Abe. Cannot tell a lie. Yes, Father Kashnoski, I did chop down that chunk of coal."

He ignored the children as he followed Victoria through the yard to the kitchen. "You know, Abe, there's an abandoned bootleg mine on the side of Manley's Mountain. Taps right into the Mammoth Vein. Honest to God, Honest Abe, Saint Abe, there is. Jinx Evert used to bootleg it. Got blackdamped to death. No canaries. Dumb bastard. Good name for him, Jinx."

"I have that pit in mind, don't worry."

"Hotcakes," he said when they reached the porch.

While Victoria was fixing his breakfast, Casimir pretended to be cracking coal, saying, "Wwwwwhack," with each thrust of his arms. When he tired of that, he pretended to be a newspaper reporter doing a story on Victoria, writing on the table with his finger. "'Hard-Coal Abe Rolls Up Sleeves and Digs into Hard Work.' How's that headline? Ha, ha. 'Hard-Coal Abe Rolls Up Sleeves—' No, wait! Not sleeves—skirt. 'Hard-Coal Abe Rolls Up Skirt to Pay Grocery Bills.'" He went into a long, knee-slapping laugh. Then with no explanation, he stood up and headed for the back door.

Victoria rushed ahead of him, opened the door, and told the children to come inside.

"Afraid the coal-miner husband bites children?" Casimir said.

Victoria spoke softly. "Hurry, children! Come inside."

When the children reached the door, Casimir got down on all fours. He growled and snapped at them like a mad dog. He hooked his finger in the back of Julie's boot. She fell flat, her voice a wretched squeak as her chest hit the floor. She twisted around, pleading with her wide, brown eyes.

Casimir grinned and wrapped both hands around her ankle as Victoria tried to lift her. Julie threw her head back and looked up toward the ceiling. "Dear Jesus, please! Make my daddy stop!"

Casimir looked up at the same spot. He felt a rush of self-contempt, of hatred for his own brazen defiance as he found himself going after Julie all the more, grabbing her leg, her skirt, her braids. She screamed one long scream.

Casimir silently begged Jesus to help him stop, but his hands only tightened their grip. He heard a train whistle and said, "It's now my heart, chug CHUG, chug CHUG, chug CHUG, chug CHUG, chug CHUG. It's too big. Too late. A locomotive!"

Still gripping the child's ankle, he pressed his lips against his hands. "Make me stop, Saint Joseph," he whispered. Then he shouted, "I'm tired! I went to the slagpiles at three this morning. I'm tired. Walking, walking, walking on the rocks. I'm tired."

"Dear Jesus, help!" Julie cried.

Casimir, pinching and twisting the skin on Victoria's wrist as she tried to peel his fingers from the little girl's ankle, wished she'd grab something—a chair, a pan, a bucket—something, and smash him over the head with it, knock him out, make him stop.

Suddenly, Julie, pulled free by her mother, ran to the parlor, wailing. Casimir slumped against the wall and sighed. "Julie, wait. I have something for you. I'll get it." He opened the door and called to her over his shoulder. "Don't go away, Julie. I have something for you." He went to the school field. Victoria watched from the window as he crawled along the ground in search of the silver dollars. He stood up and pulled his pockets inside out. He looked confused and sad, as if he were about to cry. He sat on the ground and shook his head. He said nothing about the money when he came into the house, but sat on the rocker in the middle of the kitchen, silent and brooding, rocking slowly, nodding, jerking awake, then nodding, nodding, until he was in a deep sleep.

He dreamed he was sitting on the slagpiles. At the Ebony Gem below him, he could see a train parked, thirteen coal cars behind the engine. The engine was marked, LEHIGH VALLEY, the coal cars, PENNSYLVANIA. Behind the last one was a brown passenger coach with the words PHILADELPHIA & READING COAL & IRON POLICE painted in dull green letters, and behind that, a red caboose with no lettering at all. A pair of hands parted the bushes near the caboose. Two uniformed officers stepped out and held the bushes apart like curtains. Victoria, carrying Frank, was pushed out into the clearing. An officer stepped out behind her, his rifle at her back. He shoved her with the butt of it, and she stumbled a few more yards. Then three Coal & Iron Police, each dragging one of Casimir's daughters by the hand, stepped from the bushes. The officers made the family climb into an empty coal car, the thirteenth and last one. The prisoners sat on the floor of the car. Their arms were stretched wide, their hands tied to metal hooks on the sides of the car, as if they were being crucified. Casimir ran down from the slagpiles and jumped aboard the train. One by one he tore rifles away from the officers while dodging bullets from others. The train chugged faster, and officers from the passenger car, an almost endless line of them, came out and leapt over the couplings. They grabbed at Casimir as he tried to untie his family. He fought off every one, tossing them out of the car.

When he finally rid the car of the last officer, he looked toward the engine and saw that the other coal cars had disappeared. Behind him, the passenger car was gone. The caboose had disappeared. Only his car was attached to the engine. The lettering on the back of the engine now read, DELAWARE & HUDSON.

The engineer, whose face, stubble and all, looked exactly like Casimir's, turned around and grinned at him through the window as the train reached the crest of a mountain. The grin gathered itself into an O. The eyebrows twitched in mockery.

Suddenly, the engine vanished. The coal car that held him and his family started down the steep hill alone. Wired to the front of the car was a round indicator with smudged glass over the face. It showed the speed to be forty-five miles per hour, moving to fifty, to sixty.

Ahead, at the bottom of the hill, on the same tracks, a trolley had stopped to load passengers, frail old women and crusty miners bent with age and broken backs. Leaning on canes, they inched themselves up the two steps of the trolley.

The wind whistled in Casimir's ears. His wife and children, their hands still tied to the sides of the coal car, looked up at him, their eyes begging him to help. He searched for cables or pedals, anything that might bring the car to a halt. The indicator was on ninety-five, the trolley only yards ahead. He raised his eyes to the heavens, screaming, "How do you stop the train?!"

He saw St. Joseph glaring down at him from behind a cloud, his eyebrows dipped in disapproval.

He leapt from the rocker and grabbed Victoria's shoulders. "How do you stop the train? Tell me!" He fell against her, weeping, scraping his fingers down her dress as he slid to the floor.

22

AND THE SOUND OF A VOICE THAT IS STILL

Break, break, break,
On thy cold gray stones, O Sea!
And I would that my tongue could utter
The thoughts that arise in me.

O, well for the fisherman's boy,
That he shouts with his sister at play!
O, well for the sailor lad,
That he sings in his boat on the bay!

And the stately ships go on
To their haven under the hill;
But O for the touch of a vanished hand,
And the sound of a voice that is still!

—TENNYSON

The Delaware & Hudson would not let up. Its bell clanged at Casimir's back as he ran down to the cellar. Its whistle pitched to a scream. He clasped his hands behind his head and pressed his arms against his ears. Someone was hollering, "Charlie!" He looked up and saw Victoria standing in the doorway to the kitchen. He shook his fist at her. "Don't come down here!"

He charged up at her. She slammed the door. He ran down, got five nails, hammered them alongside the door, and threaded rope around the heads and across to the doorknob several times.

The engine quieted a little, but it lurked nearby, breathing its steam. Oh, if it would only stop! He grabbed his four-foot auger and hurled it through the invisible window of the locomotive. The chug-ging grew louder, mocking him.

If only his papa would speak to him. He could tell him how to stop the train. Somewhere in this basement Ignacy was waiting for the right time to speak. Casimir was sure of it. The thing to do now was spend all his time in the cellar, listening.

He hung four chains from the beams and threaded them through four holes he drilled in a board with a miner's drill. He made a mat-tress of a sack of rags and lay listening, listening for that voice. With the engine chugging constantly, sleep was a consolation almost entirely lost to him. The only way he could make himself doze off was to take a fire poker into his beambunk, press the tip against the furnace, and set the bunk to rocking.

Except to go out to the outhouse, he would not leave the base-ment. He would not eat supper with his family. Victoria would set his plate by the door at the top of the cellar steps. He'd remove the ties, take his plate, tie the door shut, and eat on the top step. He'd eat lifelessly, picking up one pea or bean with his fingers, holding it like a stone he had absent-mindedly picked up and forgotten.

One night while he was eating, Anna Chrissy knocked and called, "Daddy?" He did not answer. After a while, she knocked again, but said nothing. She slipped a sheet of paper under the door. Casimir heard her run through the kitchen and out the back door to the porch. She reminded him of a miner slipping a squib into a newly-drilled hole, lighting the fuse, and then scrambling like hell down the man-way into the gangway, waiting for the charge to blow.

He took the paper downstairs and unfolded it. It was a drawing, a simple drawing of a flower, a plain circle surrounded by petals. A plain leaf protruded from each side of the base of the stem. "Anna Chrissy" was printed on the bottom.

The next night, as he was rocking in his bunk, he heard a sheet of paper come through the crack under the door with a quick whoosh. It fluttered down the stairs like a falling leaf and landed by the furnace, face down. Like a bad-news penny, Casimir thought. He heard his daughter run across the kitchen and stop near the door to the back porch. He could picture Anna Chrissy, still as a statue, listening, waiting for him to look at it, waiting for him to do something after he saw. Now he heard slow steps coming toward the cellar door.

Tears came to his eyes. "Oh, what use am I? What use!" He jumped out of the bunk and picked up the paper. It was a drawing of a stickman holding hands with a stickgirl in a scallop-edged skirt. The heads were perfectly round, obvious tracings around a penny. Casimir knew the pennies had to have been face down. Dots did for eyes and noses. But the mouths were toothy crescent smiles so big that they poked beyond the penny faces.

Casimir knelt down and pressed the paper to his chest, crumpling it, weeping.

The next night, as he was eating supper on the top step, Anna Chrissy slipped him a drawing of a stickman, a stickwoman in a triangular skirt, and four stickchildren standing between them, all holding hands, all smiling oversized smiles. The beams of a big fat sun stretched to touch them.

This time Anna Chrissy did not run away. Casimir placed his fingers by the space at the bottom of the door. He could feel her breath. He jerked his hand back when the tips of four small fingers slid through. They groped along the wood, tapping gently. Casimir got to his knees. He reached toward his daughter's hand, his own floating just above it, tracking its every movement. Oh, if only he could touch her! A tightness gripped his heart. He clenched his fists and pounded them against his temples.

He ran down the stairs and put the drawing into a sack hanging from a nail in a beam. Maybe I should be hanging there, he thought. He rolled a barrel over to a spot where a knothole in one beam was wide enough for threading a rope. When the noose was in place, he lit a votive candle at his little altar. It took five matches to get the damp wick going. He climbed up on the barrel, slipped the noose over his head and looked around, waiting to hear something before tipping the barrel. If his papa cared at all, he would have something to say about this. He might even think it was the right thing to do. Casimir's eyes turned to the altar. The candle had gone out. That must mean something. He flung the noose away and jumped down.

The Delaware & Hudson chugged behind him as he went to the altar and knelt. He tried to steady one hand with the other as he held a match to light the wick of a new candle. It was slow to catch the flame only because it was damp. But Casimir took this to be a sign that his father was angry. After a while, remembering the glaring Saint Joseph in his dream, he decided that Saint Joseph was mad at him, too. Was it because he had stolen the candles from the tray before his altar in the church? He had put money in the slot for them, much more than they were worth. Didn't that make it right?

"I had to take them from your altar. You were the head of the Holy Family, weren't you? I thought Papa, being head of our family, you know, well, it seemed to fit. I thought it would make him talk to me. But if it makes you mad, I'll bring them back. And you can keep the money besides." He put the unused candles into a sack with the empty glass cups from the candles he had already burned. He draped the strings of the sack over the knob of the door that went directly outside. He would take them back the next day.

He slept on the cold, dirt floor as a penance for having stolen the candles. In the morning he looked around to see if there might be anything else displeasing to his father or Saint Joseph. He tidied up the place, making nice even spaces between his miner's tools leaning against the wall. He dusted the tools, the barrels, the tin tub, everything. He took the doilies off the altar and shook them outside, spacing them evenly when he replaced them.

To continue his penance, he went without breakfast, without lunch. In the middle of the afternoon, he took the sack of candles to the church, the Delaware & Hudson chugging after him. He went to the altar of Saint Joseph, leaned over the rail, and set the sack under the candle tray. He had no money to light a candle while he prayed to Saint Joseph, and he wondered if there was any use in praying then. He tried closing his eyes and waiting for a sign of approval.

"Charlie," he heard a man whisper. It couldn't be his papa. Ignacy would never call him Charlie. Casimir began to tremble. He didn't dare open his eyes. "You did the right thing, bringing the candles back," the voice said.

"Who is it? Who's talking to me?"

"Saint Joseph. Be still and listen."

Casimir folded his arms on the railing and pressed his forehead to them, humbling himself as best he knew how.

"Charlie, do you want the train to stop?"

"Yes," he whispered.

"And your father. You want to hear his voice. You've waited a long time."

"Yes."

"You'll find him in the coal mine."

"The Ebony Gem?"

"Yes. Breast Number Six."

"The one I worked with Joe McDonald. That one? It's all mined out now. All boarded up. That one?"

"Yes. Put on your miner's clothes. Blacken your face and hands before you get to the mine yard. Get ready tonight. Spend the night on the slagpiles. Show up tomorrow when they bring the mules up."

"Then what?"

"You'll know what to do."

"How? How will I know?"

"You'll feel right."

"Feel right? How!"

He heard no reply. He didn't know whether to open his eyes, be still, or what. Suddenly he was aware of an aching in his chest. It felt as if something had reached inside, clamped around his breastbone, and begun pulling him, pulling him. Somehow it seemed to have been there all along. But now it was pulling with all its force. He thought it would pull him right over the altar rail. He pushed against the rail with both hands. He was pulled forward with a terrible yank. But the thing lost its grip and almost sent him reeling backwards. He was free. Uncoupled, he realized, as he heard the Delaware & Hudson chugging away without him. He was free from its spell. He could rest in peace. He sank down onto his heels and pressed his forehead comfortably on his forearms, his wrists dangling over the altar rail.

After a while he felt that it was right to open his eyes. Right. You did the right thing, he remembered Saint Joseph saying. Right. How wonderful it felt to be right about something. He opened his eyes and saw the statue of Saint Joseph smiling down on him. He thought he saw the saint's green robe flutter, his light brown hair lightly lifted in a breeze that Casimir could feel sweeping across his own face now. Casimir smelled sea salt in the wind and the sweet smell of wild roses. Above the fading whistle of the Delaware & Hudson, he could hear water sloshing between wharf pilings and fishing boats. Papa must be nearby.

Casimir stood up and walked to the center of the altar rail. He opened the gates and let himself in. Then he walked over and kissed the feet of Saint Joseph, saying, "Thank you for giving me this sign."

It was not until he started down the aisle to leave that he noticed an old woman in a babushka kneeling in the last pew, saying the rosary, whispering her prayers aloud. He wondered if she had been watching him. Had she seen him put the sack of candle cups under the tray? Would she tell the priest he was the one? Oh, what did it matter? Let her tell. As he got closer to her, he realized she was praying her beads in Polish. Oh, you greenie, he thought. Learn English, why don't you? He chuckled and slid into the pew in front of her. He clasped his hands around hers and kissed her on the cheek. Then he skipped out to the vestibule, smiling to think how she must be twisted around staring at him.

He all but skipped down the street. The sun was bright and buds were swelling on the trees. He wished he'd run into Anna Chrissy. He'd whisk her into the air and kiss her all over the face and call her "Daddy's girl," like when she was very little. She'd like that. When she came home from school, he'd do that.

He walked up Saylor Street, nodding politely to neighbors. He took his shoes off on the front porch of his house, unlocked the door, and let himself in. No one was home. He went into the kitchen and looked out the window to the back yard. He could see that Victoria had constructed a miniature bull shaker for screening coal. She had hammered together some planks to make two chambers, one atop the other. The top one had a screen with larger holes, the bottom one a screen with holes small enough to let pea coal drop through. He could hear her smashing coal in the shanty.

The children, wearing blackened leather gloves, were working in the yard. Felicia was standing on an overturned bucket, rubbing her palms over the top screen, spreading the coal around, making the smaller pieces fall through the holes. Julie was rubbing the coal on the lower screen. They picked off all the chunks that were too big to drop through, and they put them in two wicker baskets alongside the shanty steps. Victoria came out. She took the basket with the large pieces back into the shanty, smashed them to smaller pieces, brought them back out and dumped them onto the bull shaker. She set the empty basket by the steps and went back inside.

The girls said, "Come on, Frank." Frank reached up and grasped the frame. The three children shook it as hard as they could, forcing the smallest pieces through to the bottom. Felicia and Julie each palmed their screens and emptied the larger pieces from the upper chamber. Then they helped Frank, who was scooping up the dust and slivers with a toy shovel and putting them into an ash can.

Casimir did not know why, but he got the feeling it was best not to let them see him. It was only for a moment that he was not sure what to do next, for though he could not actually hear Saint Joseph instructing him, he got a good feeling whenever his mind hit upon this or that idea, and he knew—he felt sure—it was right. It must be Saint Joseph guiding me, he thought. I must trust and keep trusting.

Miners, some with tools strapped to their backs, some gripping them or pressing them against their sides, were passing by on their way home from work, a little earlier than usual. They passed the gate and slowed down, looking into the yard as they walked along the fence toward the shanty. Some of them smiled at the children but exchanged sad and serious looks among themselves that made Casimir feel ashamed. They tipped their hats at Victoria when she came out to the step with another basketful of coal. She nodded and looked away quickly. Then she dumped the coal into the top screening bin.

Casimir heard Vladimir Urkov exclaim in that booming voice that erased any question of which dusty-faced miner he might be, "Oykhh! No good, such life!"

After the group moved on, Donny Wilson stayed behind, resting his arms on the fence. Casimir saw him reach for the coal shovel leaning against the fence inside the yard. The D-handle dangled from one rusty, bent side. Donny bent it back into its normal position at the top of the handle and seemed to be imagining it with the broken metal strip replaced. He unbuckled the belt that held the augers and shovel against his back. Then he lifted the broken shovel over the fence and replaced it with his own, which was almost new.

As he was strapping the broken shovel to his back, Julie noticed the new one. She jumped up and down and squealed, pointing. The others looked over. Donny greeted them with a grin and one big nod. Julie went over and hugged the new shovel, which was a little taller than she was. She dragged it into the shanty.

Casimir felt a flash of rage. What was that goddamned Donny doing helping Victoria? She didn't deserve help. She thought she was too good for everybody in the patch.

When Donny turned and began to walk away, Casimir grabbed the doorknob in an impulse to run after him, claim the broken shovel, and throw it at Victoria. He felt a stab of fear. Would he be punished? Would he not get to hear his papa's voice?

He'd better not go out there. He let his hand slide from the knob. He paced the kitchen floor, waiting to know the right thing to do. Suddenly, he knew he should dig up the key to the padlock he had put on the attic door. So he went to the basement and did that. Then he took the broom from the kitchen closet. He filled a bucket with soapy water and a few rags and took them upstairs. It was wrenching to make himself go into the attic where he had worked so hard, preparing it for Anna and Krystina. But he relied on Saint Joseph to give him the strength to face the ladies in gowns waltzing with their lovers on the wallpaper. He wondered if Anna and Krystina had found young men to dance with. Maybe they had married by now. Maybe they were dead. Maybe he'd get to see them tomorrow, too. It still angered him to think they got to fight the war for his papa and he didn't. He felt so bad at that thought that he was afraid Saint Joseph would get mad at him for getting angry with his sisters. Don't think about those things, he cautioned himself. Get to work here.

He dusted off the vanity dresser and swept and damp-wiped the floor. Then he went to the bedroom that Anna Chrissy shared with Felicia. He dragged the mattresses off the beds and hauled them to the attic. He carried up the springs and frames and put the room in order. The bed he had made for Patches sat in one corner. He took it down to the second-floor hall and set it near the top of the stairs.

He took Julie's bed apart in the back room and set it up again in the room that had been the older girls', remembering how she'd sigh like an old woman when Frank woke her with his crying at night: "Oh, I wish, I wish, I wish I had my own room," she'd say. So there it was, her own room. Casimir beheld it with delight.

He returned to the basement. He took Ignacy's watch and his sisters' address from the red cloth on the shelf under the altar, leaving the address laid out flat on his bunk by the furnace. He wound the watch and smiled, then went up and hid it under Victoria's pillow.

He left a note in Frank's crib: "A present for you under Mama's pillow. In red cloth. She'll keep it for you till you're big like me. It was your grandfather's. His name was Ignacy." Then he left a note in Patches' bed in the hall, saying, "Victoria, the children should have a cat."

He was pleased to see he had made the words come out on paper the good way. Not like a bunch of bouncing balls that made him feel frustrated and foolish as he watched Victoria try to make sense of them. Saint Joseph was fixing him, he could tell.

He walked through Frank's room and looked down into the back yard, where the children were palming another heap of coal through the screens. A very tall, thin woman with her hair tied in a kerchief stopped by the fence and called to the children. Her back was turned to Casimir, who could not guess, at first, who she might be. Must be a visitor from somewhere else. What patch woman would want to come anywhere near this house?

The woman handed the children a little sack. They threw their gloves on the ground, pulled out apples, and began to eat.

Victoria came out of the shanty and carried her basket of coal down one step before she saw the woman by the fence. Casimir was delighted with the look of embarrassment that sprang to Victoria's face. Felicia turned around and lifted an apple up toward her mother. Victoria stared at it as though she couldn't decide whether to take it. She twisted around and set the basket inside the shanty. She reached her hand toward the apple but still didn't accept it.

The woman at the fence nodded big nods, coaching her to take it.

Who the hell is that, Casimir wondered. Resentment wrapped around his heart. What's the idea giving Victoria food? Acting so friendly! Ah, he thought, I know who that is—Vladimir Urkov's woman, Vera! His mind flashed back to the Monday after the wedding when he returned all spruced up from the Hungarian boarding house to a long-winded speech about some miner's wife, some Vera Urkov, showing up to invite Victoria to pick coal.

Was this Urkov woman crazy? What did Victoria ever do for her besides tell her to get lost? Maybe Vera had confessed some terrible sin and Father Kashnoski sent her over to be nice to the princess as a penance. Or maybe—ah, yes, this was it—Victoria was pulling this bootlegging stunt to drag some pity from the people in the patch, putting struggling little children on display like that. Pretty clever, that princess, getting help for herself and shaming the father at the same time. That Urkov woman pitied the children. That's what was going on. She pitied them so much that she was willing to put up with Victoria to help the children.

Victoria was saying something to her, a sheepish expression on her face. But the longer the women talked, the more relaxed Victoria looked. Casimir saw her nod, and then Vera walked toward the porch and opened the gate.

Casimir's lips tightened. He'd put an end to this, all right. He opened the door to the high porch. "Hello, Vera Urkov!" he shouted.

The children ran into the shanty.

"Did she ask you yet?" Casimir said. He positioned both hands in such a way as to make it appear he was holding a bottle. Pressing one fist to his lips, he tipped his head way back, pretending to drink.

"Ask me what?" Vera said, shading her eyes as she looked up.

"For money. I heard her telling someone you'd be a good one to hit up for cash. Or maybe a few buckets of coal on your way back from the slagheaps. A real sucker with a big heart, she called you."

Victoria's face flushed. She shook her head fast and hard. "I never said—"

"She did so!" Casimir shouted. "She—" A train passing through the Joy Junction Station at the bottom of the mountain blew its whistle. "She— Victoria— She— The whistle blows and you wonder. She'll be at you for money or coal and—and you wonder if it's coming for you after all. So she comes out of the shanty, cracking coal, and makes the children screen it and clean it, hoping some sucker will come by to hit up, and before you know it, you hear that whistle just when you thought you were rid of it. She's got her eye on your purse right now."

"If that was my man," he heard Vera say, "I'd dump every drop of hooch down the sink."

"He's not drunk," Victoria said. "He's out of his mind."

"Sounds like hooch to me. Look! He's taking another swig right now! Look!"

Casimir dragged up a dollop of phlegm and spat over the banister. "Sounds like this! Sounds like that! La-di-da, you two." Another train whistle blew. Its scream filled the whole valley. Casimir ran back inside and slammed the door, a train chugging at his back. He crawled under Frank's crib, pulled his knees up to his chest, and pressed his fists over his ears. "I'm sorry I'm sorry I'm sorry I'm sorry I'm sorry I'm sorry…"

"That was the Delaware & Hudson," a man's voice said. "This is your last chance."

"Saint Joseph?"

"Yes. This is your last chance. I released you from that train at Saint Hedwig's today, and look what thanks you show. Why should I help you?"

Casimir rolled out from under the crib and rose to his knees. He bowed his head and covered his face. "I'm disgusting. I—I'll leave everybody alone. I promise." Tears trickled over his knuckles. "I won't do it again. I'll be nice. I'll get to hear Papa's voice. I will, won't I?"

"One last chance."

"Ohhhhh. God bless you, Saint Joseph!" He sat back on his heels and rocked in silence till he heard the voices of many children outside as the James Buchanan School let out. He got up and looked down into the yard. Vera had gone, but he did not permit himself to rejoice. Anna Chrissy was crossing the street, her canvas schoolbag hanging from her shoulder. She came through the gate, tossed her bag onto the porch, ran to the back of the yard and stooped down by the bull shaker, ready to pitch in.

Casimir wanted to call out to her, say he was sorry for everything, call her Daddy's girl. But he remembered the children running into the shanty the last time he came out to the porch. They were calm and happy just now. He should just leave them alone. That decision made him feel right again. Right. He was doing the right thing.

Victoria came out of the shanty. She gestured for Anna Chrissy to wait in the yard. Then she took off her grimy gloves and coat and started for the house. She left her boots on the porch.

Casimir met her in the kitchen. "You wanted to see how I was acting before you let Anna Chrissy in to change her school clothes."

"Yes."

"I won't be mean to her." He paced across the kitchen and looked out at the children. "They think it's fun, sorting the coal."

"For now."

"I'm sorry." He slapped his forehead. "God, what use am I?" He looked at his wife, who was standing across the room with her hands locked across her stomach. "Victoria, you're an angel."

She stared, motionless, expressionless, like one obliged to be still through an airy sermon before getting back to her real life.

"Yes, an angel. Remember when I came to your house for dinner in Dickson City? Your mother— 'Eat!' she hollered, when we gazed at each other. Some dream I pictured. Me cleaning the coal dirt off my boots on the porch. You beside me, smiling, supper inside. A little boy with yellow hair between us. But the Delaware & Hudson. The first time you saw me. There it was. I remember, now. You on the platform. Me, stepping out from behind that devilish Delaware & Hudson. Can you hear it? Doomed from the start, we were. And your father. He knew. He knew all along. It was his idea, that train. And now look. Your boots on the porch. Look whose face is filthy, sooty black. Look what a rotten life I made. But if you think *you* hate me, and the *children* hate me—" He walked over to the cellar door and looked in the mirror. "Well!" He laughed softly.

When he turned around, he thought Victoria's stare had softened a little. "You pity me, don't you, even after the miserable life I made here. You are an angel."

He took a key from his pocket. "This is for the padlock right here on this door to the cellar. If you don't trust me not to bother Anna Chrissy, lock the door after me. The only way I can get out is through the yard. You'd see me if I got out." He felt grateful that she did not hold an open palm out for the key, but let him set it on the table. "Don't put supper by the door for me. I don't deserve it."

He did not lift his eyes to her on his way to the cellar. He pulled the door shut after himself, stepping hard on each step so she'd hear him get to the bottom. Then he took his shoes off and crept back up listening at the door. He heard her slip the lock on and clamp it shut.

He went and sat on the bottom step. "Mama?" He heard no answer. She was probably at the Ebony Gem, too. He picked his sisters' address up from the bunk, slipped it between the buttons of his shirt, and pressed it against his chest. He lay down and pushed the poker against the furnace to make the bunk rock. He fell asleep waiting for instructions.

If he had dreamt anything, he did not remember it when he was wakened by footsteps overhead and the sound of chairs sliding at the supper table. He lay rocking in his beambunk, still waiting, hoping Saint Joseph would tell him what to do. Suddenly, his eyes fell upon the spot where he had buried Patches. He hated himself for never having put some kind of monument up for her, a little stone with her name. Mercifully, his attention was drawn away, and he felt directed to pack up his tools, and then his bunk blankets, which he put into a burlap sack. He took Anna Chrissy's drawings from the sack hanging from the nail, and without looking at them, slipped them into the sack with the blankets.

He left his sisters' address on the bare boards of the bunk for Victoria to find. He was doing all this on a hunch, unable to explain any of these behaviors, even to himself, until he felt something like a cold hand press against his heart and stop him from making another move until he figured it out. I'm packing up and putting things in order like a man who might never come back, he thought. "A man who will never come back," he said aloud. "Ain't I?"

His eyes searched every corner of the basement, as he waited for an answer. They all knew, all of them—Saint Joseph, his mother, his sisters, his father. They knew all along, and no one had the heart to tell him. They just prompted him somehow, in silence, knowing the moment would come when he'd get the picture. He felt sad for himself, deeply mournful. His eyes burned with tears. Then he lashed himself with ugly memories of his hateful ways. Who was he to ask anyone to spill tears for him, even himself?

Thoughts from his own memories, guilts, loves, vows, hates, joys overwhelmed him like arrows shot from all directions as fear of his end overtook any promise that seemed to direct his actions up until now. He tried to feel some control by doing some sensible thing. If this is the end, he must try to say good-bye. He must write a note. To put words in any kind of order seemed impossible. Words bounced about his brain like rubber balls. How could he ever manage it?

He paced the dirt floor till he got an idea. "Papa," he said. "I know you can hear me. Help me write. It's to Victoria, only devoted to you. I'll prove it! Here's what I'll do. I'll do all the letters in your name in capitals: I-G-N-A-C-Y. So, if a word in my note has letters from your name, like, 'sincerely yours,' I'll write, 'small s, then capital I, then capital N, then capital C, then small e-r-e-l, then capital Y, another capital Y, then o-u-r-s.' And you'll know. You'll know it's dedicated to you. Just me and you will know."

He waited to hear his father say something. Though he received no answer, he felt right. He managed to write the letter, steadying one hand with the other. Then he stole up to the top of the stairs, and slipped the note under the door and into the kitchen. He knocked on the door and hurried down the stairs. He heard a chair slide away from the table. A child's footsteps approached the door.

Quietly, Casimir slid the bolt back on the door to the yard, let himself out onto the stone steps, and pushed up the wooden bulkhead, just a crack, at first, enough to look out and make sure no one could see him. He stepped into the yard and crawled toward the gate. He knew that if he looked over the porch banister through the window, where the curtains were probably wide open, he would see the children sitting around the table. He imagined that the kitchen must be a bustle of talk and laughter without him there to spoil it. Happy with talk of the presents Anna Chrissy must have discovered when she went upstairs to change out of her school clothes. But if they saw him, their eyes would widen in dread of their father coming in to ruin everything. What kind of sight was that for him to carry away? He wanted to remember them screening the coal, happy. So he crawled, dragging his burlap sack, until he was out of the yard. He got to his feet, then, but bent over as he walked alongside the house.

As he neared the kitchen window, he asked Saint Joseph for the strength to resist looking through the small space where the cafe curtains were spread apart. He cupped his palm along the side of his eye, like a blinder on a horse. "Good-bye," he muttered, and walked on.

He felt right.

23

THE VIGIL

Anna Chrissy stood by the cellar door, holding Casimir's note. "Another letter! Another surprise for us! More presents, I bet!" She began to read, "'Dear Vic-tor—Victoria—' Mama, the letters are all mixed up. Capital ones and small ones. Look. See? Our teacher said not to do that. And this is so long. Will you read it?"

Victoria took the letter from her and read silently:

> deAr vICtorIA,
> I wIll mAke A stoNe IN the CellAr, If I Get bACk. If I doN't, mY sIsters Address Is there tell them I wIll sAY hello to fAther for them. GIfts Are for ChIldreN feed the New CAt. I pulled the boArds off ANd wAshed the floor for the GIrls. tell them kIss them, kIss frANk. Good-bYe, I thINk, If joseph sAYs. pleAse doN't reAd the Address. uNlessYou Are sure joseph told me to do It. You wIll fINd pAtches burIed IN the CellAr floor. doN't dIG, pleAse. I hAve to Go ANd lIsteN Now, so I kNow. Good-bYe. sAY I'm sorrY. vICtorIA, You Are AN ANGel. pleAse doN't wrIte CAsImIr oN the stoNe. I'm AshAmed of thAt boY. frANk Is Good.
> > sINCerelY Yours,
> > ChArlIe.

Victoria folded the letter. She closed her eyes and pressed it flat against her forehead.

"Mama, what's wrong? It's not about more presents, is it?"

"No, just the ones you already discovered. He wants to make sure you found the notes upstairs and the nice room he fixed for you."

"What else does it say?"

"It says he's going somewhere."

"On a trip? Where?"

"It doesn't say where. Come, sit down for supper. We'll talk about it more later. Maybe I'll know more tonight." Victoria put mashed potatoes, roast beef, and creamed corn on everyone's plate. A stone, she thought. His name on a stone. He expects to be dead. But he'll make a stone in the cellar if he gets back. What stone, then? What kind of patches did he bury? And who is this Joseph?

Julie smiled up at her mother. "I have my own room, now. My own, own room. Mama, can I lock it so Daddy don't come in and do mean, scary things?"

"Yes. I'll get you a key. And I'll have one in case you need me."

Felicia said, "What about us? Can we have a key for the attic so he can't tear our blankets off?"

"Yes."

"Good. Anna Chrissy, we can make a big, big tent up there with blankets!"

Victoria left her plate and went into the parlor. She opened her sewing basket and rummaged through the patches she kept for mending. Nothing seemed to be missing. What patches was he talking about?

She unlocked the padlock on the cellar door and called down, "Charlie?"

She stood by the table, looking out over the cafe curtains. The school field, except for Casimir, was deserted. She saw that he was dressed in his work clothes. A burlap sack lay on the ground beside him. He was kneeling at the edge of the field, near the corner, scraping his finger between the cobblestones on Girard Street. He rubbed his hands on his face. He took his miner's hat off and filled it with coal dirt as he dug it out. He put the hat on and twisted it, grinding the dirt into his scalp.

Victoria watched him until she felt the children's eyes on her and heard the silence of their stilled hands. It was the kind of silence that freezes every person in a patch when the mine whistle blows beyond all the patterns of weather forecasts or simple ends to a workday, when it blows and blows and blows to warn that someone—some-one's husband, someone's father, someone's brother, someone's son, someone's neighbor, someone's friend—someone is in trouble inside the mine, and will probably die.

Victoria felt that familiar urge to scoop up her children and run with the throng to see what was the matter. Reading again her husband's letter, seeing images of the attic bedroom, the gifts, the other notes, watching him blacken his face, his neck, his hands, his arms, she thought, this really is his end. He is, in his own strange way, preparing his body for the grave, scrubbing it, not with water, but with coal dirt.

She did not go out to him. Her hands clung to the back of a chair. Guilt washed over her. His own wife, watching, doing nothing. It couldn't be right.

She pulled Felicia's chair away from the table. "Remember that nice lady, that Vera, who came and gave us apples today?"

"She said we were welcome to visit any time."

"Yes. Remember which house she told us?"

Felicia's straight black bangs dipped below her eyebrows when she rolled her eyes upward and thought about it. "Go up Girard. Turn left onto Saylor. Don't cross the street. Go one block. In the middle of the next block her house is. She said the bottom step was rotten, to be careful."

"Run there as fast as you can. Ask Vera to come to our house to stay with you right away. It's very, very important. Tell her I'll be back as soon as I can." She handed Felicia her jacket. "Don't go up Girard to Saylor. Your daddy's there. You mustn't let him see you. Go through the shanty and out the back to the alley. Then up to Saylor. Hurry!"

Felicia ran out.

"Anna Chrissy, you stay and watch Julie and Frank till Felicia comes back with Vera Urkov."

Victoria looked out the window. There was still time to follow him. He had just turned onto Saylor Street. He was walking toward the mine.

She tied a brown rag over her hair. From the pegs in the cellar stairway, she took the old black pants and brown jacket Casimir always wore to haul ashes out. She unbuttoned her dress, shoved it down her body, stepped out of it and into Casimir's clothes, hoping he would not recognize her if he saw her.

She went out to the alley through the shanty, crossed Girard Street and walked two blocks toward the mine through the alley. She caught sight of Casimir crossing Downs Street. She stopped, asking herself, what am I doing, following? Why should I stop him? Let him die, the cruel bastard! A moment later she thought, no, I can't just let him die.

She went up to Saylor Street and started walking directly behind him, only at a block's distance. He turned down an alley two blocks before the Ebony Gem Colliery and started to climb the slagpiles.

Victoria followed. When he reached the top, she went to the foot of the culmbank some distance from the spot where he had started up. She blackened her face and hands, rubbed coal dirt into her blonde hair along the edge of the rag. She climbed toward an area where some white birches and a few white pines had sprung up. The tallest birch had a triple trunk that gave her a place to hide.

A few yards ahead Casimir was spreading a blanket behind some bushes, his back to Victoria. Only his shoulders and head were visible to her. The sun had set behind the Ebony Gem. Everything was black against a deep red sky. Casimir seemed a silhouette of himself.

When he stooped down, Victoria could not see him at all. A crooked row of baby white pines stretched between her hideout and his. When the darkness deepened, she moved toward him, keeping low, hiding behind the little pines.

She saw a faint light shining from within the circle of bushes. She saw that Casimir had lit a tall candle inside a canning jar. He was on his knees, his hands folded in prayer. His hands began to move in gestures of supplication, contrition, fear, relief, confusion. He seemed to be taking turns speaking and listening.

Victoria crept toward his campsite and listened from behind a bush.

"Let this cup pass from me," he said. Then he waited. "No! No, I didn't mean I wouldn't. I will! I'll do exactly as you said. Tomorrow, in the afternoon, when they bring the mules up." He paused and listened. Then he said, "Yes, yes, Rebekah, the one who loves me most, I know. Take the boards off Breast Number Six. Never mind the blackdamp in there, I know. It will help me to hear Papa's boots, his voice. Forget about the cup. I won't ask anymore. Oh, I can't wait!"

Victoria wanted to pray for help. But for what kind, she didn't know. She could not bring herself to ask God to stop her husband from walking into the deadly blackdamp, but she dared not wish him dead either. Thy will be done, she remembered Jesus saying in the Garden of Gethsemane after he prayed to let the cup pass from him. But what if his will was to let Casimir live and come home? How could she accept that? What kind of a God would— This was a question for a priest. She must go to the priest. Then she would have till tomorrow afternoon, when the mules came up, to think over whatever he said.

She crept back from pine to pine and scrambled back down the culmbank. She hurried home, went into the cellar, and washed quickly. Then she went up to the kitchen.

"Are you all right?" Vera said. "I was afraid you were hurt or—"

"No. It's just that we have a lot of trouble. I can't explain right now. Vera, can you stay a little while? I need to speak with the priest. Then I'll be back."

"Yes, I can stay." She picked up a washcloth, rinsed, and wrung it out, saying, "Here, you might want to wipe your face a little better."

Victoria ran the cloth once across her face and tossed it into the sink. She changed back into her dress and hurried out.

She went up to the front porch of the rectory and knocked. She looked through the glass in the outer door and saw the stained-glass portrait of the Good Shepherd dismembered by the metal dividing it up. Through that she saw Father Kashnoski coming from a back room. He opened the door.

Mrs. Wozniak, holding a dishtowel, followed. She remained behind the priest and stretched her neck out to the side, narrowing her eyes coldly at the visitor.

The priest raised his eyebrows. His head nodded slowly while his mouth made a tight-lipped smile. "So! So you finally came to me.

I've been wondering how long it would take." He swung the door wide and gestured for her to come in.

"You know, then. You know how troubled my husband is."

"Come into my office, Mrs. Turek." She followed and he pointed to the plain wooden chair in front of his desk, a huge, heavily carved structure that looked impossible to budge. The wooden posts on the chair behind it rose in spirals almost a foot higher than the padded leather back. The tips of the spirals were sharp, like spearheads.

The priest stood beside the desk, watching Victoria sit down. He stood there staring, and she found herself squirming, smoothing her skirt and her hair, and pressing her shoes together. Coal dirt clung to the roots of her yellow hair. There were smears of black along her hairline and on one side of her nose.

"Looks like you've been cracking coal. That's what I hear," Father Kashnoski said, still standing.

"I just came from the culmbank. My husband is up there now. He's got a candle in a jar and he's kneeling in front of it, praying. He's—" Her voice broke off. Where should she begin?

Mrs. Wozniak was standing in the doorway, frowning. Her dishtowel was twisted and taut between her fists, as though she were poised to strangle someone with it.

The priest walked toward Victoria. He squinted like someone trying to read a smudged gauge. Now he was standing directly in front of her, his knees almost touching hers.

She pressed her knees together. She pulled both shoulders forward and inward, toward her heart.

The priest folded his arms. He nodded slowly as he spoke. "You know, Mrs. Turek, I could put a new roof on the church with the money that poor man has spent lighting candles since he married you. He's always in there with his head buried in his arms, begging something of Saint Joseph."

Saint Joseph, Victoria thought. That's the Joseph he meant in his letter. The voice he thinks he hears.

"Oh, he mutters into his sleeves," Father Kashnoski continued, "but I've caught a word here and there, always something about being a better husband, a better father. Knocked himself out making a fancy place for you. Is it any wonder he's 'troubled,' as you call it? Oh, and lest you think I'm just an eavesdropper, Charlie's been in here himself begging me to pray for him. So he receives the grace to put down that bottle he's taken up trying to please you. He shows up here so drunk you can hardly make heads or tails of what he's trying to say. Isn't that right, Mrs. Wozniak?"

The housekeeper, glaring at Victoria, said, "Yes, Father."

The priest went around to the back of the desk and sat down. He picked up a fountain pen and dipped it into a bottle of ink. As he spoke, he doodled little circles and crosses, steeples and coal buckets. "You know, Mrs. Turek, it's women like you, never satisfied, who drag men down and spread discontent among the other men's wives, damage their family life."

Victoria moved forward in her chair, her mouth dropping. "Father, what—"

The priest turned to his housekeeper. "Mrs. Wozniak, look in the drawer with the marriage files. Get the one on the Tureks. Remember this one lived too far away to come for pre-Cana conferences, and we sent her a letter with questions to answer before I'd announce the Banns?"

"Yes, Father, I remember. I will get it." She marched to a wooden cabinet behind Victoria's chair, opened a drawer, and flipped through some papers.

Victoria gripped the arms of her chair as though she might push herself up any moment and run out. "Father, drag men down, spread discontent among— Father, what—"

"You know what I'm talking about. Every woman in the patch thinks she should have what you have."

Mrs. Wozniak handed the priest a large envelope. From that, the priest removed a small envelope, which Victoria recognized as the one she had sent from Dickson City in answer to his questions. He took the letter out and dangled it from one corner as if it were someone else's soiled handkerchief. "Remember the question about whether you understood the lot of a coal miner's wife? Just the other day I read it again, after your husband paid me another visit. Thought I'd look it over and see if perhaps I missed something that should have made me realize you were not prepared to accept your lot. But no, judging by this letter, I'm sure God won't blame *me* for this tragedy. I'd never have guessed you had no heart or stomach for this life. You listed the hardships and toil with no judgment or scorn. But

I guess it's one thing to write about your lot and another to live it. Here, listen to your own words."

"Father, I thought you were asking about any coal miner's wife. I didn't realize— Oh, I know what I wrote! God knows what I wrote. You needn't rub it in."

"See here! You come to my door, telling me your husband's troubled. Anybody in the patch could tell you why. It's not enough that he's forgiven you—yes, he told me he forgave you for that little black-haired girl—but you still want more, more, more."

"Little black-haired girl! Who?"

"If this were two thousand years ago, your husband could have had you stoned to death for that."

"Felicia?"

"Whatever her name is. The one from that Italian photographer you hired for your wedding pictures. From Pottsville, Charlie said he was."

"Charlie told you I—"

"And that Evert fellow. Charlie forgave you for him too, he told me."

"Jinx Evert?"

"Everybody in the patch saw him going in through the back door of your shanty. Didn't they, Mrs. Wozniak?"

Mrs. Wozniak nodded firmly.

Victoria shook her head.

The priest stood up and leaned over the desk. "Do you deny it?"

"Jinx Evert brought me coal."

The priest came around to the front of the desk. He leaned over her. "Well, yes, he came with a wheelbarrow all the time. Something to explain himself." He slouched back against the desk, folded his arms, and sighed through a smile. "You know, I guess I'm a foolish man, Mrs. Turek. When I saw you on my porch tonight, I thought you'd finally come to make a good confession. A good confession. That's the one thing you need right now, to make a good confession. But no, you came to complain about your troubles. Your hard life. Your miserable lot. I know about the money, Mrs. Turek. I know Charlie started holding back on you, and you know what? I'm glad.

"But I think your place is in the kitchen, not bootlegging out back to make ends meet. I'll talk to the Ebony Gem, see if I can get him his job back. In the meantime, the man's bound to be troubled and irritable, hard to live with. If you let it get to you, you have no one to blame but yourself." His voice grew louder. "You brought this whole thing on yourself in the first place. Face it. You got no more than what you had coming to you."

Victoria raised her eyes toward the ceiling and said, "No use coming to him. He won't help us." She stood up. "Let me by."

"Mrs. Turek! You are talking to a priest! You should, you should— You need to make a good confession. Mrs. Wozniak, go get the stole so I can hear this woman's confession. Then go back into the kitchen till she's finished."

"I be glad to do for you, Father," Mrs. Wozniak said. Her tone was flat. Her mouth clapped open and shut like the mouth of a puppet. She marched out of the room.

The priest wagged his finger. "You! You should drop to your knees and thank God I'm even willing to hear your confession. If you prefer not to show your face, we can go over to the church and use the confessional."

"I don't want to go to the church," Victoria said coldly.

"Fine. We can do it right here."

Victoria looked upward again and folded her hands in prayer. "Father in Heaven, listen to him. What does he know about what I need, what my husband needs, my children? Yet he shouts at me and tries to force me to my knees. It's true what Papa always said: empty barrels make the most noise."

"Mrs. Turek!"

Mrs. Wozniak returned, a look of triumph on her face. Across her palm was draped the official silk stole, a long, white, narrow, scarf-like vestment with gold crosses embroidered at both fringed ends.

Father Kashnoski stepped sideways and reached for the vestment. His rage seemed to melt as he bowed his head at the sight of it. He lifted one end, the gold fringes dangling from between his fingers, and kissed it.

Victoria, determined to leave without speaking another word, fixed her eyes on the dark rug and felt her way to the end of the desk like a blind person. For a moment, she looked up. She saw the beautiful, white silk bridge between the hands of the priest and the housekeeper. It caught the flickering light from the candles burning on the mantle. "Oh!" she uttered, suddenly lifted. She brushed her fingers across the silken light as she continued toward the door.

"How dare you!" Father Kashnoski said, snatching the stole and hugging it.

His voice dashed her into a well of fright. She ran through both doors, across the porch and down to the gate.

"God, help me! I don't know what's right or wrong anymore! I don't know what to do, who to ask. My husband is up there devising his own death. I'm the only one who knows besides you, God. I know, and I can't decide whether to do anything about it. Help me to know!"

She started for home, praying to know what to do. Pictures of past days came to her, days with laughter and good-natured teasing, his good little greenie making a Christmas Eve dinner in the Polish tradition. The mountain laurel, blooming early in June, picked for her on his way home from the mine. The evenings he dozed off at her feet with a baby sleeping on his chest, while she was mending. What happened? What happened to it all?

She reached her back yard. She crept up onto the back porch. Through the window, she saw her daughters skipping into the kitchen from the parlor, showing Vera things they had drawn. Vera accepted their gifts with hugs and smiles of great delight, and they skipped back into the parlor. Anna Chrissy took her school satchel down from the peg by the cellar door and spread her books and writing tablet on the table. She showed each book to Vera, who nodded encouragement. Then she sat down and began to write her lessons in her tablet.

Victoria remembered nights when Casimir would burst in and pick on everything the child wrote, making her erase again and again till she was in tears. He would hear her spelling words and snap his fingers to push her past each hesitation. He'd squeeze her fingers together if she used them to count during arithmetic. When she read from her primer, he'd make her repeat a corrected word fourteen times, and she wasn't allowed to keep track of the times on her fingers. Successful rescuing by Victoria resulted only in shifting Casimir's urge to torment to one of the other children.

Now, Anna Chrissy sat calmly at the table, delighting in the serene companionship of Vera, who sat sipping tea and acknowledging the child's good work with nods of approval and occasional, but gentle, instructions to erase a mistake. Felicia and Julie brought in more drawings. Then they brought their tablets out and sat at their neighbor's feet, absorbed in their art.

Little Frank crawled out from under the table. He rolled a ball across the floor and tried to catch it when it bounced back from the woodwork. It rolled through the space between his feet, and he tumbled into a somersault, laughing.

Suddenly, all the children sprang to their feet, their smiles gone. They clung to Vera. She comforted them and went into the front room alone. She returned laughing, waving her palms downward in a gesture of reassurance. She puffed up her cheeks to make a big blowing wind. Then she opened the cellar door and pretended to blow it shut, helping it along with her foot. The girls laughed. Then Anna Chrissy repeated Vera's performance, but blowing the door open, which they had seen happen many times in their parlor when the catch didn't catch right. In a moment, everyone was playing calmly again.

It was then that Victoria made up her mind. "God, forgive me," she said. "But you can see for yourself, either way I'd have to beg you to forgive me."

She went inside and gathered the children against herself. "I don't think Daddy will be coming home tonight," she said.

"Good," Felicia said.

"Yeah, good," Julie said.

"Shame, girls," Vera said. "He's your daddy. You mustn't say things like that."

Victoria waved her hand. "Don't shush them. Let them speak the truth. Don't make them feel ashamed of it. Vera, thanks for watching the children. I just want to be alone with them right now. I'll explain tomorrow night if you'll come back then." Tears broke forth in silent sobs.

Vera said, "Are you sure? Tell me what's going on. I can stay."

"No, I just want to be alone with my children."

Vera put her coat on and said, "I'll come back tomorrow night, for sure."

When she was gone, Anna Chrissy said, "Will Daddy come back tomorrow night?"

"I don't think so."

"Will he come back the next night?"

"I don't think so.

"Will he—"

Victoria put her finger to her lips and pulled Anna Chrissy's head against her stomach. She remembered that the first line of Casimir's note said something about if he got back home.

"Please," she prayed silently, "don't let those voices send him back here."

24

THE PEBBLE IN THE PEGBOARD

Goddamn you, you rotten, stubborn mule!"

Ah, Casimir thought, watching from behind the bushes outside the mine yard, Rebekah! That boy was finally bringing Rebekah up to the yard. It was time. "Thank you, Saint Joseph."

He tucked his burlap sack of blankets and tools among the bushes, crept toward the fence and watched. Isaac was led out from the cage without a fuss, but Rebekah stayed put, her front end on the ground, her hind end still in the cage. The cage operator in his small wooden station by the double shaft, laughed at the miner's efforts to budge her.

Casimir whistled the soft whistle he knew Rebekah would recognize as his. Then he backed in among the bushes. Rebekah rose to all fours and lurched forward, almost knocking the miner down.

The cage operator stuck his head out the window and said, "There! A kiss for all your trouble!"

"She'll wait her turn now," the miner said. His voice was very young. "Isaac, let's go, you and me. To hell with Rebekah. She can walk herself, for all I care." He strutted off, leading Isaac, turning once to give Rebekah a look of spite.

Casimir whistled again.

Rebekah walked out of the cage. The adjoining cage had a set of rails leading out. The set branched off to two, one heading for the tipple, the other curving and meeting up with a set that went from the breaker chute to the slag heaps. In her blindness, Rebekah took a few steps and stumbled over a rail. She moved her head about.

Casimir, convinced that she was seeking the touch of the only hand she had ever allowed to lead her, pitied her. "Saint Joseph, look at her. Should I go to her now or wait? Give me a sign." He took a penny from his pocket. It was face down. But Rebekah managed to position herself between the rails, a place where she was sure-footed, and began to walk forward.

Casimir crept along the fence and looked through the window of the mine office. Relieved to see that Thatcher's head was bowed over his desk, a pencil in his hand, he went around to the back of the yard where neither the cage operator nor Thatcher could see him jump the fence.

Rebekah followed his soft whistle and met him back there. He rubbed his face against hers as though he himself were a long-time companion from the same stable. He began to walk her around the back of the yard, his head bowed, in case his blackened face might still be recognized. Even that wouldn't help for long. Rebekah was walking for him like a saint. Who else would she do that for?

The sheave wheels at the mouth of the mine turned, bringing up a cage. Casimir heard a car of coal being pulled out of the cage by a mule. He knew it would take a few moments for the car to be hooked to the cable that would hoist it up the rails to the tipple. Another car, loaded with waste from the breaker chute and headed for the culm-bank, went by on another set of tracks, pulled by a mule. Casimir took advantage of this busy moment to slip around to the front and lead Rebecca into the cage.

The miner walking Isaac hurried in. His face, dusty and young, did not show the deep caked lines mapped in the faces of miners with years of work in the mines. Casimir took him to be about sixteen. "Where'd you come from?" the boy demanded. "What do you think you're doing?"

Casimir, hiding his face from the shaft operator, said, "They said you were having trouble. You're supposed to meet Fairbanks on Level Three. I'll take these mules back." Casimir pulled the signal cord for the cage to descend.

"But this is *my* job! I just started here this week. They should give me a chance. I worked in a Hazleton mine for two years. All stable work, like this. I know what I'm doing. I'm a miner's apprentice, too. I know what I'm doing."

"Sure. But now and then, they make me walk Rebekah 'cause she gives everybody a hell of a time, not just you. Too late today. I'll just take her back down."

"My name's Gabe O'Connor. Ask anybody in Hazleton about me. They'll tell you I can handle a mule."

"I'll tell Fairbanks you don't need my help. It's plain to see. But you better go look for him down on Three like he says for now. I'll put in a word for you."

O'Connor grinned. "Thanks! What's your name, by the way?"

"Tim Brennan."

At the topmost underground level Casimir led the mules out of the cage and to the stable. O'Connor tugged the signal cord for the cage to drop to Level Three.

Casimir walked the rails with the mules till he reached the stable. No one was around. "Thank you, Saint Joseph, for getting me this far safely." He put Isaac in his stall and got back into the cage with Rebekah.

They got out on Level Four. The sound of coughing came from the various gangways that converged near the cage. Casimir put out the light on his hat. Now he was as blind as Rebekah. But he knew she would lead him to Breast Number Six. She knew he belonged there.

"Hurry," Casimir mumbled. "No, wait. Wait on the tracks for a minute." He walked a few feet along the gangway, feeling for the pegboard. He picked up a pebble. His fingers groped along the holes, some already plugged, some empty, till they came to number thirty-one. Casimir plugged the pebble in there. Then he shuffled back to the mule and said, "Tell you a secret, Rebekah. That stone stands for me."

He gave her a pat on the rump and she led him down the tracks. The five wooden rungs that led up to Breast Number Six were soft and splintered, but he climbed them. He took a crowbar from his burlap sack and pried off two of the boards that were nailed over the entrance. "All mined out, this breast," he said to Rebekah. "Finished, like me."

She snorted, as if to agree.

"Thick with blackdamp, I bet." He raised his eyes in the darkness and whispered to Saint Joseph, "Are you sure I should wait in there?" There was no voice, no sign. He didn't dare draw attention to himself by lighting his hat lamp and consulting with a penny. He counted to ten. Still no voice. So he pried away the remaining boards and pushed his sack through the space.

Then he climbed down and kissed Rebekah between the eyes. "Oh, I wish you could understand what you just did for me. At last I'll hear Papa's voice!"

He slapped her hard on the rump to send her off, but she sat down. "Go!" Rebekah stood up and nuzzled his arm. "Go!" he said, slapping her harder. But she stepped in front of him and breathed on his face. He could hear her scrape the ground with her right front hoof, something she always did to let people know she had no intention of doing as she was told. "Okay, then, stand there. But don't be insulted when I have to block up this opening behind me. Don't think I'm being mean, shutting you out."

He climbed back into the breast, lit the lamp on his hat, and began nailing the boards back over the entrance. He stayed low to the ground to make sure his lamp didn't hit a pocket of methane and blow him to bits before he got a chance to hear his papa's voice. No, Saint Joseph wouldn't let that happen, any more than he let him be poisoned by the copperheads slithering on the slagpiles the night before. As he pounded the nails, he got a weak feeling in his chest, as if his ribs were turning soft, melting. "Are you sure this is what you want me to do, Saint Joseph? Tell me with your voice." It was difficult for Casimir to draw in a full breath. "I'm not getting the right feeling. I need to hear." He rummaged through his sack for more nails. He pulled them out and dropped them. "Does this mean I picked the wrong thing to do? Tell me!"

The light went out on his hat. He trembled violently. He must have picked the wrong thing. He tore the boards away and slipped back into the gangway. Rebekah snorted to him. He spread his feet apart and stood on the rails where the mine cars ran. In the distance ahead of him he heard a loud hiss, like the first blast of a great locomotive starting up. A slow, laboring chug began. The whistle blew softly from a distance, growing louder as it approached. Casimir almost fainted. "The Delaware & Hudson!"

He scrambled back up into the manway of Breast Number Six and groped for the nails he had dropped. He managed to light his hat again. He nailed the boards in place and sat with his back against them, his fingers in his ears as the whistle screamed in the gangway on the other side of the boards, fading, then, with the distance as it passed. Casimir sat still, breathless.

His light shone dimly up the steep manway, but only for a moment before it went out. "Blackdamp," he muttered. He listened for rats. He heard nothing. "So this is it, huh? The end of the line. This is why you sent me here. This is how to stop the train. Okay, I'm here. I'll be brave. But remember, you promised. My papa's voice. You promised."

It took a while for him to stop shaking and get control. He was able, finally, to pull the blankets and pillow from the bag. He spread the blankets in the space between the incline and the boards he had nailed back. With great effort, took off his boots and socks. His arms and legs felt so heavy. He laid his head against the pillow. Was there something else he should do? Or should he just wait?

He listened again for rats. There were none. In the silent, absolute blackness, he knew that from under the heaps of loosed rock, that sneaky, heavy gas was slithering toward him, winding its way down the rungs of the manway and coiling itself around his ankles.

"Casimir," a woman's voice said. It was a young, delightful, dancing voice.

"Mama?" Casimir tried to raise his head.

"Yes, it's Mama. Lie back." The voice spoke in Polish.

"Mama, you sound so young," Casimir said, his tongue free, skipping joyfully through the syllables of his first language. "Young, like in Gdansk. Where's Papa?"

"Shh. He'll be here soon. I promise."

"You won't fight, will you?"

"No. Hush, now." He felt her remove his hat. Then her hand came down and stroked his hair. Softly, the hum of an old Slavic tune breathed over him and made his hair dance on his forehead. He felt the warm wood of the porch banister against his bare feet. The salty breeze from the Baltic carried the smell of late summer wild roses.

A bright light like a sunset shone red through his eyelids. He tried to open them to see his father coming up the steps of the porch. But his lids fluttered feebly with the weight of sleep. The clock tower on the hill struck nine. Heavy boots came up the wooden steps and across the porch. The amused chuckle had to be coming from behind a big grin. Casimir smelled the shirt of a fisherman just home from the docks. Two strong arms slid under him. He felt his father's breath on his cheek. "Up you go, *muy synku*."

A mule brayed in the distance.